ALL IS NAT LOST

MARIA SCRIVAN

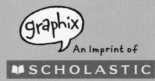

graphix

An Imprint of

SCHOLASTIC

There is always a way.

All rights reserved. Published by Graphix, an imprint of Scholastic Inc.,
Publishers since 1920. SCHOLASTIC, GRAPHIX, and associated logos are
trademarks and/or registered trademarks of Scholastic Inc.

The publisher does not have any control over and does not assume any
responsibility for author or third-party websites or their content.

Library of Congress Control Number: 2022949224

ISBN 978-1-338-89109-6 (hardcover)
ISBN 978-1-338-89058-7 (paperback)

10 9 8 7 6 5 4 3 2 1   24 25 26 27 28

Printed in China 62
First edition, March 2024
Edited by Megan Peace
Book Design by Carina Taylor
Creative Director: Phil Falco
Publisher: David Saylor

CONTENTS

SCHOOL TRIP

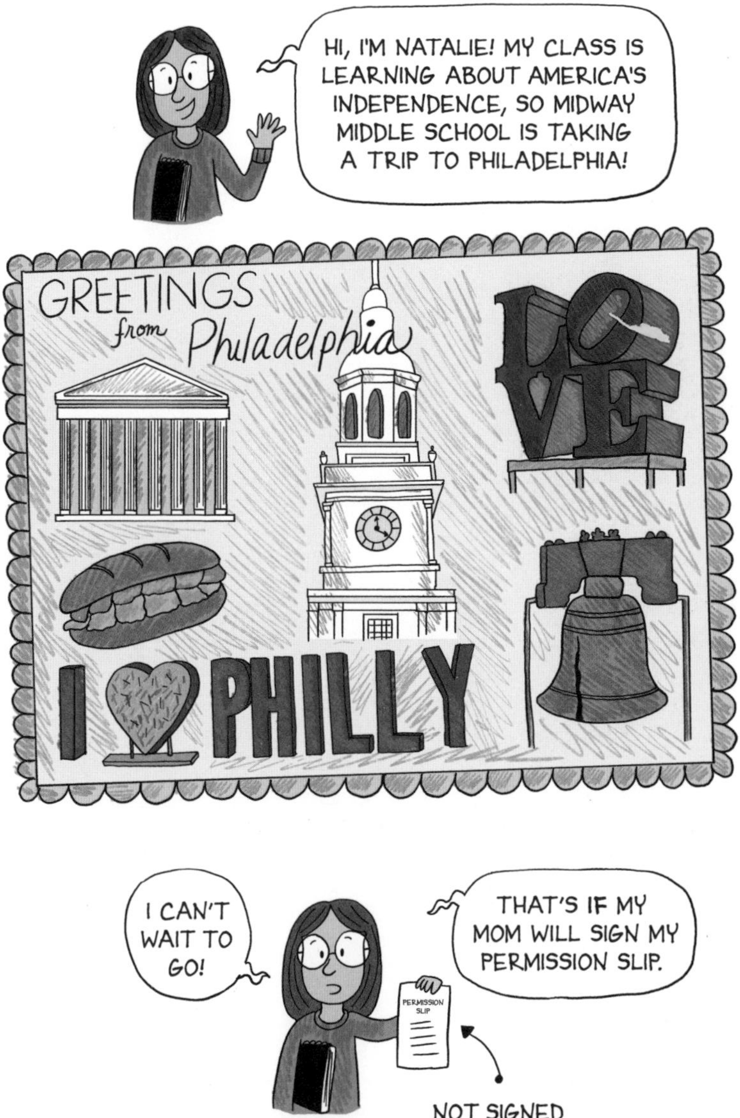
HI, I'M NATALIE! MY CLASS IS LEARNING ABOUT AMERICA'S INDEPENDENCE, SO MIDWAY MIDDLE SCHOOL IS TAKING A TRIP TO PHILADELPHIA!
GREETINGS from Philadelphia
LOVE
I ♥ PHILLY
I CAN'T WAIT TO GO!
THAT'S IF MY MOM WILL SIGN MY PERMISSION SLIP.
PERMISSION SLIP
NOT SIGNED

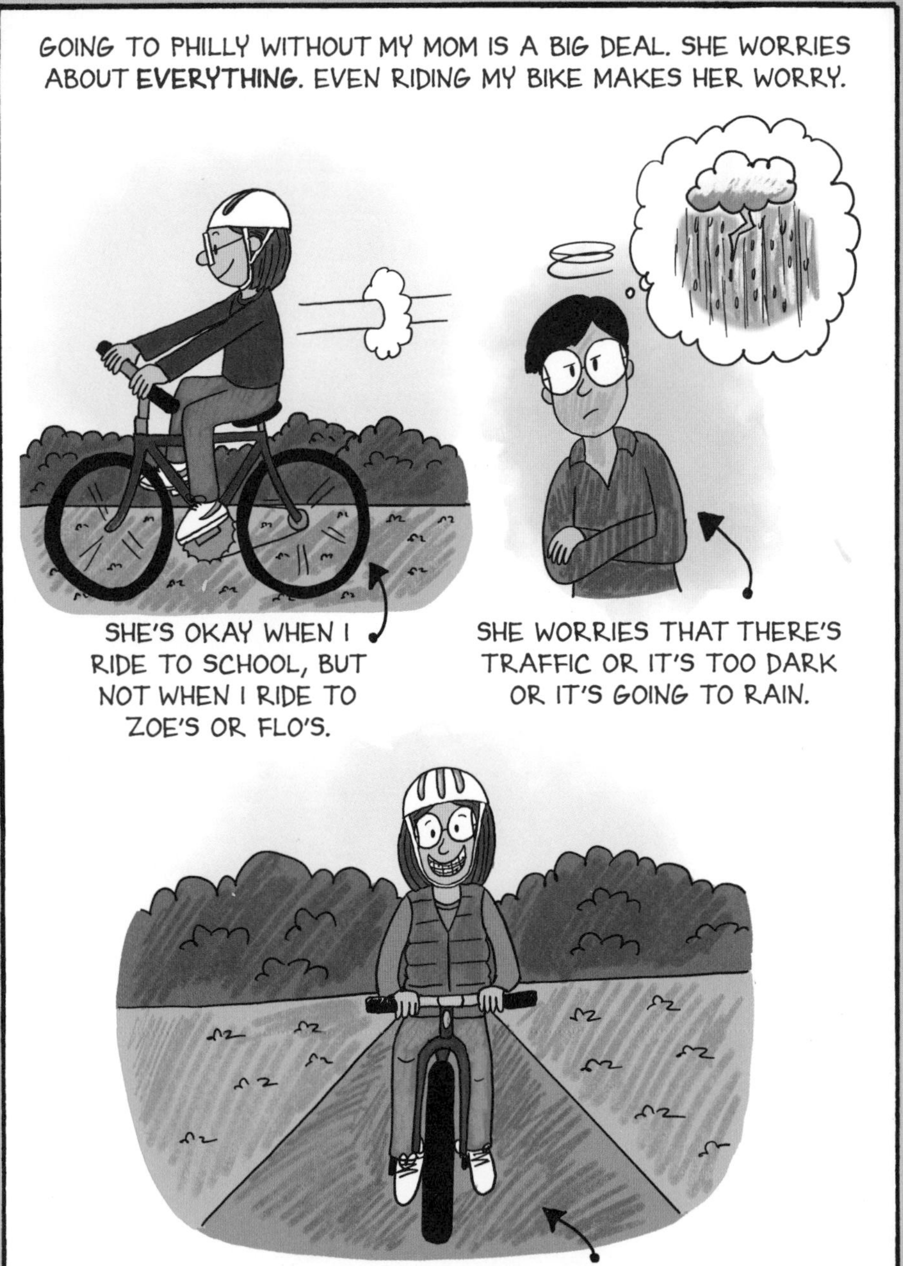
GOING TO PHILLY WITHOUT MY MOM IS A BIG DEAL. SHE WORRIES ABOUT **EVERYTHING**. EVEN RIDING MY BIKE MAKES HER WORRY.
SHE'S OKAY WHEN I RIDE TO SCHOOL, BUT NOT WHEN I RIDE TO ZOE'S OR FLO'S.
SHE WORRIES THAT THERE'S TRAFFIC OR IT'S TOO DARK OR IT'S GOING TO RAIN.
RIDING MY BIKE IS MY FAVORITE THING! IT GIVES ME INDEPENDENCE!

THIS TRIP WILL BE MY FIRST TIME GOING TO A BIG CITY!

I WENT TO CAMP LAST SUMMER, BUT OTHER THAN BEARS, POISON IVY, AND A LAKE MONSTER, THERE WASN'T MUCH TO WORRY ABOUT.

BEAR

LAKE MONSTER

POSION IVY

KNOWING MY MOM, SHE'LL PROBABLY THINK THERE'S A LOT MORE TO WORRY ABOUT WITH THIS TRIP.

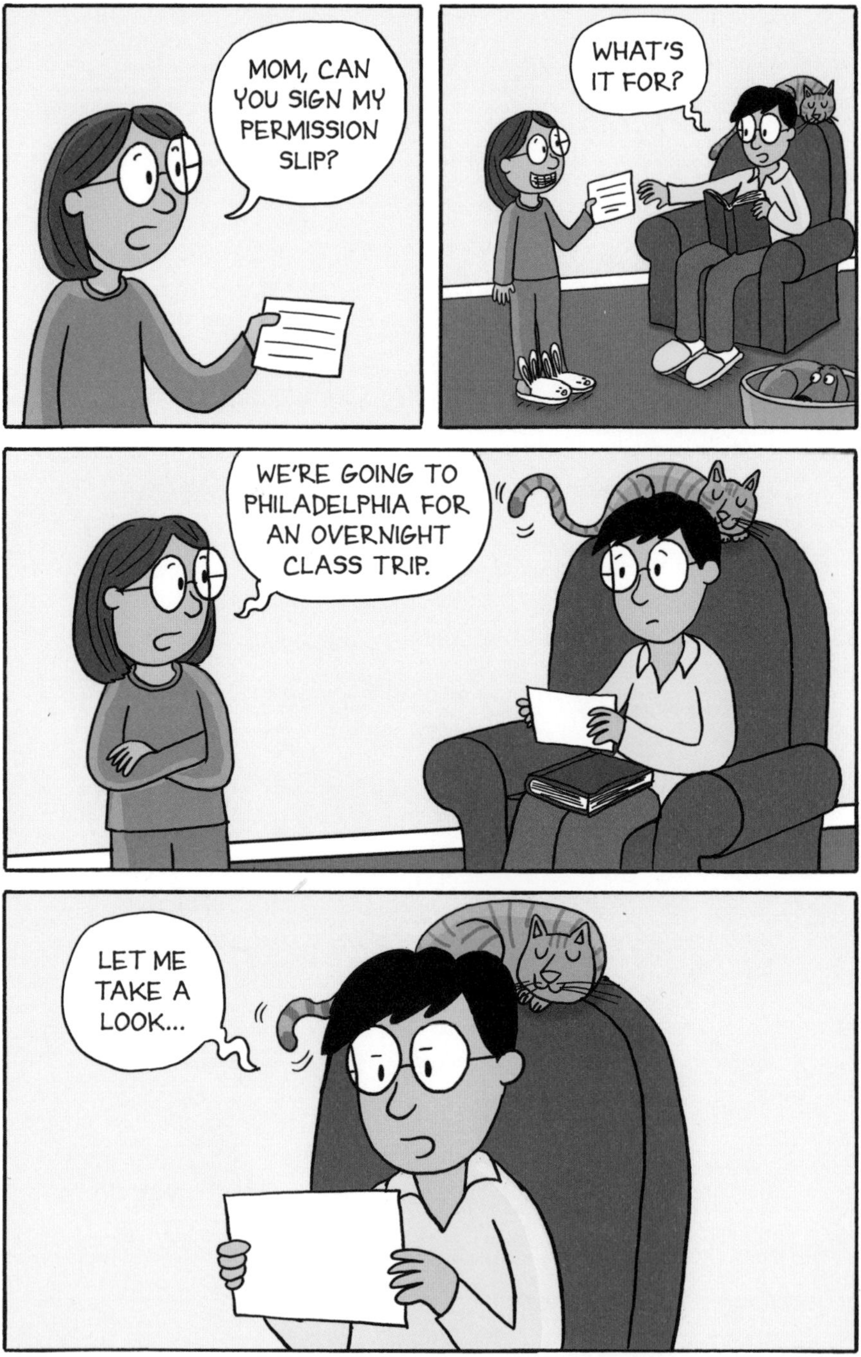
MOM, CAN YOU SIGN MY PERMISSION SLIP?
WHAT'S IT FOR?
WE'RE GOING TO PHILADELPHIA FOR AN OVERNIGHT CLASS TRIP.
LET ME TAKE A LOOK...

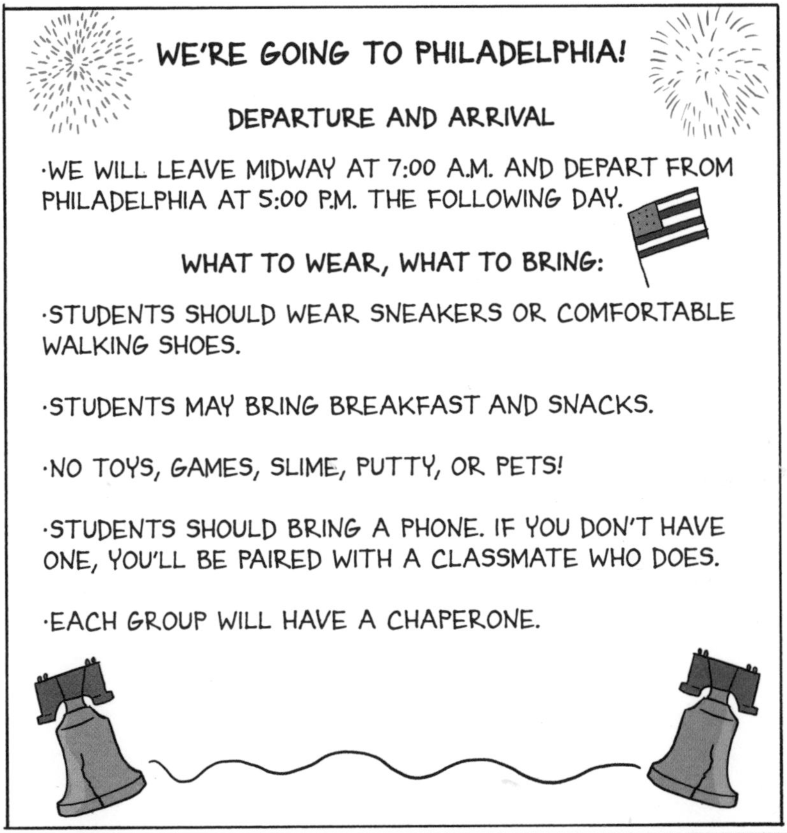
WE'RE GOING TO PHILADELPHIA!
DEPARTURE AND ARRIVAL
·WE WILL LEAVE MIDWAY AT 7:00 A.M. AND DEPART FROM PHILADELPHIA AT 5:00 P.M. THE FOLLOWING DAY.
WHAT TO WEAR, WHAT TO BRING:
·STUDENTS SHOULD WEAR SNEAKERS OR COMFORTABLE WALKING SHOES.
·STUDENTS MAY BRING BREAKFAST AND SNACKS.
·NO TOYS, GAMES, SLIME, PUTTY, OR PETS!
·STUDENTS SHOULD BRING A PHONE. IF YOU DON'T HAVE ONE, YOU'LL BE PAIRED WITH A CLASSMATE WHO DOES.
·EACH GROUP WILL HAVE A CHAPERONE.

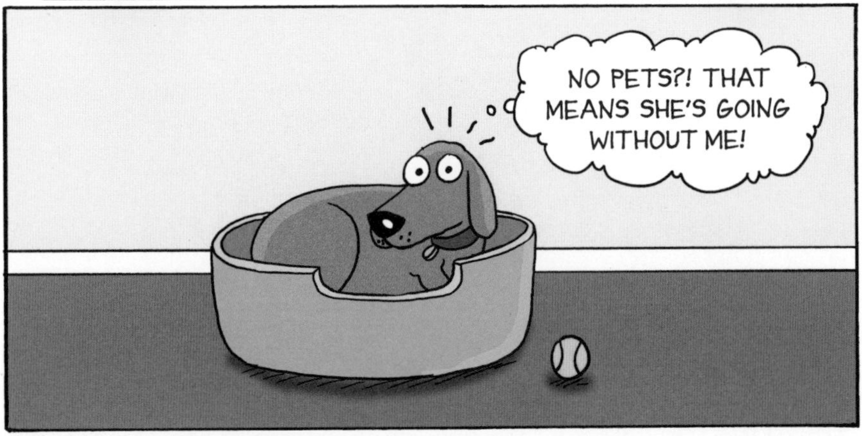
NO PETS?! THAT MEANS SHE'S GOING WITHOUT ME!

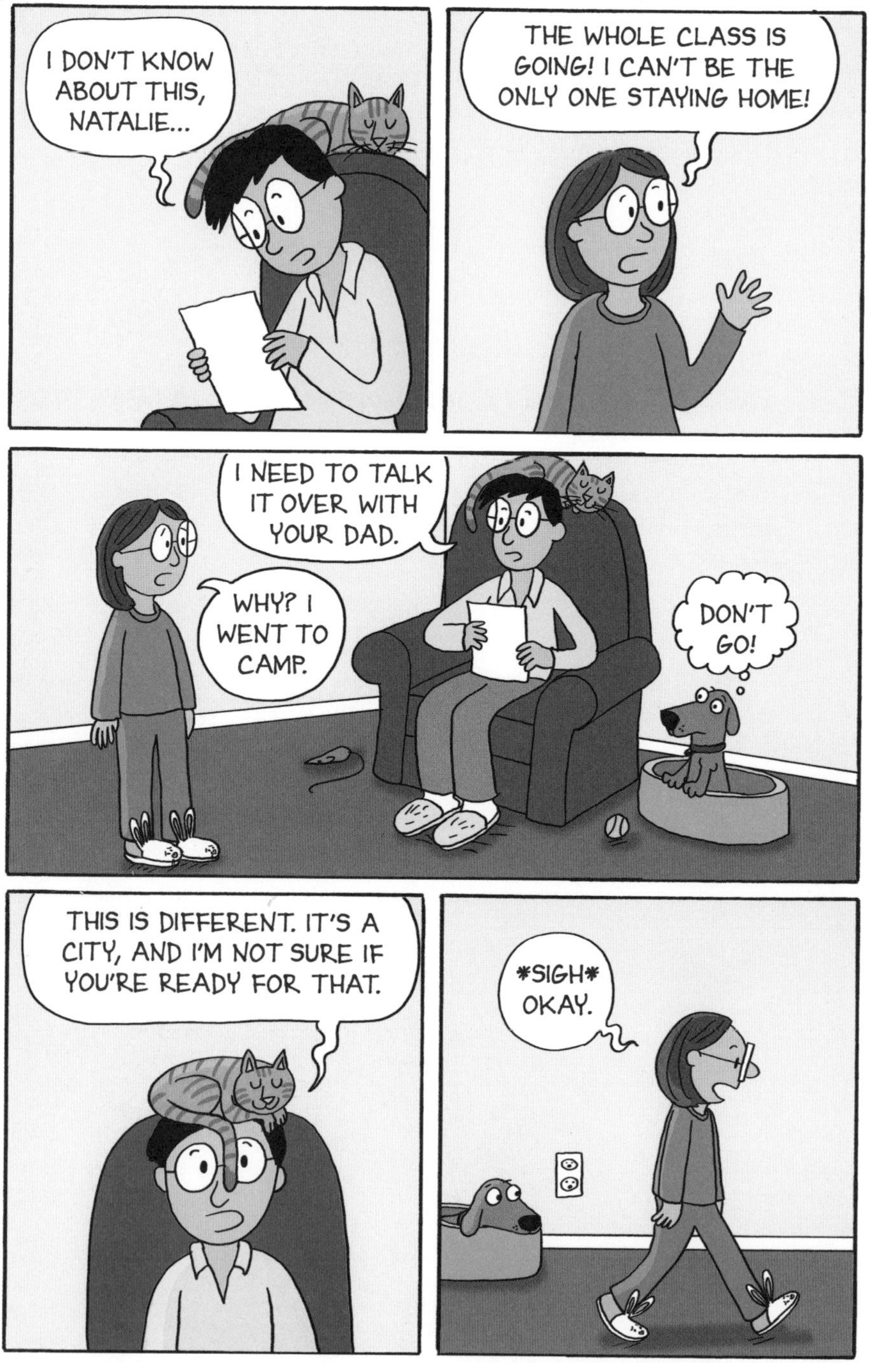
I DON'T KNOW ABOUT THIS, NATALIE...
THE WHOLE CLASS IS GOING! I CAN'T BE THE ONLY ONE STAYING HOME!
I NEED TO TALK IT OVER WITH YOUR DAD.
WHY? I WENT TO CAMP.
DON'T GO!
THIS IS DIFFERENT. IT'S A CITY, AND I'M NOT SURE IF YOU'RE READY FOR THAT.
SIGH OKAY.

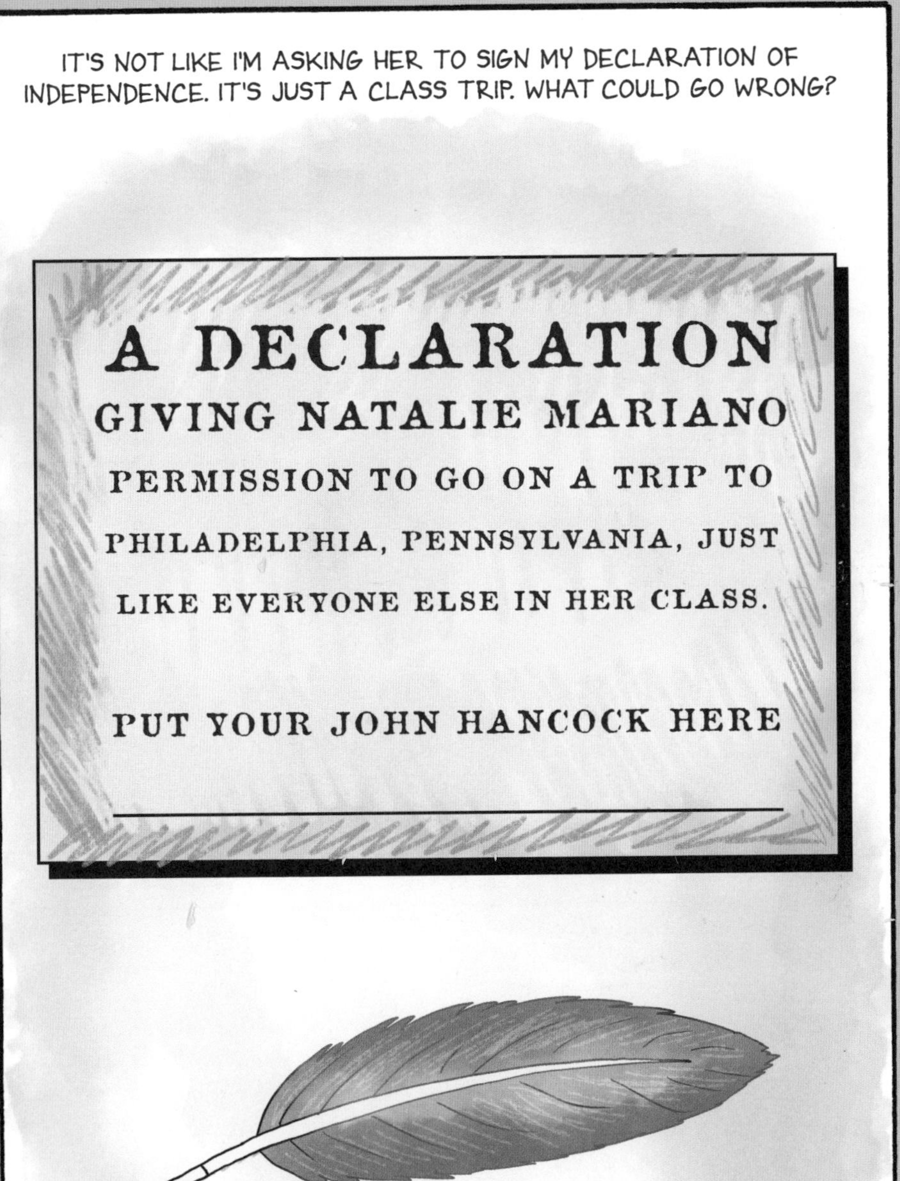
IT'S NOT LIKE I'M ASKING HER TO SIGN MY DECLARATION OF INDEPENDENCE. IT'S JUST A CLASS TRIP. WHAT COULD GO WRONG?
A DECLARATION
GIVING NATALIE MARIANO
PERMISSION TO GO ON A TRIP TO
PHILADELPHIA, PENNSYLVANIA, JUST
LIKE EVERYONE ELSE IN HER CLASS.
PUT YOUR JOHN HANCOCK HERE

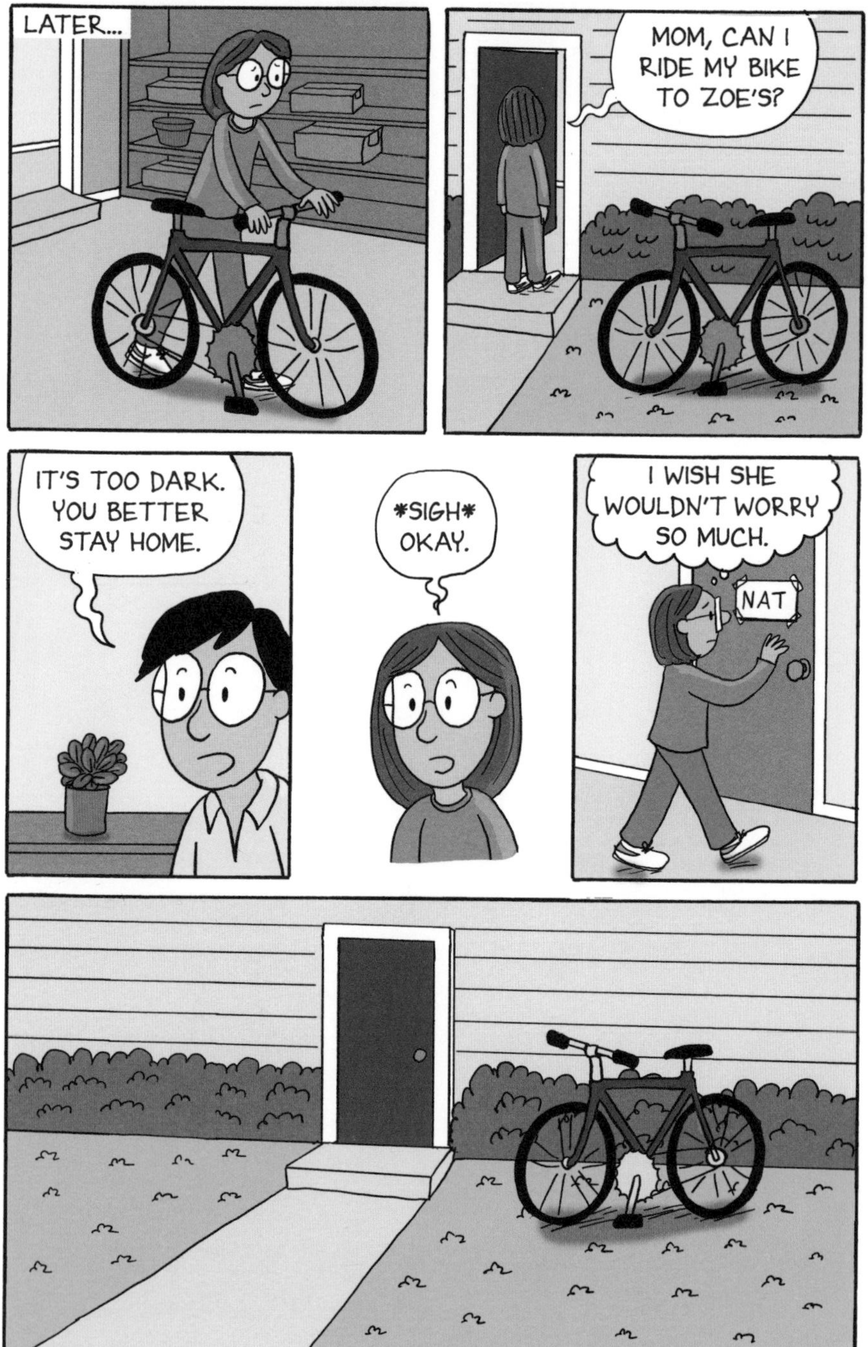

LATER...
MOM, CAN I RIDE MY BIKE TO ZOE'S?
IT'S TOO DARK. YOU BETTER STAY HOME.
SIGH OKAY.
I WISH SHE WOULDN'T WORRY SO MUCH.
NAT

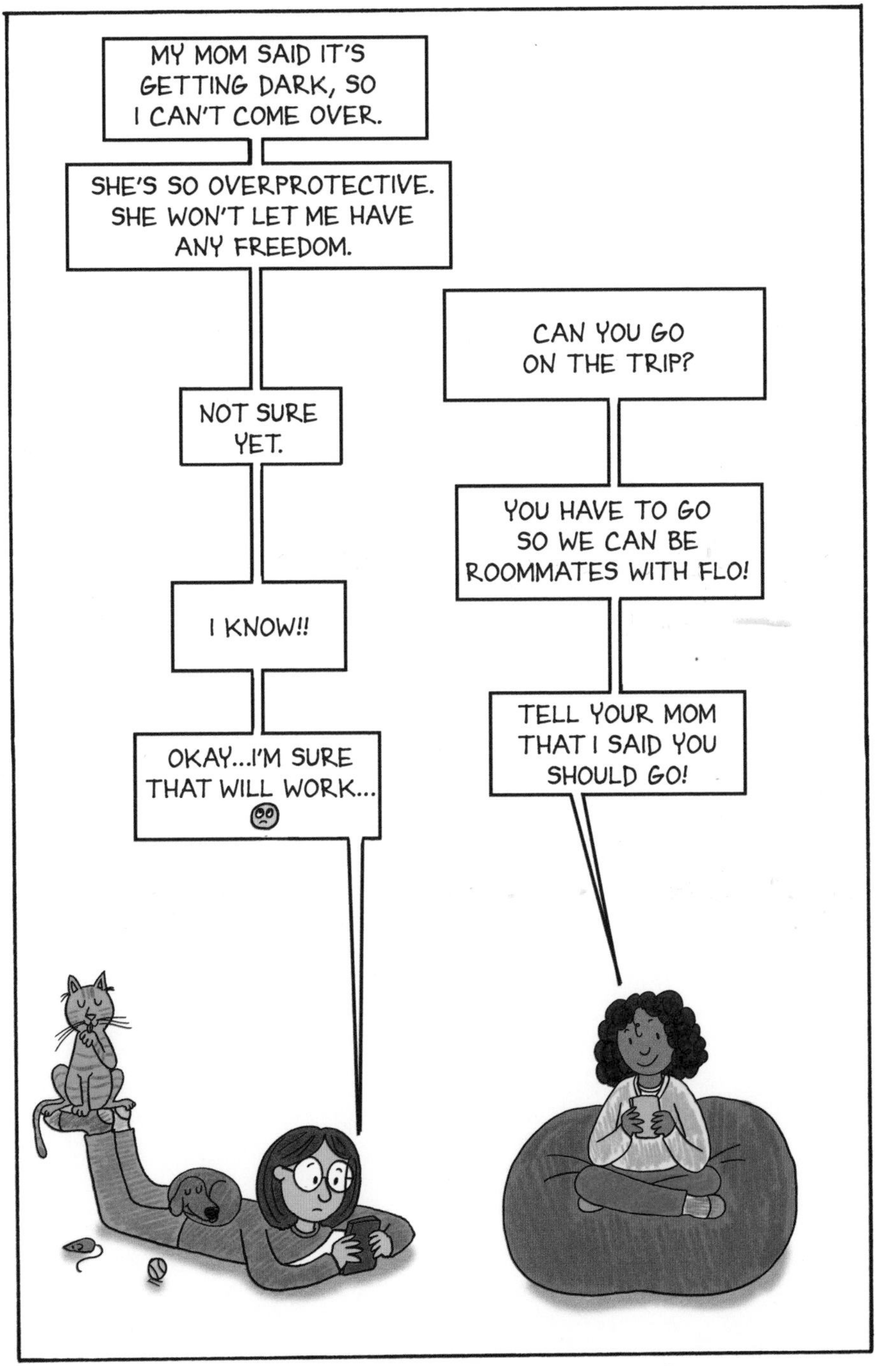
MY MOM SAID IT'S GETTING DARK, SO I CAN'T COME OVER.
SHE'S SO OVERPROTECTIVE. SHE WON'T LET ME HAVE ANY FREEDOM.
CAN YOU GO ON THE TRIP?
NOT SURE YET.
YOU HAVE TO GO SO WE CAN BE ROOMMATES WITH FLO!
I KNOW!!
TELL YOUR MOM THAT I SAID YOU SHOULD GO!
OKAY...I'M SURE THAT WILL WORK...

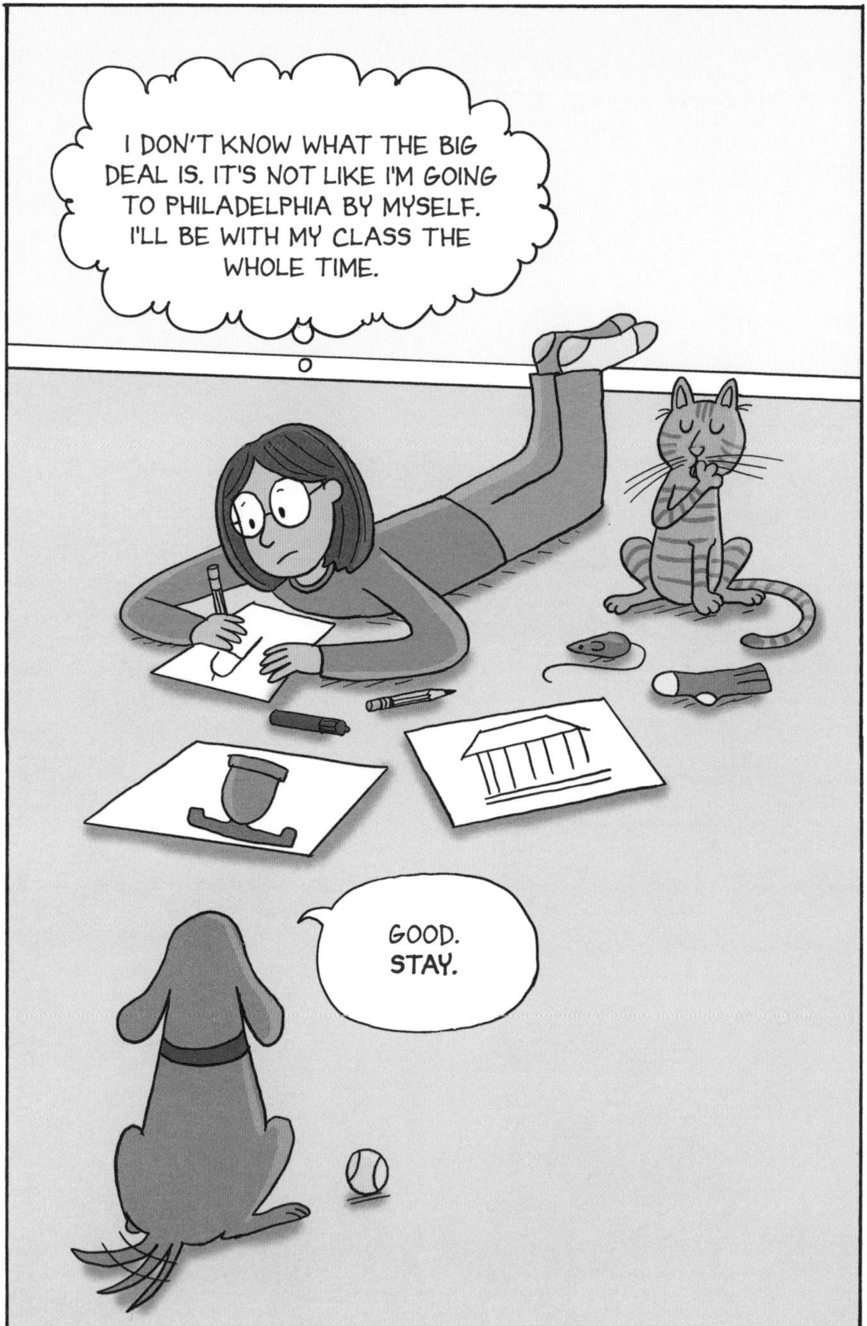
I DON'T KNOW WHAT THE BIG DEAL IS. IT'S NOT LIKE I'M GOING TO PHILADELPHIA BY MYSELF. I'LL BE WITH MY CLASS THE WHOLE TIME.
GOOD. **STAY.**

CHAPTER 1
MISSING

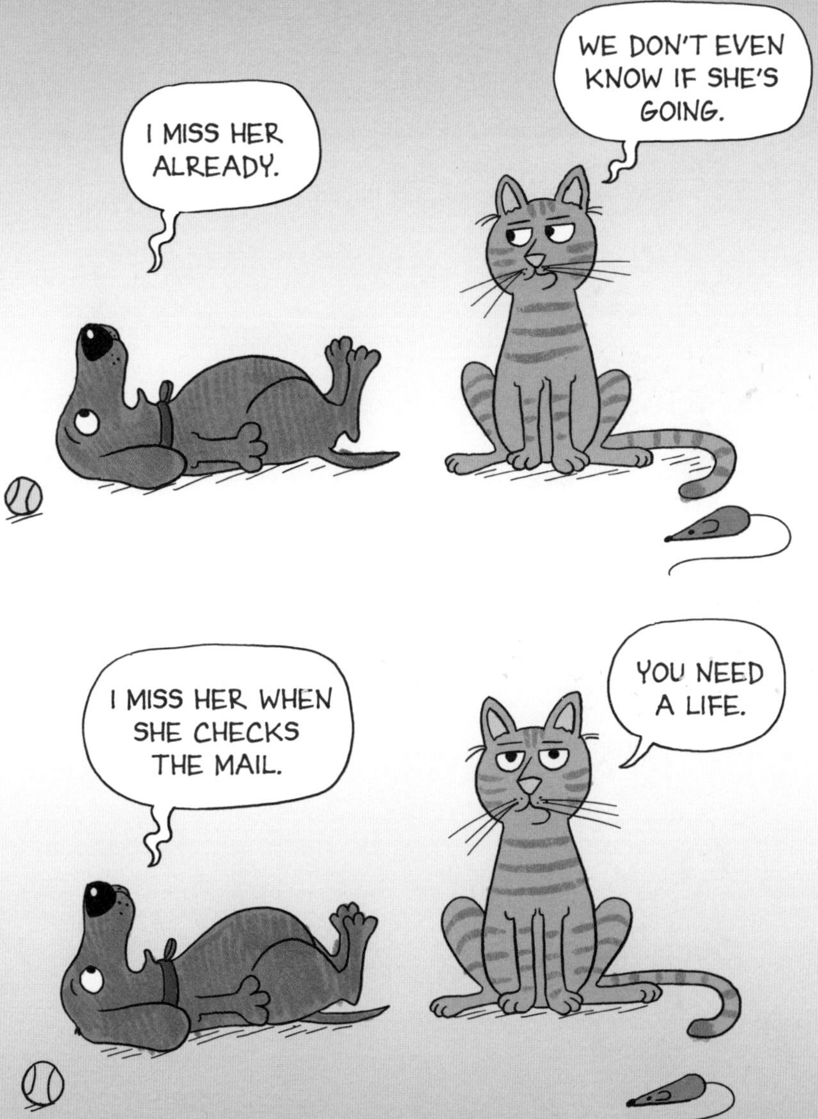

I MISS HER ALREADY.
WE DON'T EVEN KNOW IF SHE'S GOING.
I MISS HER WHEN SHE CHECKS THE MAIL.
YOU NEED A LIFE.

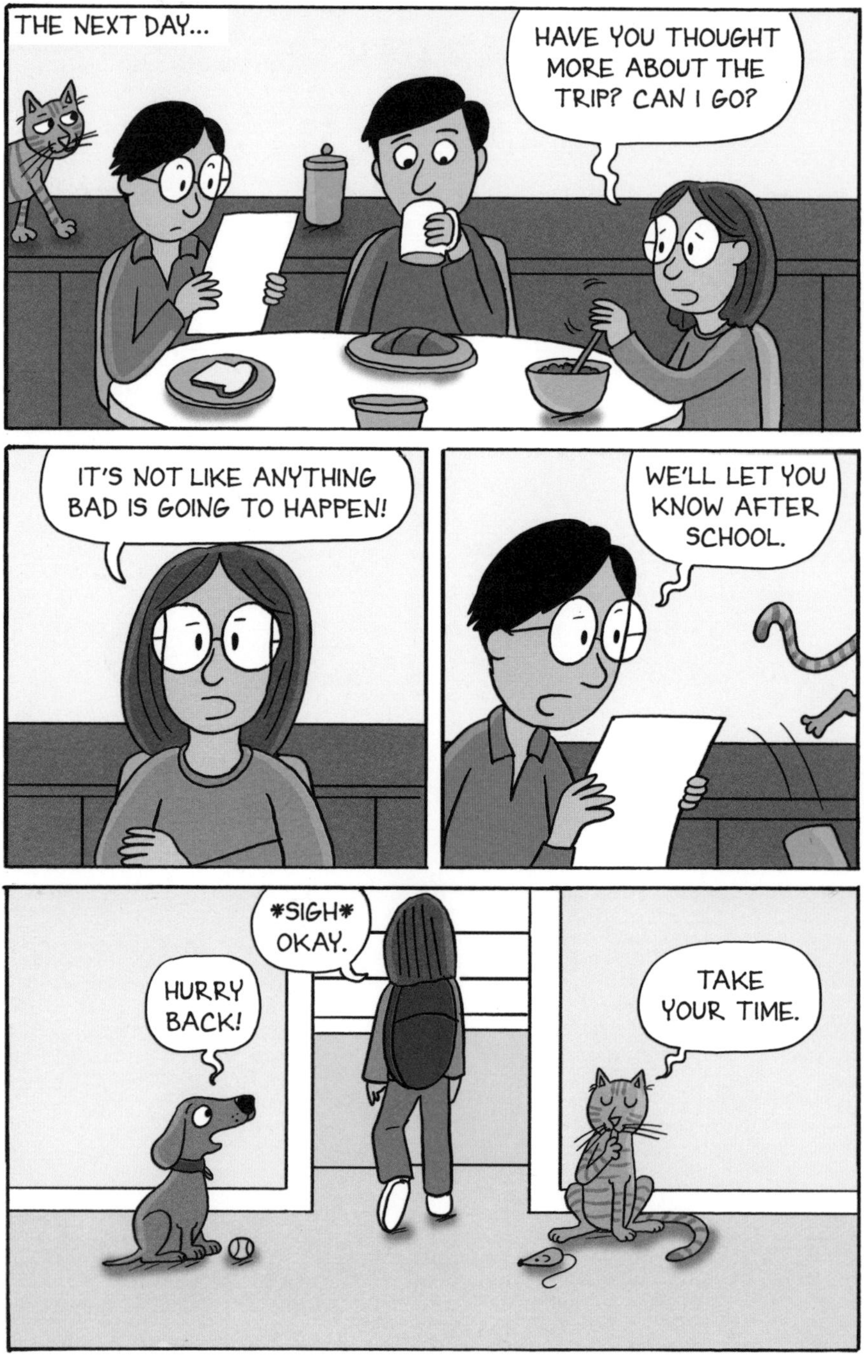
THE NEXT DAY...
HAVE YOU THOUGHT MORE ABOUT THE TRIP? CAN I GO?
IT'S NOT LIKE ANYTHING BAD IS GOING TO HAPPEN!
WE'LL LET YOU KNOW AFTER SCHOOL.
SIGH OKAY.
HURRY BACK!
TAKE YOUR TIME.

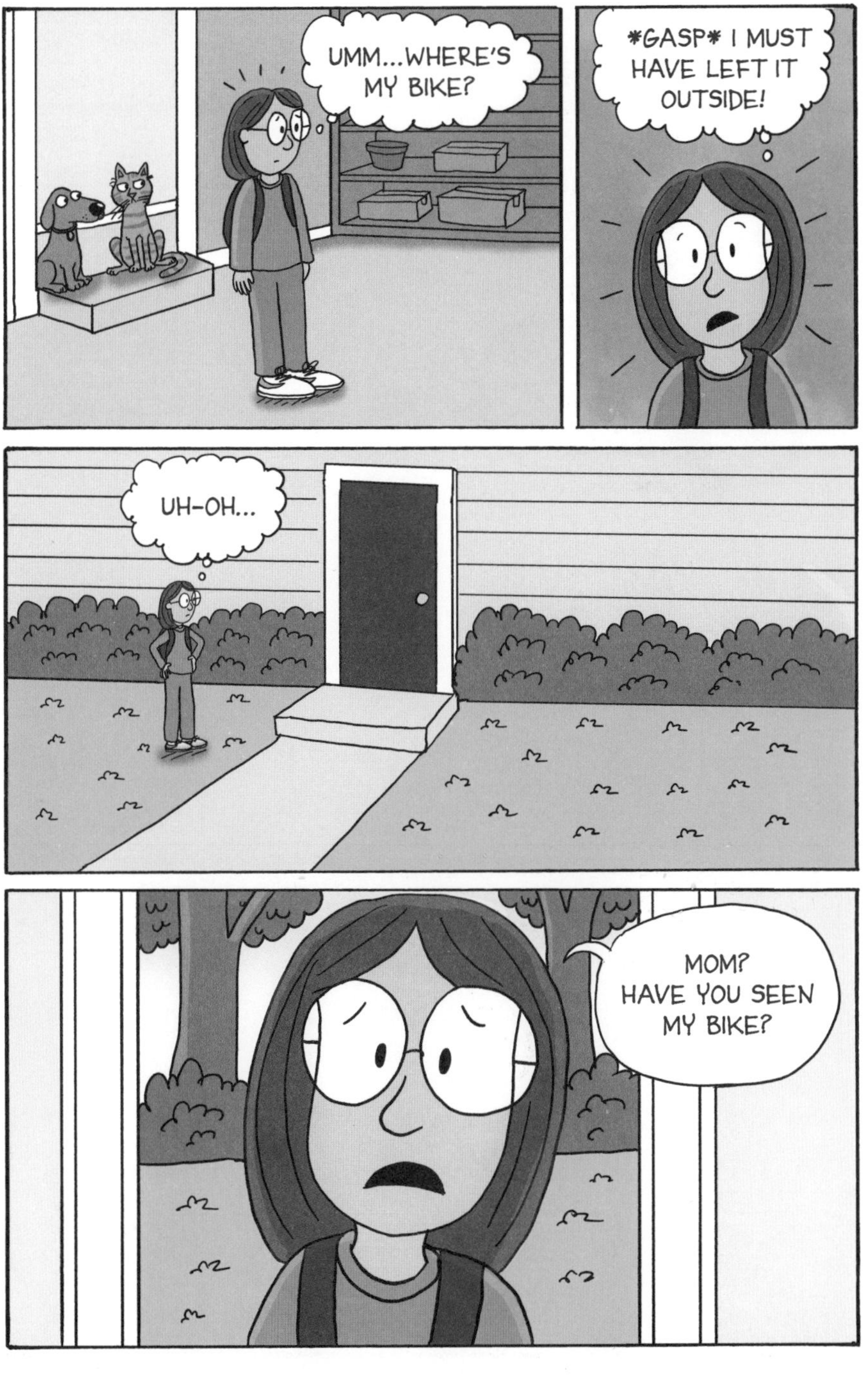
UMM...WHERE'S MY BIKE?
GASP I MUST HAVE LEFT IT OUTSIDE!
UH-OH...
MOM? HAVE YOU SEEN MY BIKE?

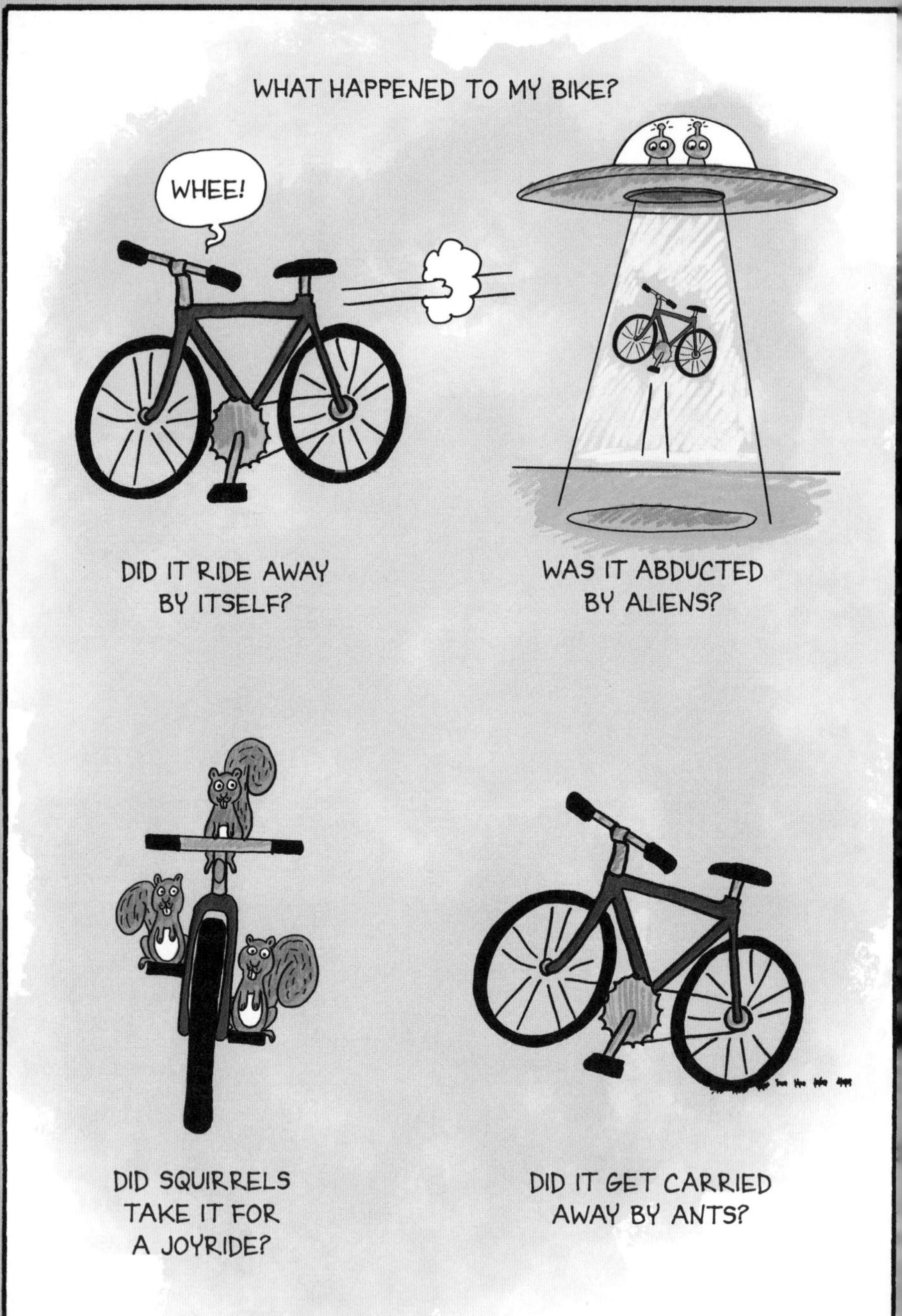
WHAT HAPPENED TO MY BIKE?
WHEE!
DID IT RIDE AWAY BY ITSELF?
WAS IT ABDUCTED BY ALIENS?
DID SQUIRRELS TAKE IT FOR A JOYRIDE?
DID IT GET CARRIED AWAY BY ANTS?

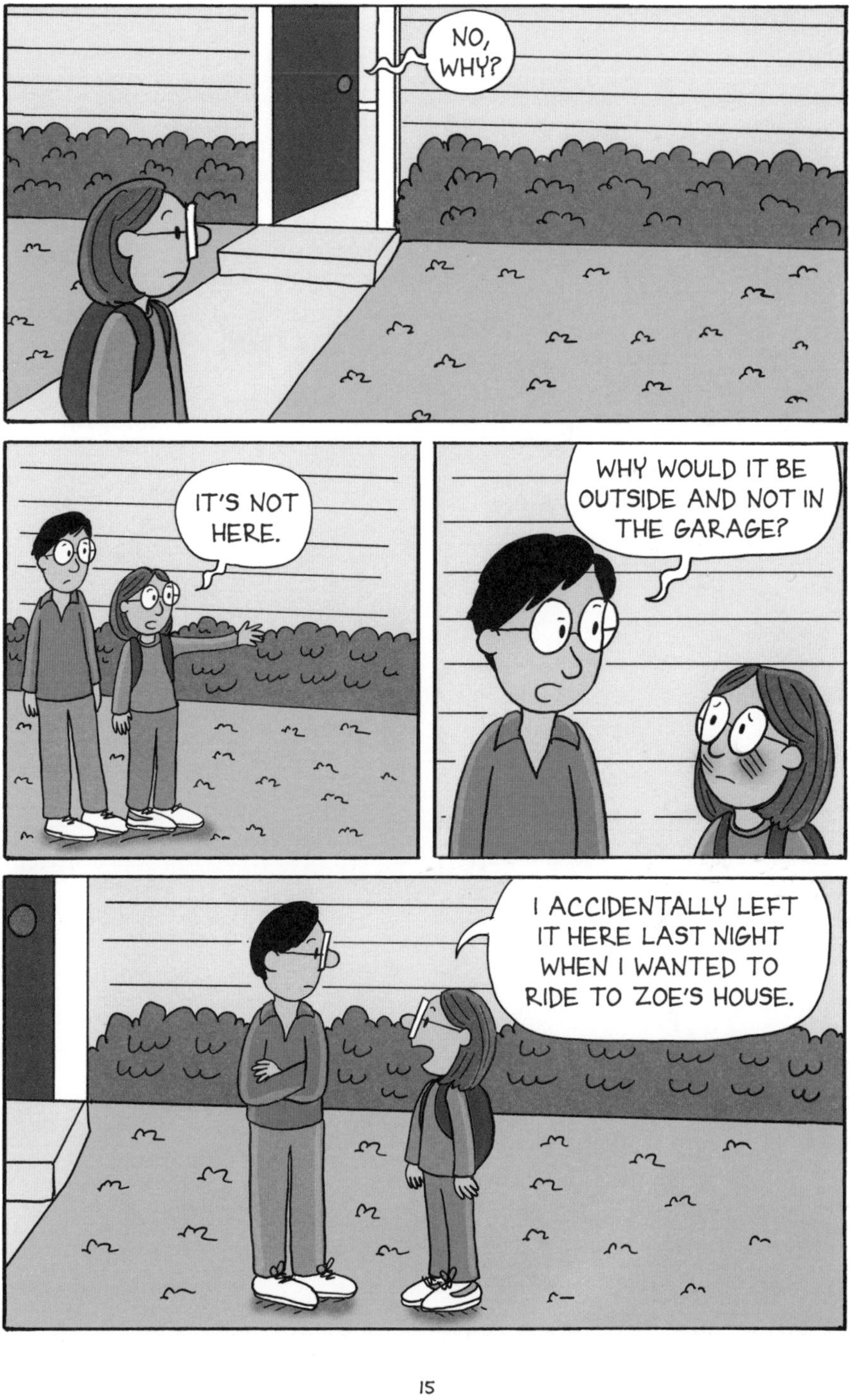
NO, WHY?
IT'S NOT HERE.
WHY WOULD IT BE OUTSIDE AND NOT IN THE GARAGE?
I ACCIDENTALLY LEFT IT HERE LAST NIGHT WHEN I WANTED TO RIDE TO ZOE'S HOUSE.

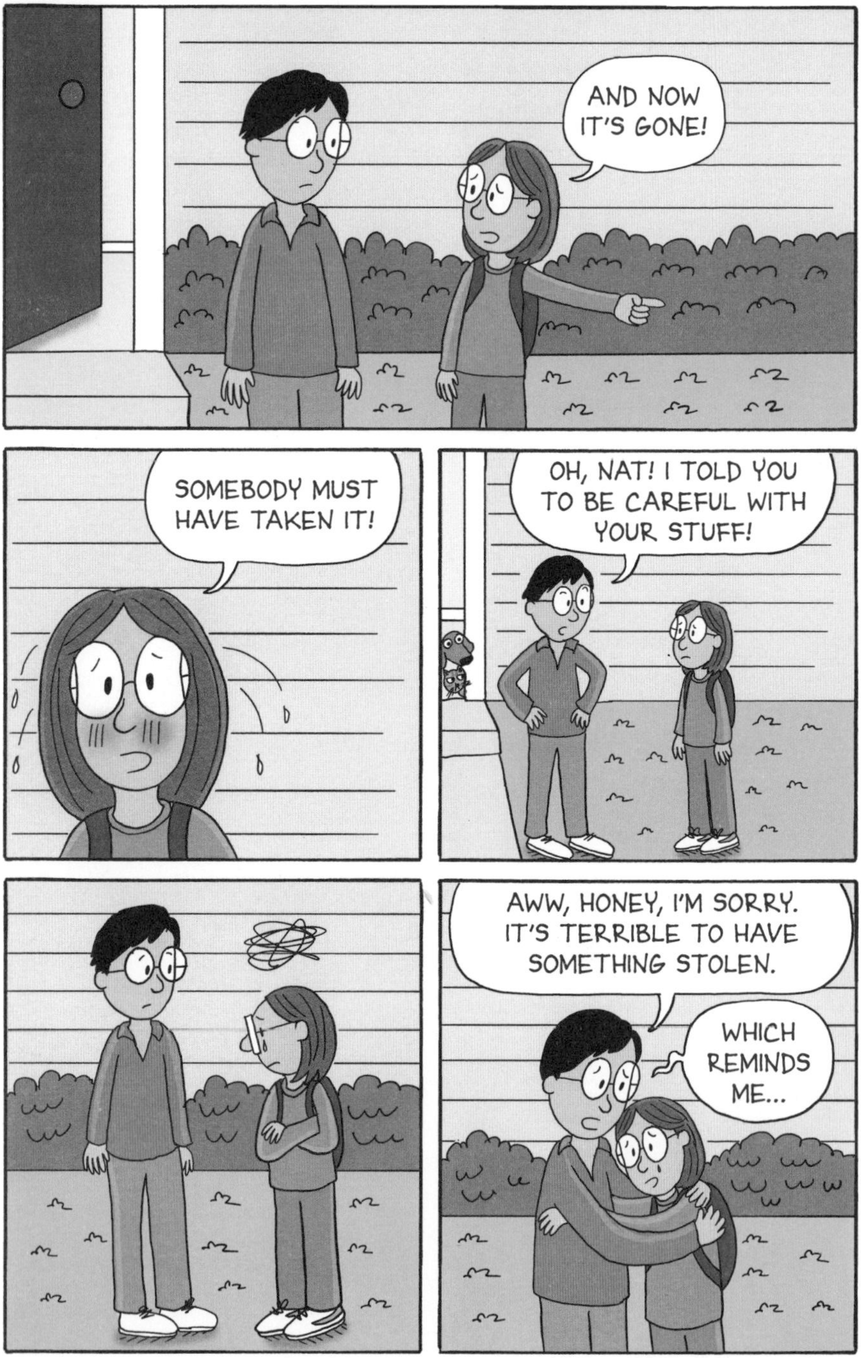
AND NOW IT'S GONE!
SOMEBODY MUST HAVE TAKEN IT!
OH, NAT! I TOLD YOU TO BE CAREFUL WITH YOUR STUFF!
AWW, HONEY, I'M SORRY. IT'S TERRIBLE TO HAVE SOMETHING STOLEN.
WHICH REMINDS ME...

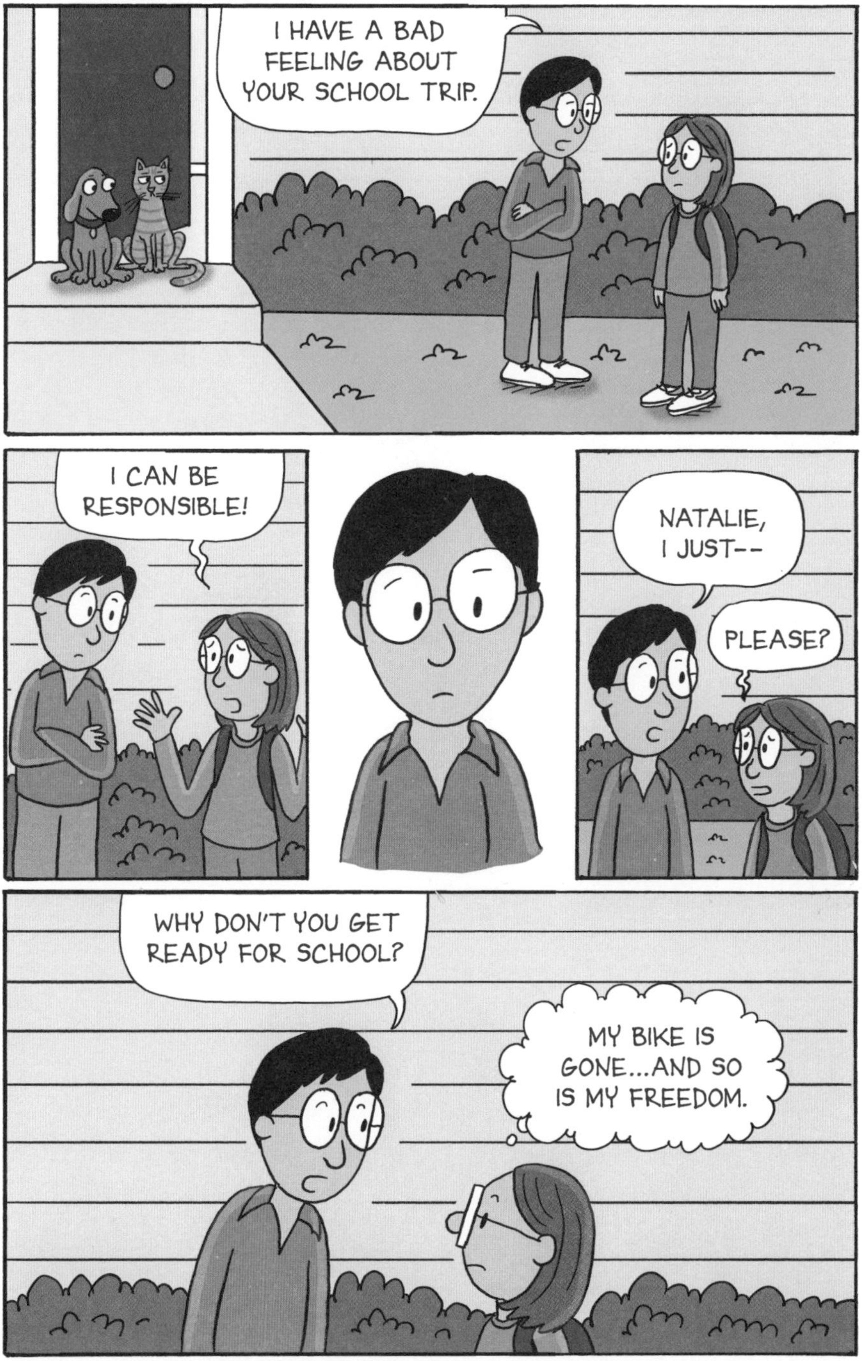
I HAVE A BAD FEELING ABOUT YOUR SCHOOL TRIP.
I CAN BE RESPONSIBLE!
NATALIE, I JUST--
PLEASE?
WHY DON'T YOU GET READY FOR SCHOOL?
MY BIKE IS GONE...AND SO IS MY FREEDOM.

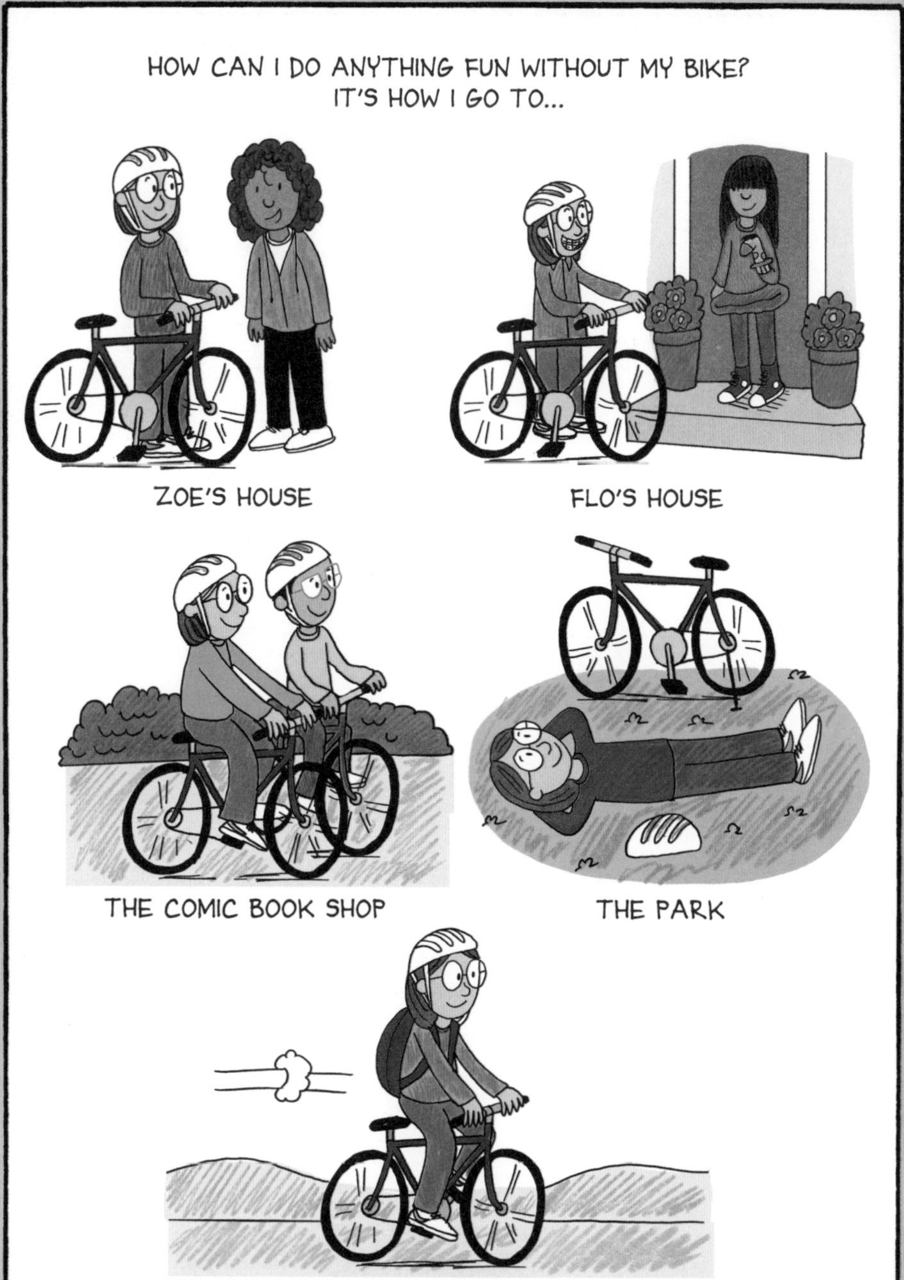
HOW CAN I DO ANYTHING FUN WITHOUT MY BIKE?
IT'S HOW I GO TO...
ZOE'S HOUSE
FLO'S HOUSE
THE COMIC BOOK SHOP
THE PARK
AND TO SCHOOL.

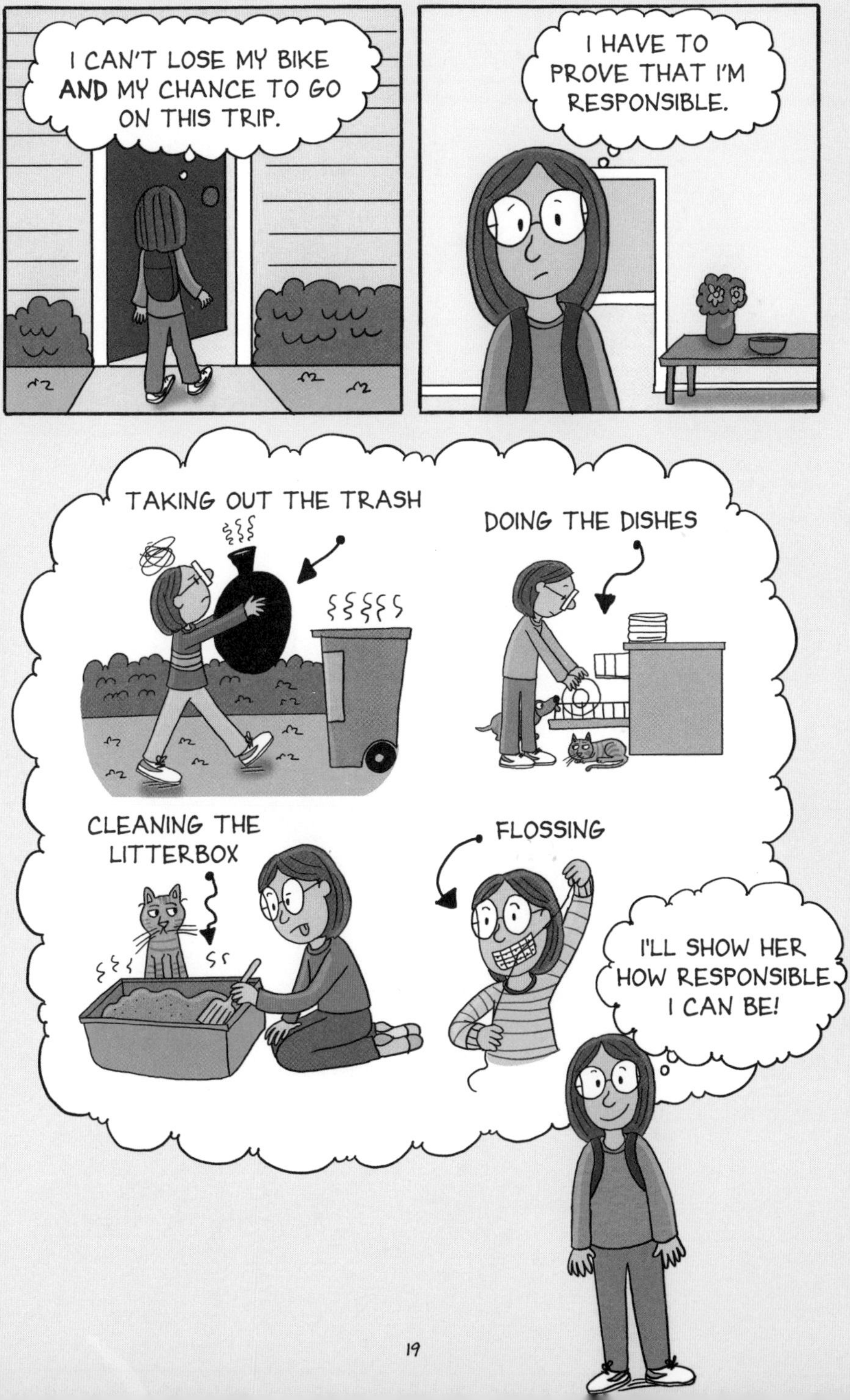
I CAN'T LOSE MY BIKE **AND** MY CHANCE TO GO ON THIS TRIP.
I HAVE TO PROVE THAT I'M RESPONSIBLE.
TAKING OUT THE TRASH
DOING THE DISHES
CLEANING THE LITTERBOX
FLOSSING
I'LL SHOW HER HOW RESPONSIBLE I CAN BE!

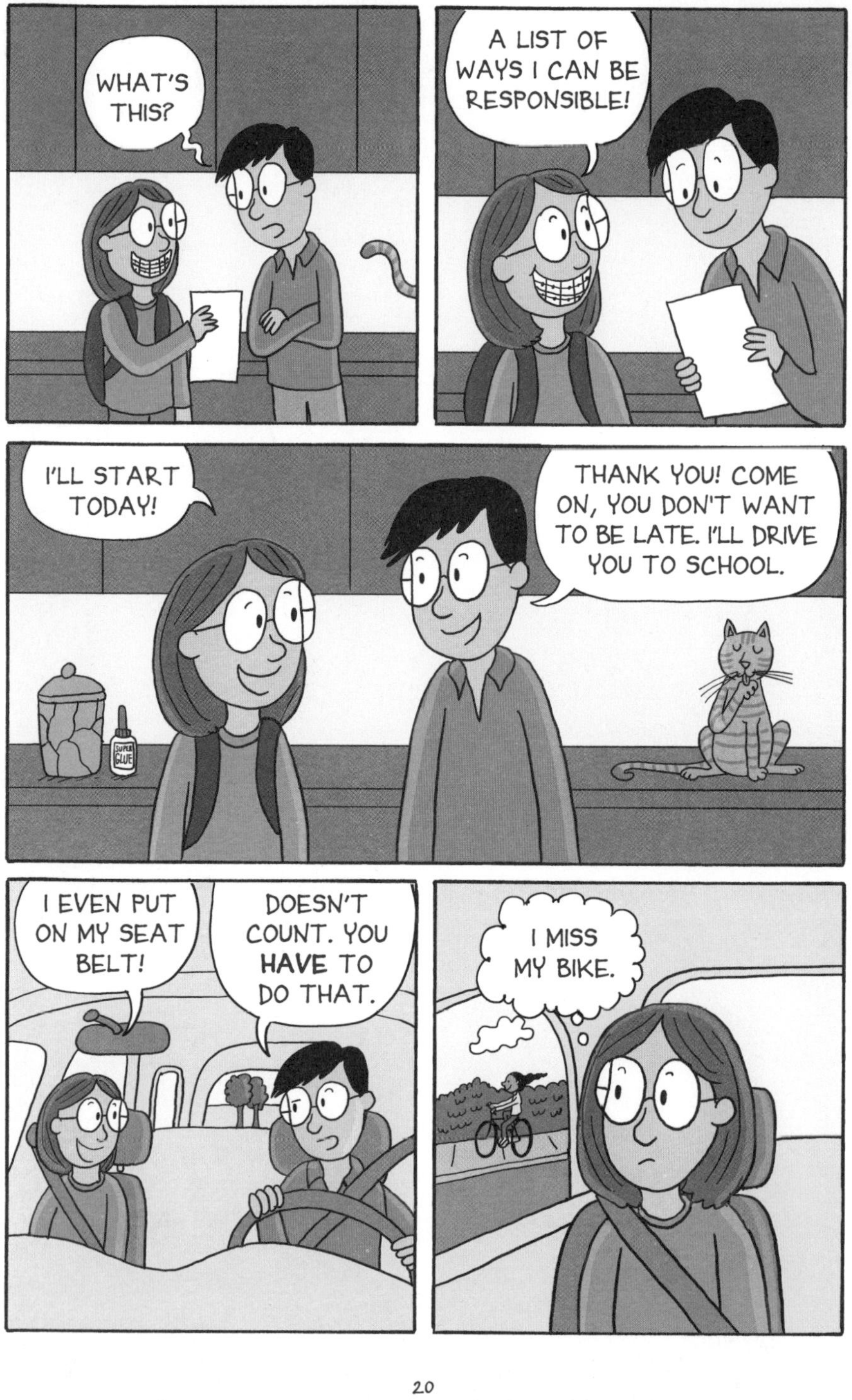
WHAT'S THIS?
A LIST OF WAYS I CAN BE RESPONSIBLE!
I'LL START TODAY!
THANK YOU! COME ON, YOU DON'T WANT TO BE LATE. I'LL DRIVE YOU TO SCHOOL.
SUPER GLUE
I EVEN PUT ON MY SEAT BELT!
DOESN'T COUNT. YOU **HAVE** TO DO THAT.
I MISS MY BIKE.

CHAPTER 2
BACK TO SCHOOL

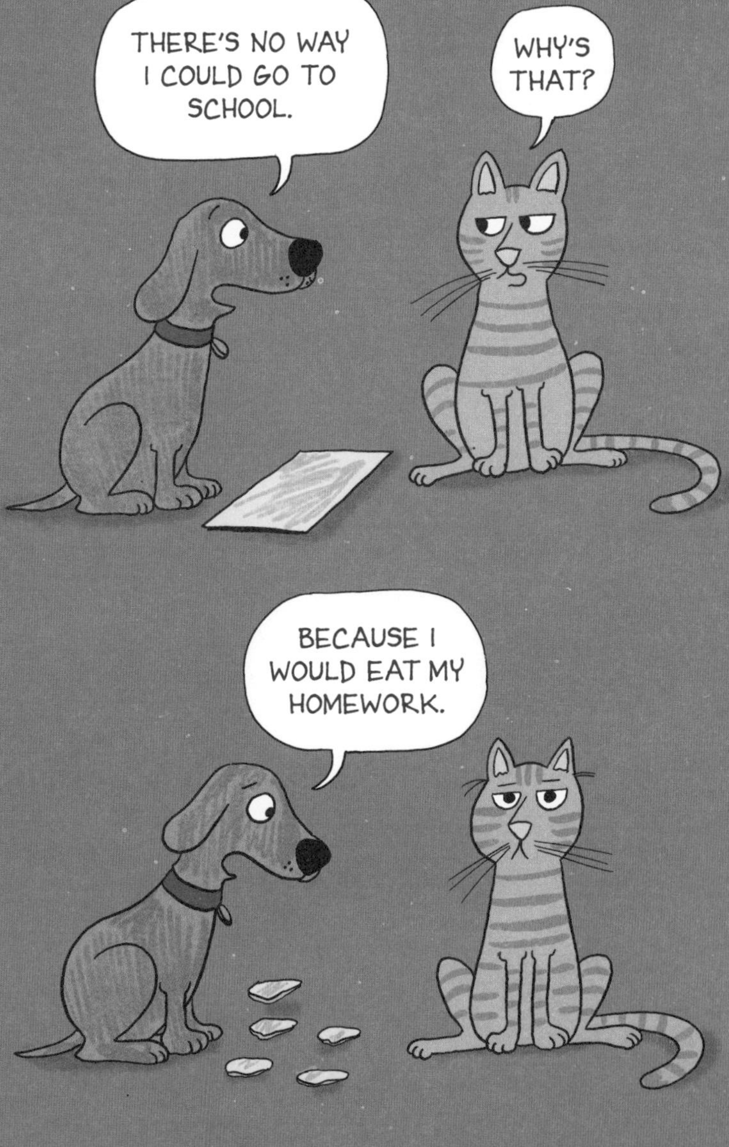
THERE'S NO WAY I COULD GO TO SCHOOL.
WHY'S THAT?
BECAUSE I WOULD EAT MY HOMEWORK.

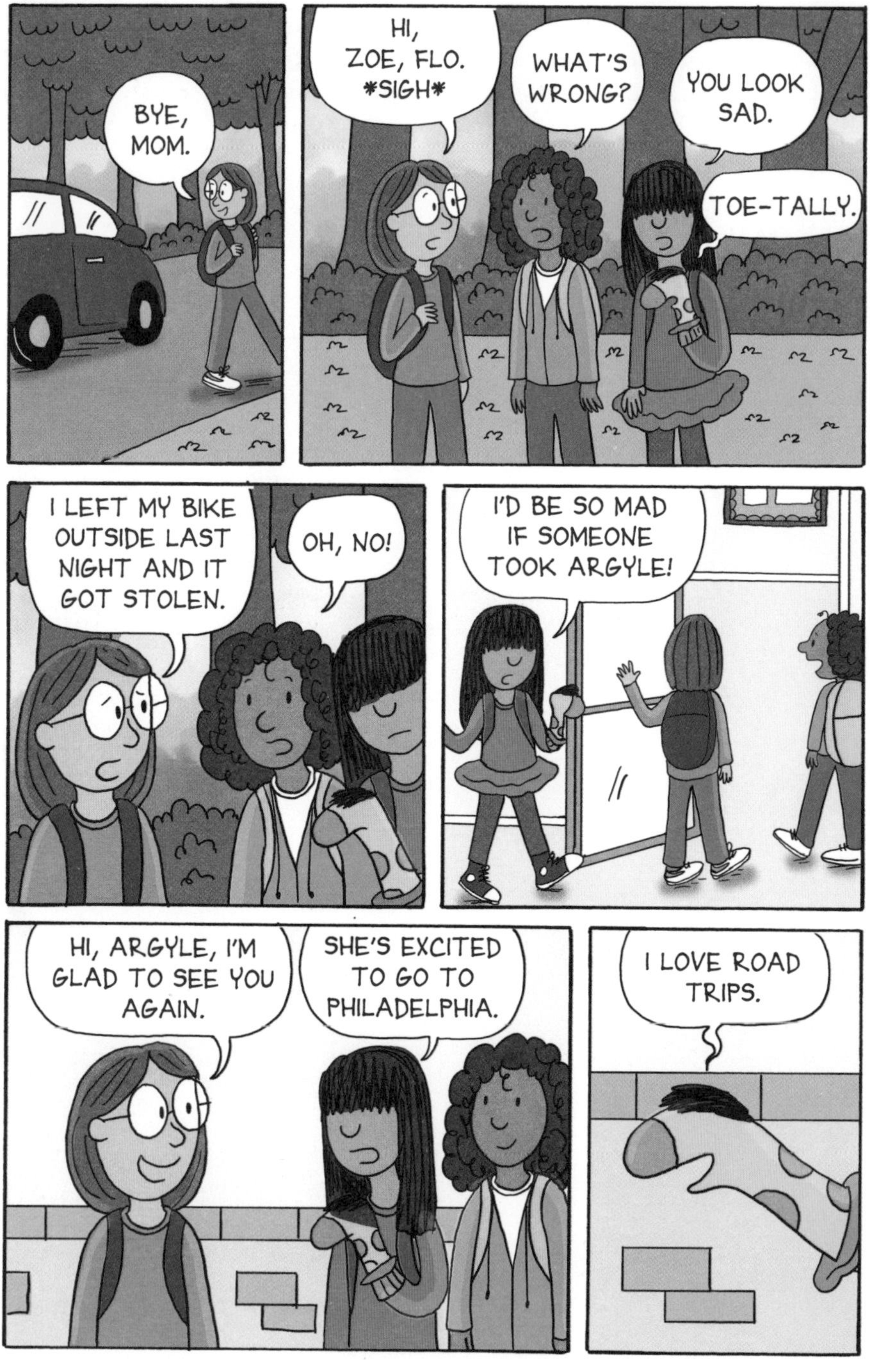
BYE, MOM.
HI, ZOE, FLO. *SIGH*
WHAT'S WRONG?
YOU LOOK SAD.
TOE-TALLY.
I LEFT MY BIKE OUTSIDE LAST NIGHT AND IT GOT STOLEN.
OH, NO!
I'D BE SO MAD IF SOMEONE TOOK ARGYLE!
HI, ARGYLE, I'M GLAD TO SEE YOU AGAIN.
SHE'S EXCITED TO GO TO PHILADELPHIA.
I LOVE ROAD TRIPS.

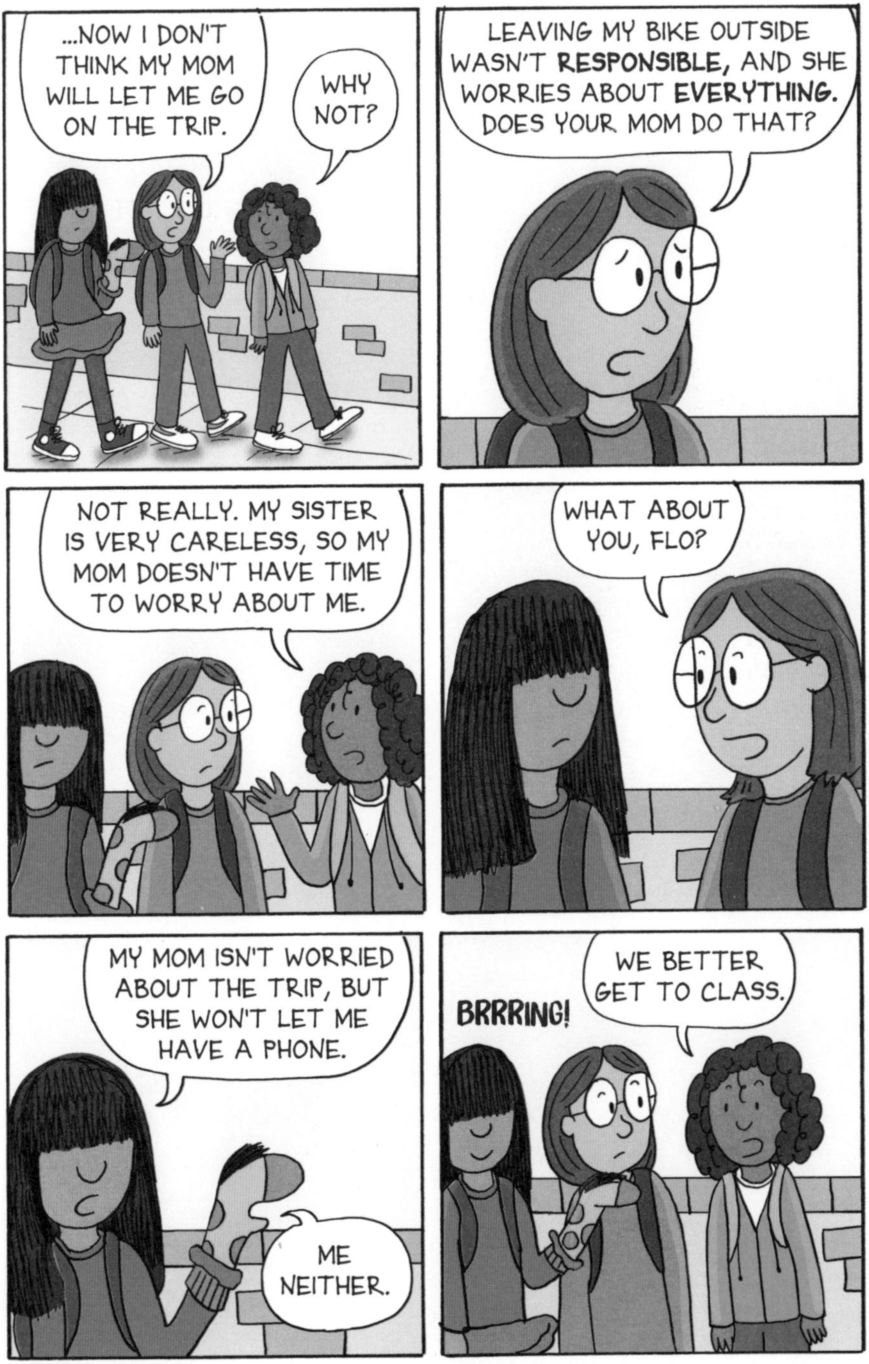
...NOW I DON'T THINK MY MOM WILL LET ME GO ON THE TRIP.
WHY NOT?
LEAVING MY BIKE OUTSIDE WASN'T **RESPONSIBLE,** AND SHE WORRIES ABOUT **EVERYTHING.** DOES YOUR MOM DO THAT?
NOT REALLY. MY SISTER IS VERY CARELESS, SO MY MOM DOESN'T HAVE TIME TO WORRY ABOUT ME.
WHAT ABOUT YOU, FLO?
MY MOM ISN'T WORRIED ABOUT THE TRIP, BUT SHE WON'T LET ME HAVE A PHONE.
ME NEITHER.
BRRRING!
WE BETTER GET TO CLASS.

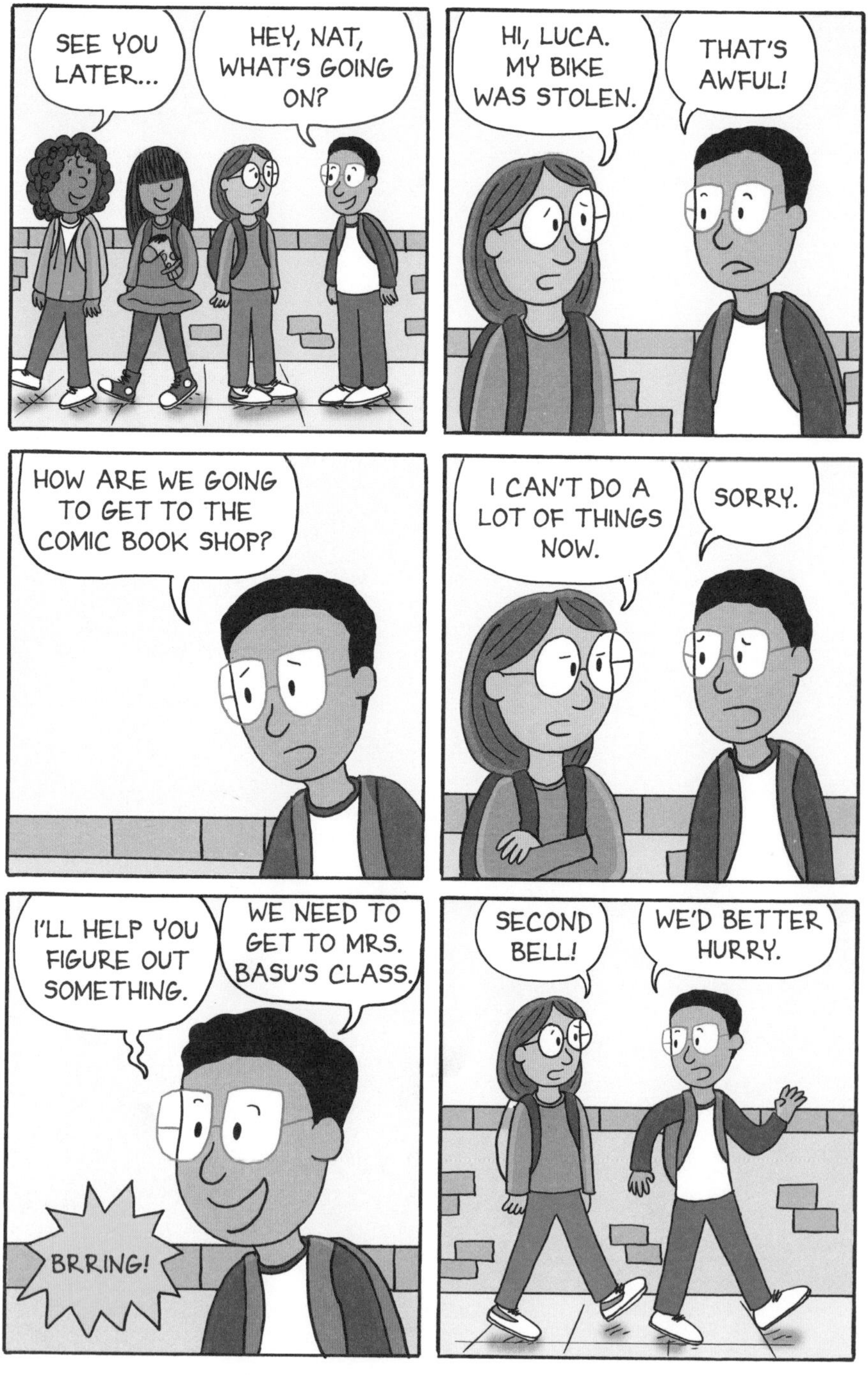
SEE YOU LATER...
HEY, NAT, WHAT'S GOING ON?
HI, LUCA. MY BIKE WAS STOLEN.
THAT'S AWFUL!
HOW ARE WE GOING TO GET TO THE COMIC BOOK SHOP?
I CAN'T DO A LOT OF THINGS NOW.
SORRY.
I'LL HELP YOU FIGURE OUT SOMETHING.
WE NEED TO GET TO MRS. BASU'S CLASS.
BRRING!
SECOND BELL!
WE'D BETTER HURRY.

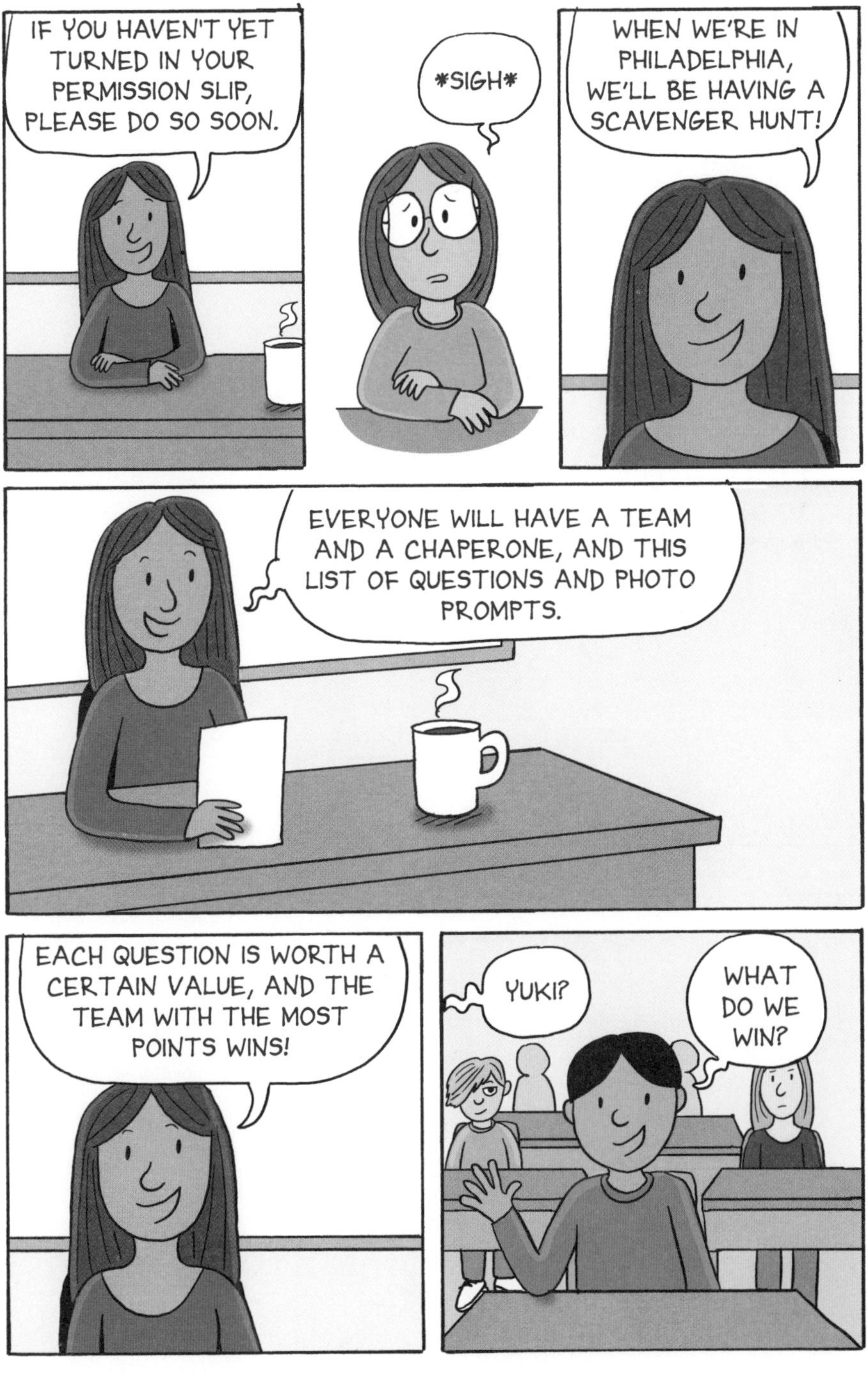
IF YOU HAVEN'T YET TURNED IN YOUR PERMISSION SLIP, PLEASE DO SO SOON.
SIGH
WHEN WE'RE IN PHILADELPHIA, WE'LL BE HAVING A SCAVENGER HUNT!
EVERYONE WILL HAVE A TEAM AND A CHAPERONE, AND THIS LIST OF QUESTIONS AND PHOTO PROMPTS.
EACH QUESTION IS WORTH A CERTAIN VALUE, AND THE TEAM WITH THE MOST POINTS WINS!
YUKI?
WHAT DO WE WIN?

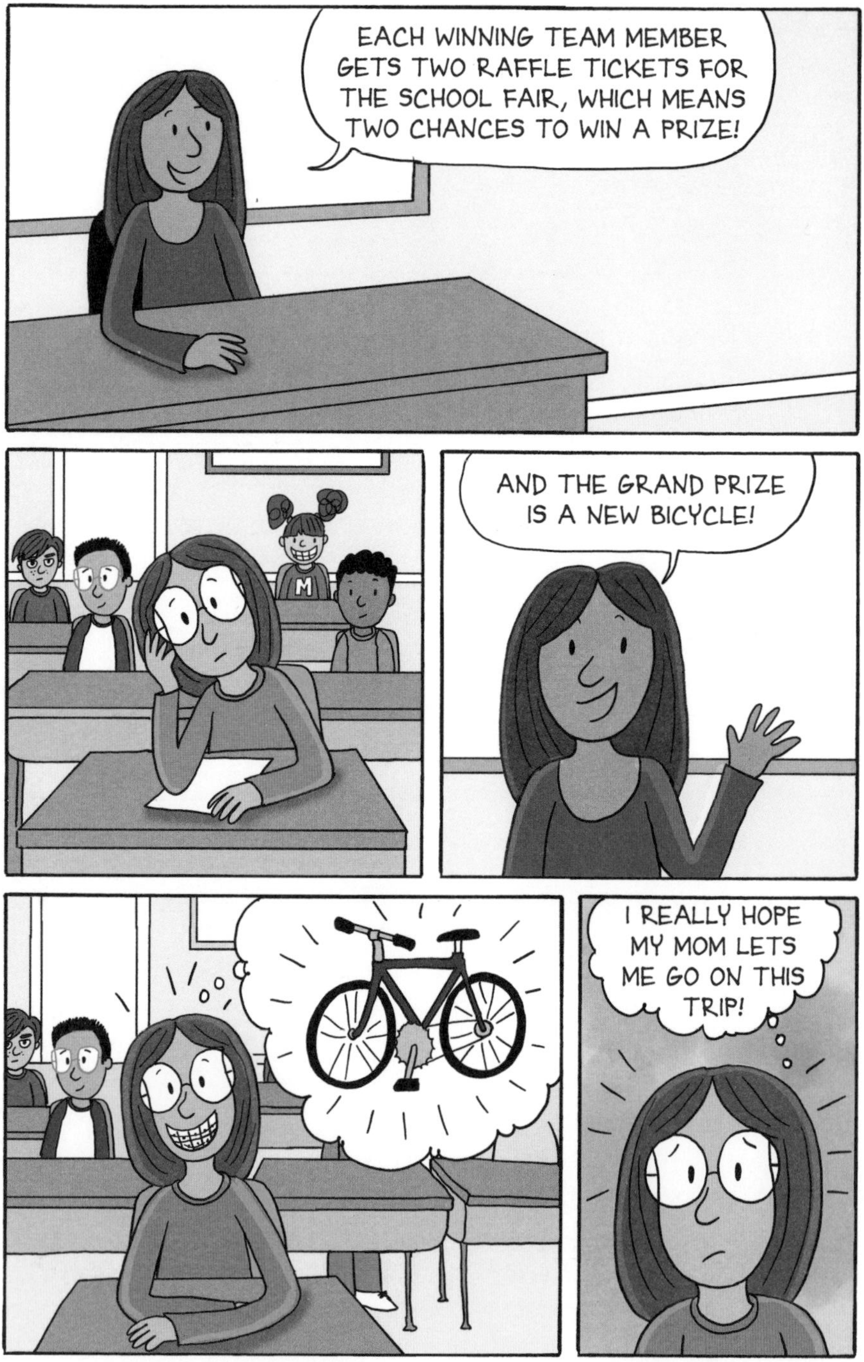
EACH WINNING TEAM MEMBER GETS TWO RAFFLE TICKETS FOR THE SCHOOL FAIR, WHICH MEANS TWO CHANCES TO WIN A PRIZE!
M
AND THE GRAND PRIZE IS A NEW BICYCLE!
I REALLY HOPE MY MOM LETS ME GO ON THIS TRIP!

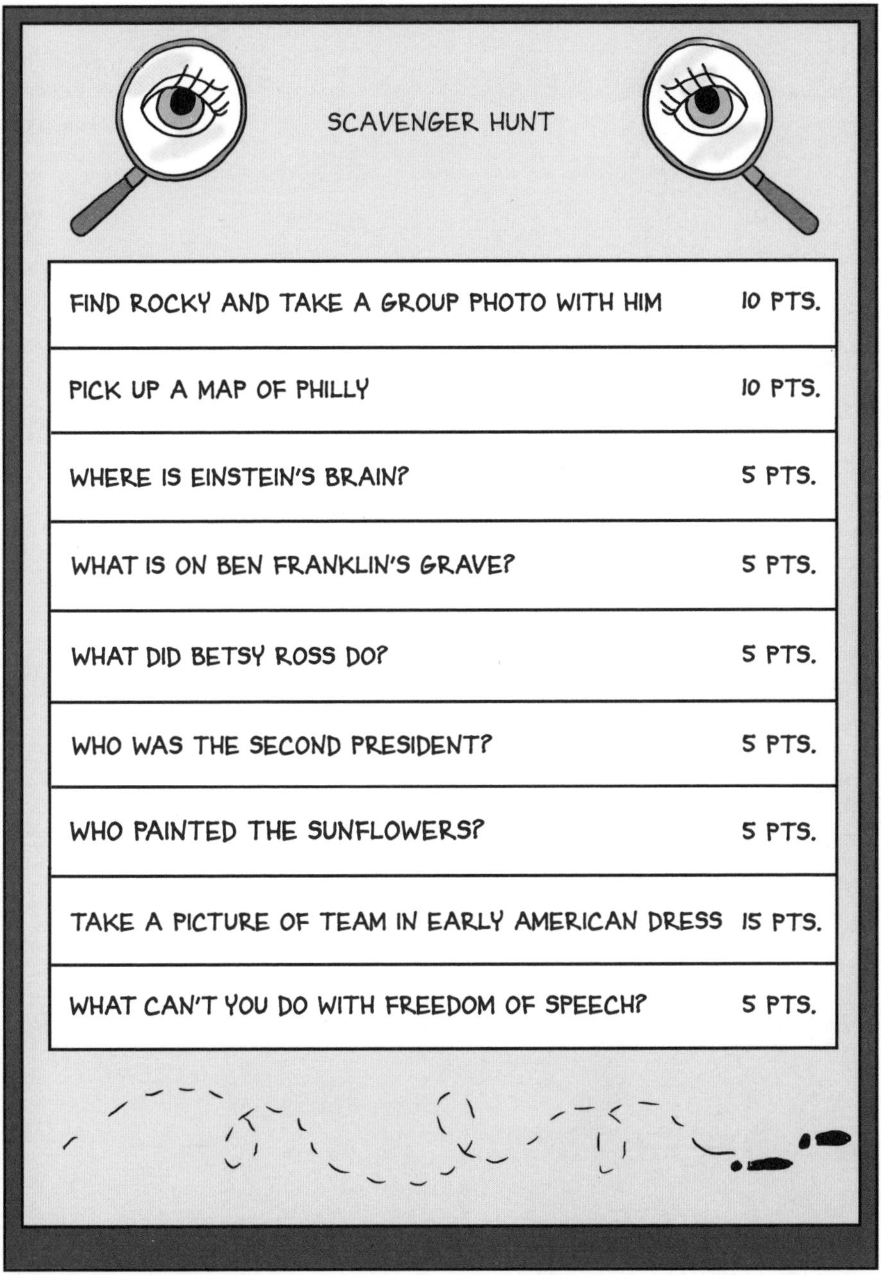
SCAVENGER HUNT
FIND ROCKY AND TAKE A GROUP PHOTO WITH HIM 10 PTS.
PICK UP A MAP OF PHILLY 10 PTS.
WHERE IS EINSTEIN'S BRAIN? 5 PTS.
WHAT IS ON BEN FRANKLIN'S GRAVE? 5 PTS.
WHAT DID BETSY ROSS DO? 5 PTS.
WHO WAS THE SECOND PRESIDENT? 5 PTS.
WHO PAINTED THE SUNFLOWERS? 5 PTS.
TAKE A PICTURE OF TEAM IN EARLY AMERICAN DRESS 15 PTS.
WHAT CAN'T YOU DO WITH FREEDOM OF SPEECH? 5 PTS.

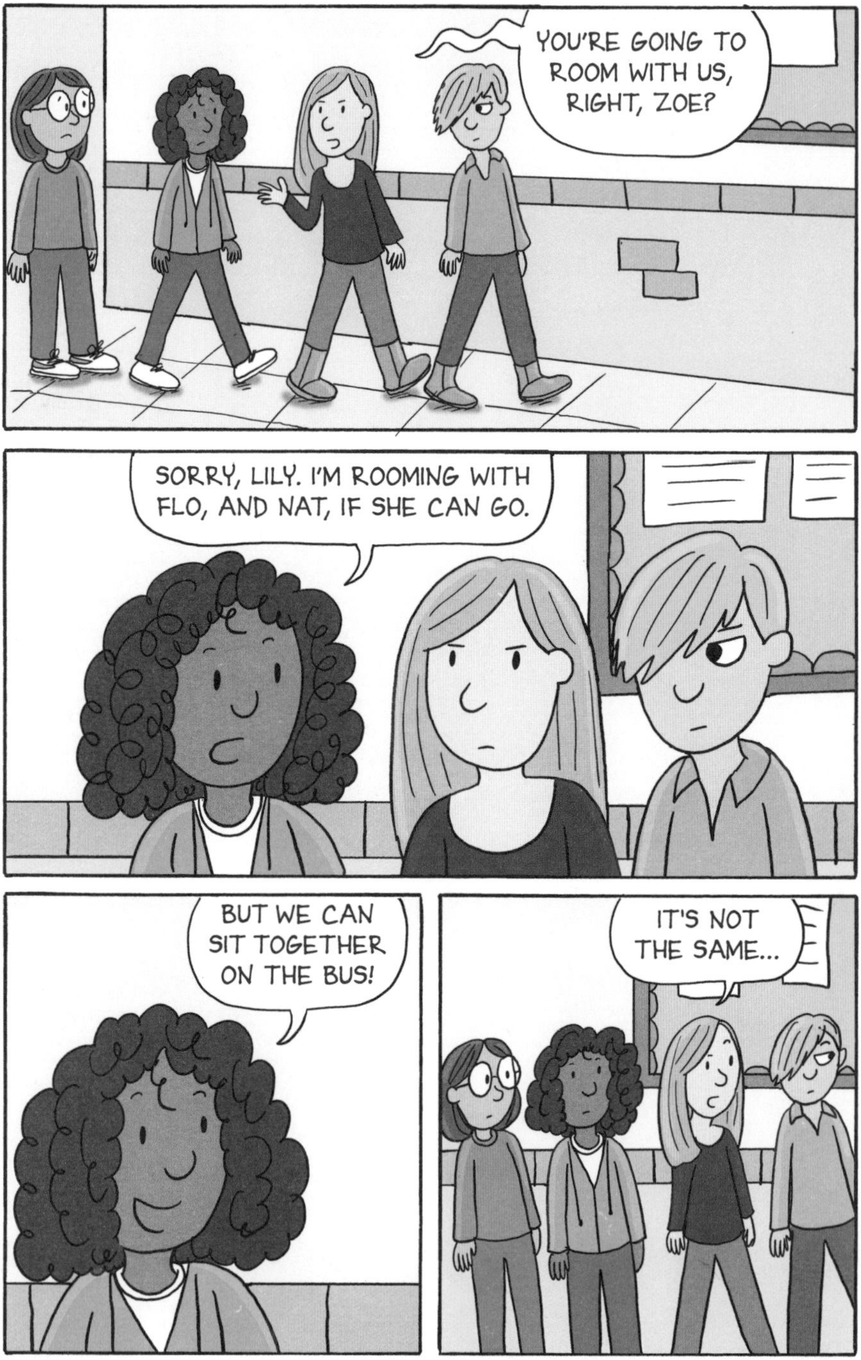
YOU'RE GOING TO ROOM WITH US, RIGHT, ZOE?
SORRY, LILY. I'M ROOMING WITH FLO, AND NAT, IF SHE CAN GO.
BUT WE CAN SIT TOGETHER ON THE BUS!
IT'S NOT THE SAME...

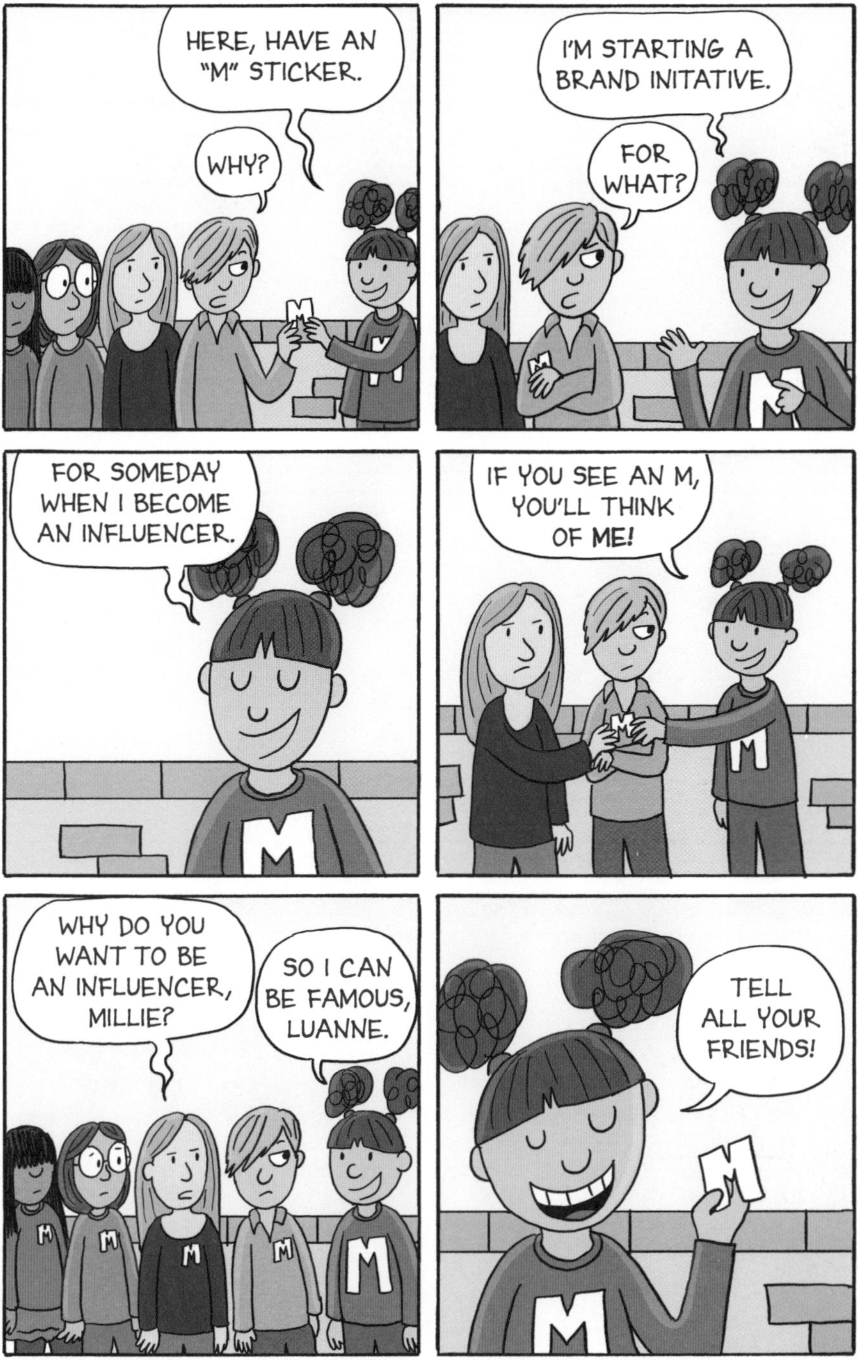
HERE, HAVE AN "M" STICKER.
WHY?
I'M STARTING A BRAND INITATIVE.
FOR WHAT?
FOR SOMEDAY WHEN I BECOME AN INFLUENCER.
IF YOU SEE AN M, YOU'LL THINK OF **ME!**
WHY DO YOU WANT TO BE AN INFLUENCER, MILLIE?
SO I CAN BE FAMOUS, LUANNE.
TELL ALL YOUR FRIENDS!

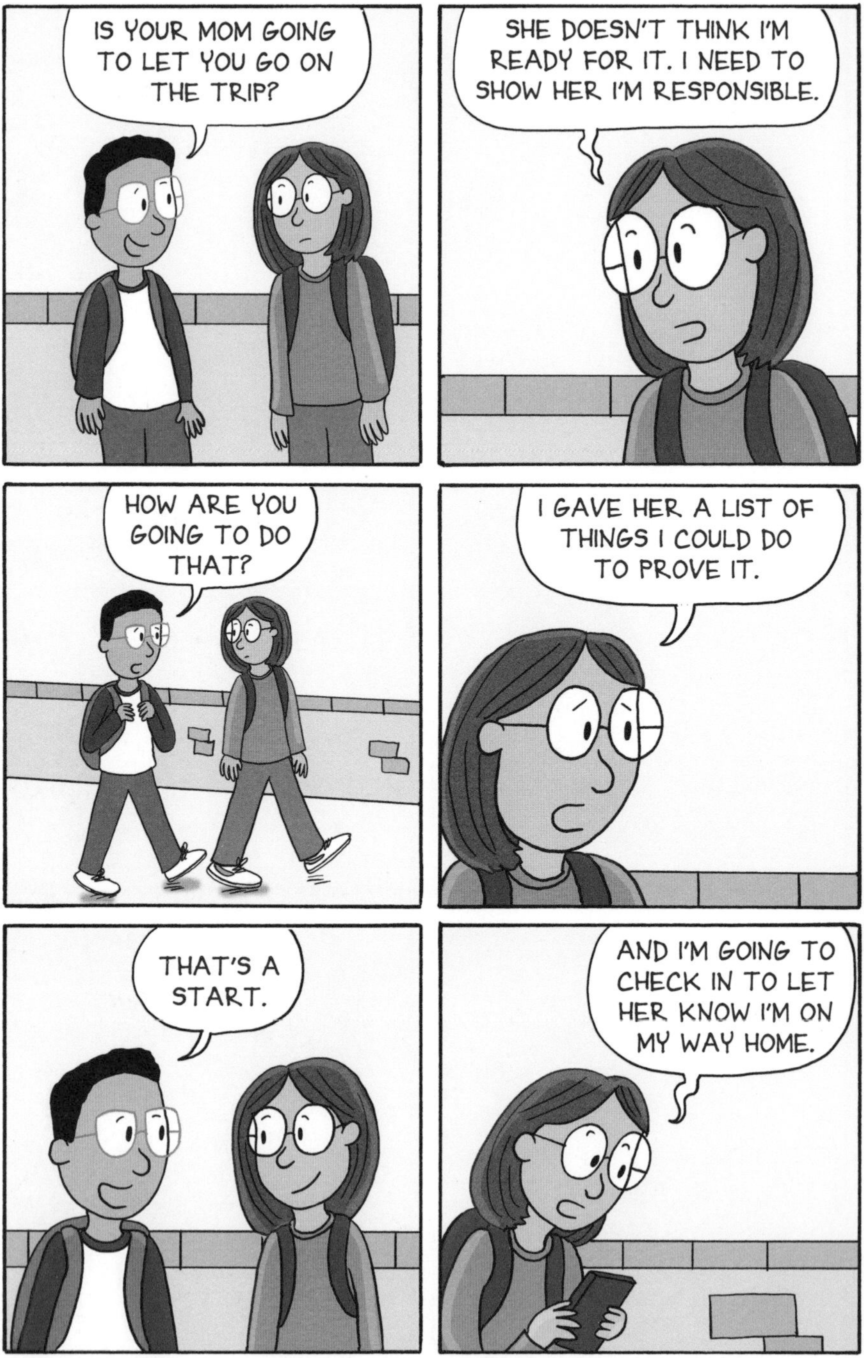
IS YOUR MOM GOING TO LET YOU GO ON THE TRIP?
SHE DOESN'T THINK I'M READY FOR IT. I NEED TO SHOW HER I'M RESPONSIBLE.
HOW ARE YOU GOING TO DO THAT?
I GAVE HER A LIST OF THINGS I COULD DO TO PROVE IT.
THAT'S A START.
AND I'M GOING TO CHECK IN TO LET HER KNOW I'M ON MY WAY HOME.

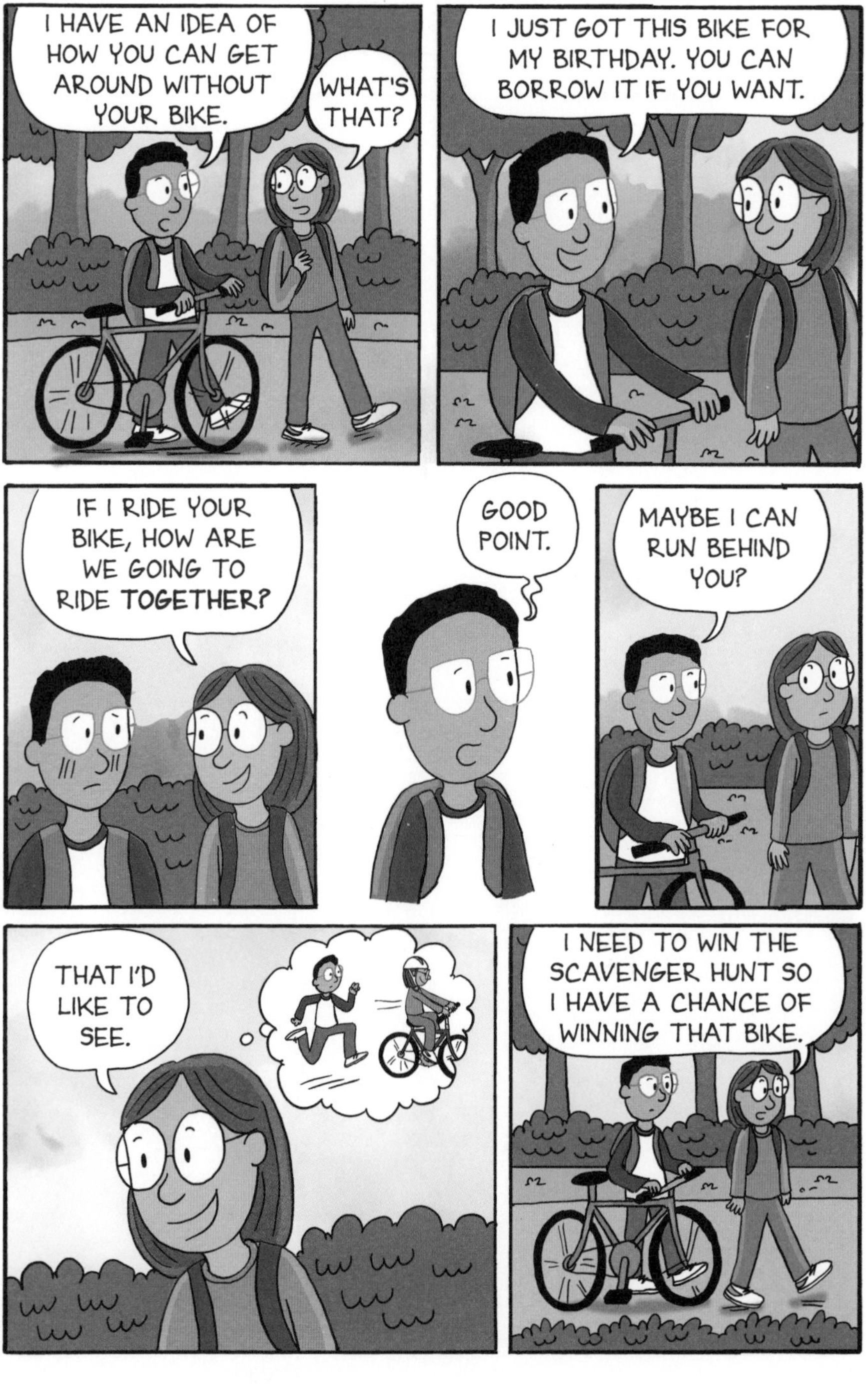
I HAVE AN IDEA OF HOW YOU CAN GET AROUND WITHOUT YOUR BIKE.
WHAT'S THAT?
I JUST GOT THIS BIKE FOR MY BIRTHDAY. YOU CAN BORROW IT IF YOU WANT.
IF I RIDE YOUR BIKE, HOW ARE WE GOING TO RIDE TOGETHER?
GOOD POINT.
MAYBE I CAN RUN BEHIND YOU?
THAT I'D LIKE TO SEE.
I NEED TO WIN THE SCAVENGER HUNT SO I HAVE A CHANCE OF WINNING THAT BIKE.

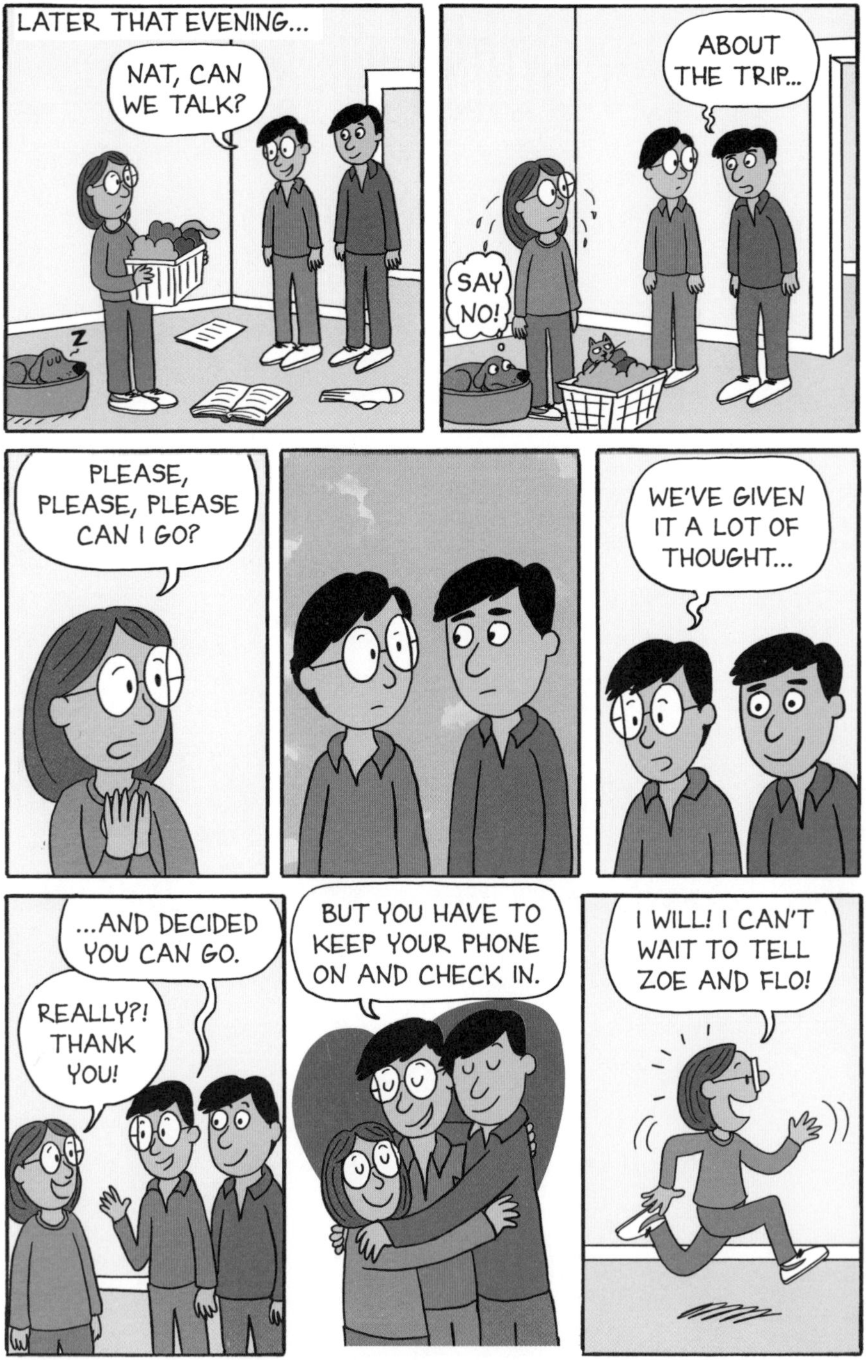
LATER THAT EVENING...
NAT, CAN WE TALK?
ABOUT THE TRIP...
SAY NO!
PLEASE, PLEASE, PLEASE CAN I GO?
WE'VE GIVEN IT A LOT OF THOUGHT...
...AND DECIDED YOU CAN GO.
REALLY?! THANK YOU!
BUT YOU HAVE TO KEEP YOUR PHONE ON AND CHECK IN.
I WILL! I CAN'T WAIT TO TELL ZOE AND FLO!

CHAPTER 3
ART

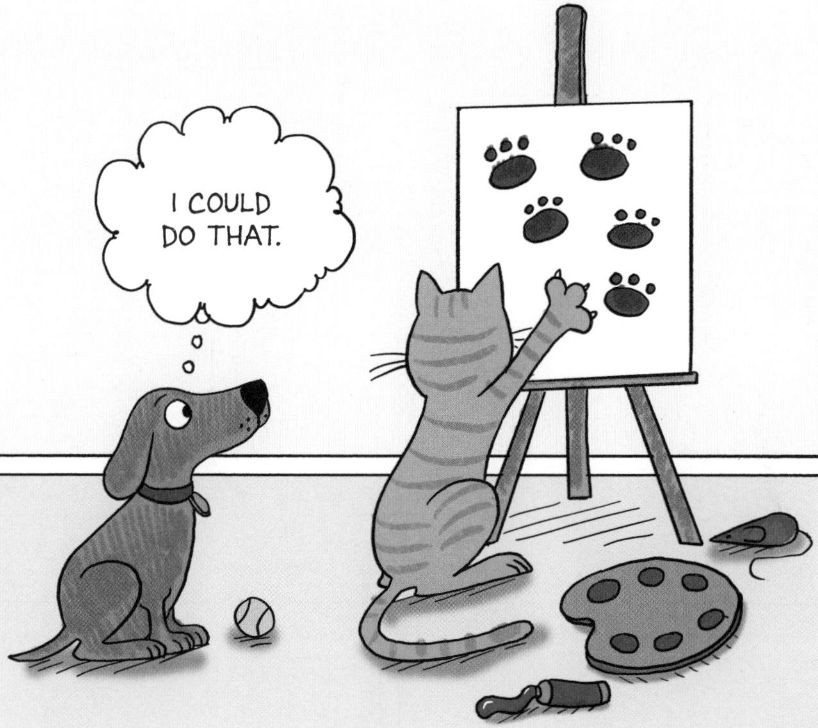
I COULD DO THAT.

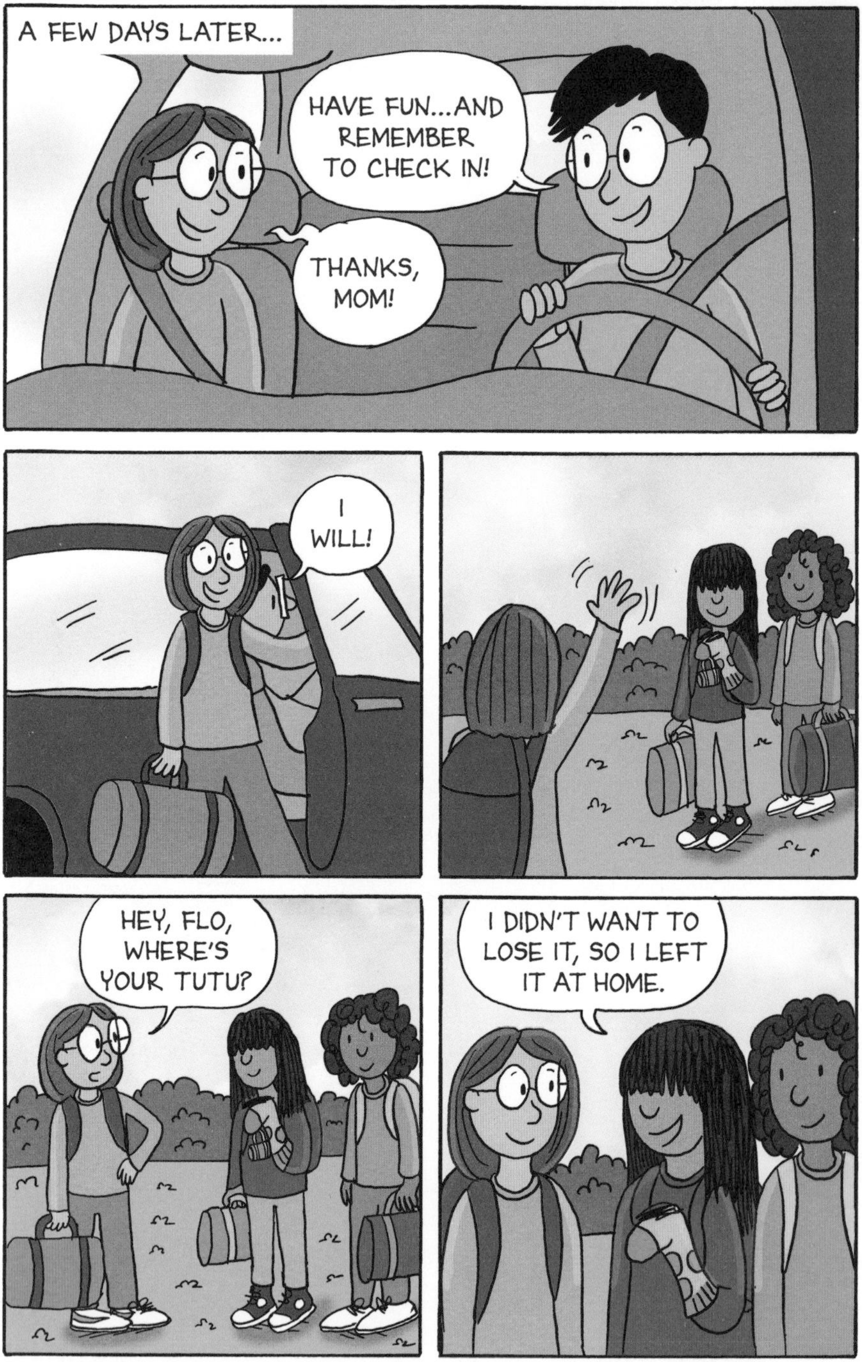
A FEW DAYS LATER...
HAVE FUN...AND REMEMBER TO CHECK IN!
THANKS, MOM!
I WILL!
HEY, FLO, WHERE'S YOUR TUTU?
I DIDN'T WANT TO LOSE IT, SO I LEFT IT AT HOME.

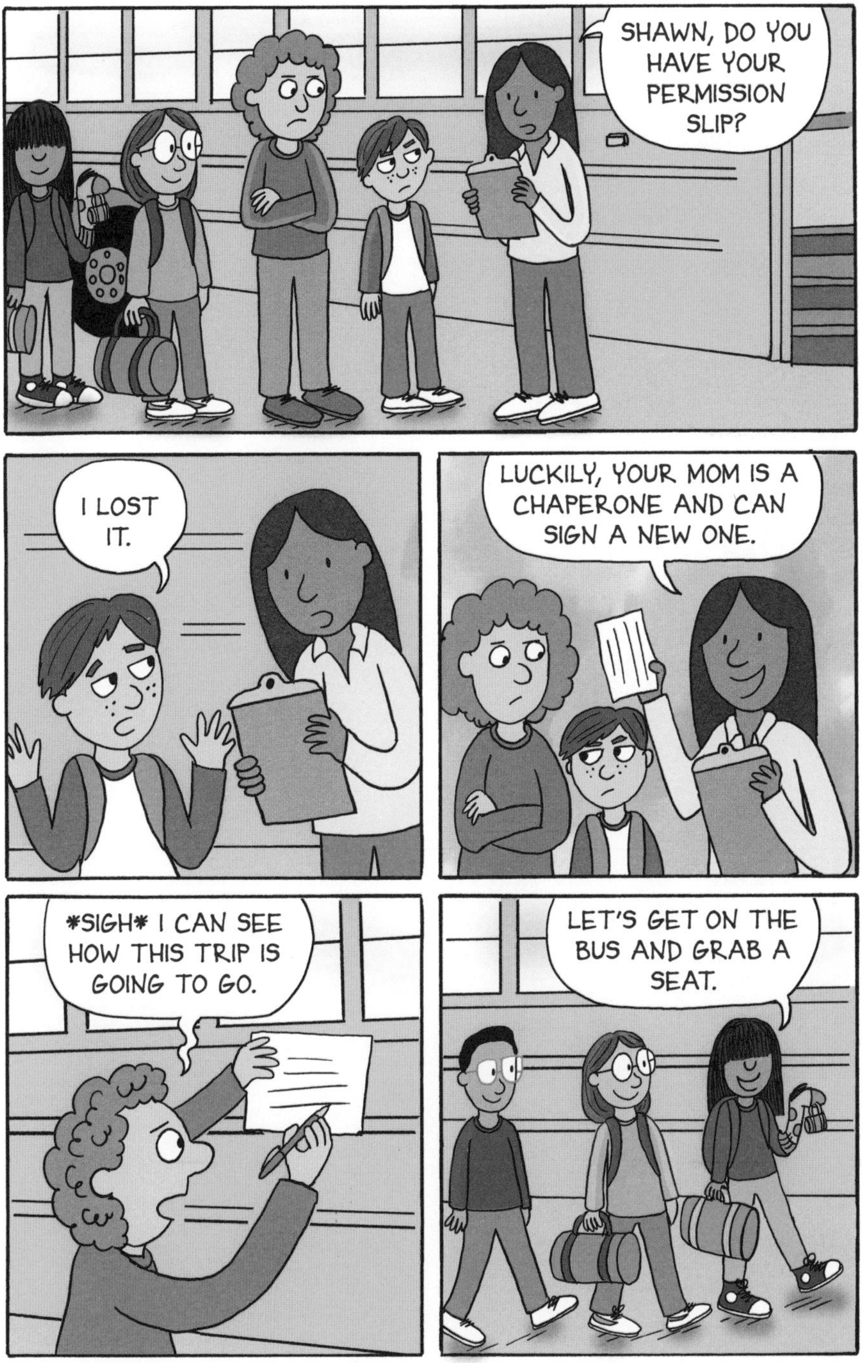
SHAWN, DO YOU HAVE YOUR PERMISSION SLIP?
I LOST IT.
LUCKILY, YOUR MOM IS A CHAPERONE AND CAN SIGN A NEW ONE.
SIGH I CAN SEE HOW THIS TRIP IS GOING TO GO.
LET'S GET ON THE BUS AND GRAB A SEAT.

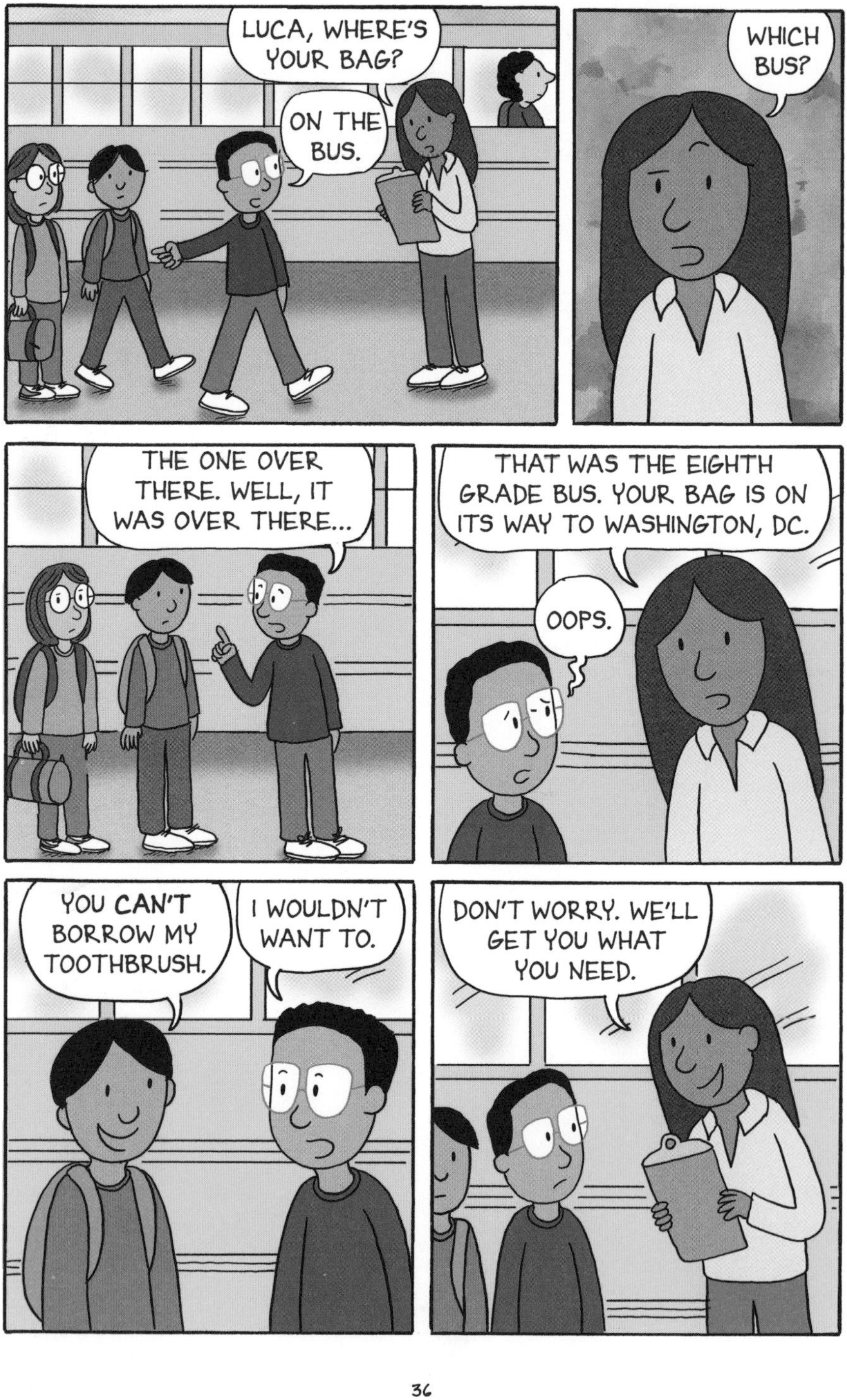
LUCA, WHERE'S YOUR BAG?
ON THE BUS.
WHICH BUS?
THE ONE OVER THERE. WELL, IT WAS OVER THERE...
THAT WAS THE EIGHTH GRADE BUS. YOUR BAG IS ON ITS WAY TO WASHINGTON, DC.
OOPS.
YOU **CAN'T** BORROW MY TOOTHBRUSH.
I WOULDN'T WANT TO.
DON'T WORRY. WE'LL GET YOU WHAT YOU NEED.

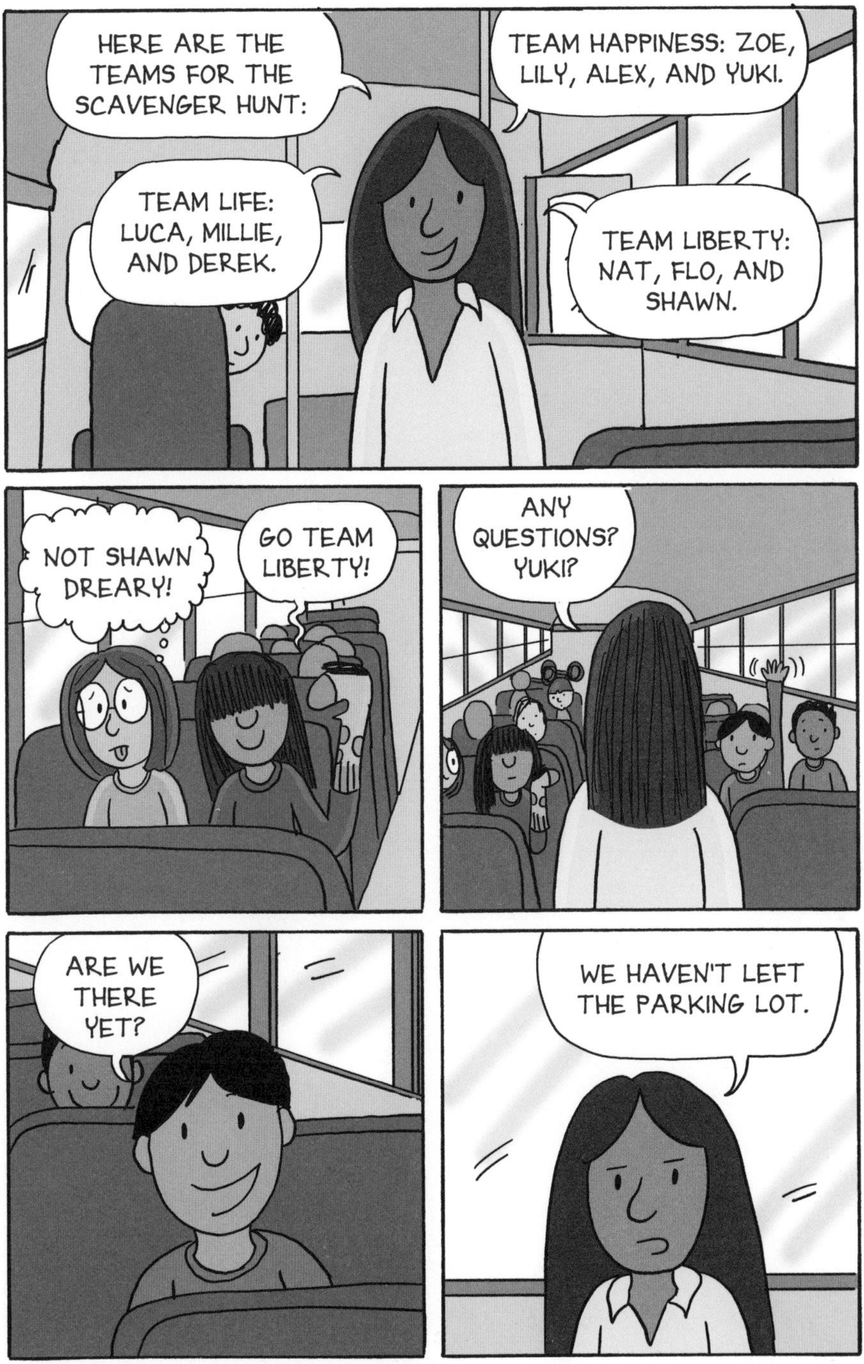
HERE ARE THE TEAMS FOR THE SCAVENGER HUNT:
TEAM HAPPINESS: ZOE, LILY, ALEX, AND YUKI.
TEAM LIFE: LUCA, MILLIE, AND DEREK.
TEAM LIBERTY: NAT, FLO, AND SHAWN.
NOT SHAWN DREARY!
GO TEAM LIBERTY!
ANY QUESTIONS? YUKI?
ARE WE THERE YET?
WE HAVEN'T LEFT THE PARKING LOT.

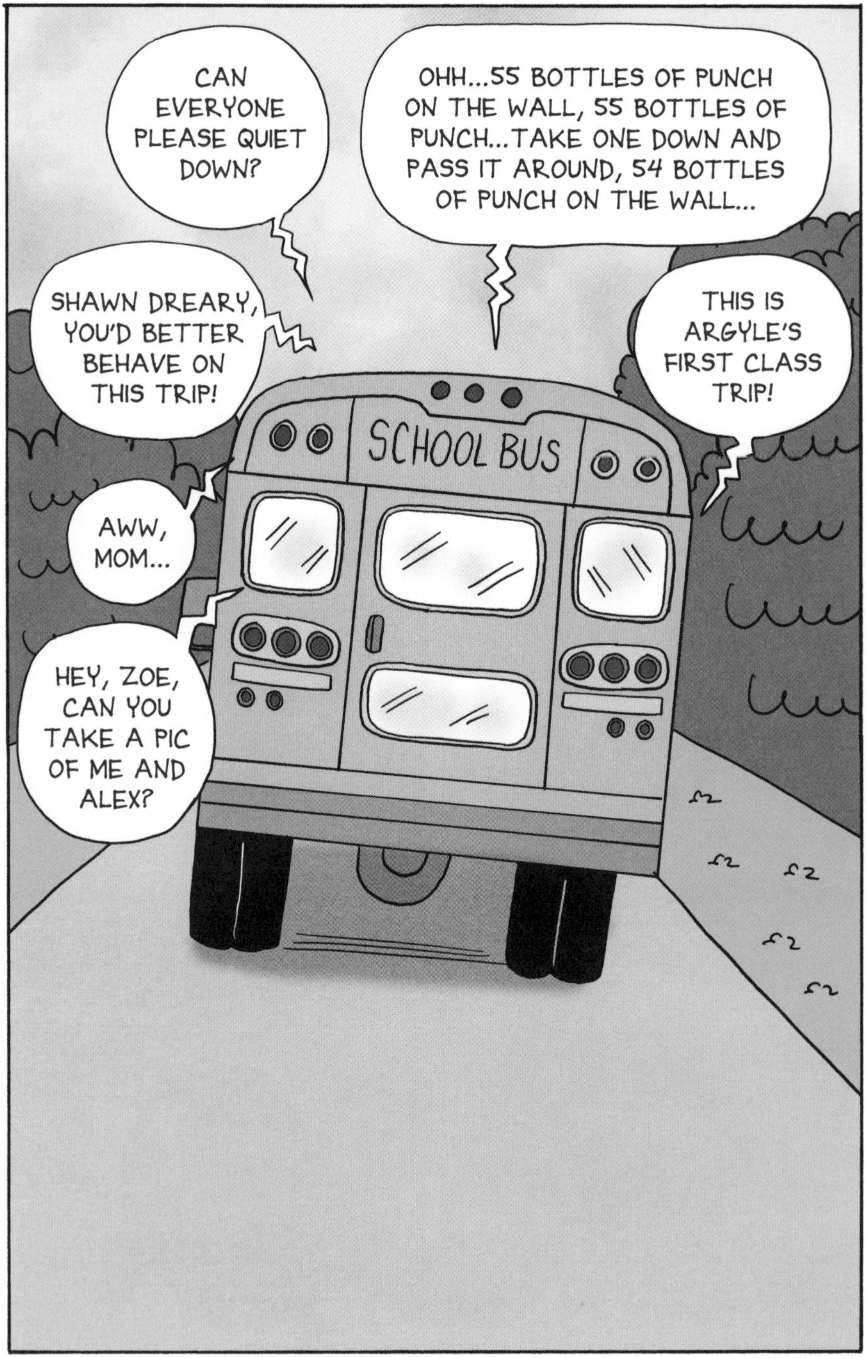
CAN EVERYONE PLEASE QUIET DOWN?
OHH...55 BOTTLES OF PUNCH ON THE WALL, 55 BOTTLES OF PUNCH...TAKE ONE DOWN AND PASS IT AROUND, 54 BOTTLES OF PUNCH ON THE WALL...
SHAWN DREARY, YOU'D BETTER BEHAVE ON THIS TRIP!
THIS IS ARGYLE'S FIRST CLASS TRIP!
SCHOOL BUS
AWW, MOM...
HEY, ZOE, CAN YOU TAKE A PIC OF ME AND ALEX?

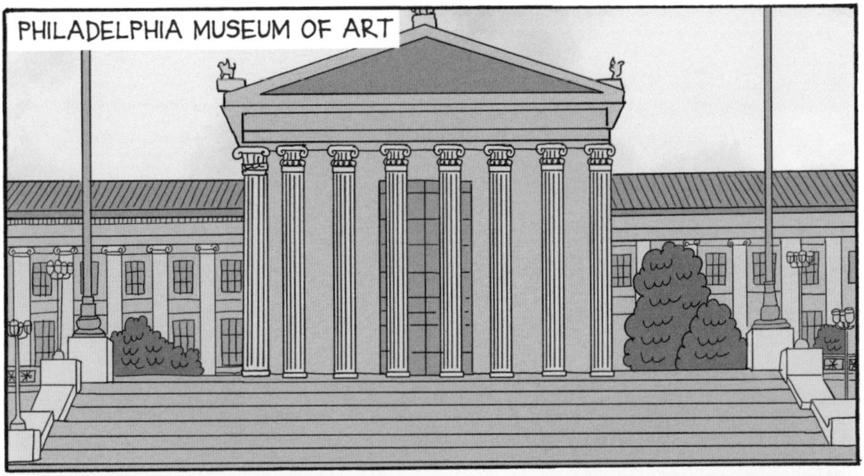
PHILADELPHIA MUSEUM OF ART

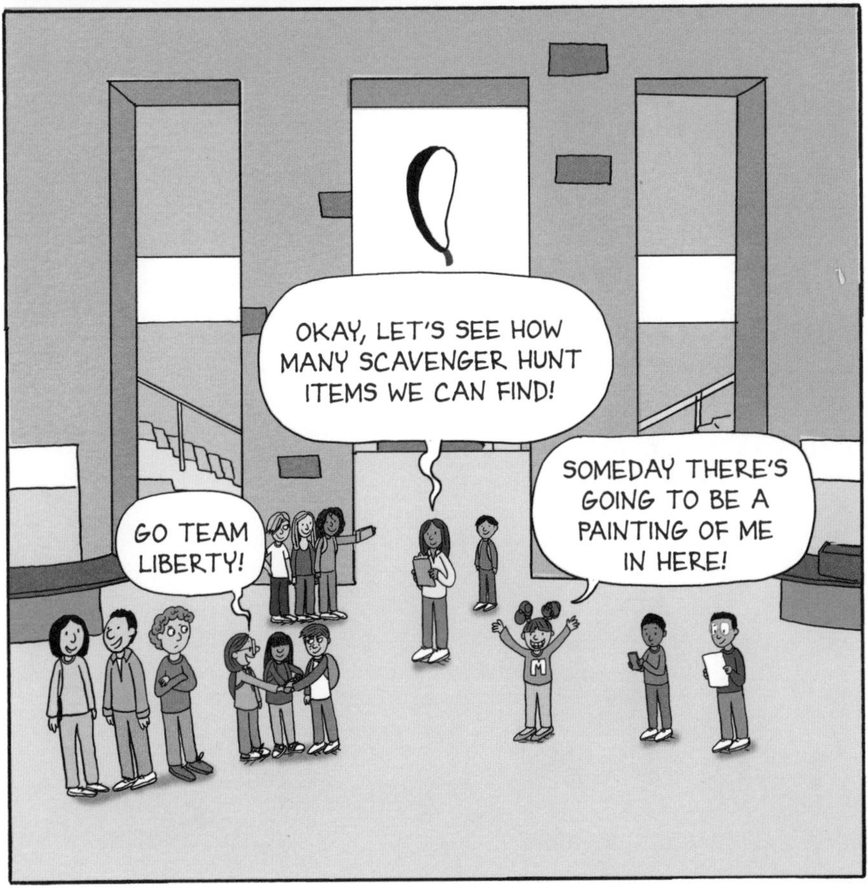
OKAY, LET'S SEE HOW MANY SCAVENGER HUNT ITEMS WE CAN FIND!
GO TEAM LIBERTY!
SOMEDAY THERE'S GOING TO BE A PAINTING OF ME IN HERE!

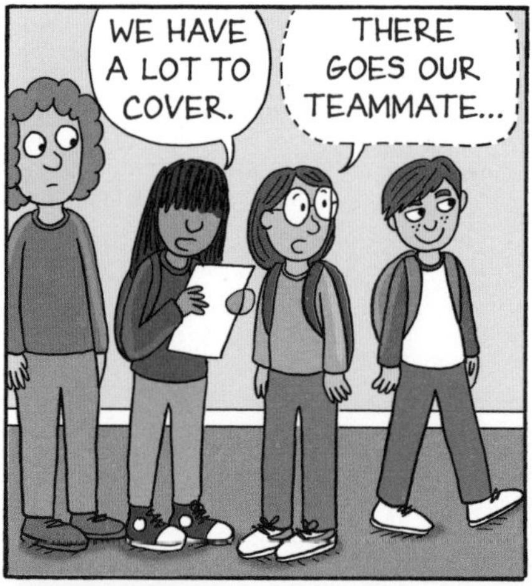
WE HAVE A LOT TO COVER.
THERE GOES OUR TEAMMATE...

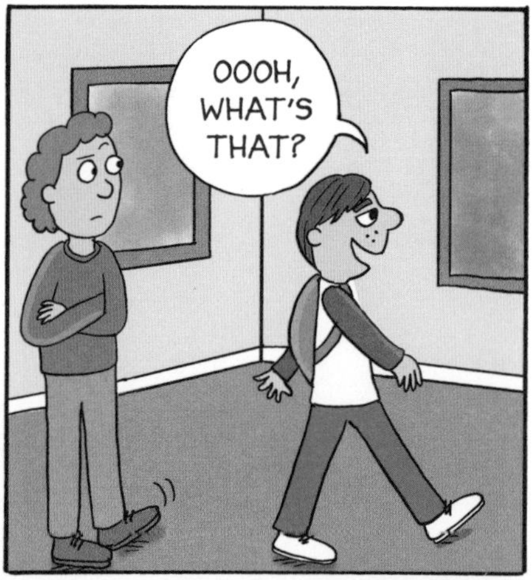
OOOH, WHAT'S THAT?

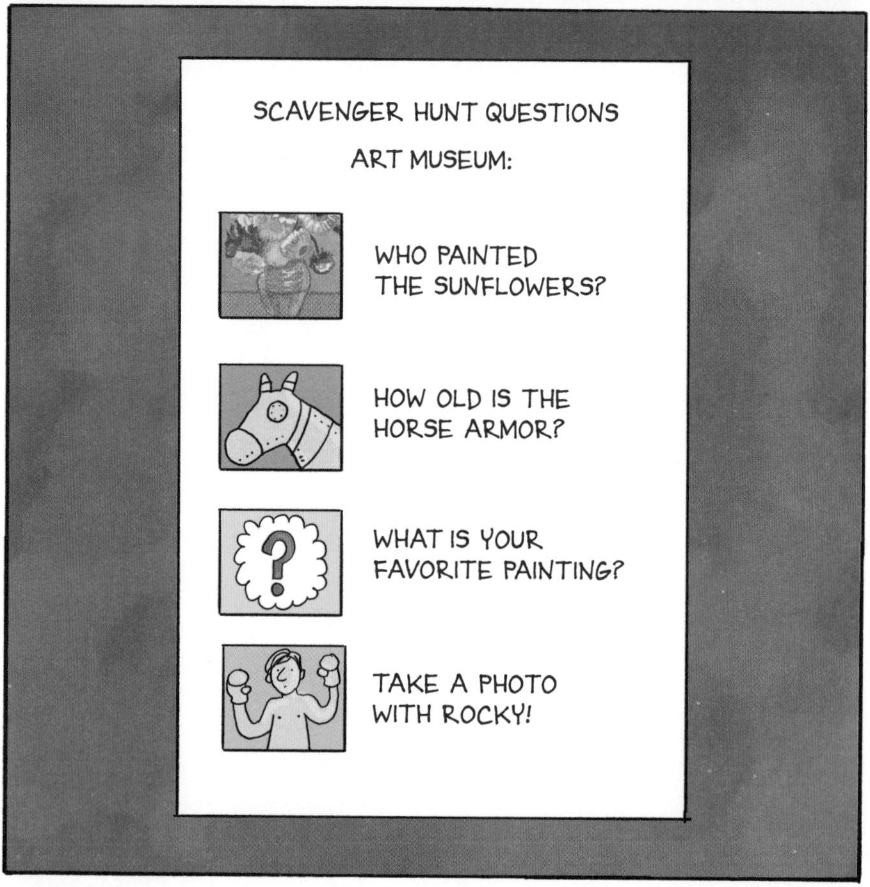
SCAVENGER HUNT QUESTIONS
ART MUSEUM:
WHO PAINTED THE SUNFLOWERS?
HOW OLD IS THE HORSE ARMOR?
WHAT IS YOUR FAVORITE PAINTING?
TAKE A PHOTO WITH ROCKY!

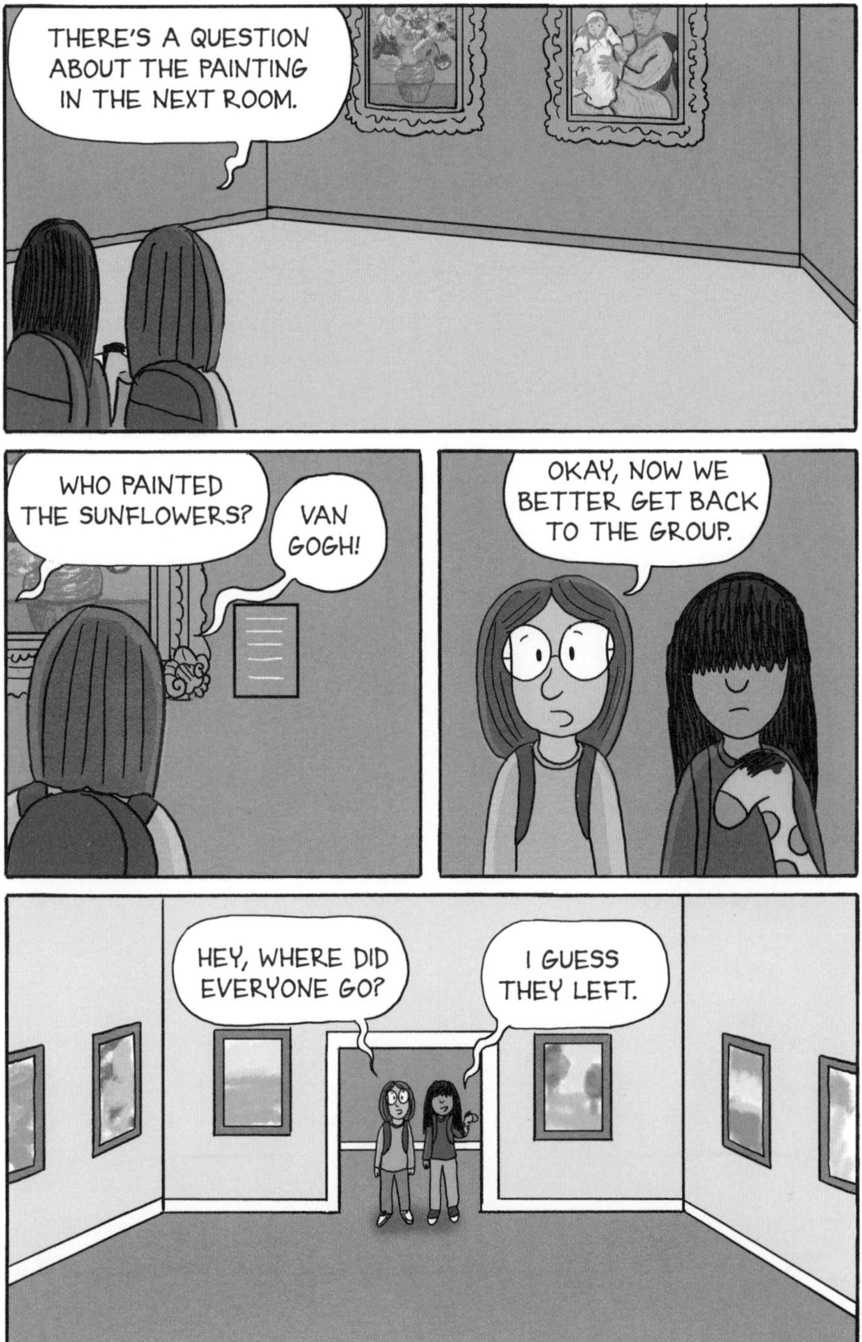
THERE'S A QUESTION ABOUT THE PAINTING IN THE NEXT ROOM.
WHO PAINTED THE SUNFLOWERS?
VAN GOGH!
OKAY, NOW WE BETTER GET BACK TO THE GROUP.
HEY, WHERE DID EVERYONE GO?
I GUESS THEY LEFT.

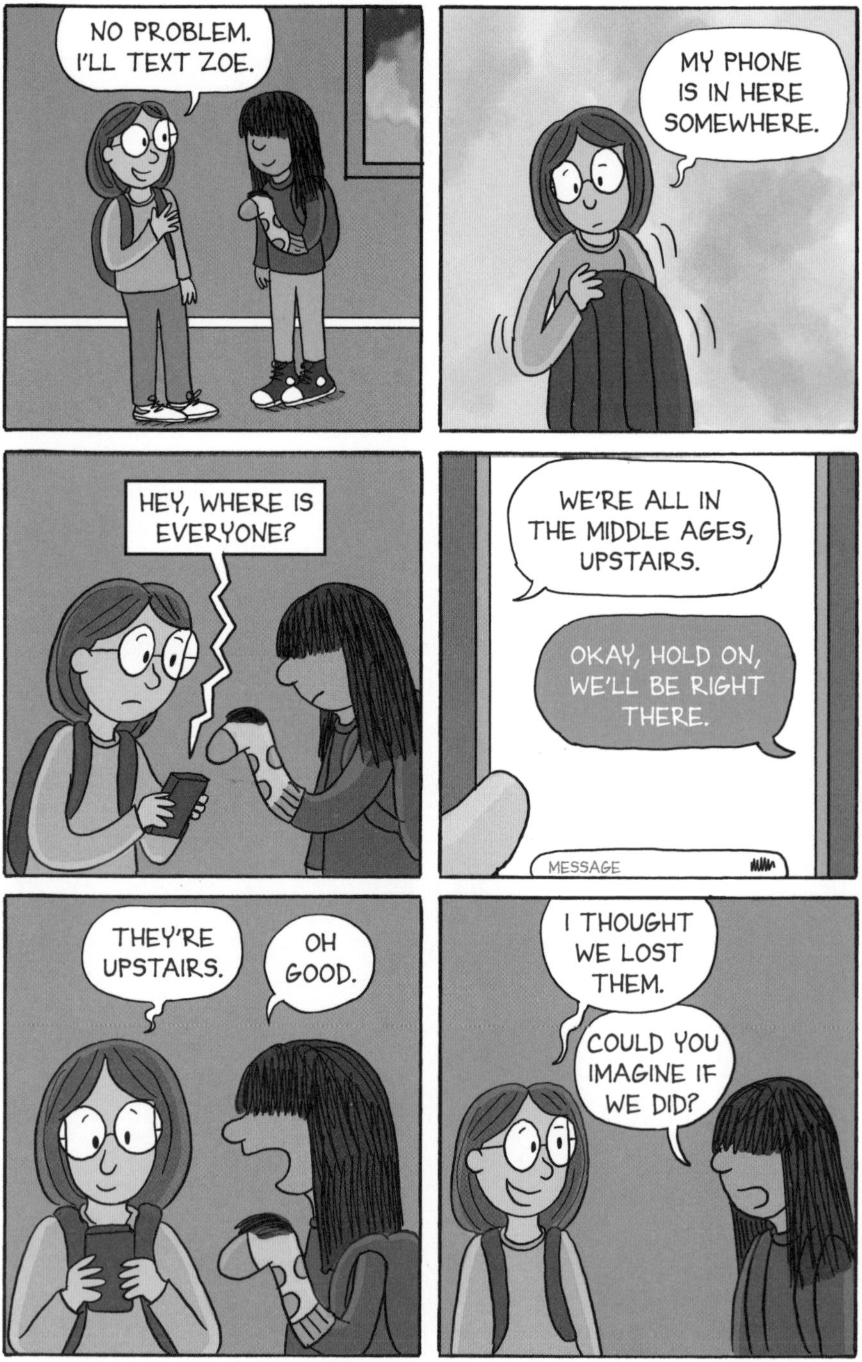
NO PROBLEM. I'LL TEXT ZOE.
MY PHONE IS IN HERE SOMEWHERE.
HEY, WHERE IS EVERYONE?
WE'RE ALL IN THE MIDDLE AGES, UPSTAIRS.
OKAY, HOLD ON, WE'LL BE RIGHT THERE.
MESSAGE
THEY'RE UPSTAIRS.
OH GOOD.
I THOUGHT WE LOST THEM.
COULD YOU IMAGINE IF WE DID?

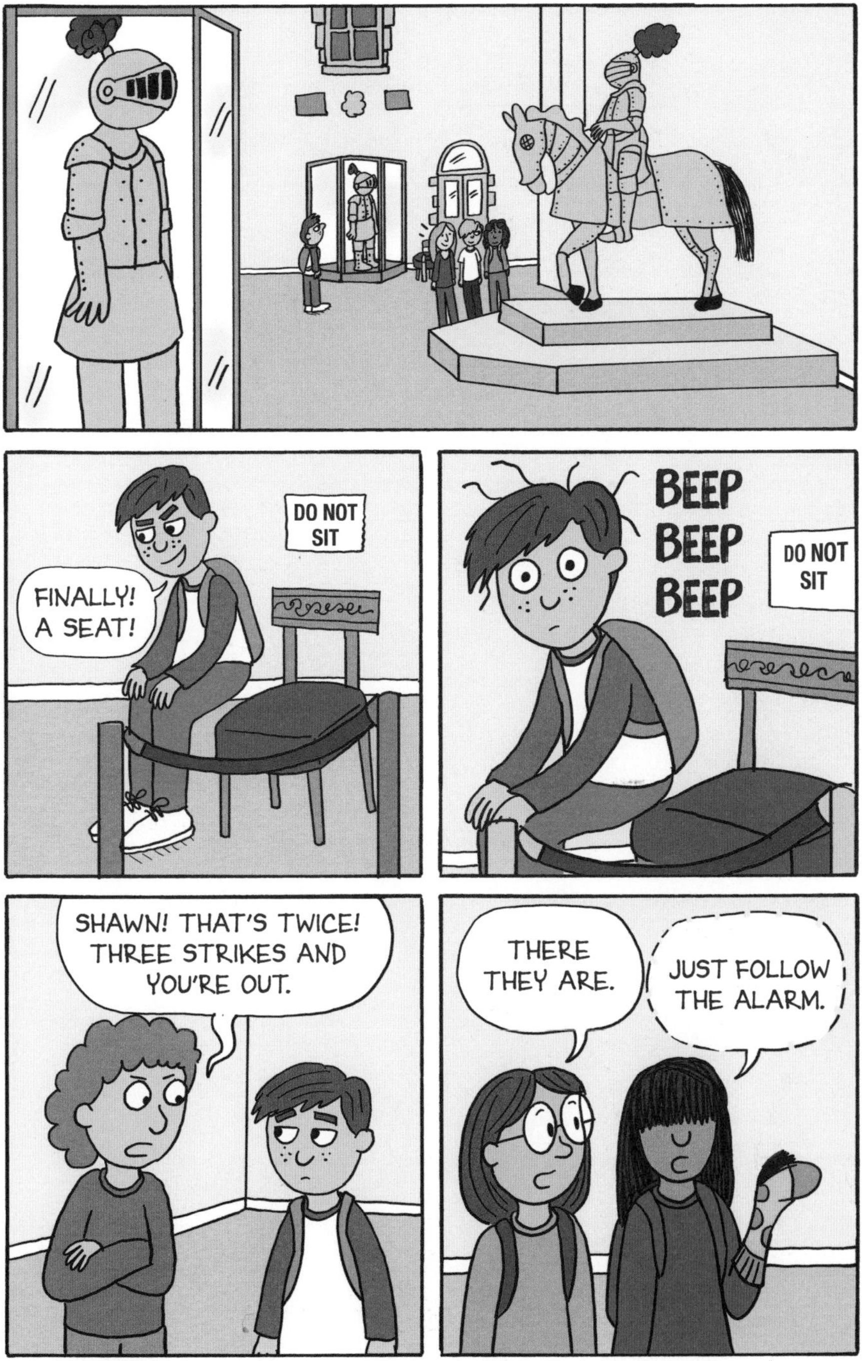
DO NOT SIT
FINALLY! A SEAT!
BEEP BEEP BEEP
DO NOT SIT
SHAWN! THAT'S TWICE! THREE STRIKES AND YOU'RE OUT.
THERE THEY ARE.
JUST FOLLOW THE ALARM.

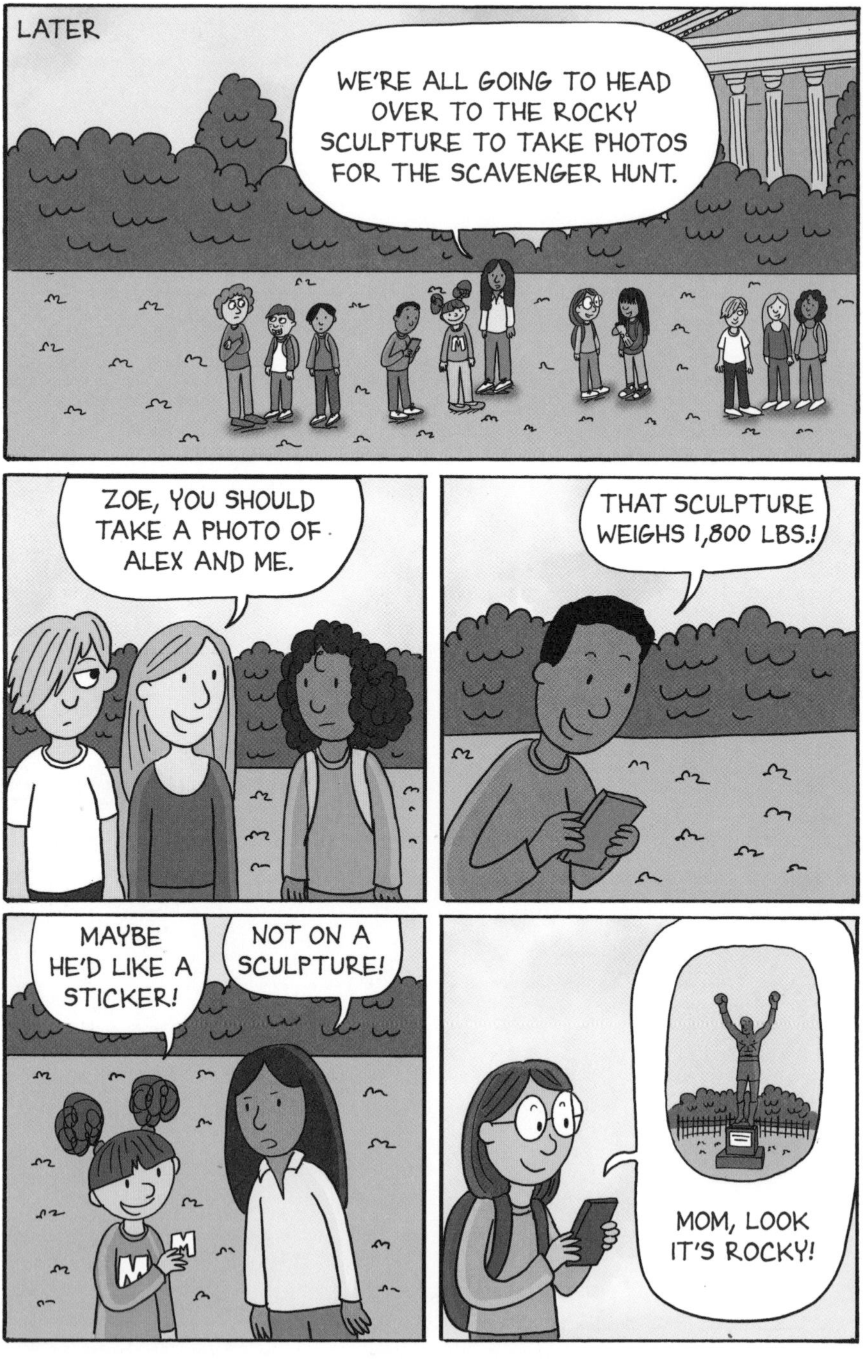
LATER
WE'RE ALL GOING TO HEAD OVER TO THE ROCKY SCULPTURE TO TAKE PHOTOS FOR THE SCAVENGER HUNT.
ZOE, YOU SHOULD TAKE A PHOTO OF ALEX AND ME.
THAT SCULPTURE WEIGHS 1,800 LBS.!
MAYBE HE'D LIKE A STICKER!
NOT ON A SCULPTURE!
MOM, LOOK IT'S ROCKY!

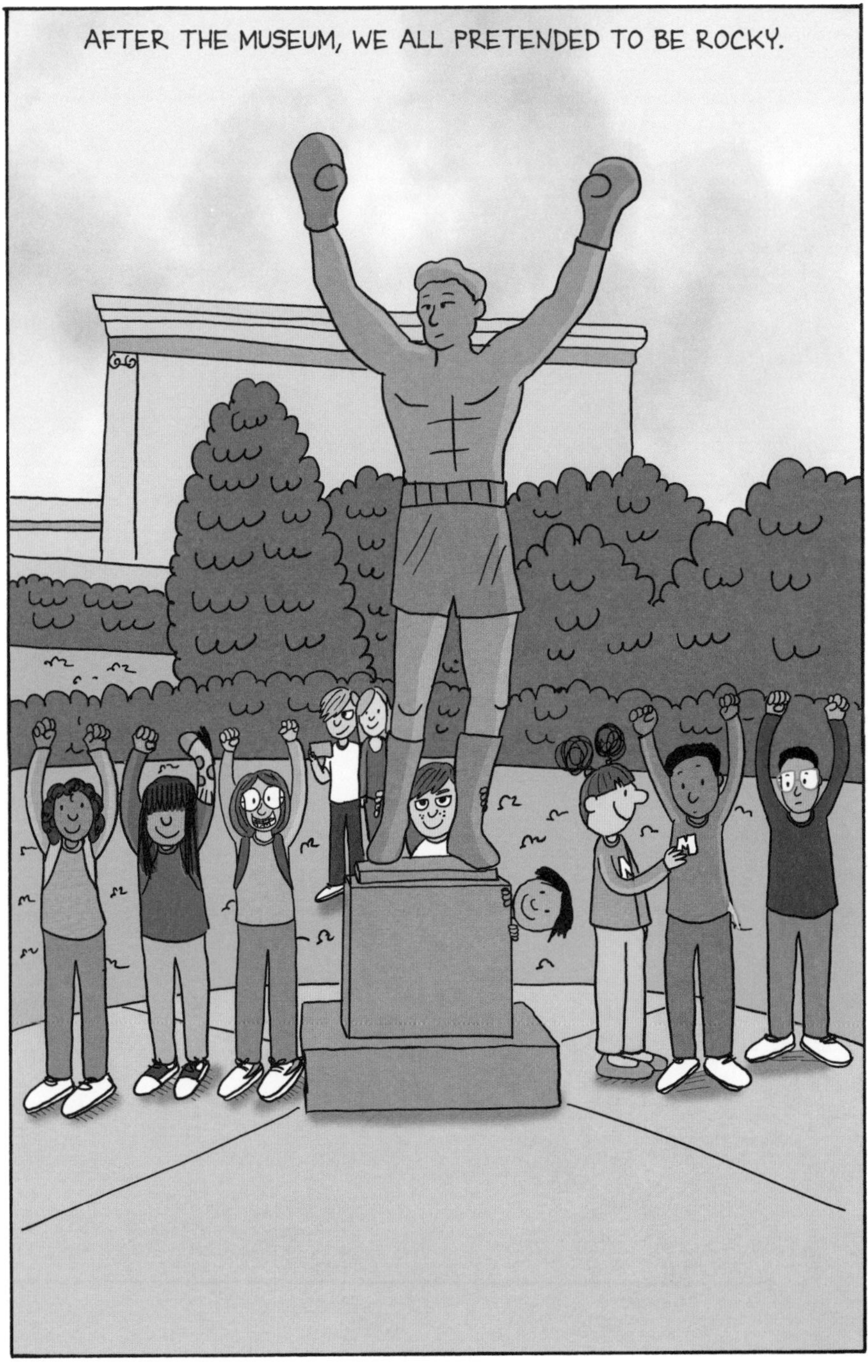
AFTER THE MUSEUM, WE ALL PRETENDED TO BE ROCKY.

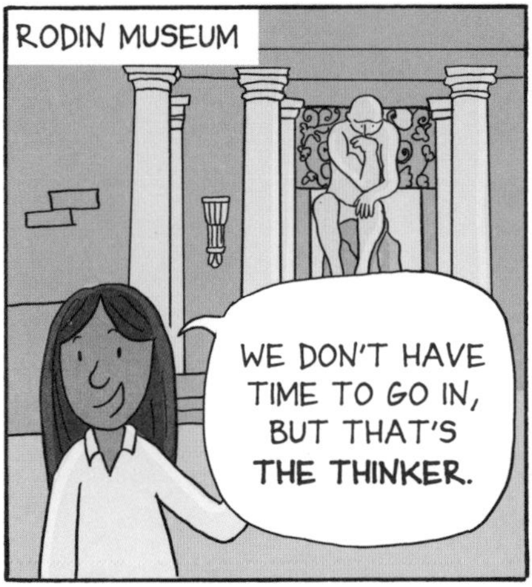
RODIN MUSEUM
WE DON'T HAVE TIME TO GO IN, BUT THAT'S **THE THINKER.**

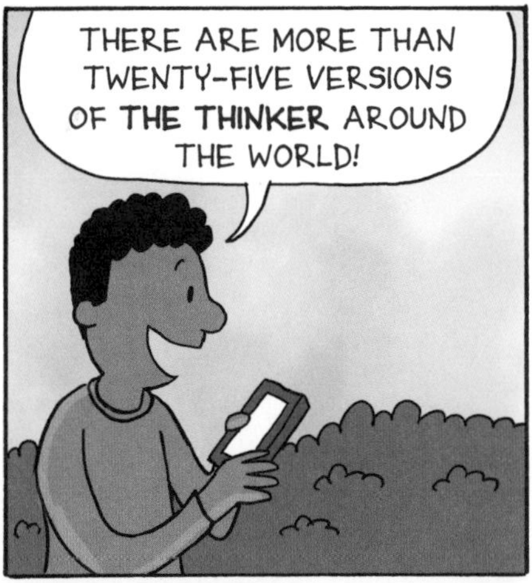
THERE ARE MORE THAN TWENTY-FIVE VERSIONS OF **THE THINKER** AROUND THE WORLD!

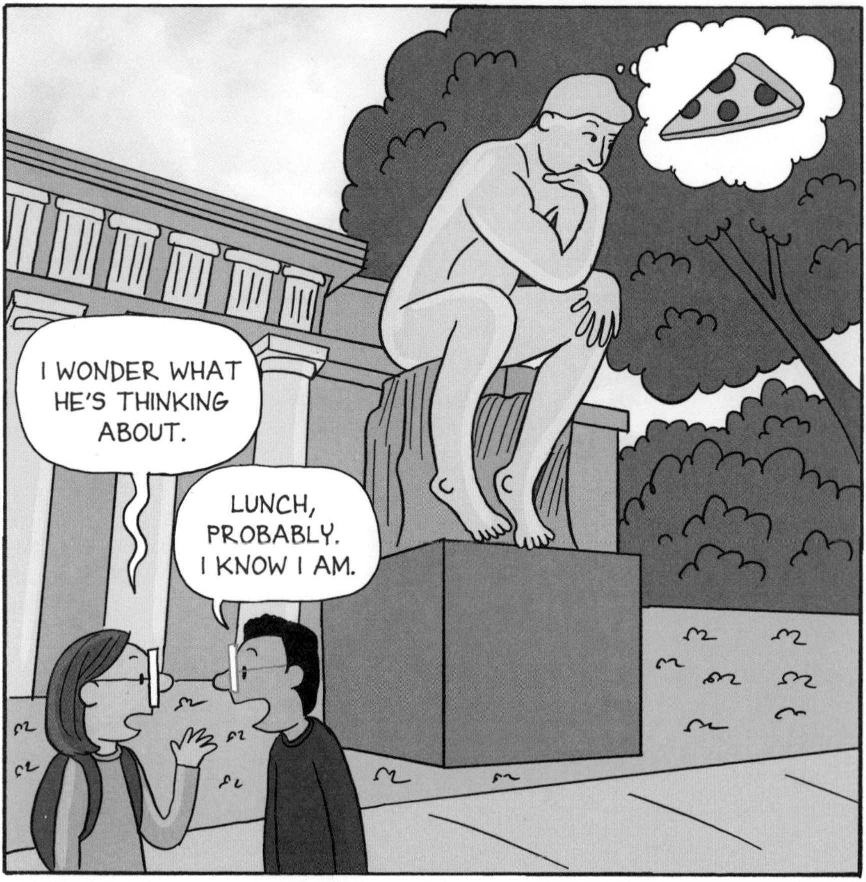
I WONDER WHAT HE'S THINKING ABOUT.
LUNCH, PROBABLY. I KNOW I AM.

CHAPTER 4
MÜTTER MUSEUM

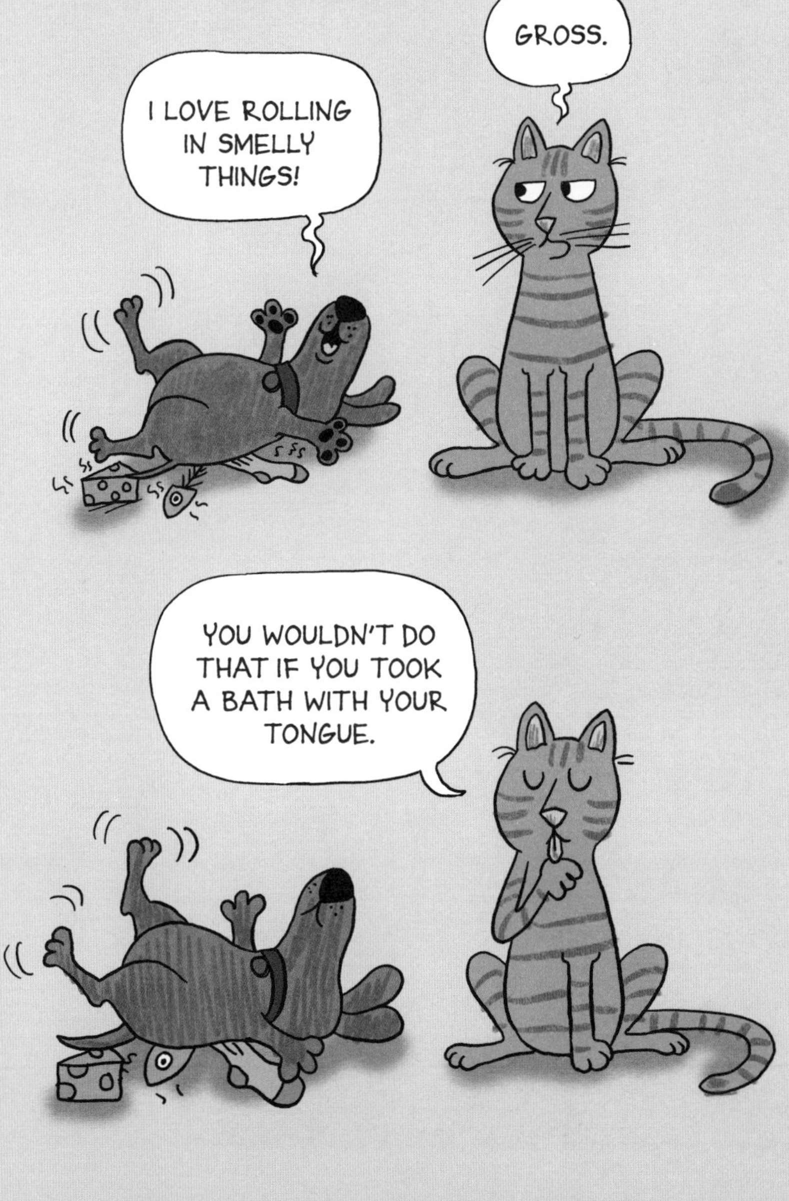
I LOVE ROLLING IN SMELLY THINGS!
GROSS.
YOU WOULDN'T DO THAT IF YOU TOOK A BATH WITH YOUR TONGUE.

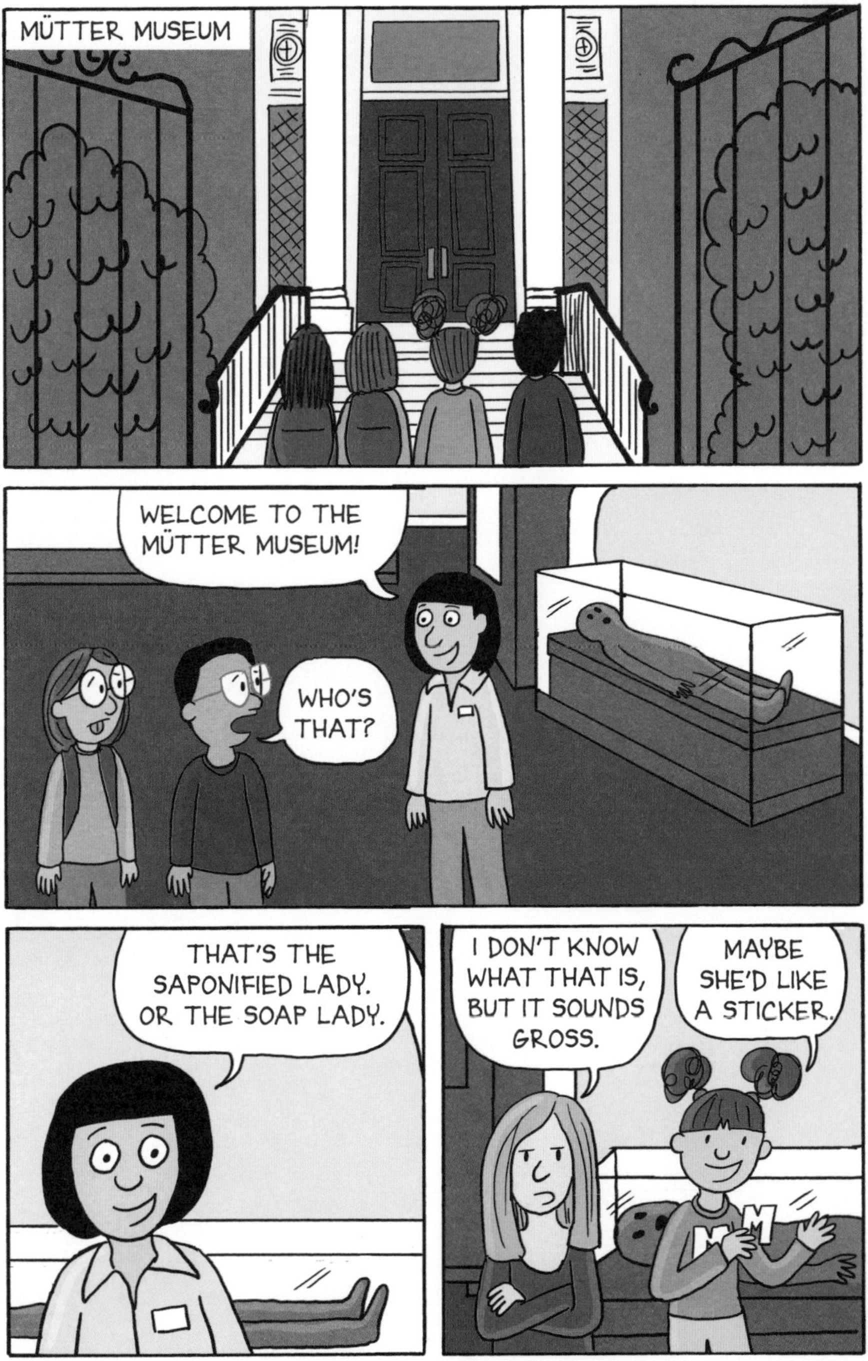
MÜTTER MUSEUM
WELCOME TO THE MÜTTER MUSEUM!
WHO'S THAT?
THAT'S THE SAPONIFIED LADY. OR THE SOAP LADY.
I DON'T KNOW WHAT THAT IS, BUT IT SOUNDS GROSS.
MAYBE SHE'D LIKE A STICKER.

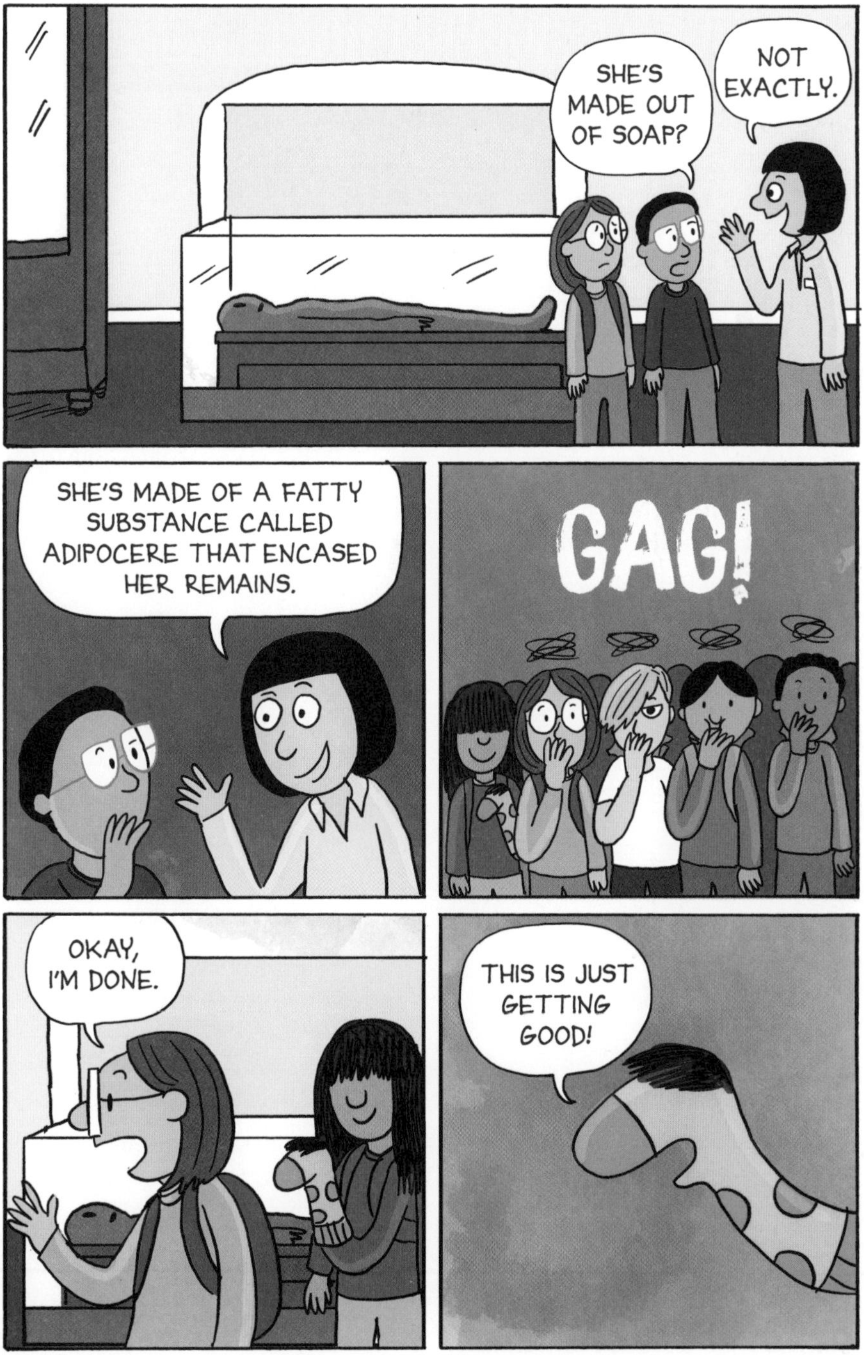
SHE'S MADE OUT OF SOAP?
NOT EXACTLY.
SHE'S MADE OF A FATTY SUBSTANCE CALLED ADIPOCERE THAT ENCASED HER REMAINS.
GAG!
OKAY, I'M DONE.
THIS IS JUST GETTING GOOD!

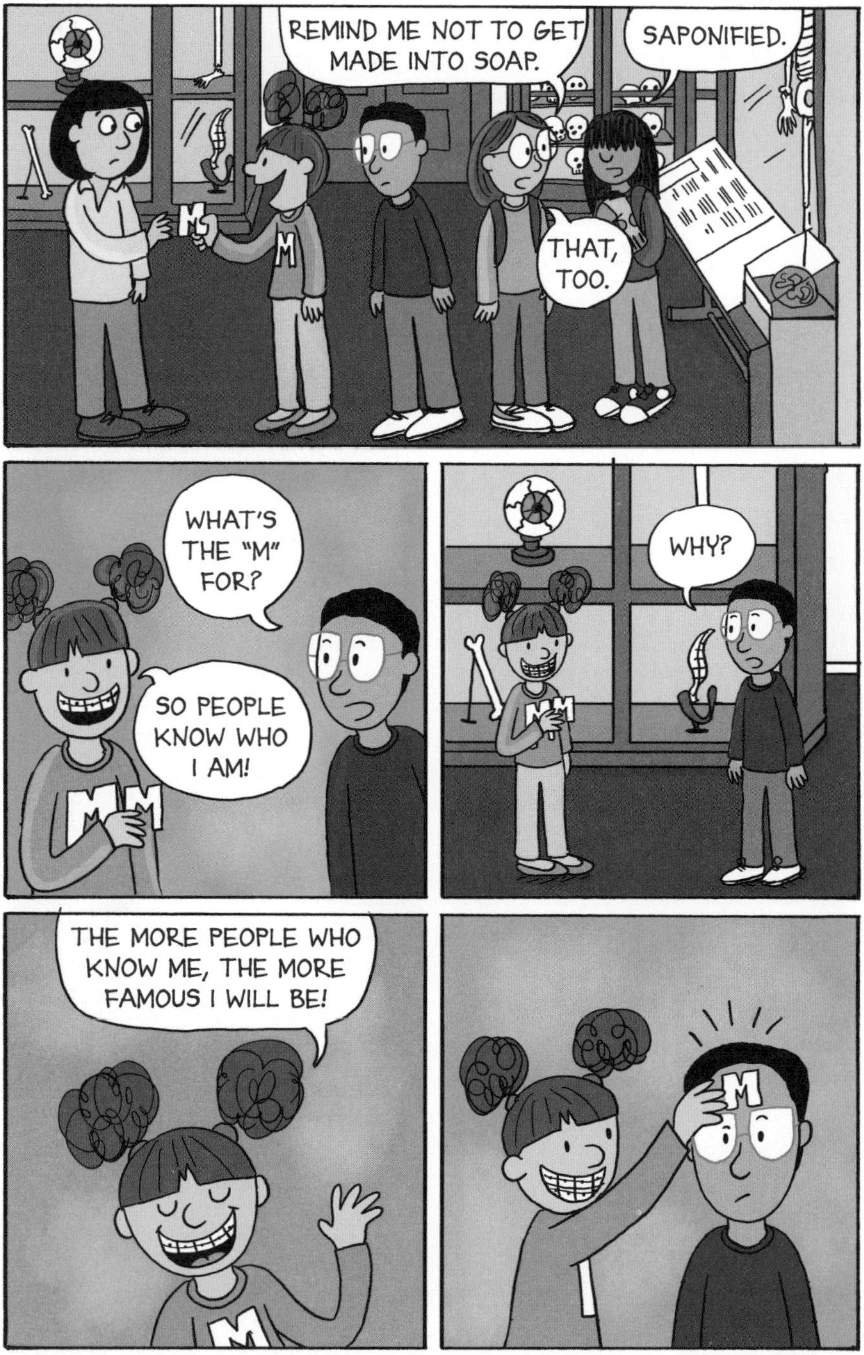
REMIND ME NOT TO GET MADE INTO SOAP.
SAPONIFIED.
THAT, TOO.
WHAT'S THE "M" FOR?
SO PEOPLE KNOW WHO I AM!
WHY?
THE MORE PEOPLE WHO KNOW ME, THE MORE FAMOUS I WILL BE!

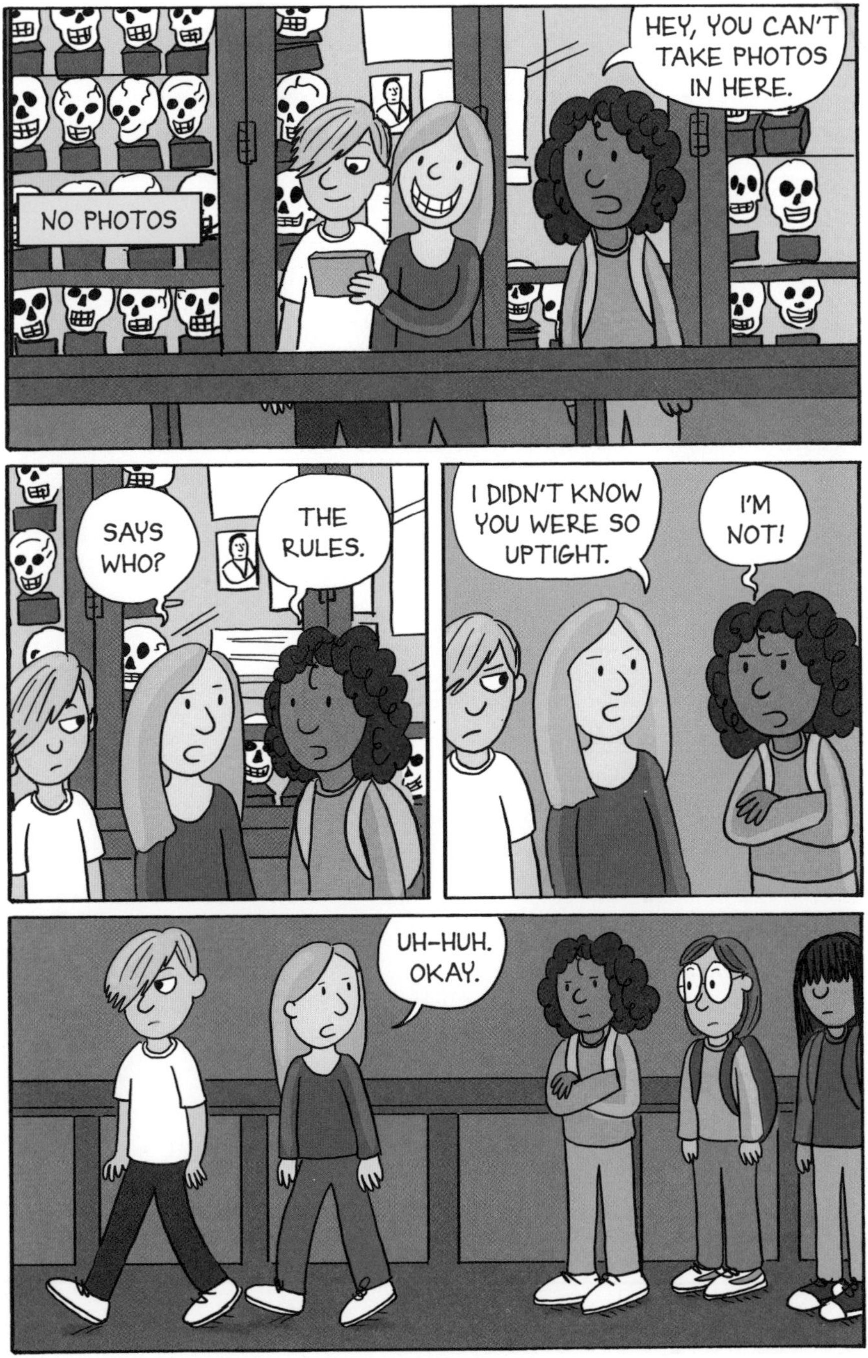
NO PHOTOS
HEY, YOU CAN'T TAKE PHOTOS IN HERE.
SAYS WHO?
THE RULES.
I DIDN'T KNOW YOU WERE SO UPTIGHT.
I'M NOT!
UH-HUH. OKAY.

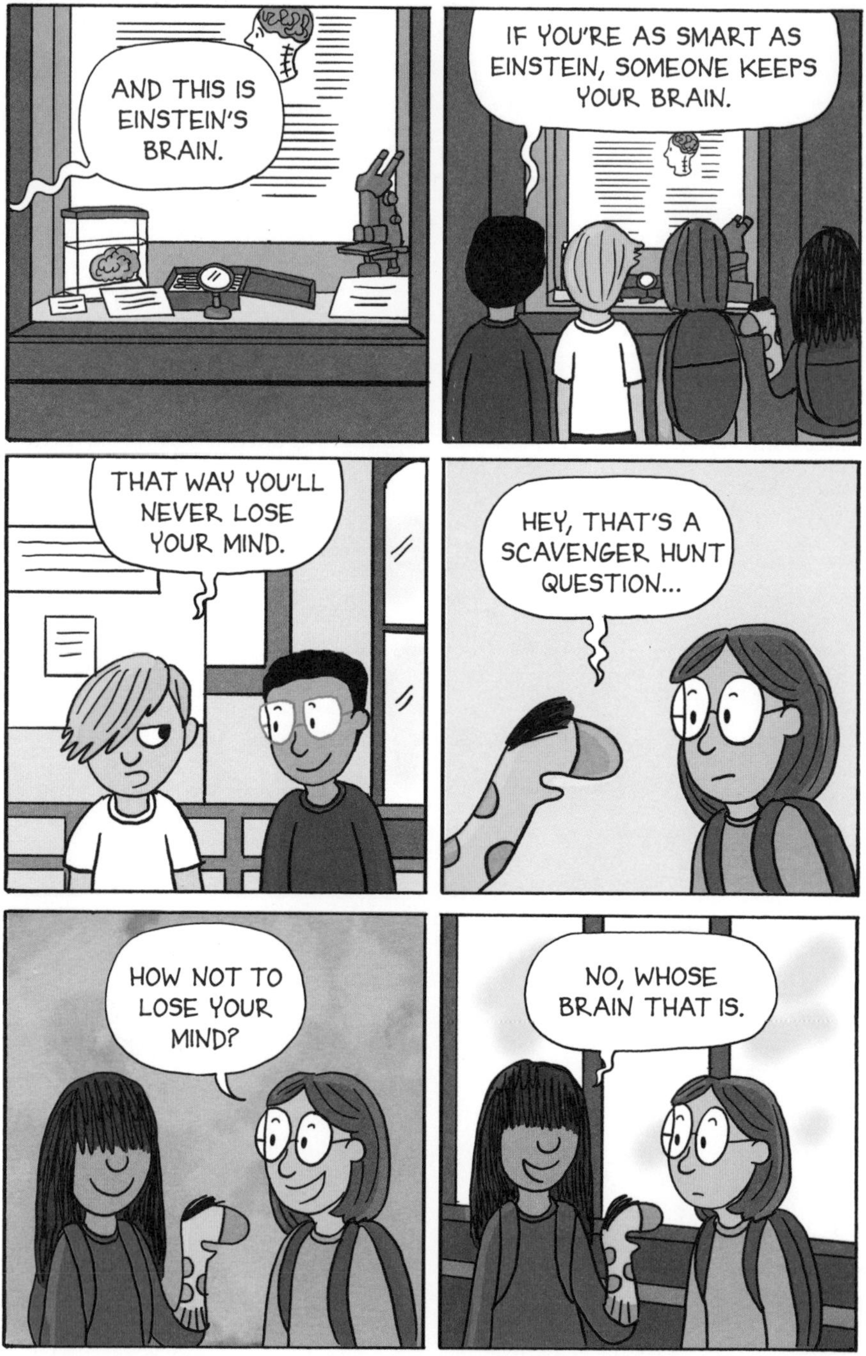
AND THIS IS EINSTEIN'S BRAIN.
IF YOU'RE AS SMART AS EINSTEIN, SOMEONE KEEPS YOUR BRAIN.
THAT WAY YOU'LL NEVER LOSE YOUR MIND.
HEY, THAT'S A SCAVENGER HUNT QUESTION...
HOW NOT TO LOSE YOUR MIND?
NO, WHOSE BRAIN THAT IS.

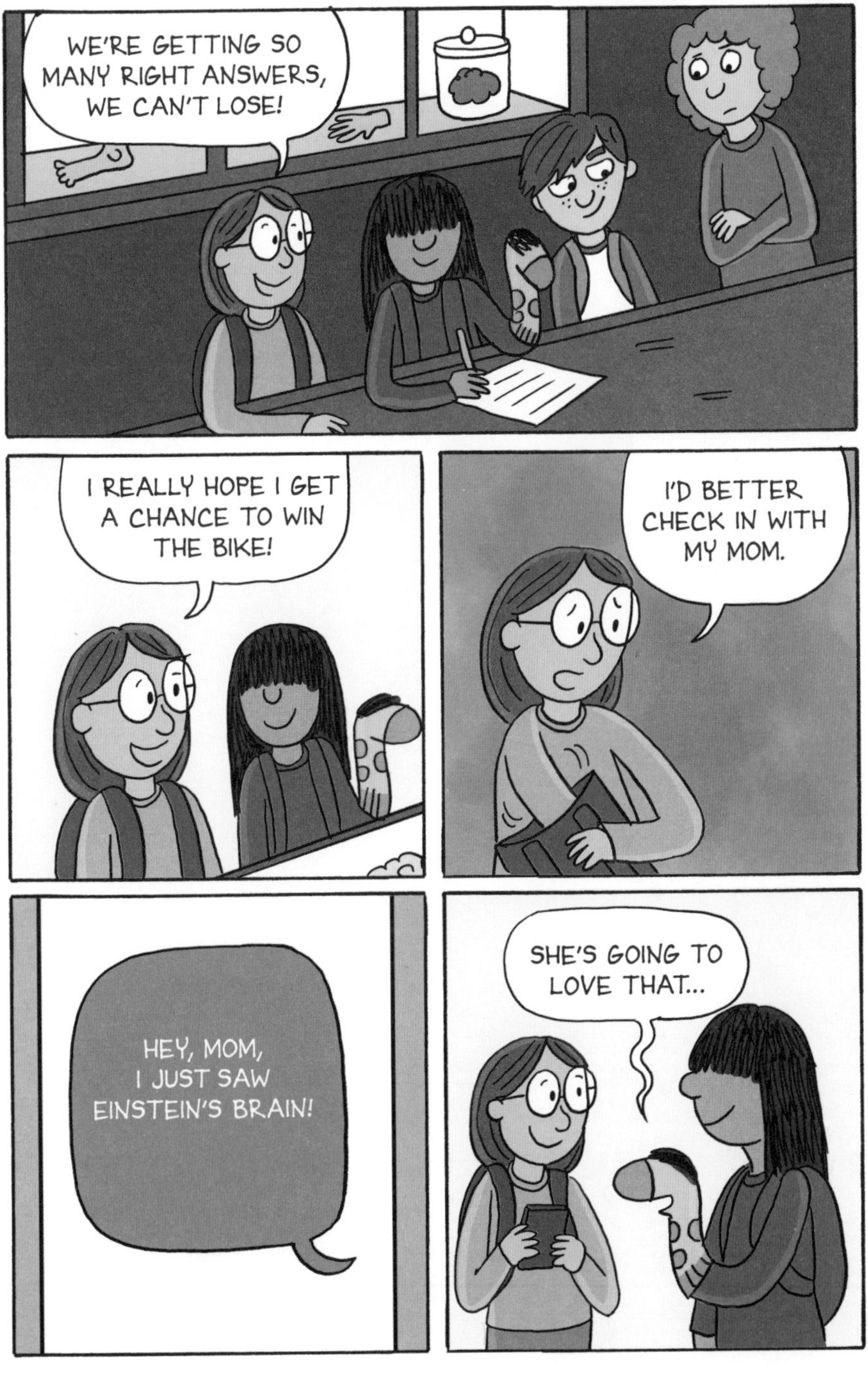

WE'RE GETTING SO MANY RIGHT ANSWERS, WE CAN'T LOSE!
I REALLY HOPE I GET A CHANCE TO WIN THE BIKE!
I'D BETTER CHECK IN WITH MY MOM.
HEY, MOM, I JUST SAW EINSTEIN'S BRAIN!
SHE'S GOING TO LOVE THAT...

THINGS YOU CAN'T UNSEE FROM THE MUTTER MUSEUM:

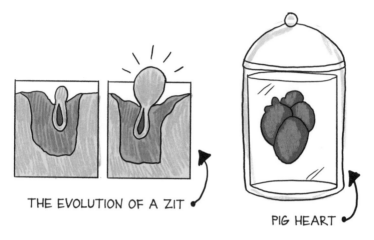

THE EVOLUTION OF A ZIT

PIG HEART

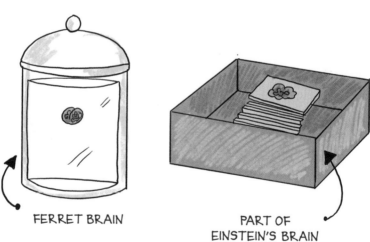

FERRET BRAIN

PART OF
EINSTEIN'S BRAIN

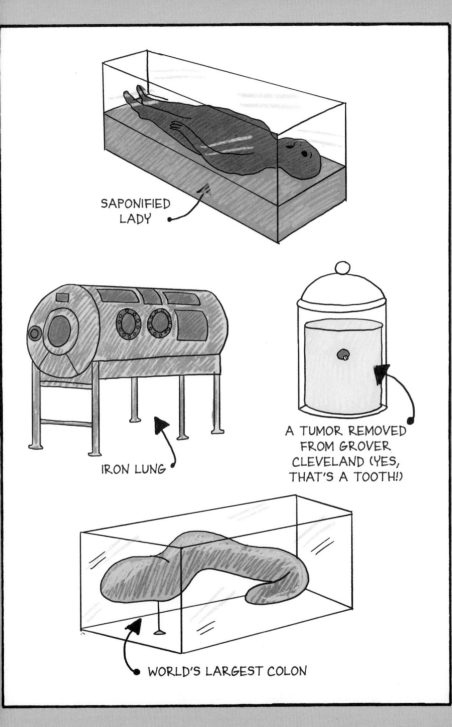

SAPONIFIED LADY

IRON LUNG

A TUMOR REMOVED FROM GROVER CLEVELAND (YES, THAT'S A TOOTH!)

WORLD'S LARGEST COLON

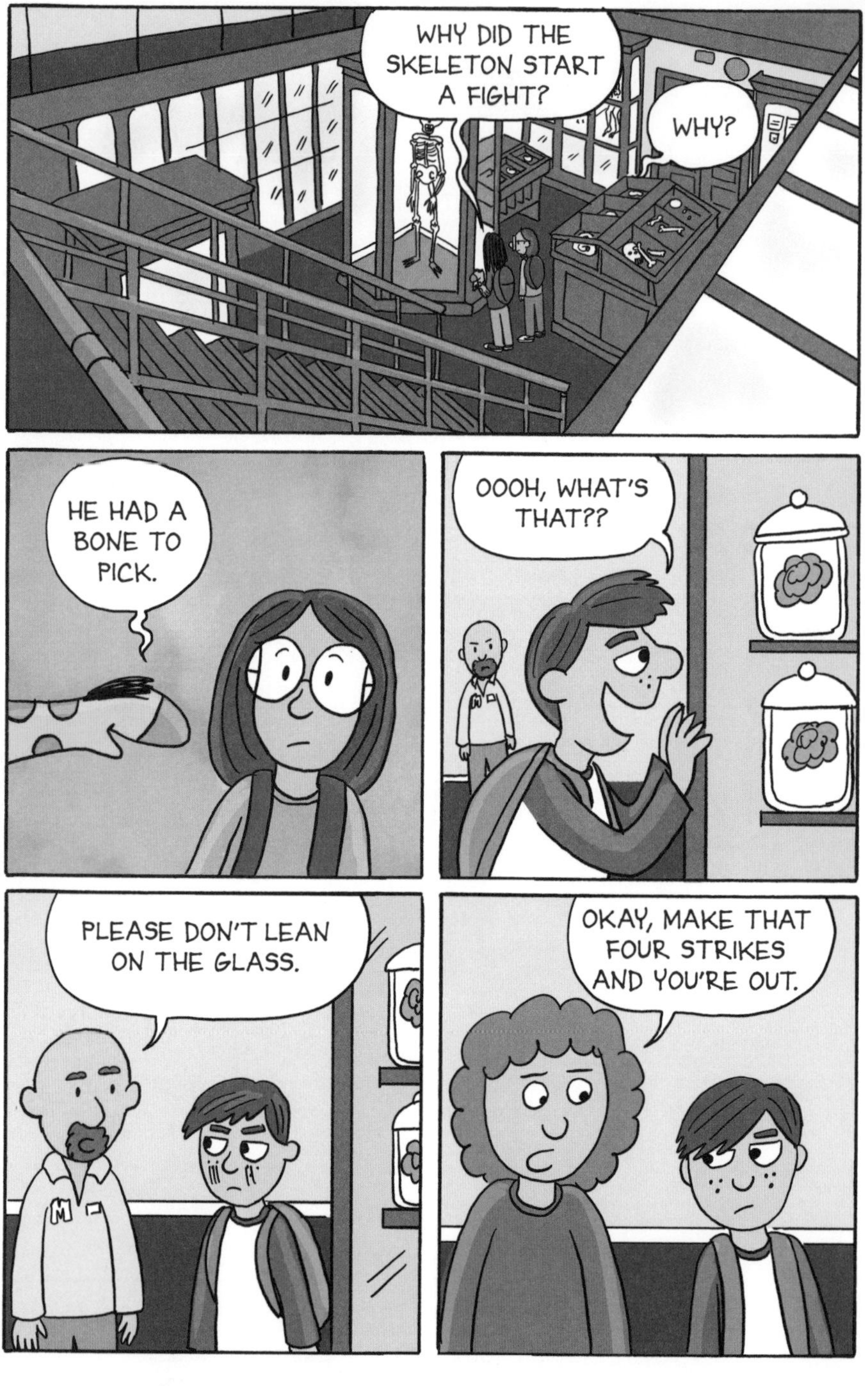
WHY DID THE SKELETON START A FIGHT?
WHY?
HE HAD A BONE TO PICK.
OOOH, WHAT'S THAT??
PLEASE DON'T LEAN ON THE GLASS.
OKAY, MAKE THAT FOUR STRIKES AND YOU'RE OUT.

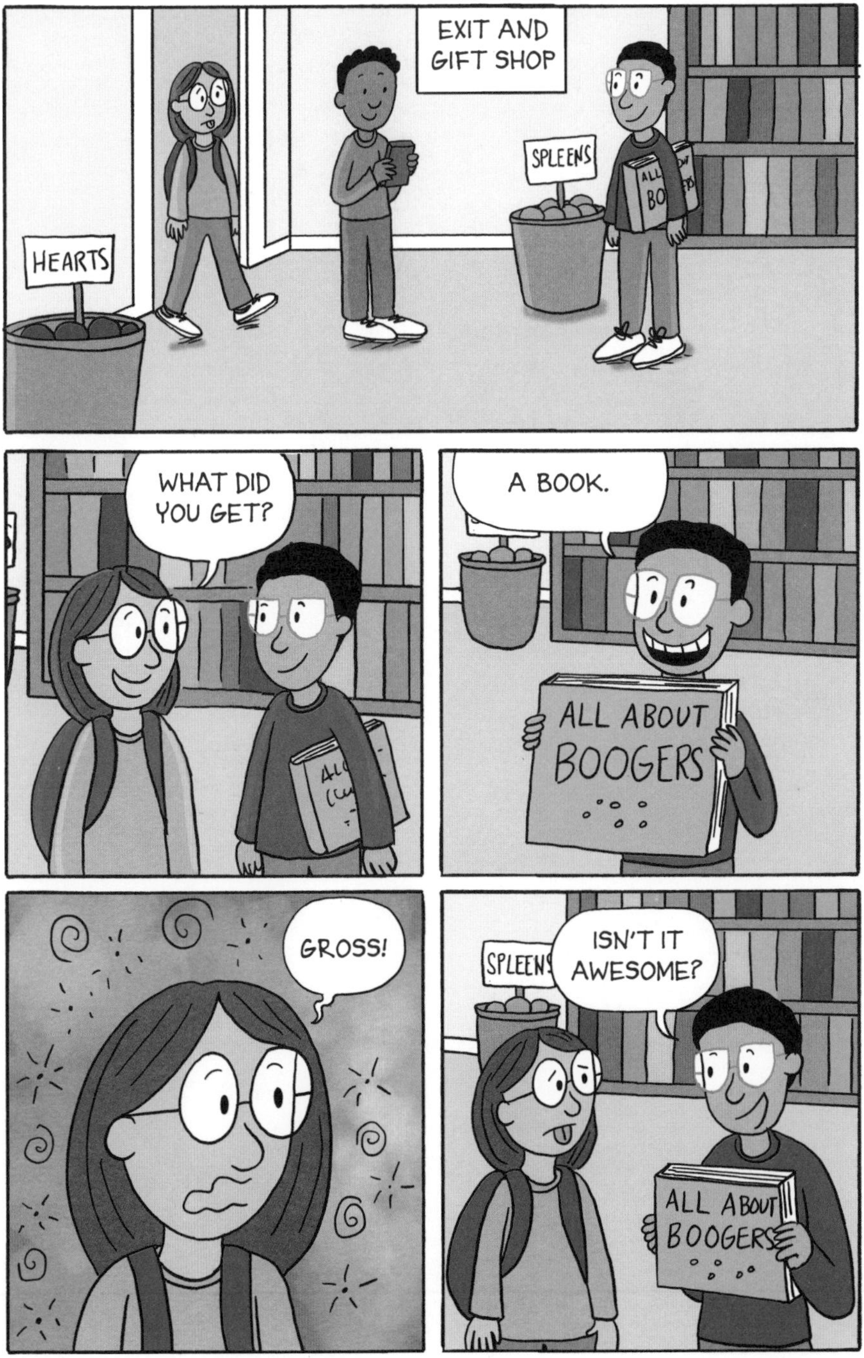
EXIT AND GIFT SHOP
HEARTS
SPLEENS
WHAT DID YOU GET?
A BOOK.
ALL ABOUT BOOGERS
GROSS!
SPLEENS
ISN'T IT AWESOME?
ALL ABOUT BOOGERS

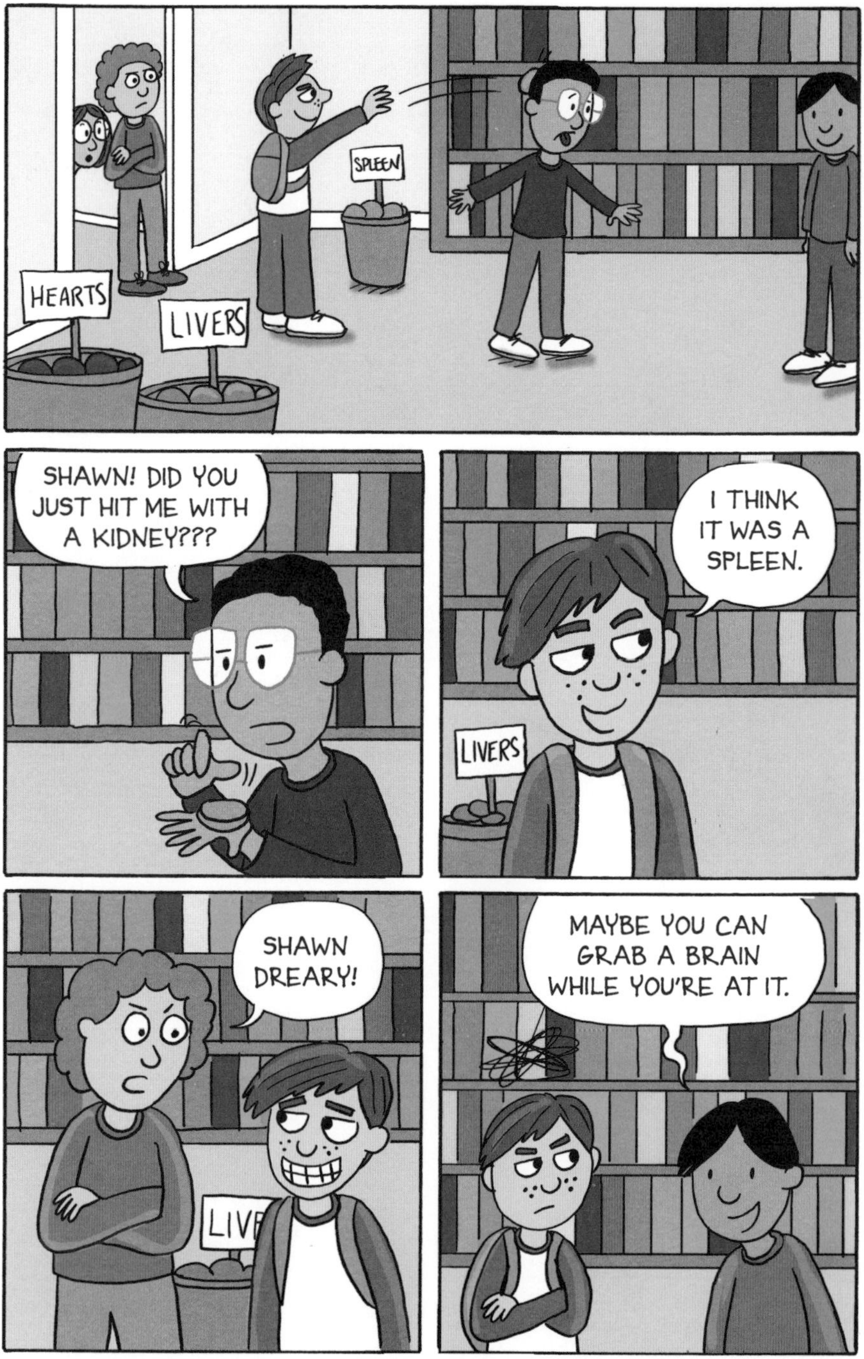
HEARTS
LIVERS
SPLEEN
SHAWN! DID YOU JUST HIT ME WITH A KIDNEY???
I THINK IT WAS A SPLEEN.
LIVERS
SHAWN DREARY!
MAYBE YOU CAN GRAB A BRAIN WHILE YOU'RE AT IT.

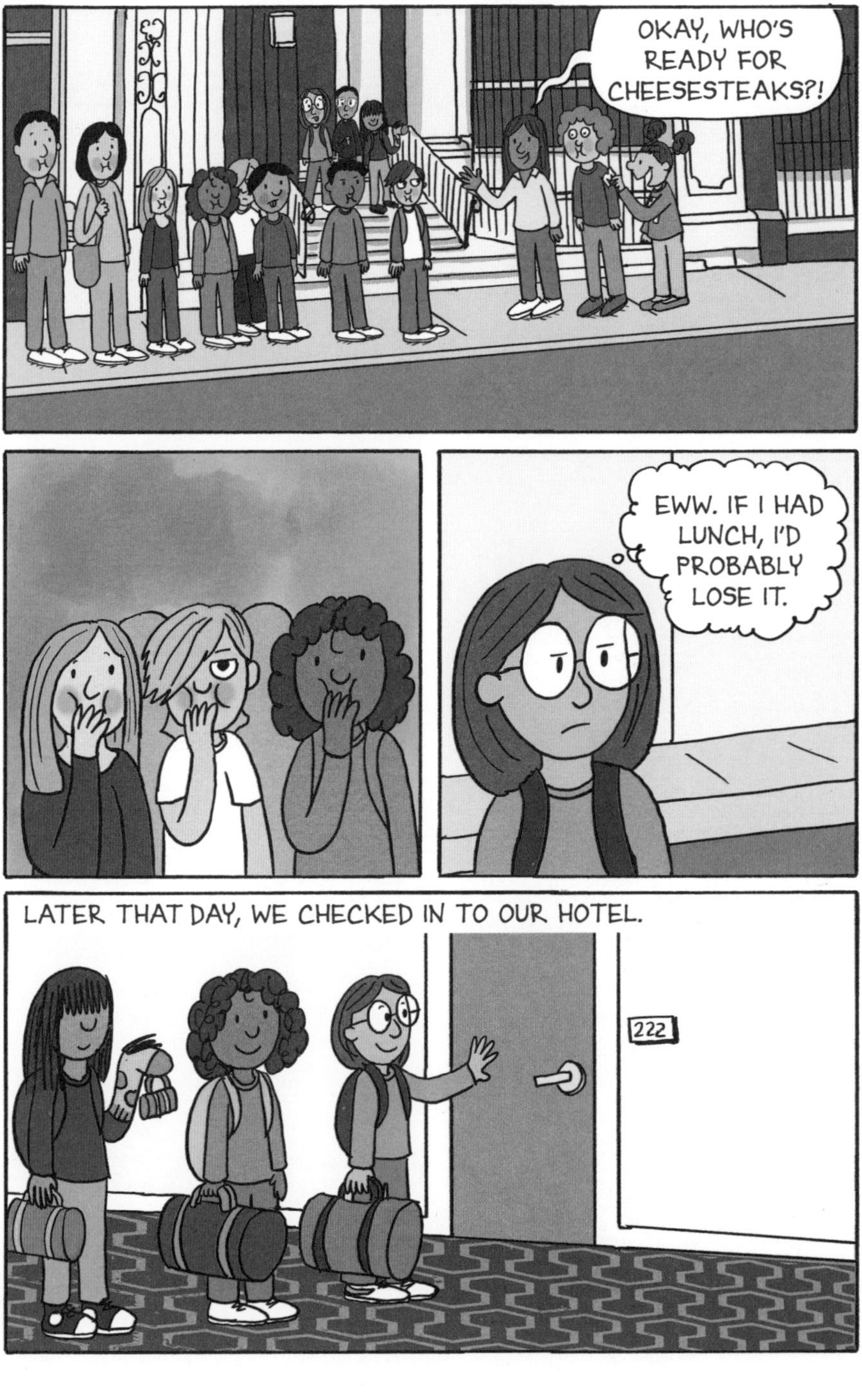
OKAY, WHO'S READY FOR CHEESESTEAKS?!
EWW. IF I HAD LUNCH, I'D PROBABLY LOSE IT.
LATER THAT DAY, WE CHECKED IN TO OUR HOTEL.
222

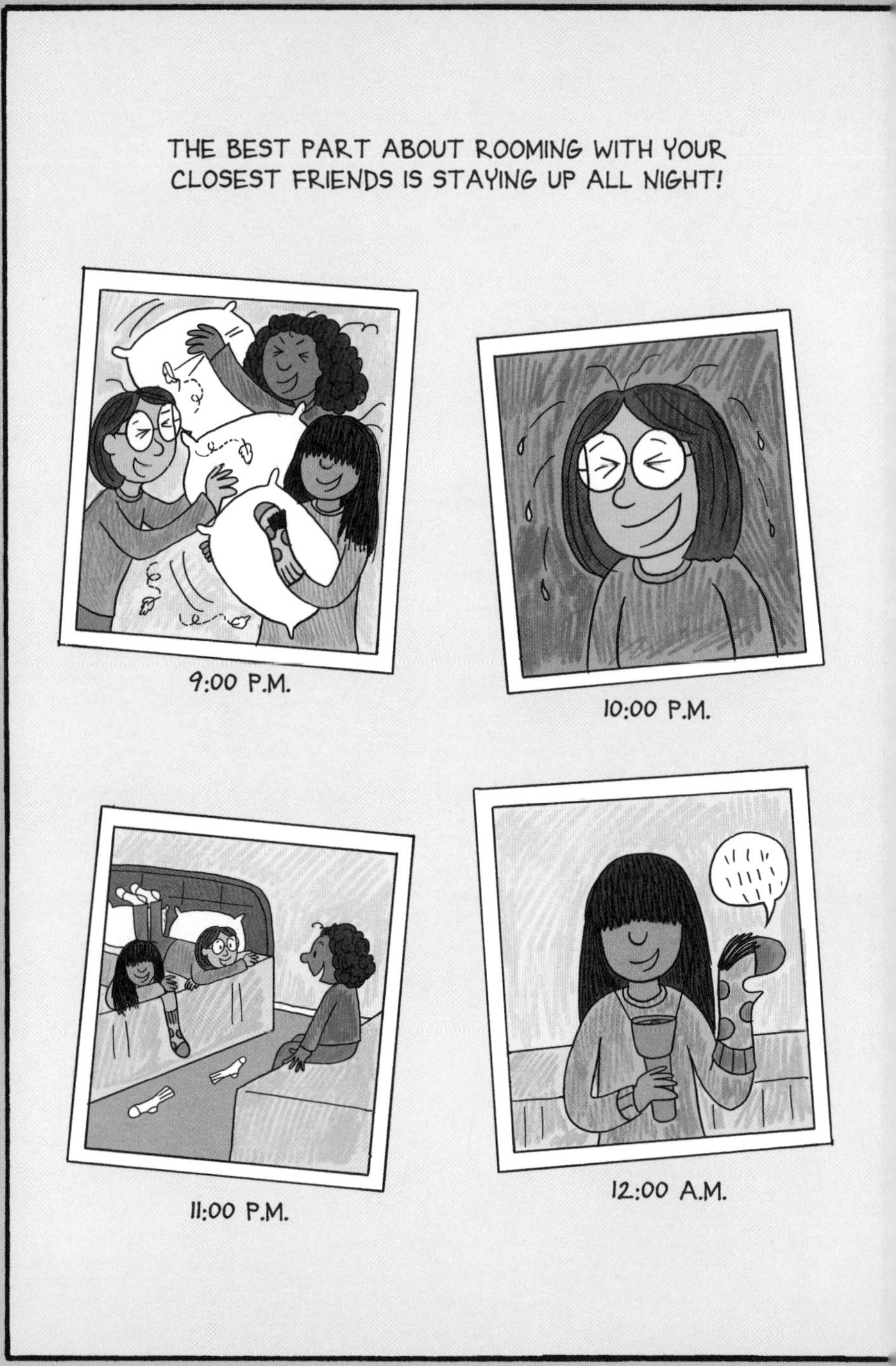
THE BEST PART ABOUT ROOMING WITH YOUR CLOSEST FRIENDS IS STAYING UP ALL NIGHT!
9:00 P.M.
10:00 P.M.
11:00 P.M.
12:00 A.M.

THE WORST PART IS BARELY SLEEPING.

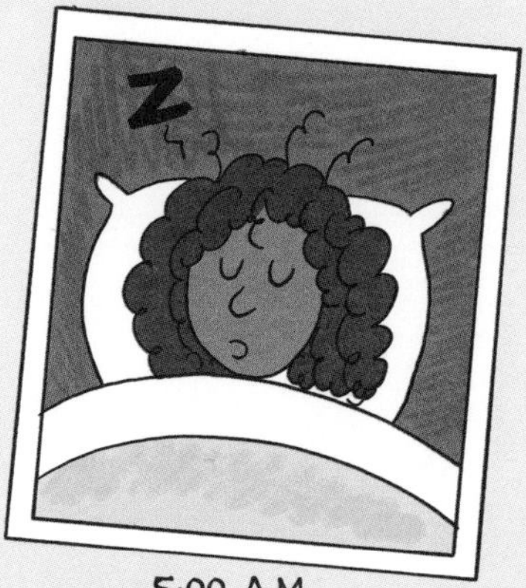

5:00 A.M.

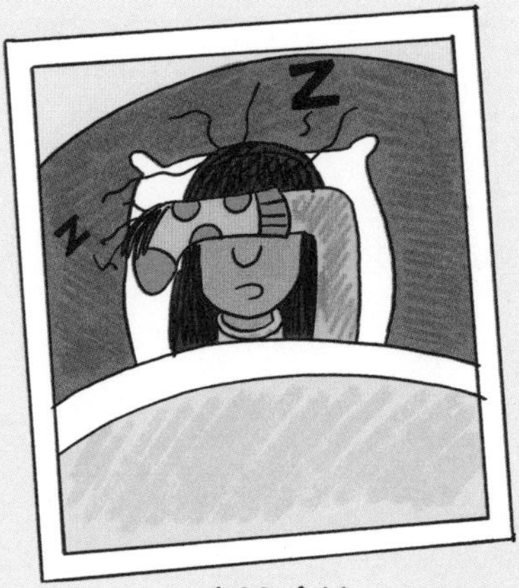

6:00 A.M.

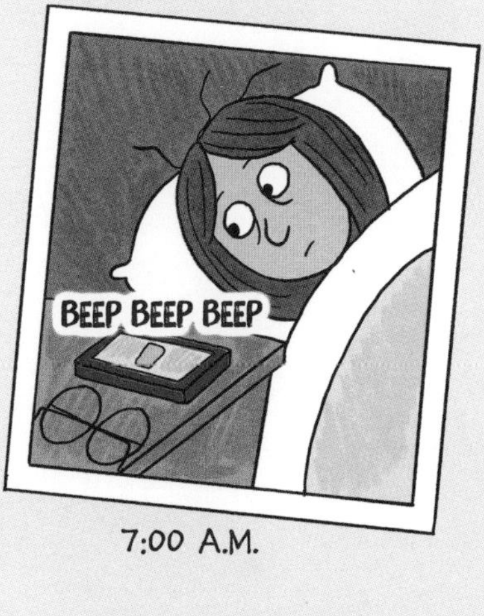
BEEP BEEP BEEP

7:00 A.M.

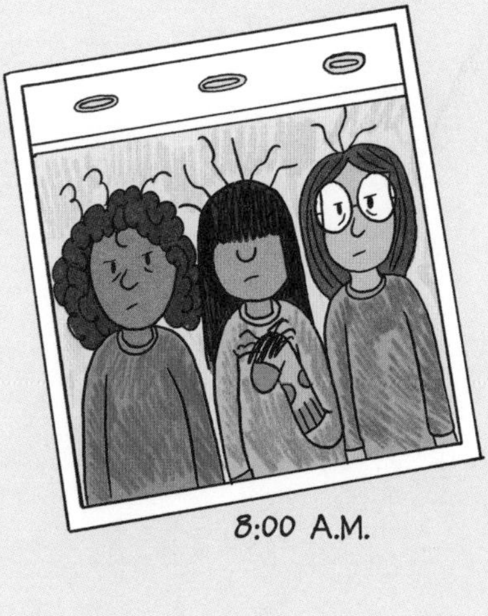

8:00 A.M.

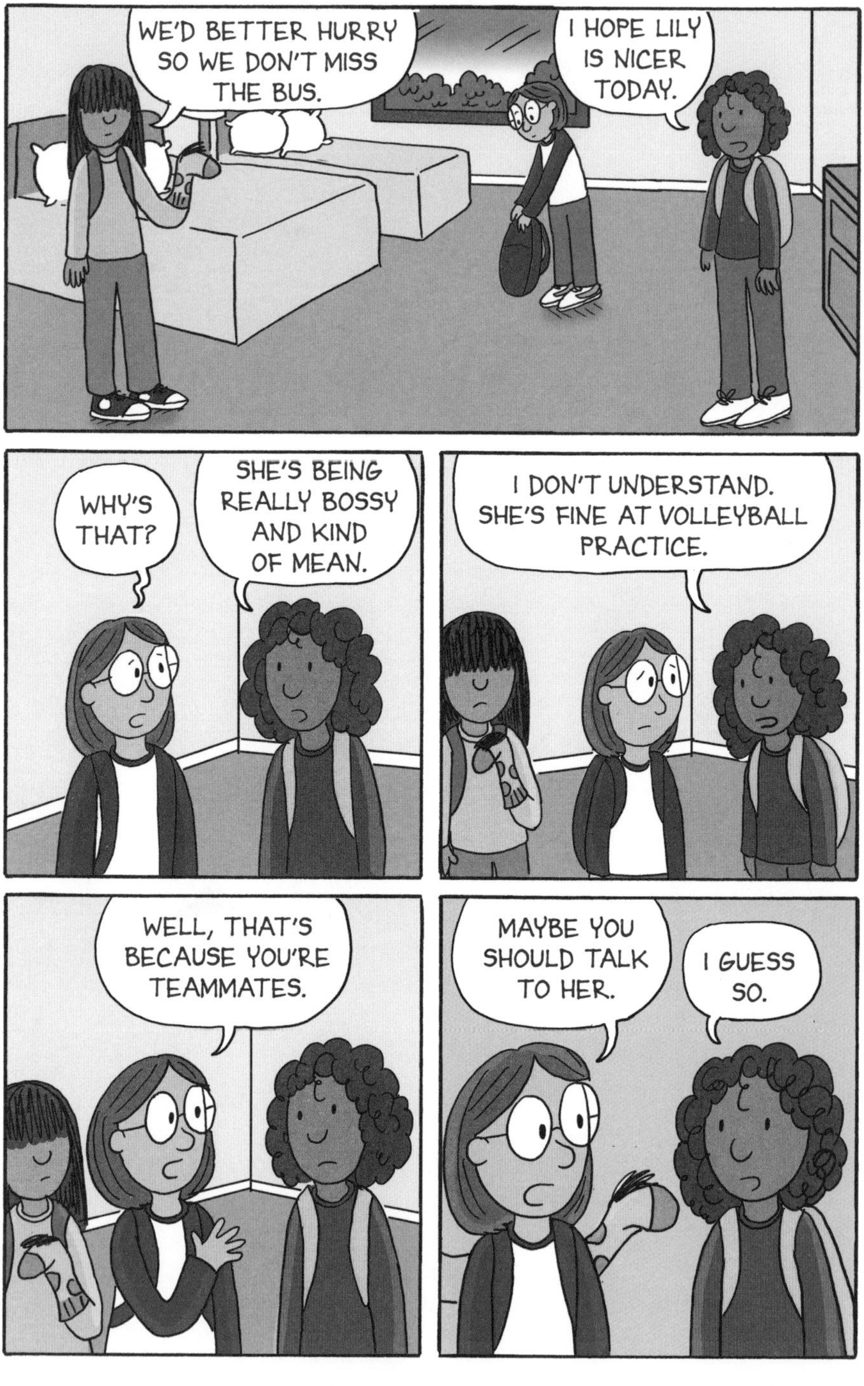
WE'D BETTER HURRY SO WE DON'T MISS THE BUS.
I HOPE LILY IS NICER TODAY.
WHY'S THAT?
SHE'S BEING REALLY BOSSY AND KIND OF MEAN.
I DON'T UNDERSTAND. SHE'S FINE AT VOLLEYBALL PRACTICE.
WELL, THAT'S BECAUSE YOU'RE TEAMMATES.
MAYBE YOU SHOULD TALK TO HER.
I GUESS SO.

CHAPTER 5
DAY TWO, HISTORIC DISTRICT

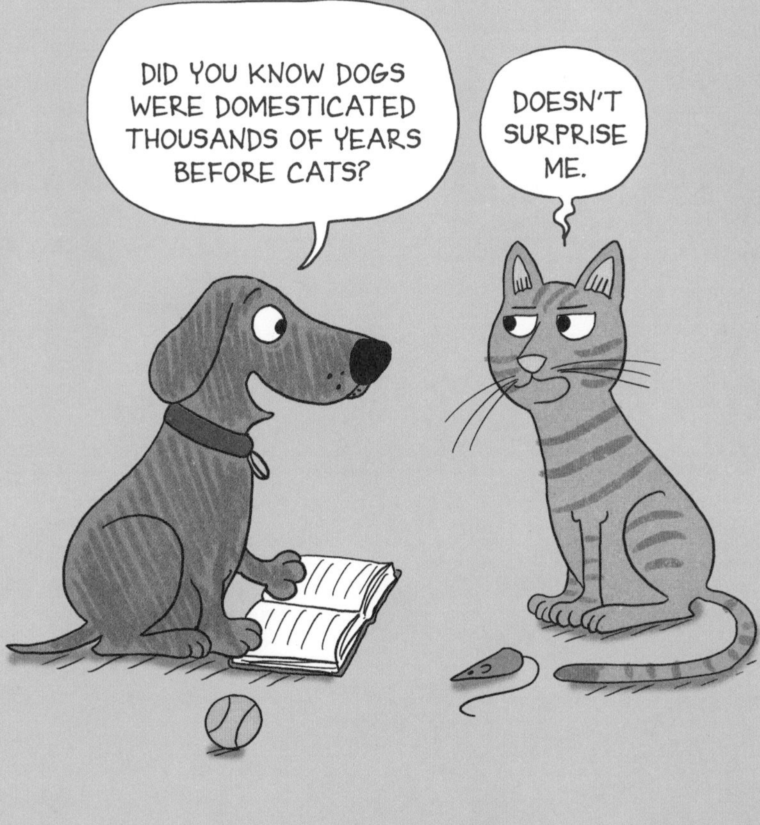
DID YOU KNOW DOGS WERE DOMESTICATED THOUSANDS OF YEARS BEFORE CATS?
DOESN'T SURPRISE ME.

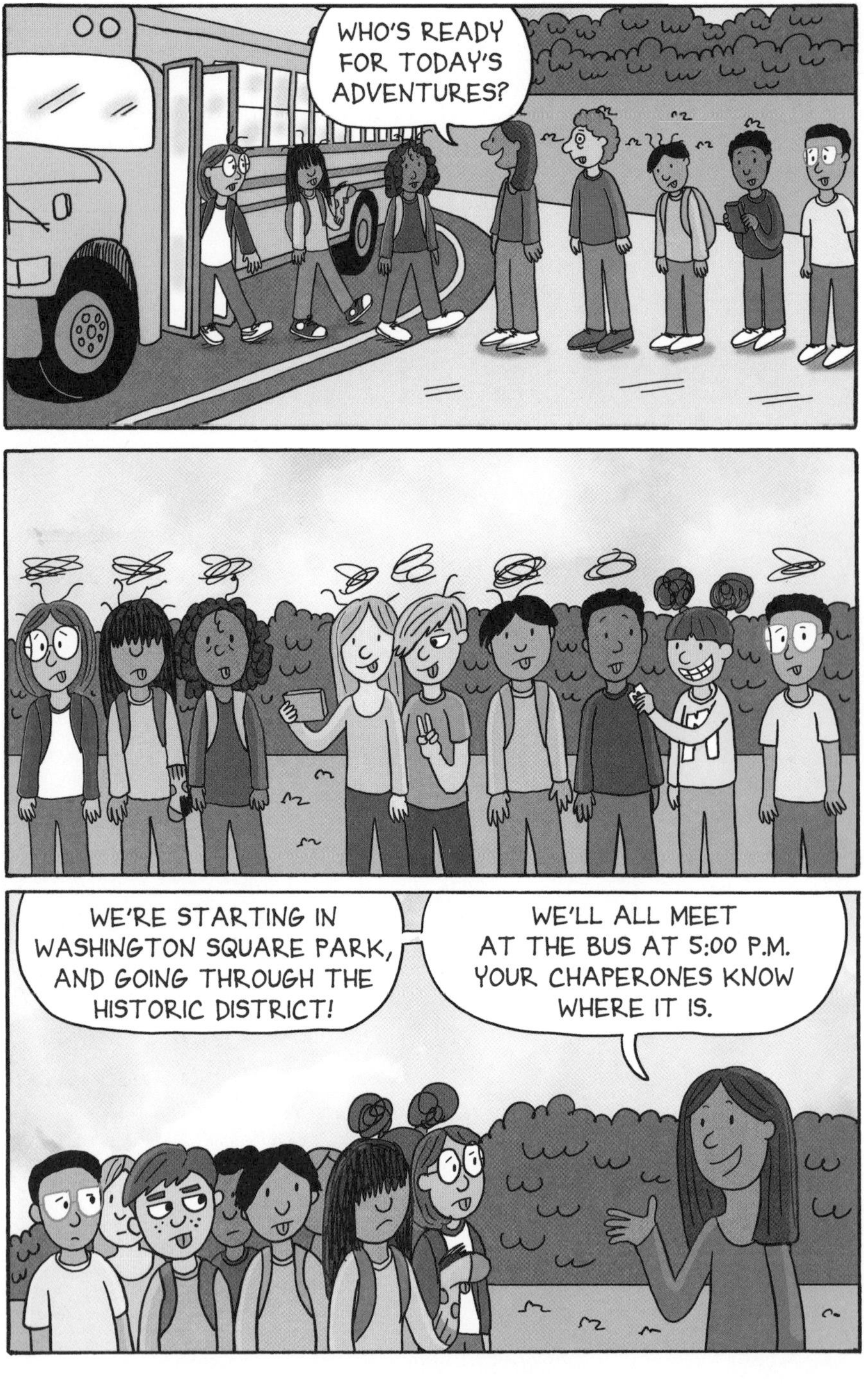
WHO'S READY FOR TODAY'S ADVENTURES?
WE'RE STARTING IN WASHINGTON SQUARE PARK, AND GOING THROUGH THE HISTORIC DISTRICT!
WE'LL ALL MEET AT THE BUS AT 5:00 P.M. YOUR CHAPERONES KNOW WHERE IT IS.

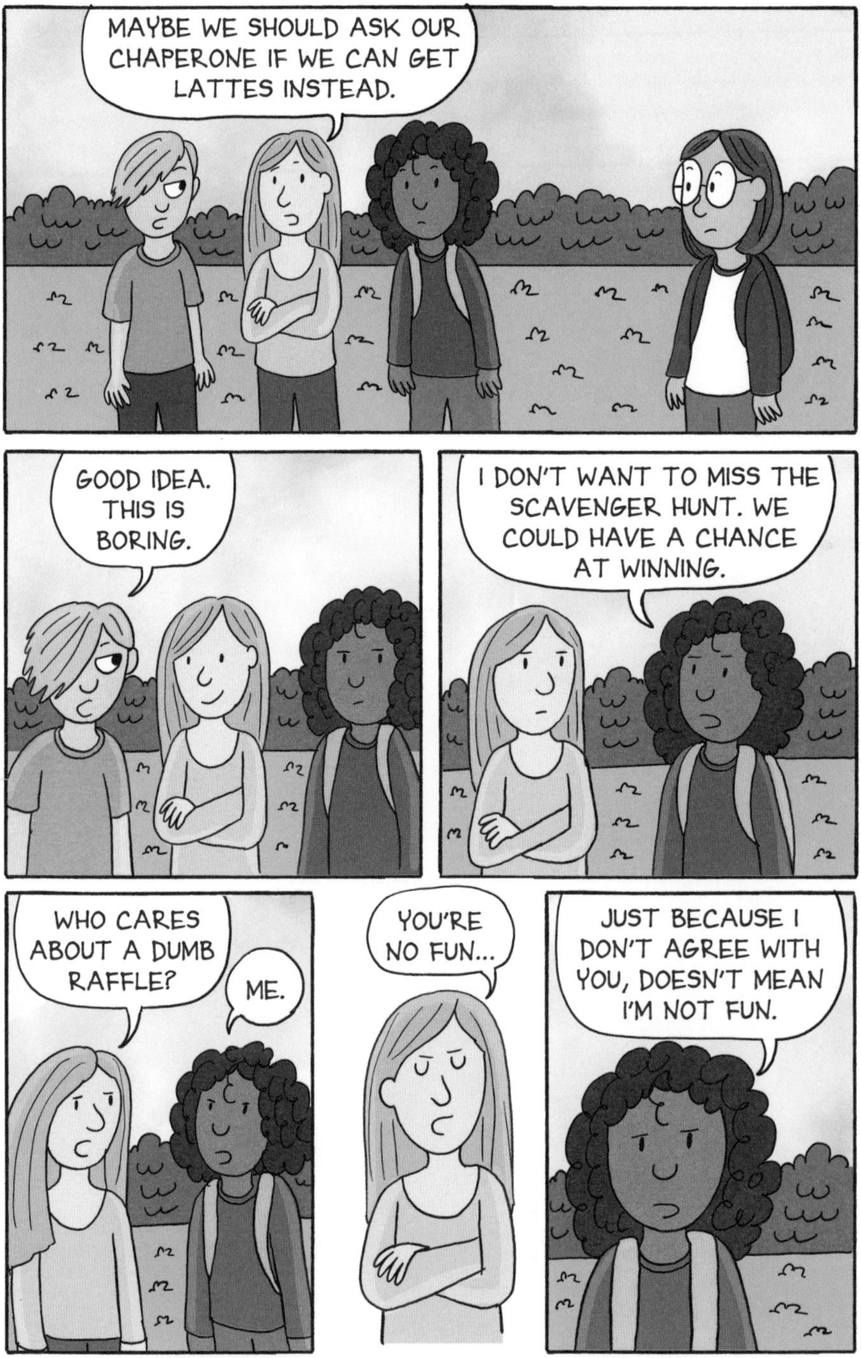
MAYBE WE SHOULD ASK OUR CHAPERONE IF WE CAN GET LATTES INSTEAD.
GOOD IDEA. THIS IS BORING.
I DON'T WANT TO MISS THE SCAVENGER HUNT. WE COULD HAVE A CHANCE AT WINNING.
WHO CARES ABOUT A DUMB RAFFLE?
ME.
YOU'RE NO FUN...
JUST BECAUSE I DON'T AGREE WITH YOU, DOESN'T MEAN I'M NOT FUN.

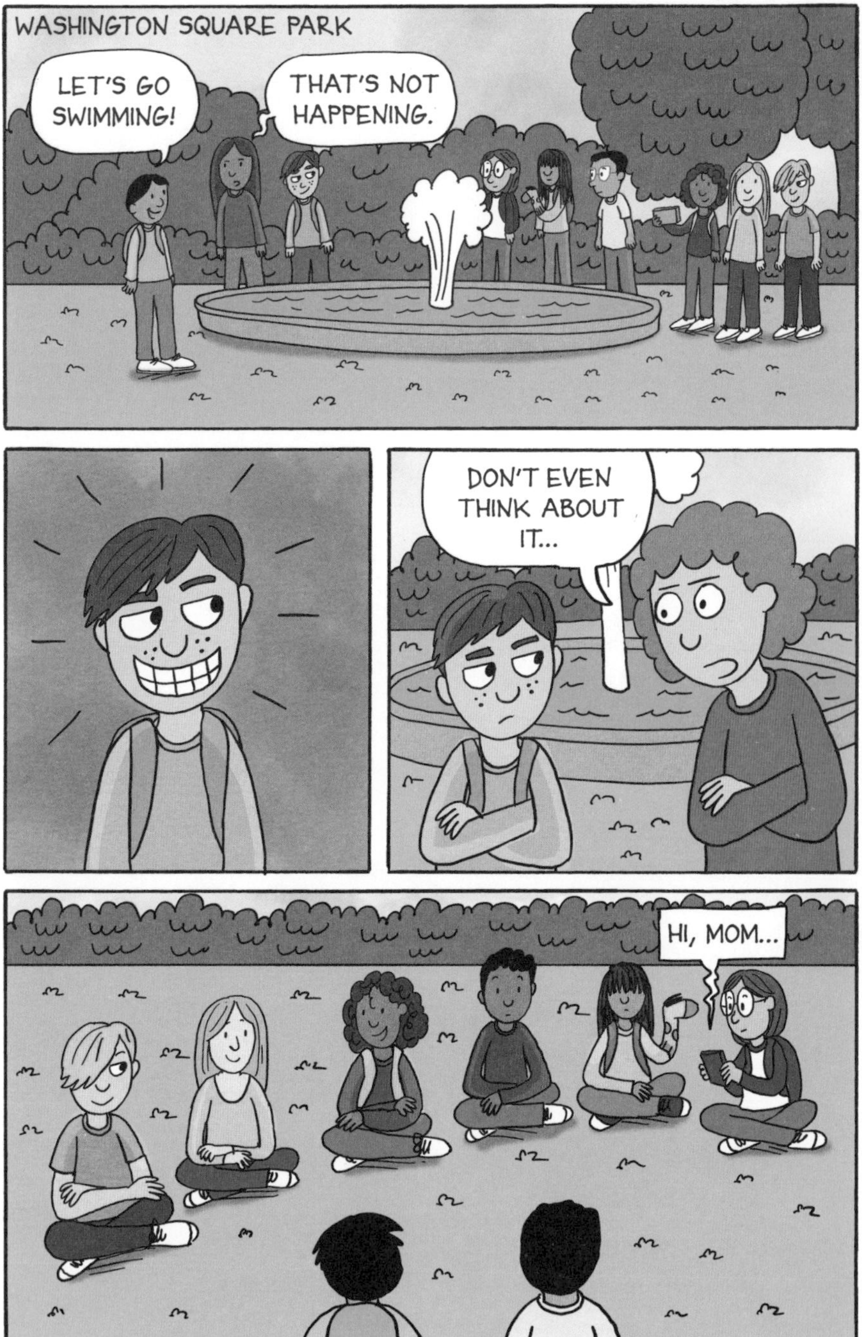
WASHINGTON SQUARE PARK
LET'S GO SWIMMING!
THAT'S NOT HAPPENING.
DON'T EVEN THINK ABOUT IT...
HI, MOM...

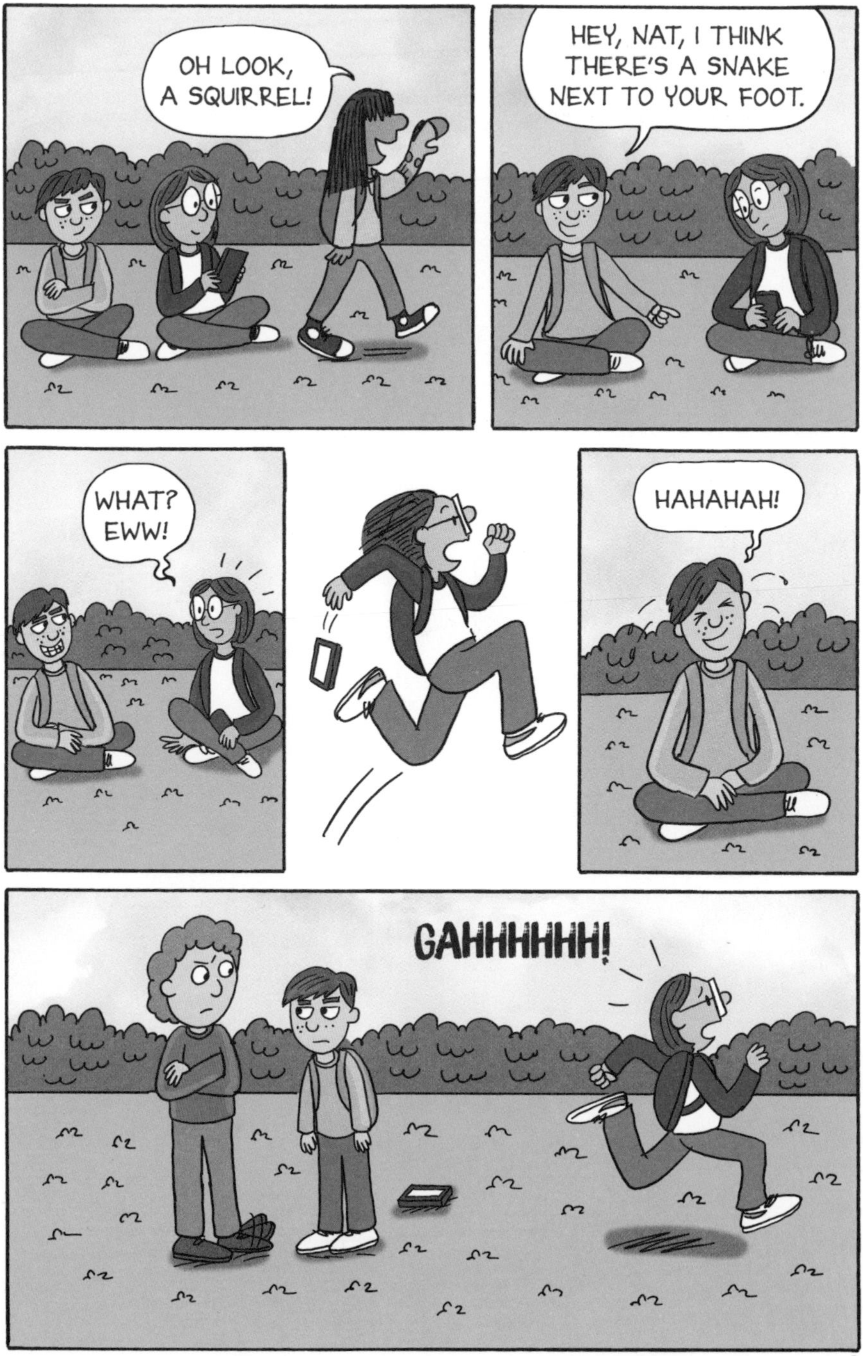
OH LOOK, A SQUIRREL!
HEY, NAT, I THINK THERE'S A SNAKE NEXT TO YOUR FOOT.
WHAT? EWW!
HAHAHAH!
GAHHHHHH!

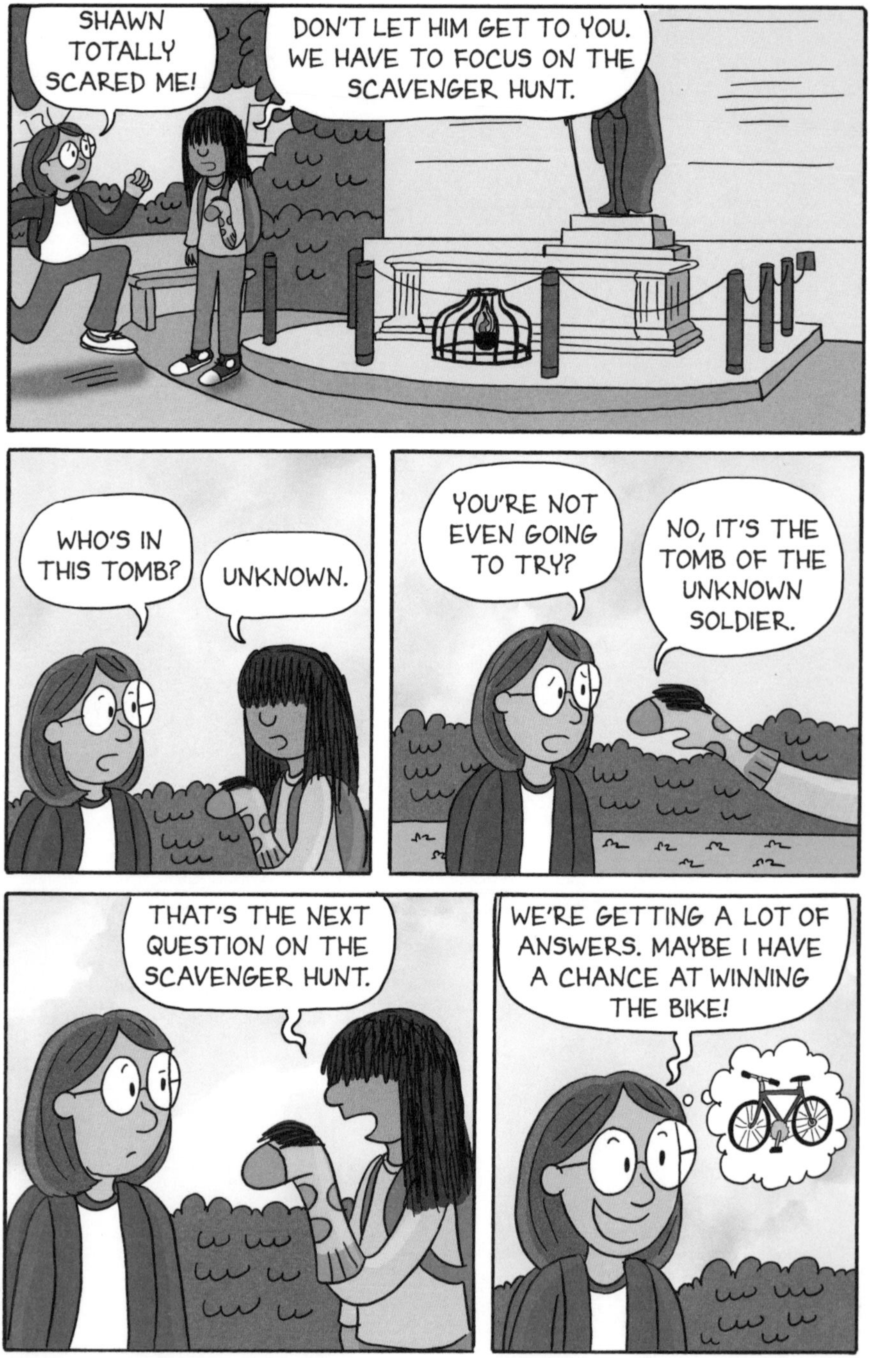
SHAWN TOTALLY SCARED ME!
DON'T LET HIM GET TO YOU. WE HAVE TO FOCUS ON THE SCAVENGER HUNT.
WHO'S IN THIS TOMB?
UNKNOWN.
YOU'RE NOT EVEN GOING TO TRY?
NO, IT'S THE TOMB OF THE UNKNOWN SOLDIER.
THAT'S THE NEXT QUESTION ON THE SCAVENGER HUNT.
WE'RE GETTING A LOT OF ANSWERS. MAYBE I HAVE A CHANCE AT WINNING THE BIKE!

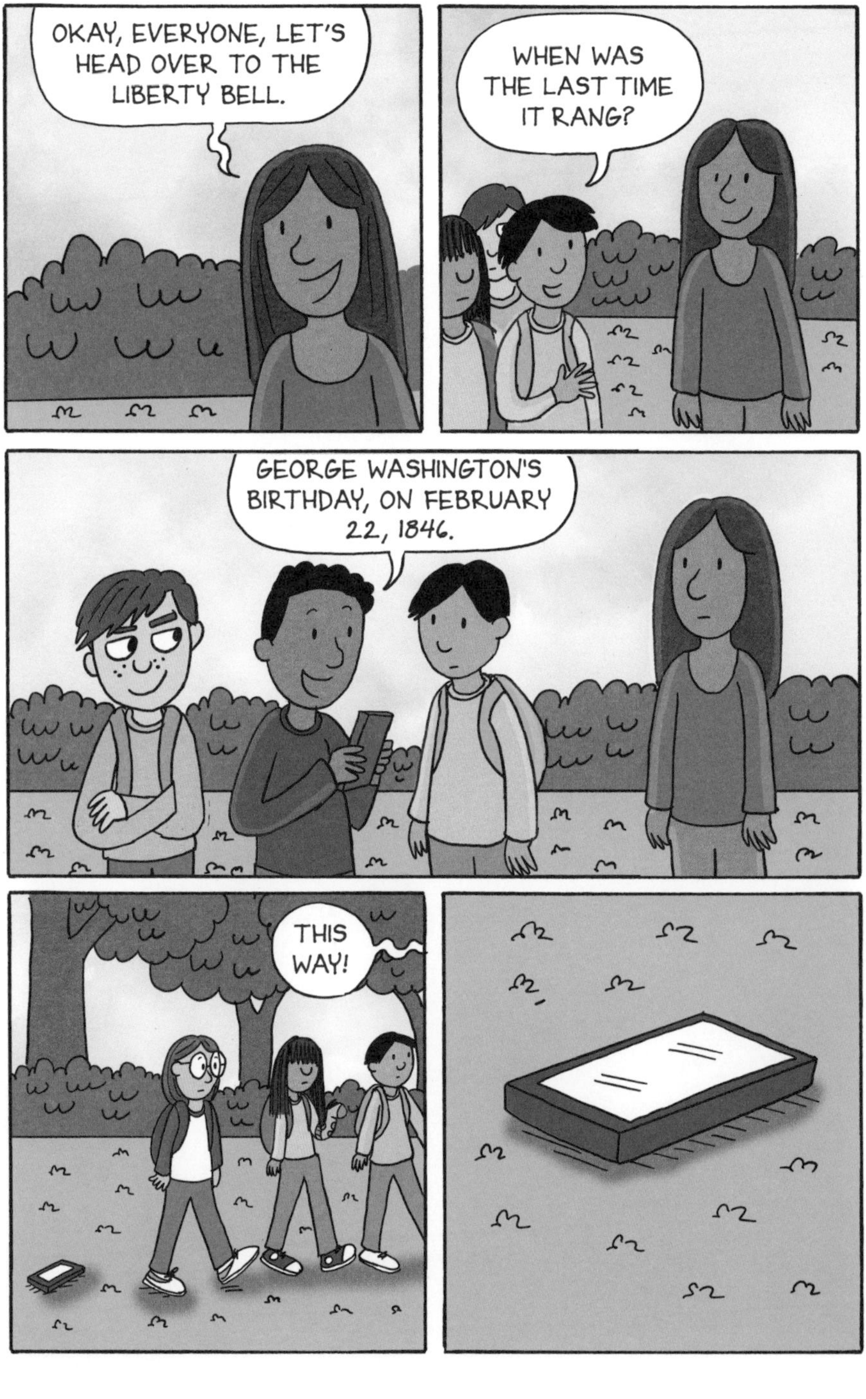
OKAY, EVERYONE, LET'S HEAD OVER TO THE LIBERTY BELL.
WHEN WAS THE LAST TIME IT RANG?
GEORGE WASHINGTON'S BIRTHDAY, ON FEBRUARY 22, 1846.
THIS WAY!

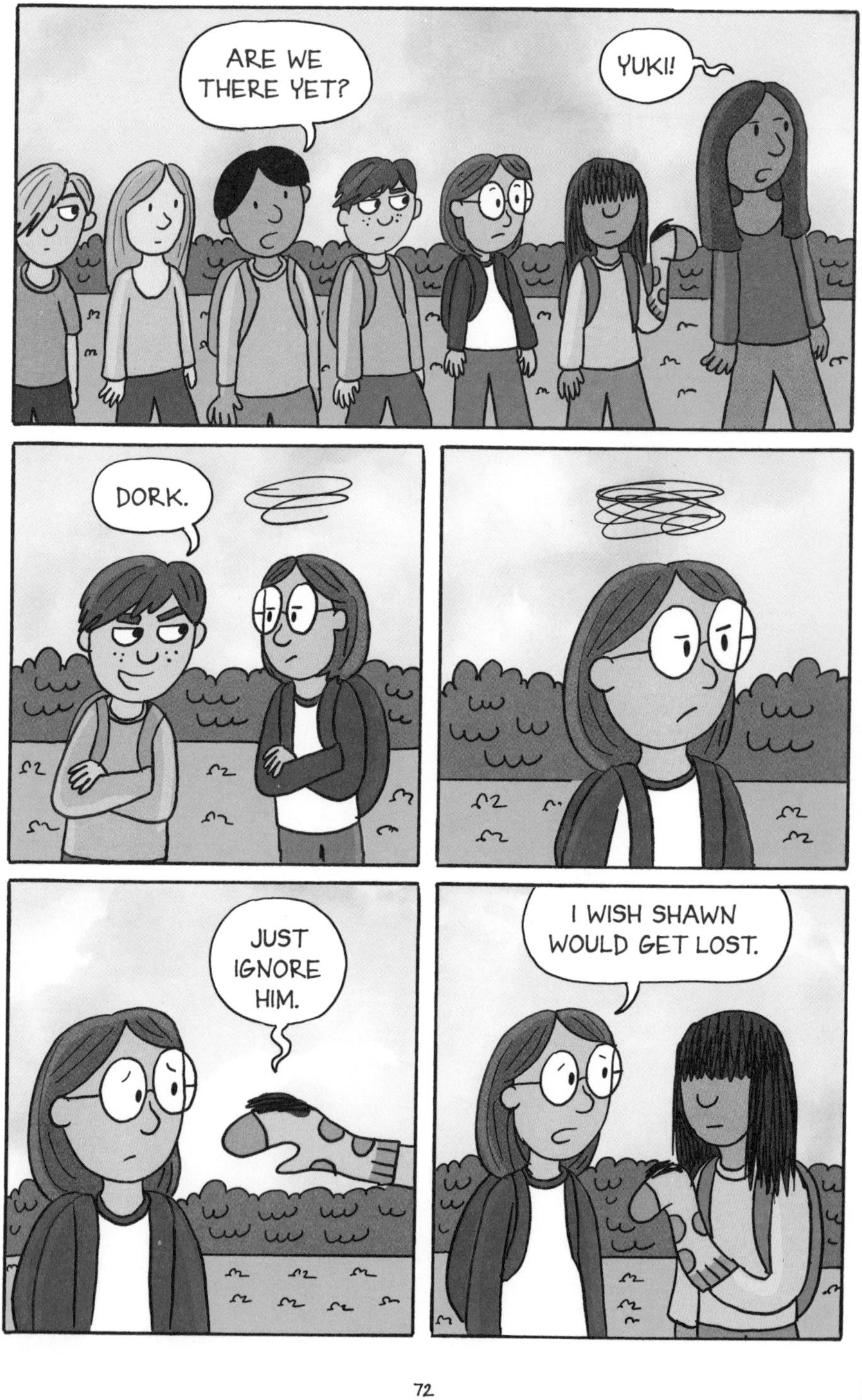
ARE WE THERE YET?
YUKI!
DORK.
JUST IGNORE HIM.
I WISH SHAWN WOULD GET LOST.

CHAPTER 6
LIBERTY BELL

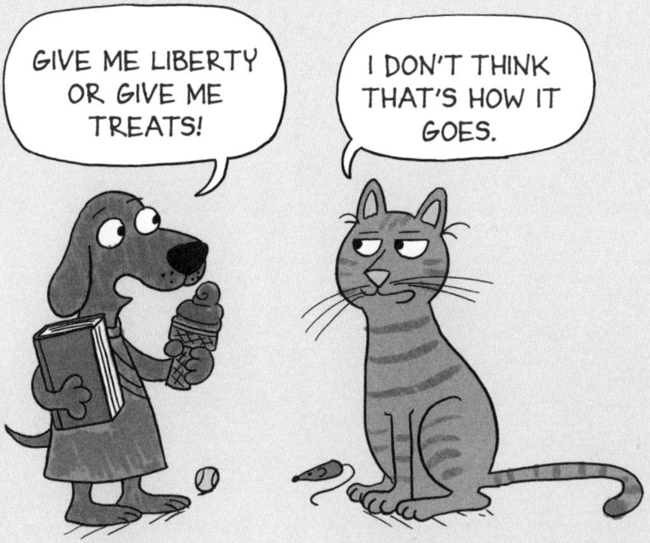
GIVE ME LIBERTY OR GIVE ME TREATS!
I DON'T THINK THAT'S HOW IT GOES.

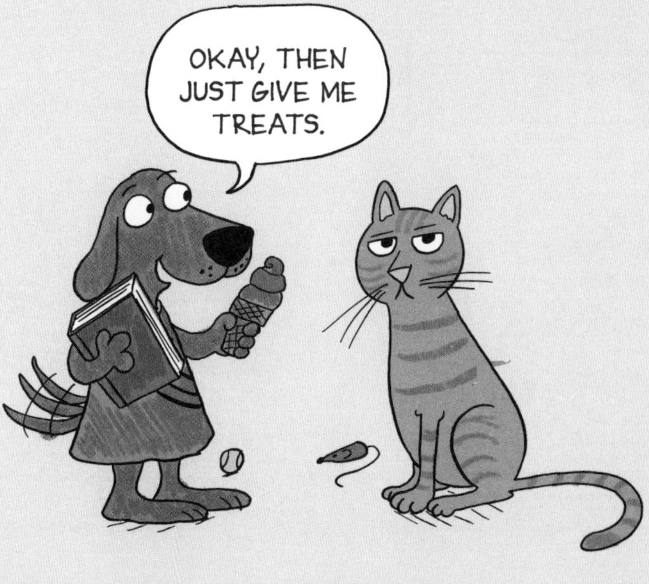
OKAY, THEN JUST GIVE ME TREATS.

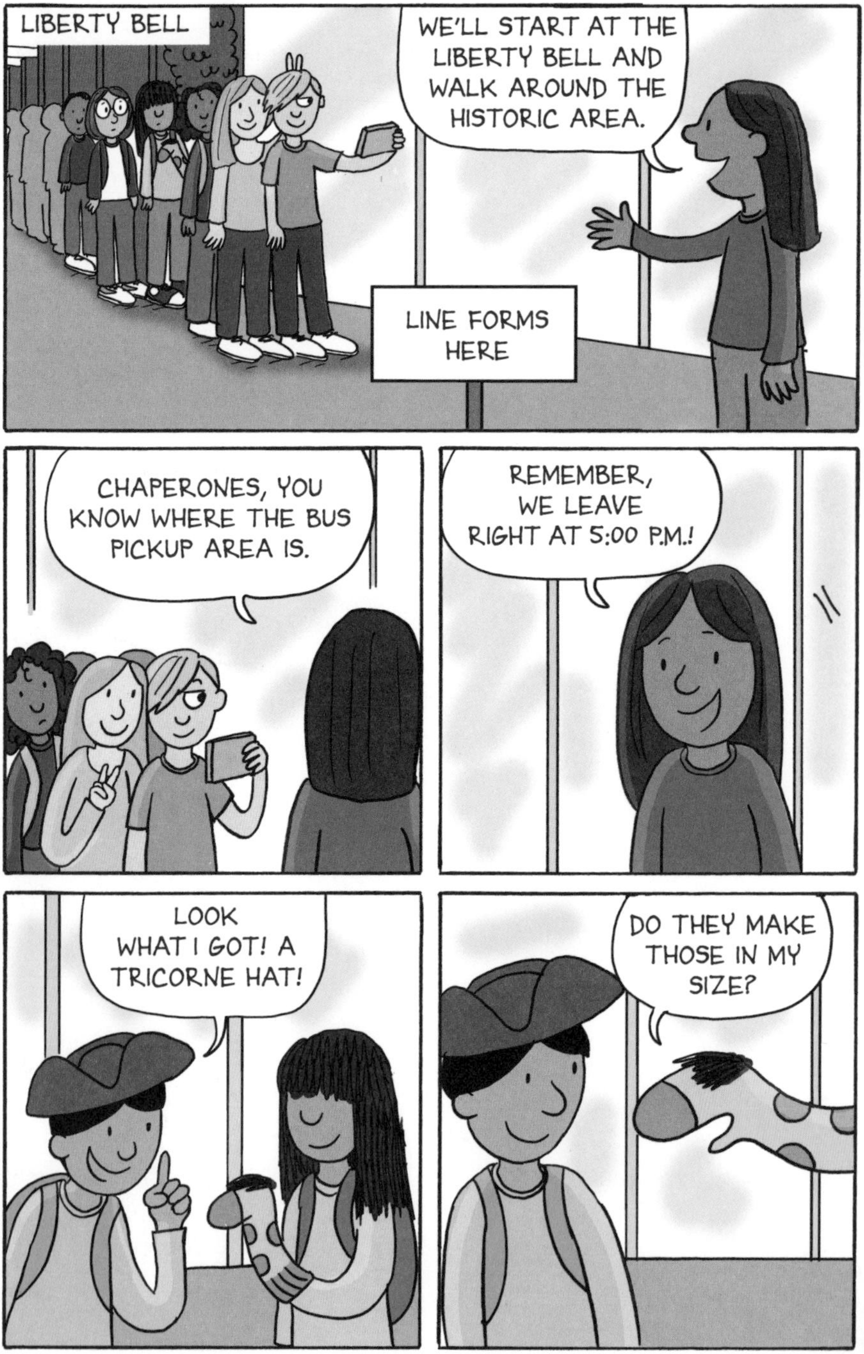
LIBERTY BELL
WE'LL START AT THE LIBERTY BELL AND WALK AROUND THE HISTORIC AREA.
LINE FORMS HERE
CHAPERONES, YOU KNOW WHERE THE BUS PICKUP AREA IS.
REMEMBER, WE LEAVE RIGHT AT 5:00 P.M.!
LOOK WHAT I GOT! A TRICORNE HAT!
DO THEY MAKE THOSE IN MY SIZE?

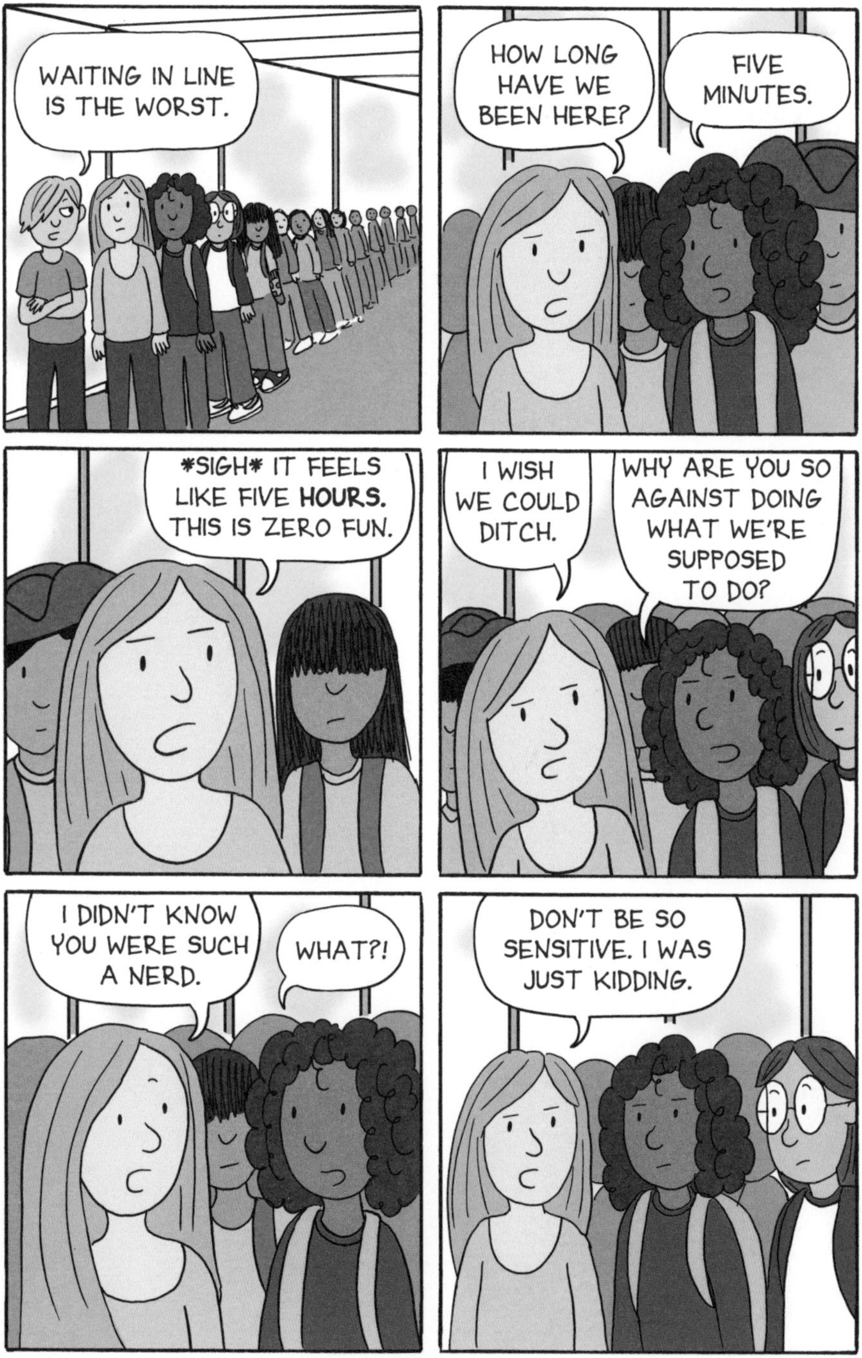
WAITING IN LINE IS THE WORST.
HOW LONG HAVE WE BEEN HERE?
FIVE MINUTES.
SIGH IT FEELS LIKE FIVE **HOURS.** THIS IS ZERO FUN.
I WISH WE COULD DITCH.
WHY ARE YOU SO AGAINST DOING WHAT WE'RE SUPPOSED TO DO?
I DIDN'T KNOW YOU WERE SUCH A NERD.
WHAT?!
DON'T BE SO SENSITIVE. I WAS JUST KIDDING.

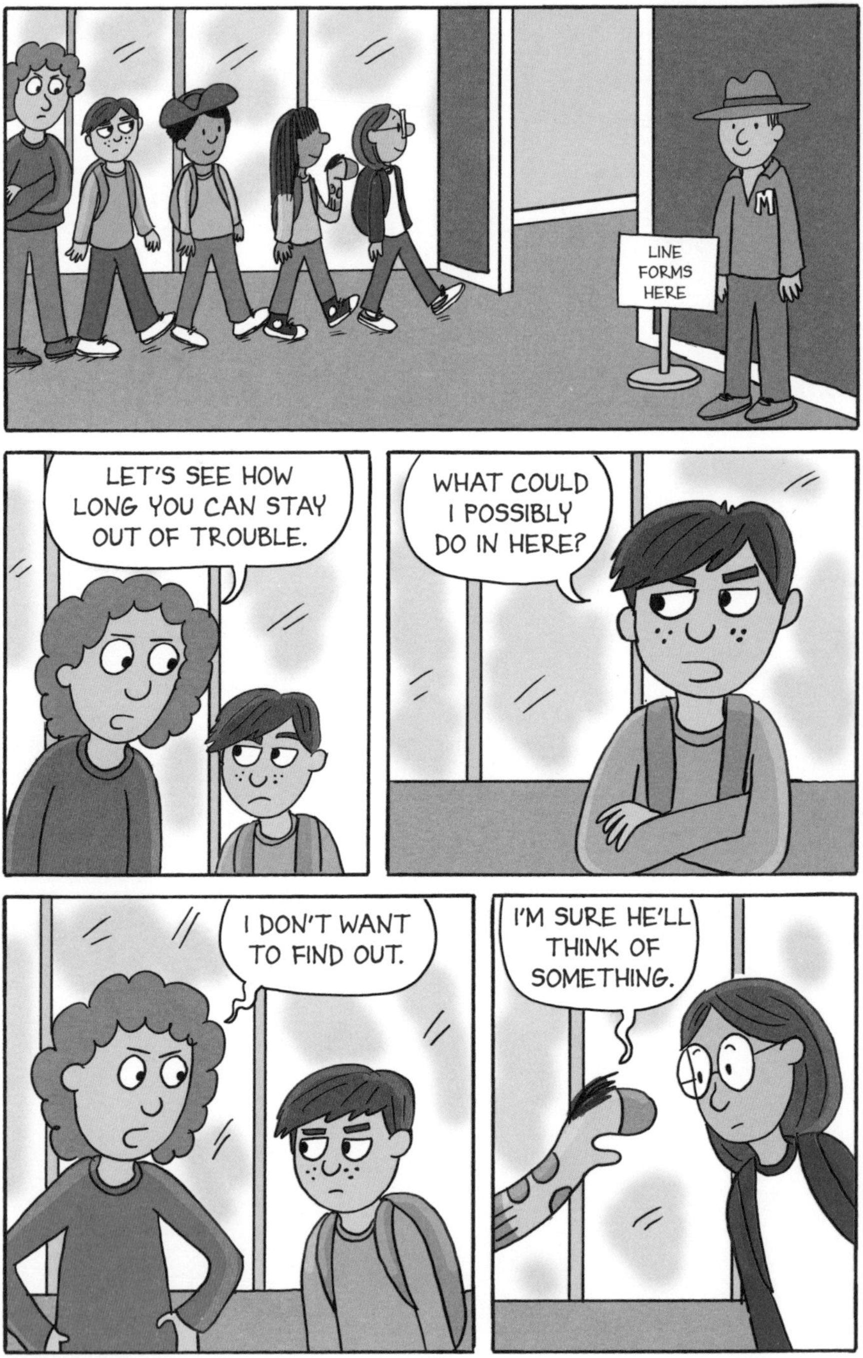
LINE
FORMS
HERE
LET'S SEE HOW LONG YOU CAN STAY OUT OF TROUBLE.
WHAT COULD I POSSIBLY DO IN HERE?
I DON'T WANT TO FIND OUT.
I'M SURE HE'LL THINK OF SOMETHING.

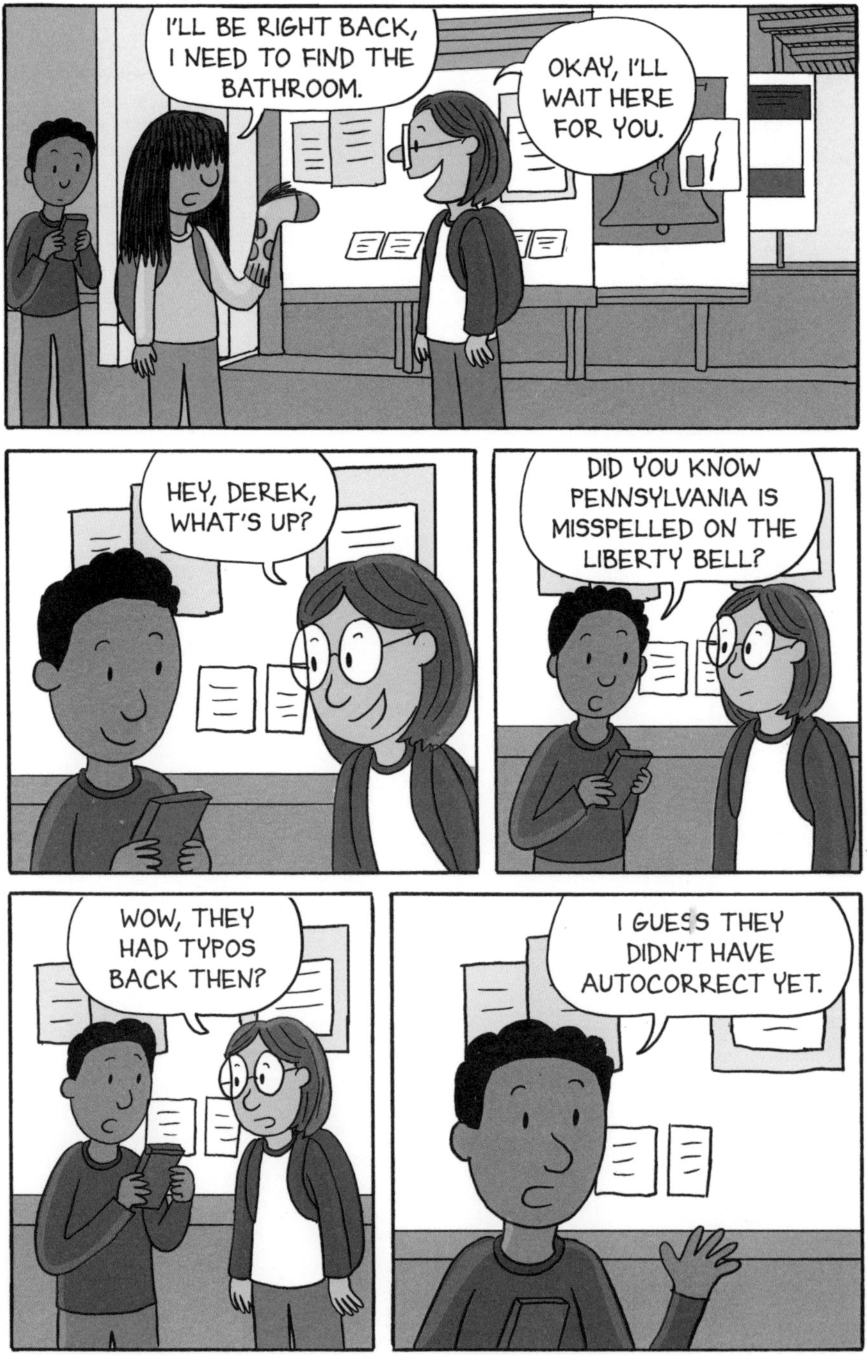
I'LL BE RIGHT BACK, I NEED TO FIND THE BATHROOM.
OKAY, I'LL WAIT HERE FOR YOU.
HEY, DEREK, WHAT'S UP?
DID YOU KNOW PENNSYLVANIA IS MISSPELLED ON THE LIBERTY BELL?
WOW, THEY HAD TYPOS BACK THEN?
I GUESS THEY DIDN'T HAVE AUTOCORRECT YET.

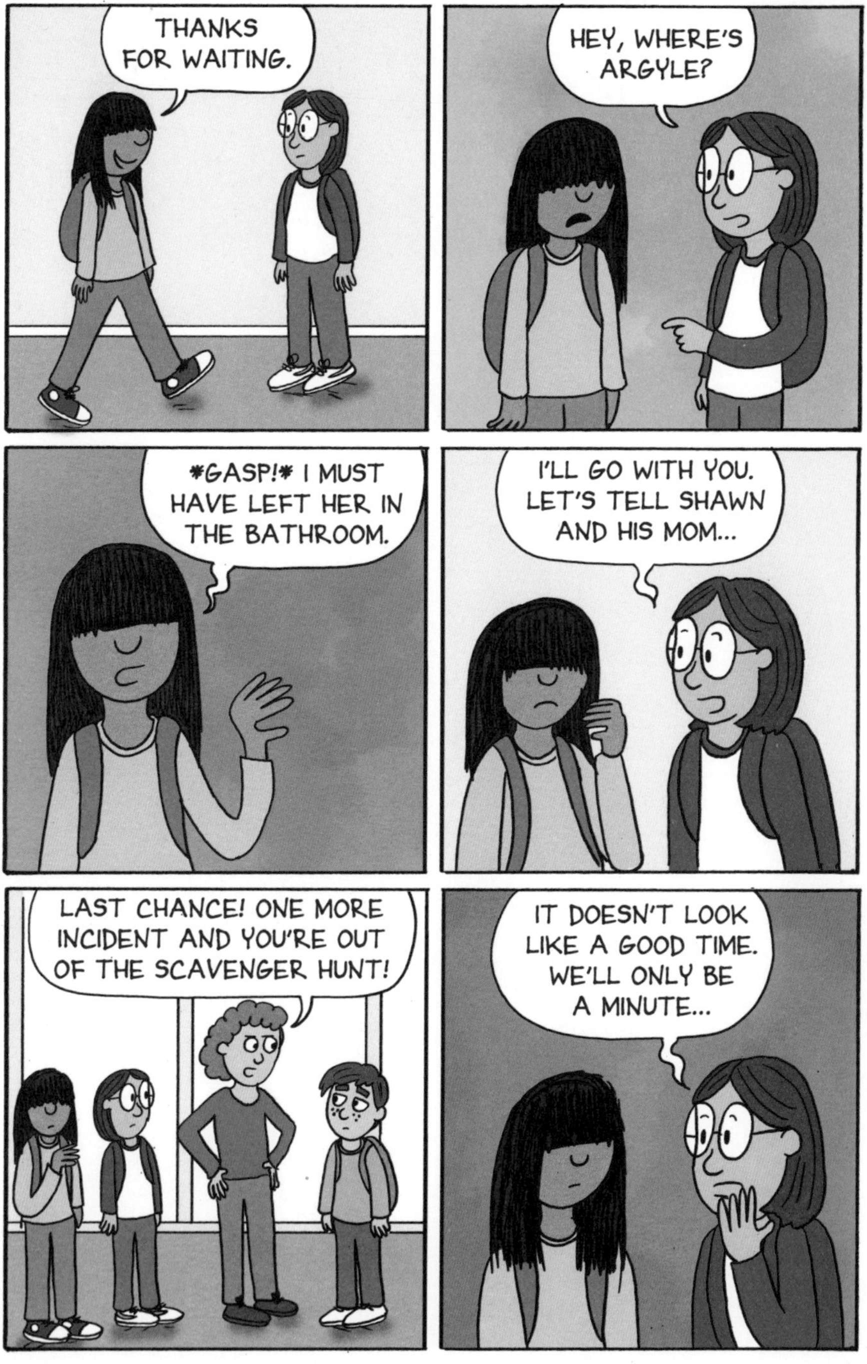
THANKS FOR WAITING.
HEY, WHERE'S ARGYLE?
GASP! I MUST HAVE LEFT HER IN THE BATHROOM.
I'LL GO WITH YOU. LET'S TELL SHAWN AND HIS MOM...
LAST CHANCE! ONE MORE INCIDENT AND YOU'RE OUT OF THE SCAVENGER HUNT!
IT DOESN'T LOOK LIKE A GOOD TIME. WE'LL ONLY BE A MINUTE...

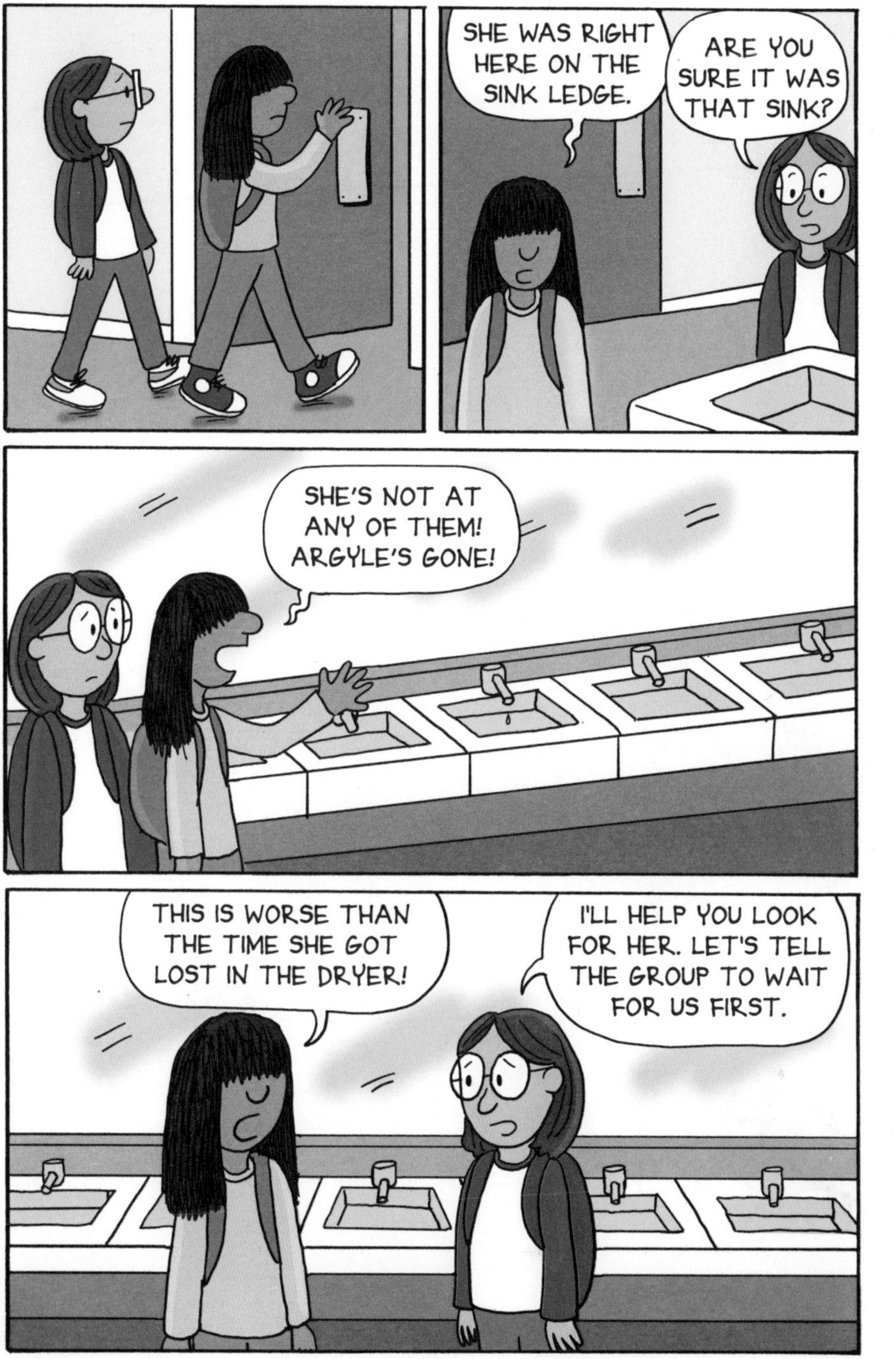
SHE WAS RIGHT HERE ON THE SINK LEDGE.
ARE YOU SURE IT WAS THAT SINK?
SHE'S NOT AT ANY OF THEM! ARGYLE'S GONE!
THIS IS WORSE THAN THE TIME SHE GOT LOST IN THE DRYER!
I'LL HELP YOU LOOK FOR HER. LET'S TELL THE GROUP TO WAIT FOR US FIRST.

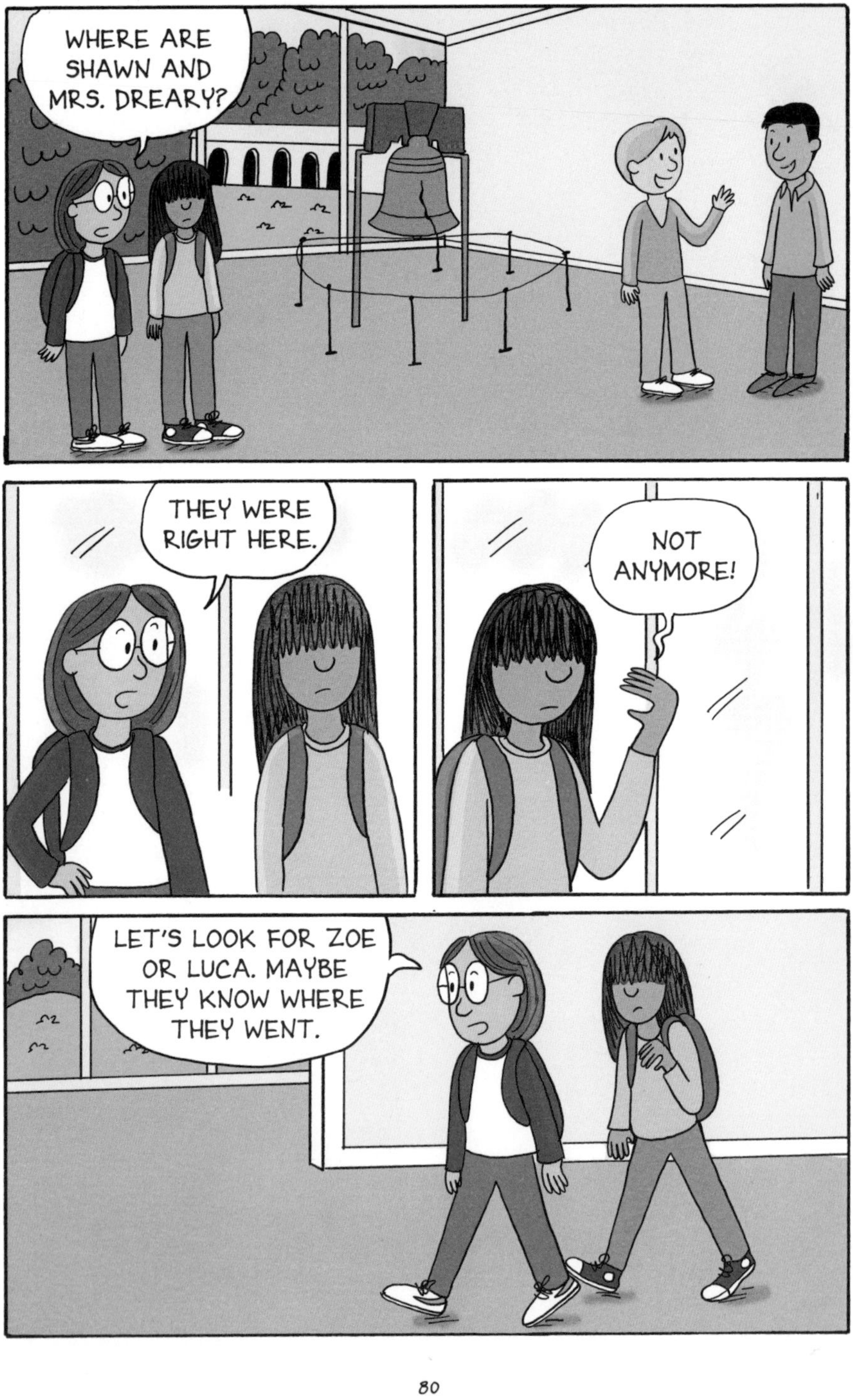
WHERE ARE SHAWN AND MRS. DREARY?
THEY WERE RIGHT HERE.
NOT ANYMORE!
LET'S LOOK FOR ZOE OR LUCA. MAYBE THEY KNOW WHERE THEY WENT.

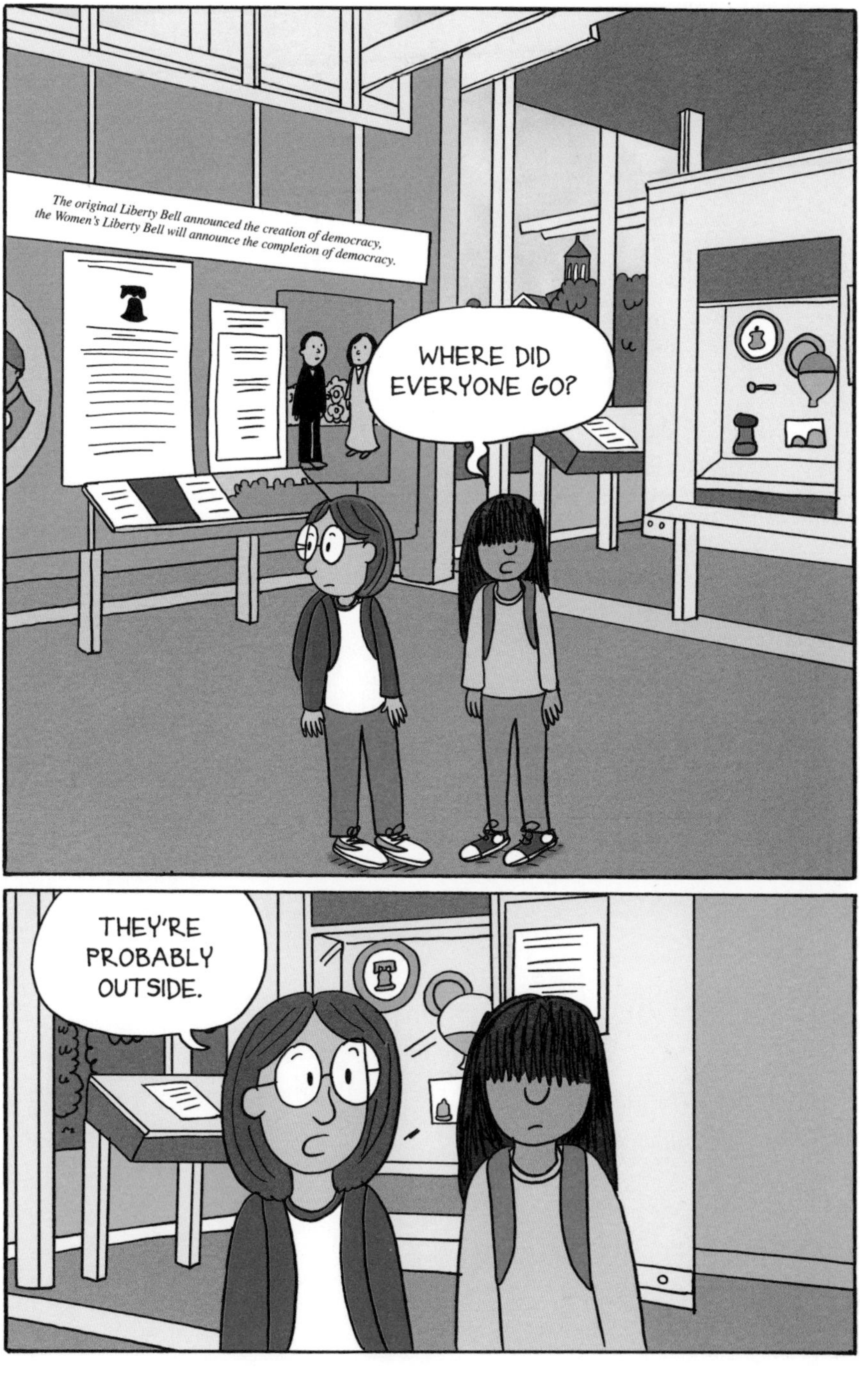
The original Liberty Bell announced the creation of democracy, the Women's Liberty Bell will announce the completion of democracy.
WHERE DID EVERYONE GO?
THEY'RE PROBABLY OUTSIDE.

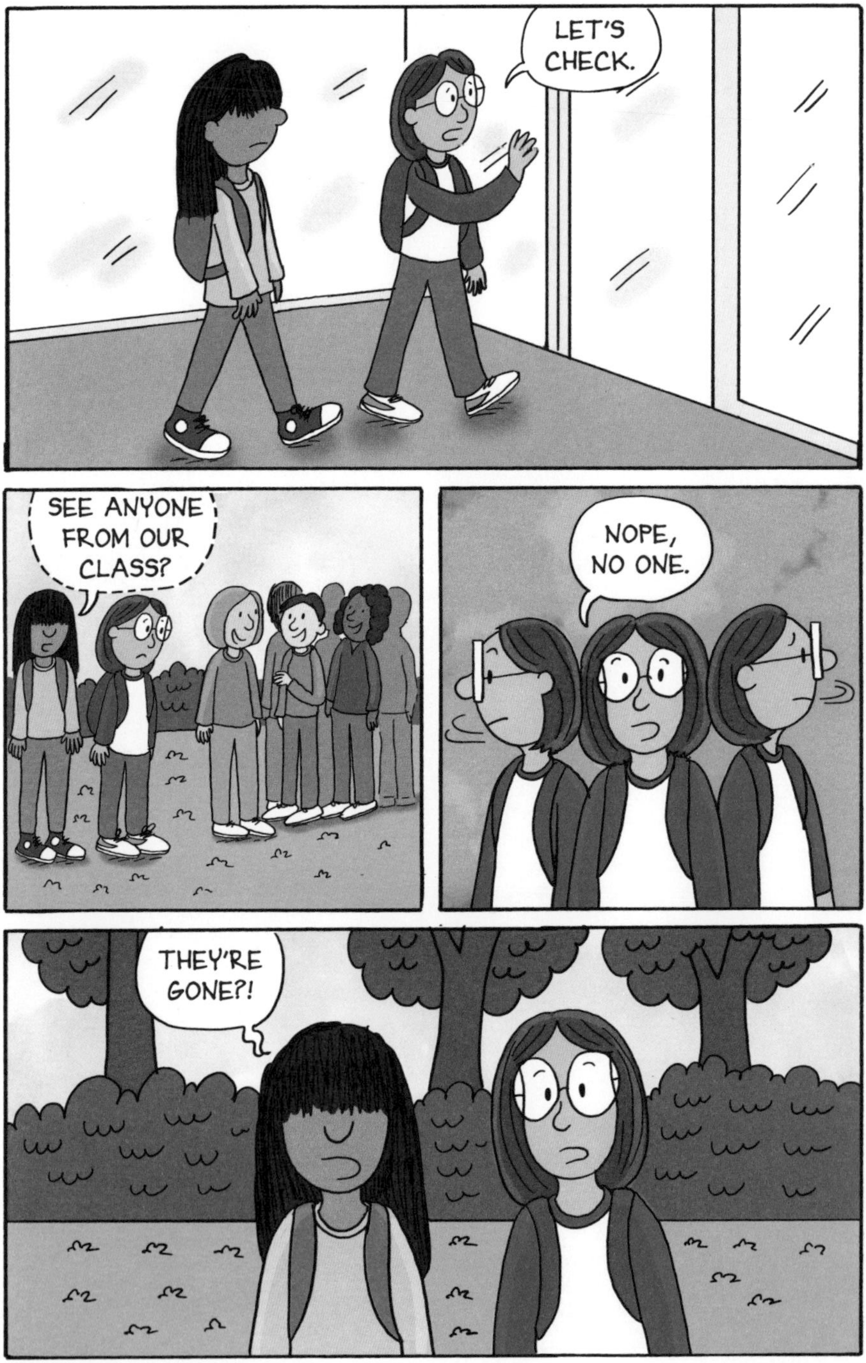

LET'S CHECK.
SEE ANYONE FROM OUR CLASS?
NOPE, NO ONE.
THEY'RE GONE?!

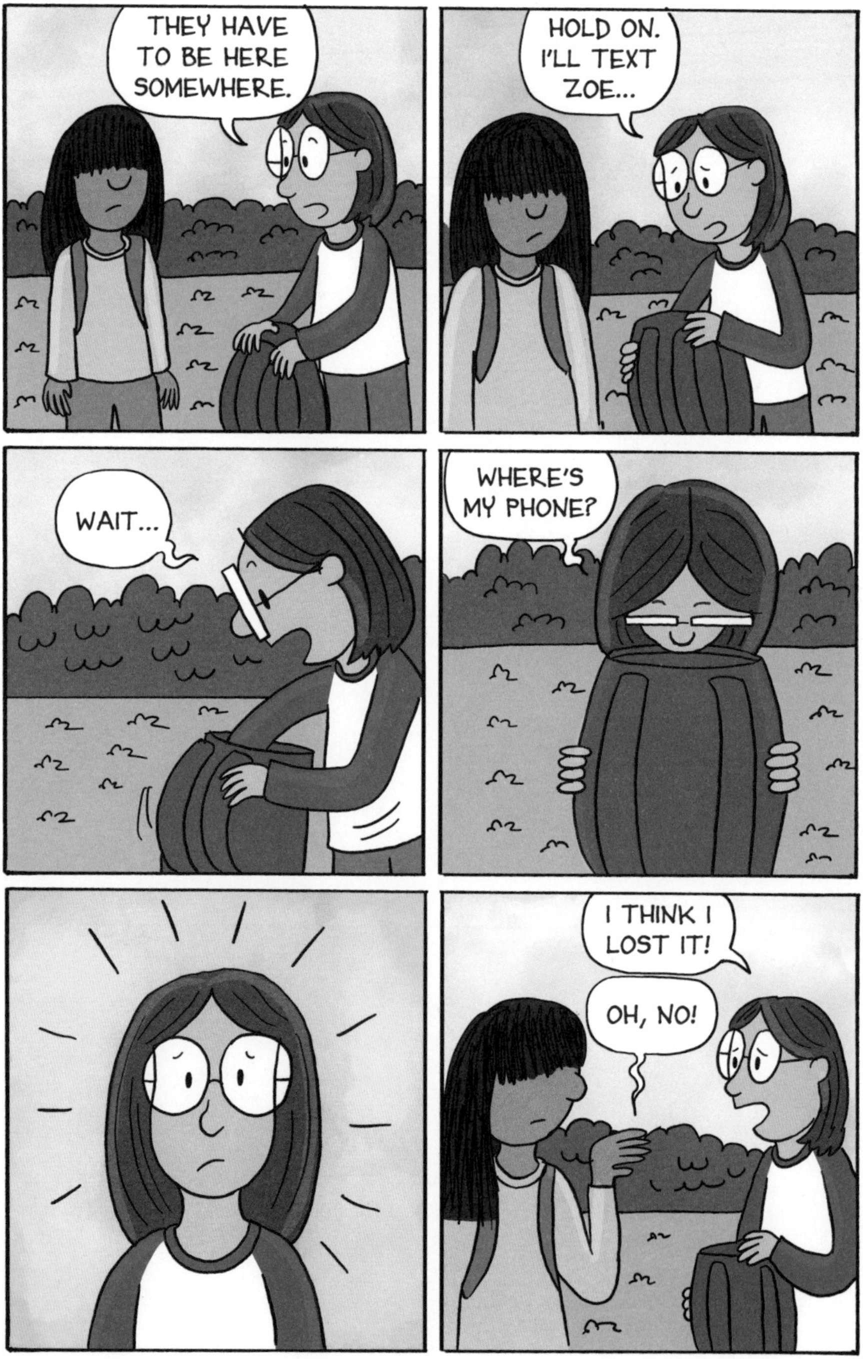
THEY HAVE TO BE HERE SOMEWHERE.
HOLD ON. I'LL TEXT ZOE...
WAIT...
WHERE'S MY PHONE?
I THINK I LOST IT!
OH, NO!

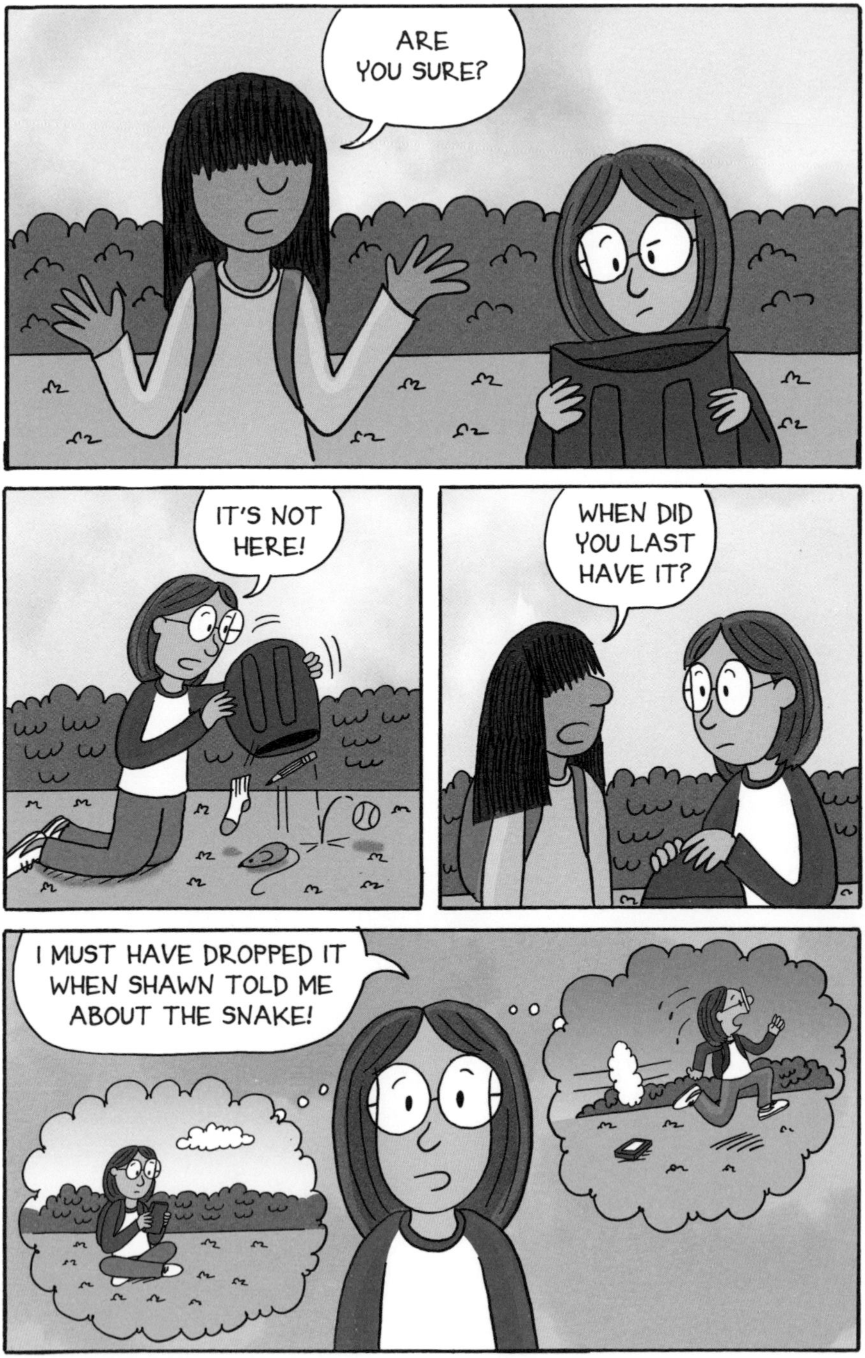
ARE YOU SURE?
IT'S NOT HERE!
WHEN DID YOU LAST HAVE IT?
I MUST HAVE DROPPED IT WHEN SHAWN TOLD ME ABOUT THE SNAKE!

CHAPTER 7
PHONE

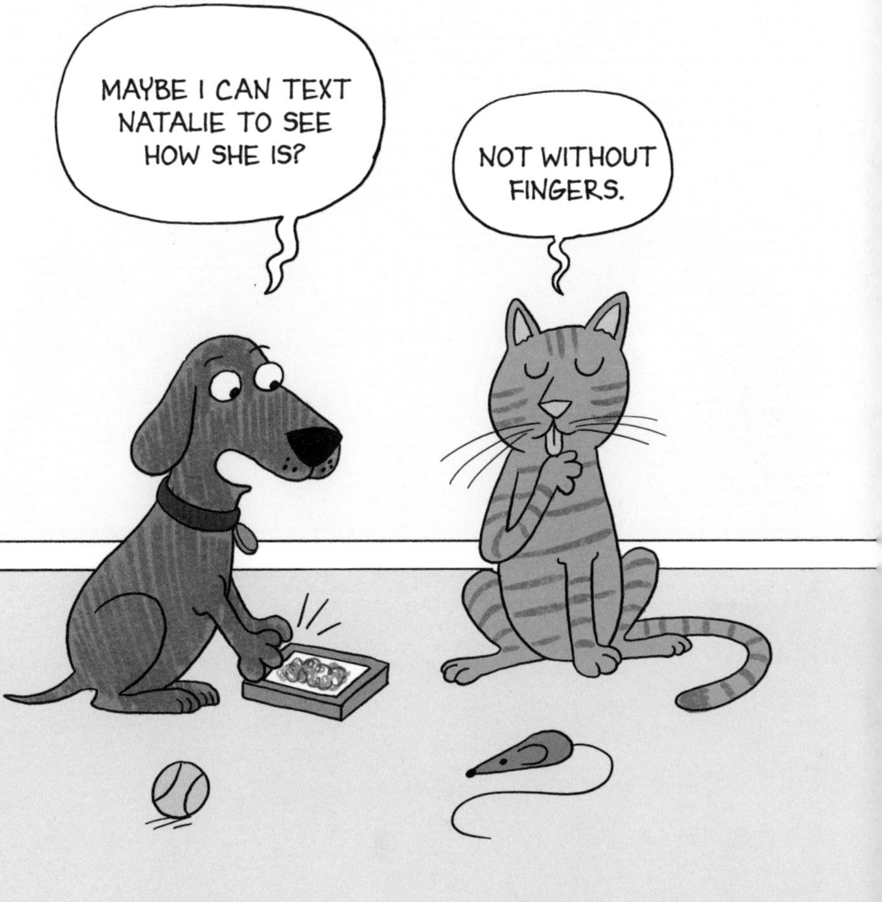
MAYBE I CAN TEXT NATALIE TO SEE HOW SHE IS?
NOT WITHOUT FINGERS.

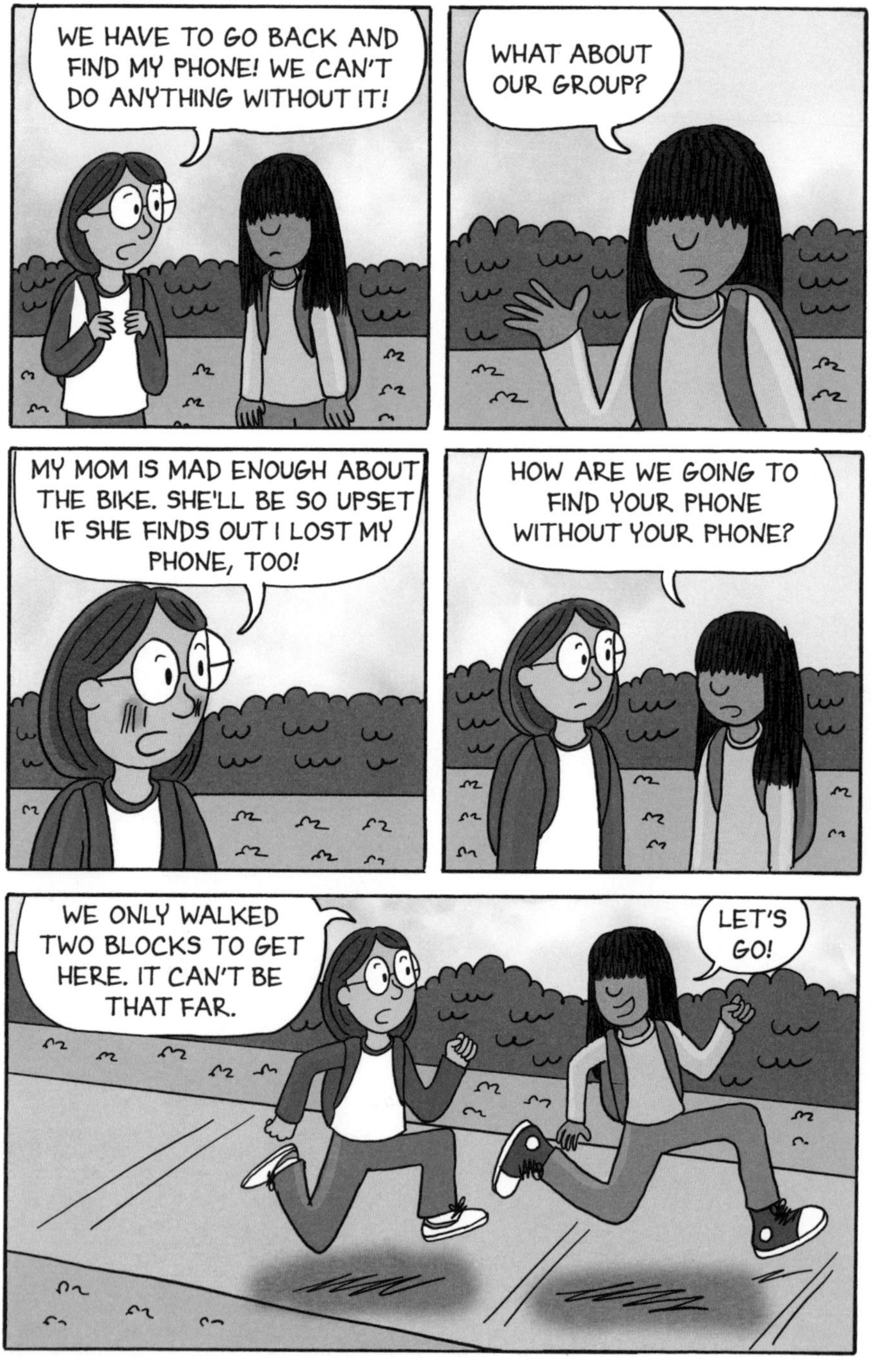
WE HAVE TO GO BACK AND FIND MY PHONE! WE CAN'T DO ANYTHING WITHOUT IT!
WHAT ABOUT OUR GROUP?
MY MOM IS MAD ENOUGH ABOUT THE BIKE. SHE'LL BE SO UPSET IF SHE FINDS OUT I LOST MY PHONE, TOO!
HOW ARE WE GOING TO FIND YOUR PHONE WITHOUT YOUR PHONE?
WE ONLY WALKED TWO BLOCKS TO GET HERE. IT CAN'T BE THAT FAR.
LET'S GO!

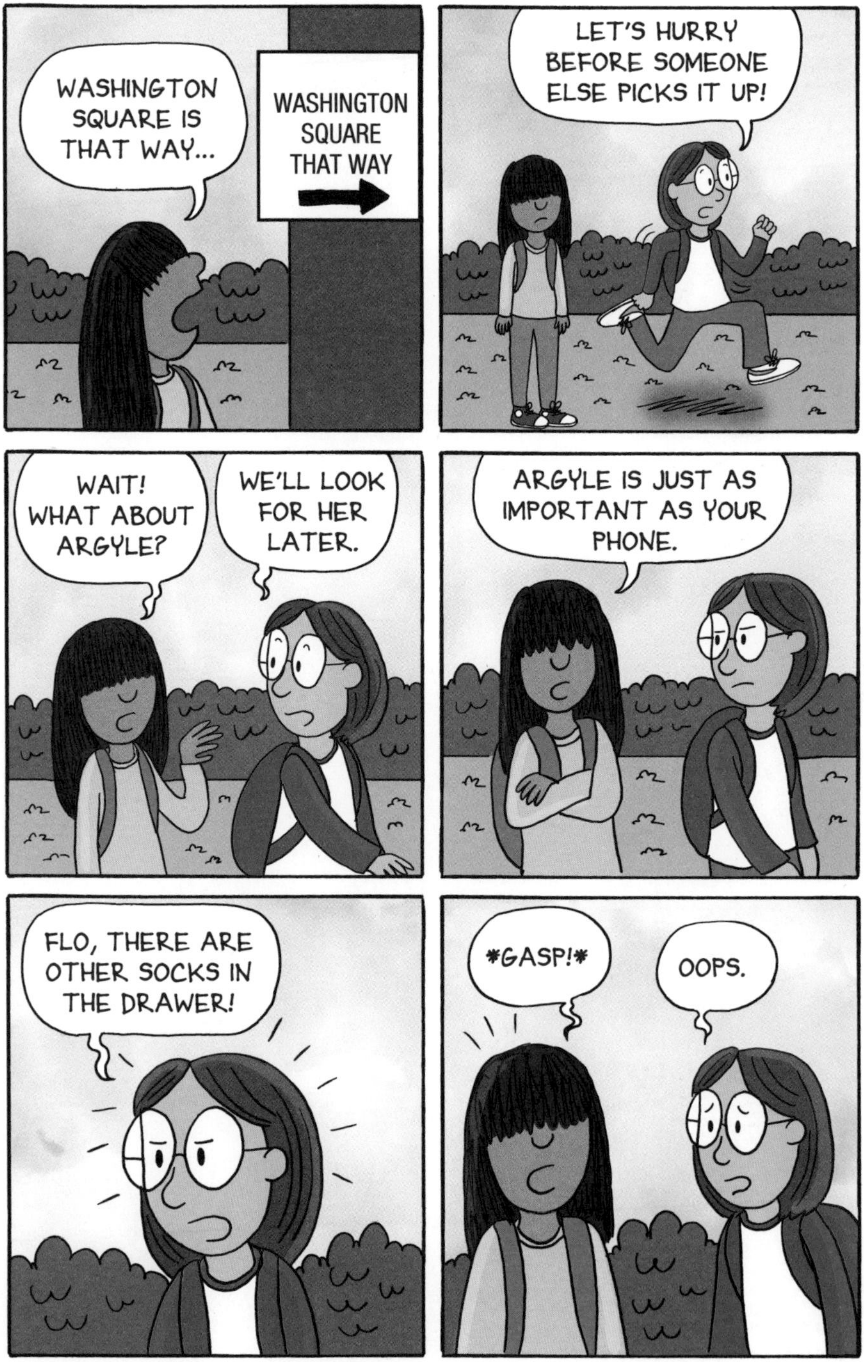
WASHINGTON SQUARE IS THAT WAY...
WASHINGTON SQUARE THAT WAY
LET'S HURRY BEFORE SOMEONE ELSE PICKS IT UP!
WAIT! WHAT ABOUT ARGYLE?
WE'LL LOOK FOR HER LATER.
ARGYLE IS JUST AS IMPORTANT AS YOUR PHONE.
FLO, THERE ARE OTHER SOCKS IN THE DRAWER!
GASP!
OOPS.

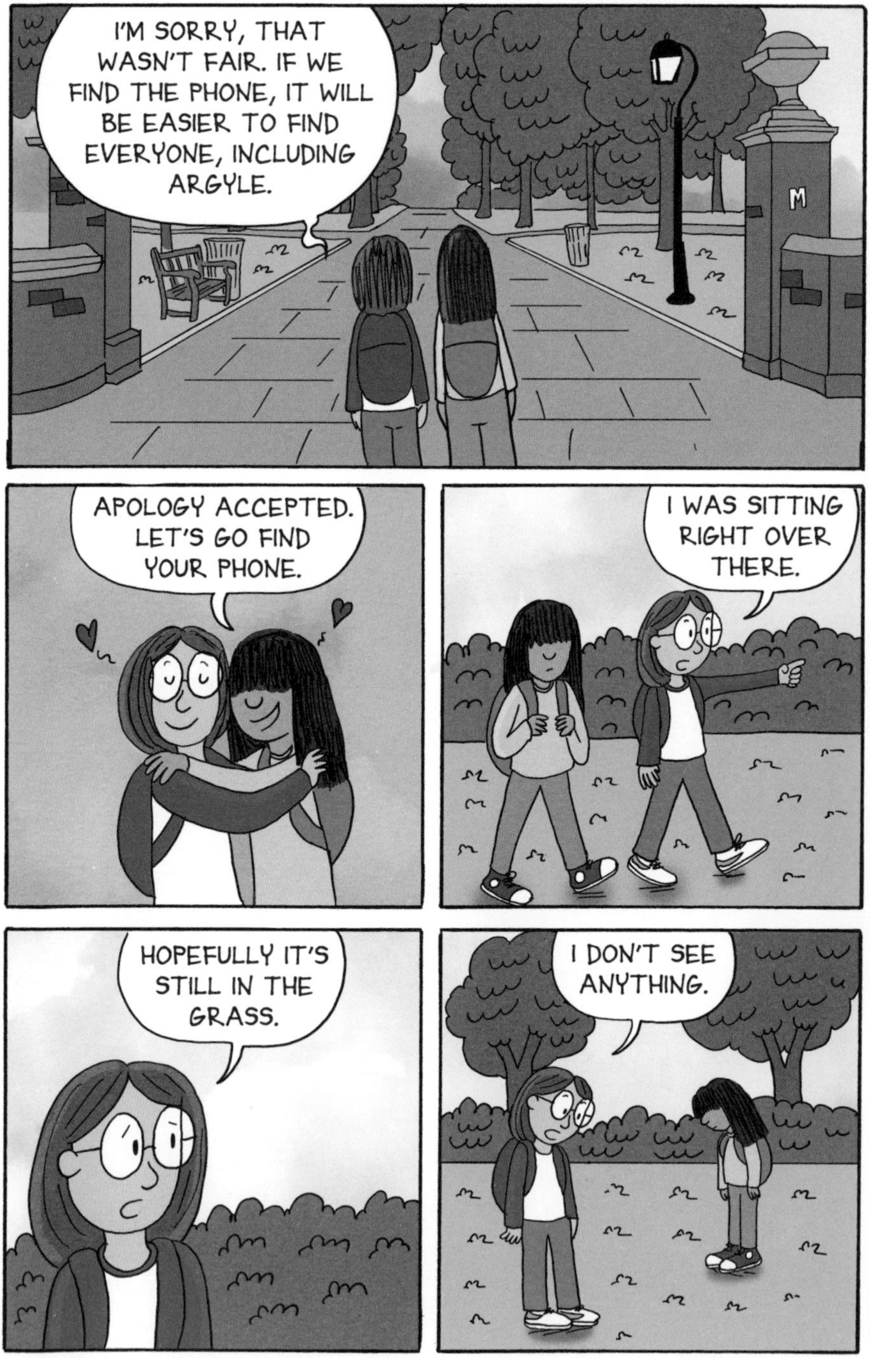
I'M SORRY, THAT WASN'T FAIR. IF WE FIND THE PHONE, IT WILL BE EASIER TO FIND EVERYONE, INCLUDING ARGYLE.
M
APOLOGY ACCEPTED. LET'S GO FIND YOUR PHONE.
I WAS SITTING RIGHT OVER THERE.
HOPEFULLY IT'S STILL IN THE GRASS.
I DON'T SEE ANYTHING.

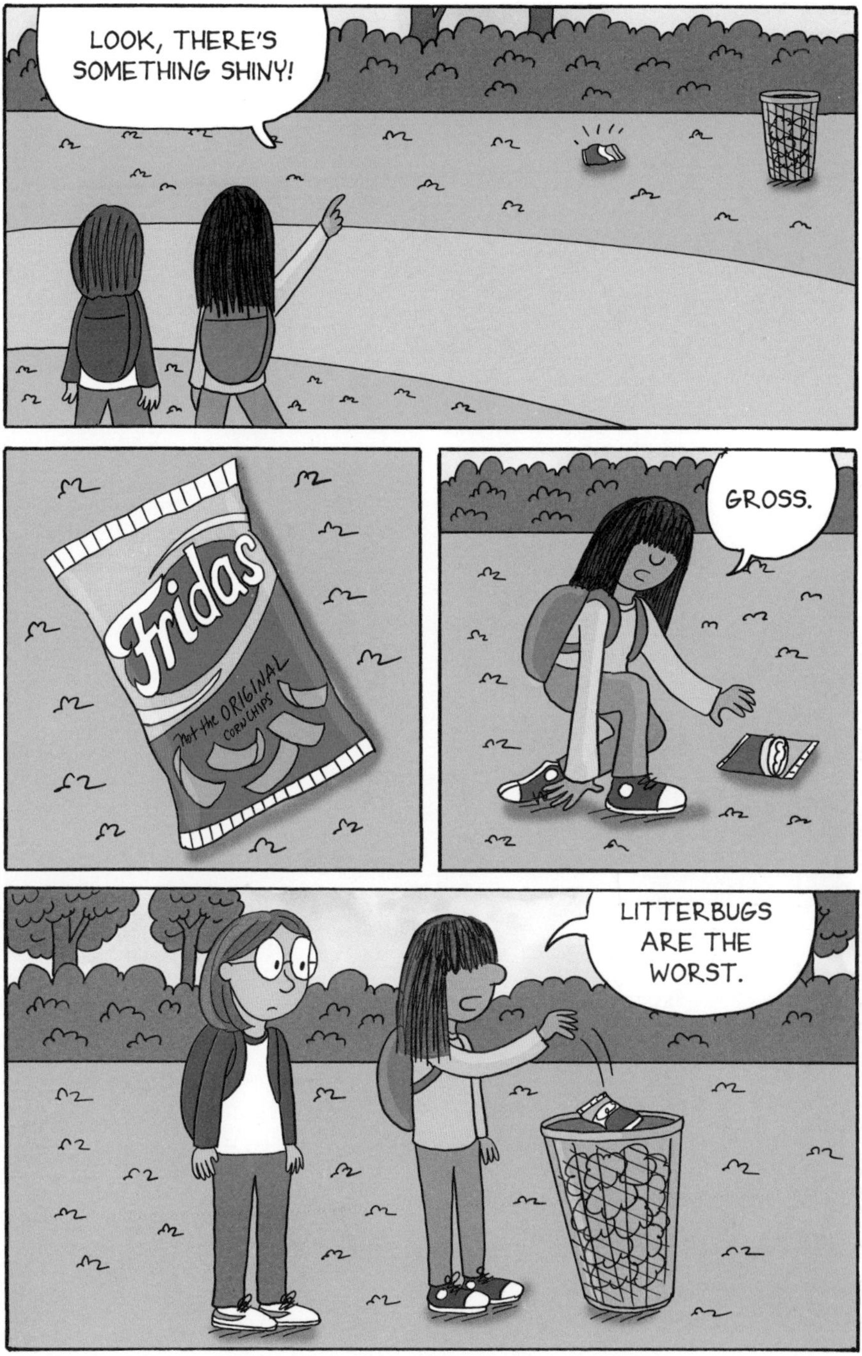
LOOK, THERE'S SOMETHING SHINY!
Fridas
Not the ORIGINAL CORN CHIPS
GROSS.
LITTERBUGS ARE THE WORST.

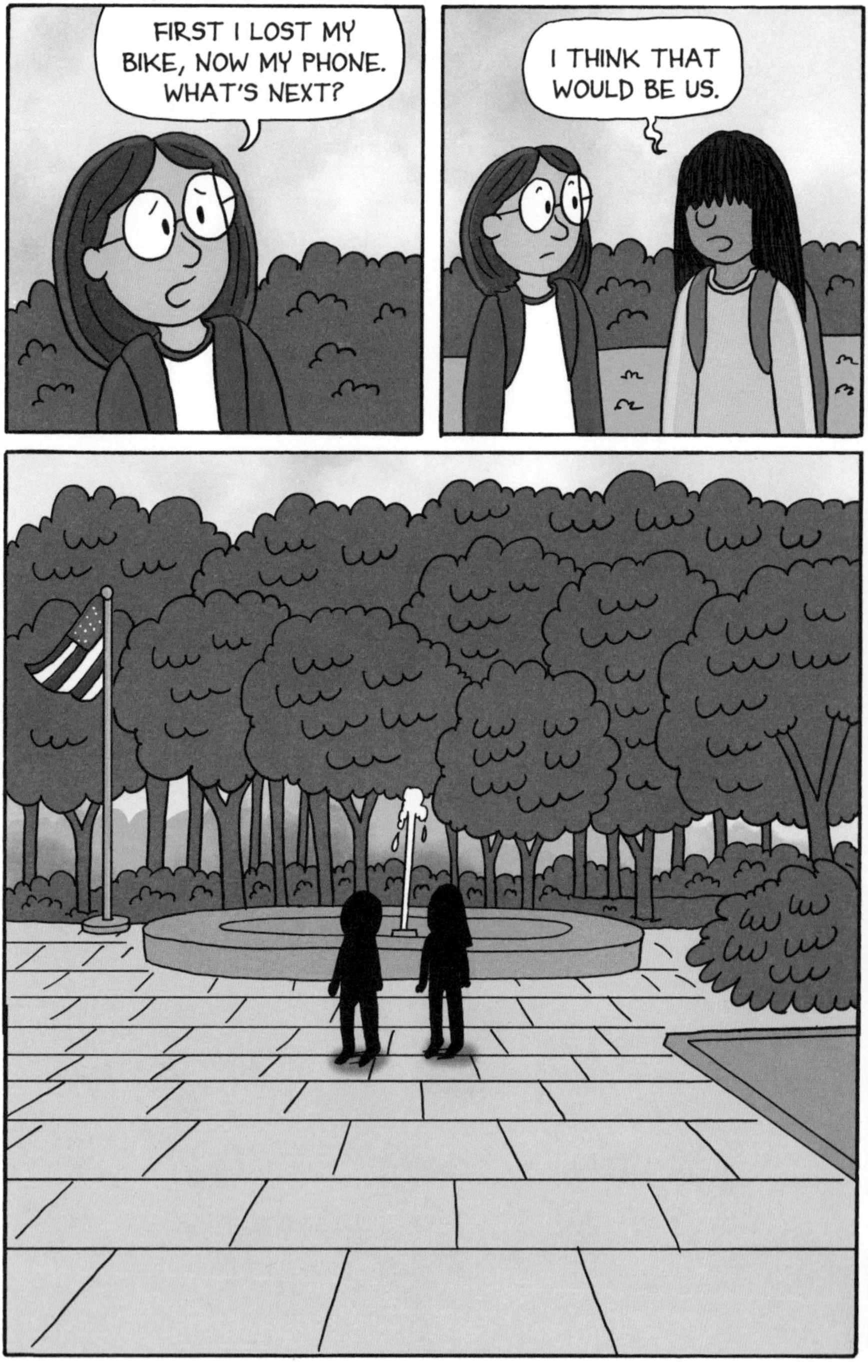
FIRST I LOST MY BIKE, NOW MY PHONE. WHAT'S NEXT?
I THINK THAT WOULD BE US.

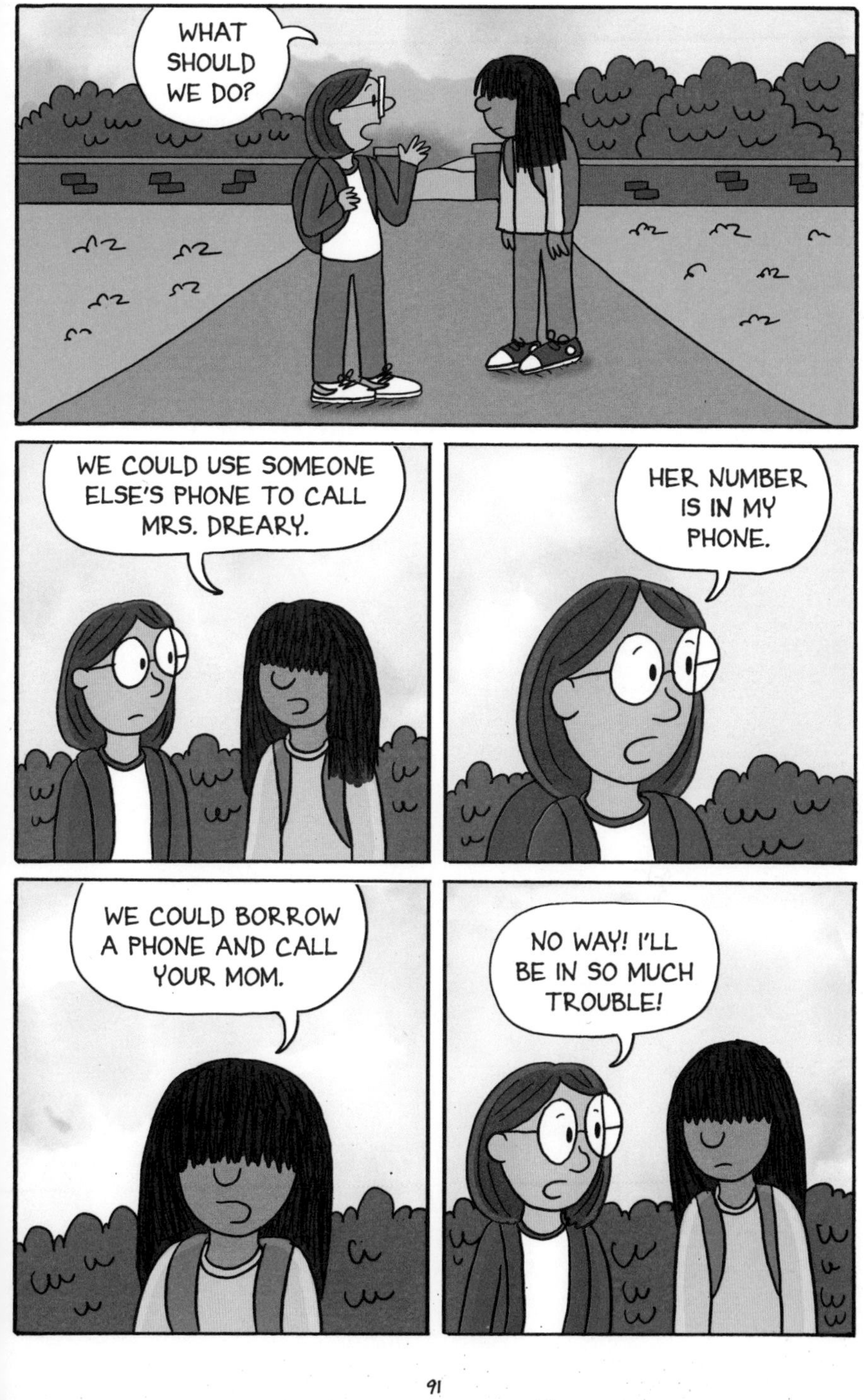
WHAT SHOULD WE DO?
WE COULD USE SOMEONE ELSE'S PHONE TO CALL MRS. DREARY.
HER NUMBER IS IN MY PHONE.
WE COULD BORROW A PHONE AND CALL YOUR MOM.
NO WAY! I'LL BE IN SO MUCH TROUBLE!

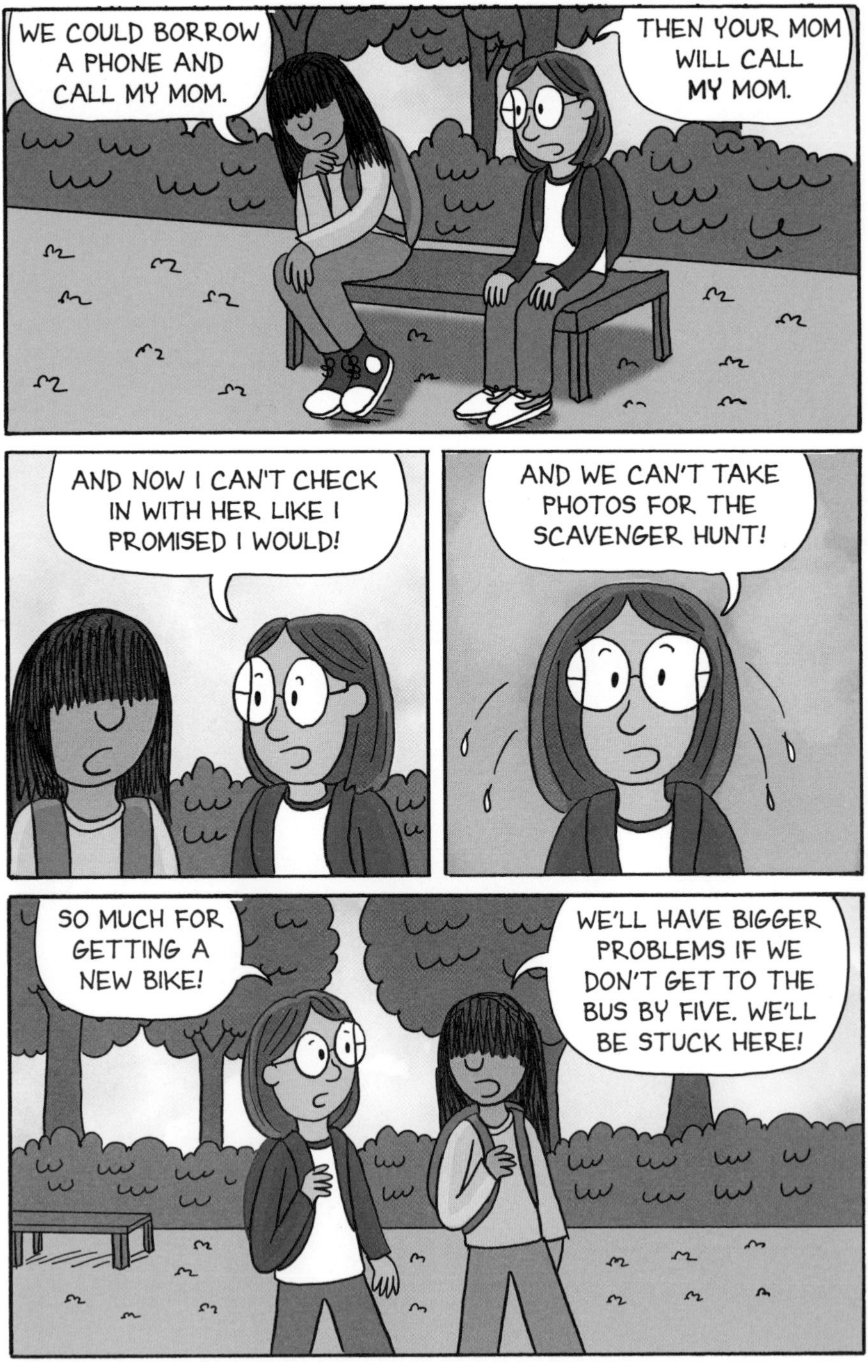
WE COULD BORROW A PHONE AND CALL MY MOM.
THEN YOUR MOM WILL CALL MY MOM.
AND NOW I CAN'T CHECK IN WITH HER LIKE I PROMISED I WOULD!
AND WE CAN'T TAKE PHOTOS FOR THE SCAVENGER HUNT!
SO MUCH FOR GETTING A NEW BIKE!
WE'LL HAVE BIGGER PROBLEMS IF WE DON'T GET TO THE BUS BY FIVE. WE'LL BE STUCK HERE!

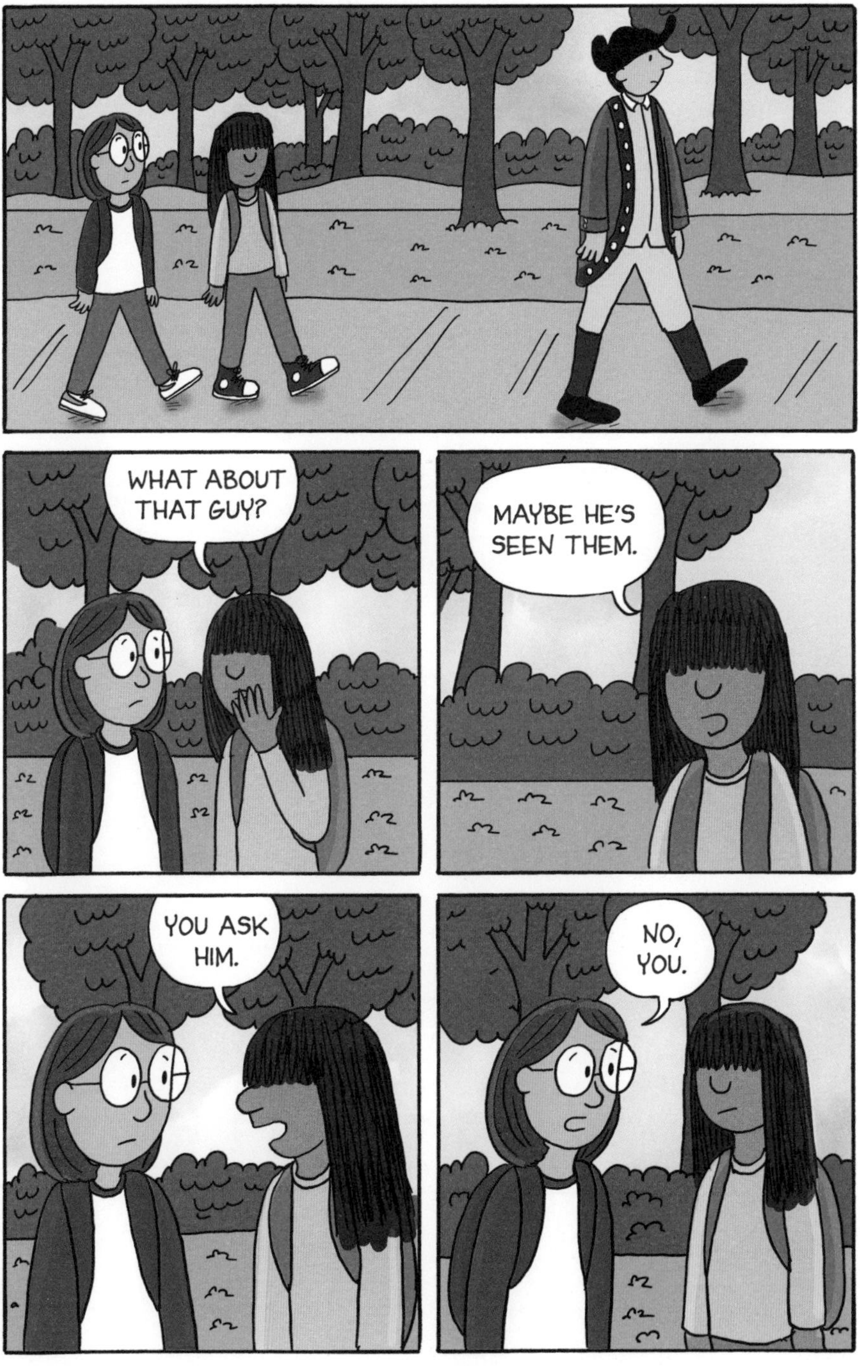
WHAT ABOUT THAT GUY?
MAYBE HE'S SEEN THEM.
YOU ASK HIM.
NO, YOU.

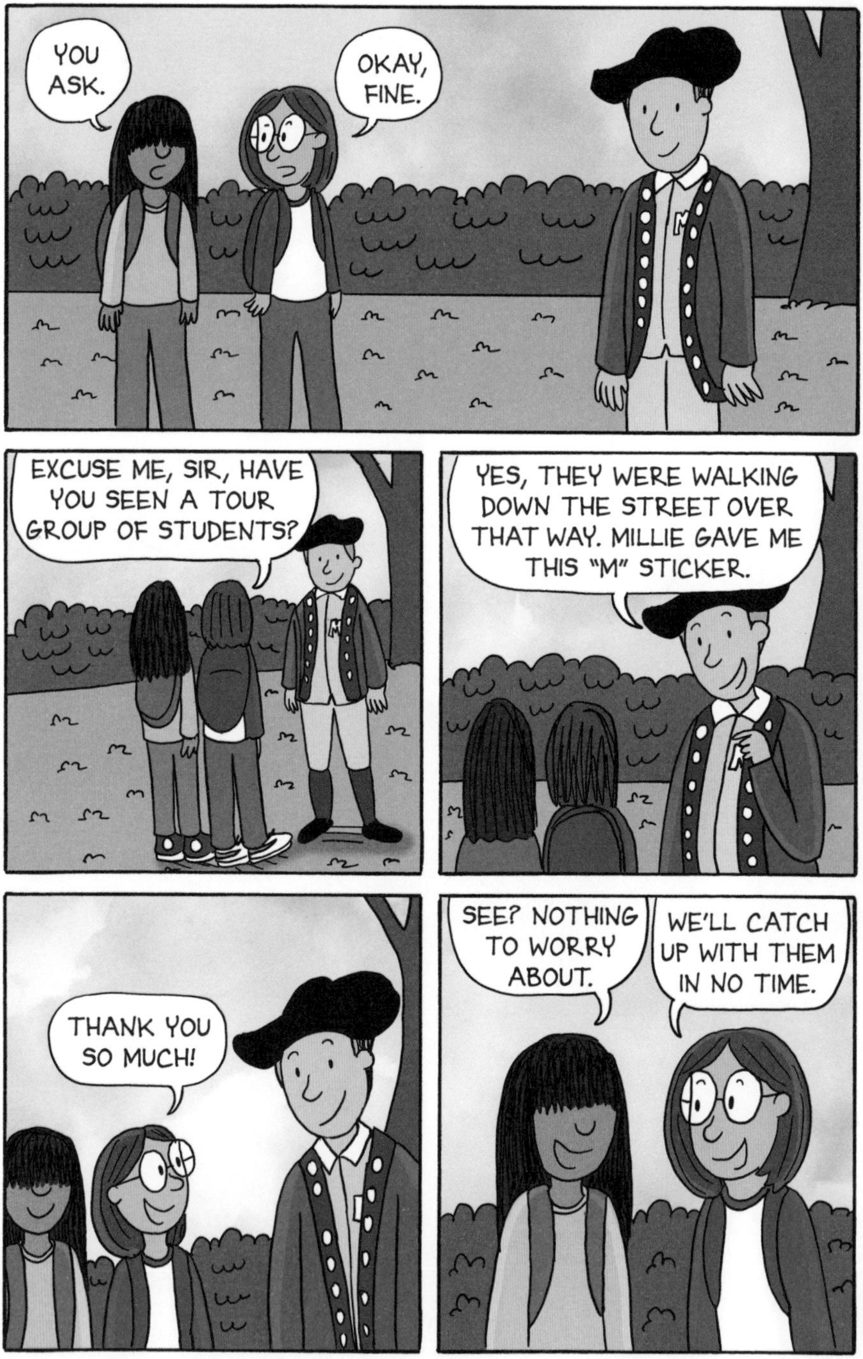
YOU ASK.
OKAY, FINE.
EXCUSE ME, SIR, HAVE YOU SEEN A TOUR GROUP OF STUDENTS?
YES, THEY WERE WALKING DOWN THE STREET OVER THAT WAY. MILLIE GAVE ME THIS "M" STICKER.
THANK YOU SO MUCH!
SEE? NOTHING TO WORRY ABOUT.
WE'LL CATCH UP WITH THEM IN NO TIME.

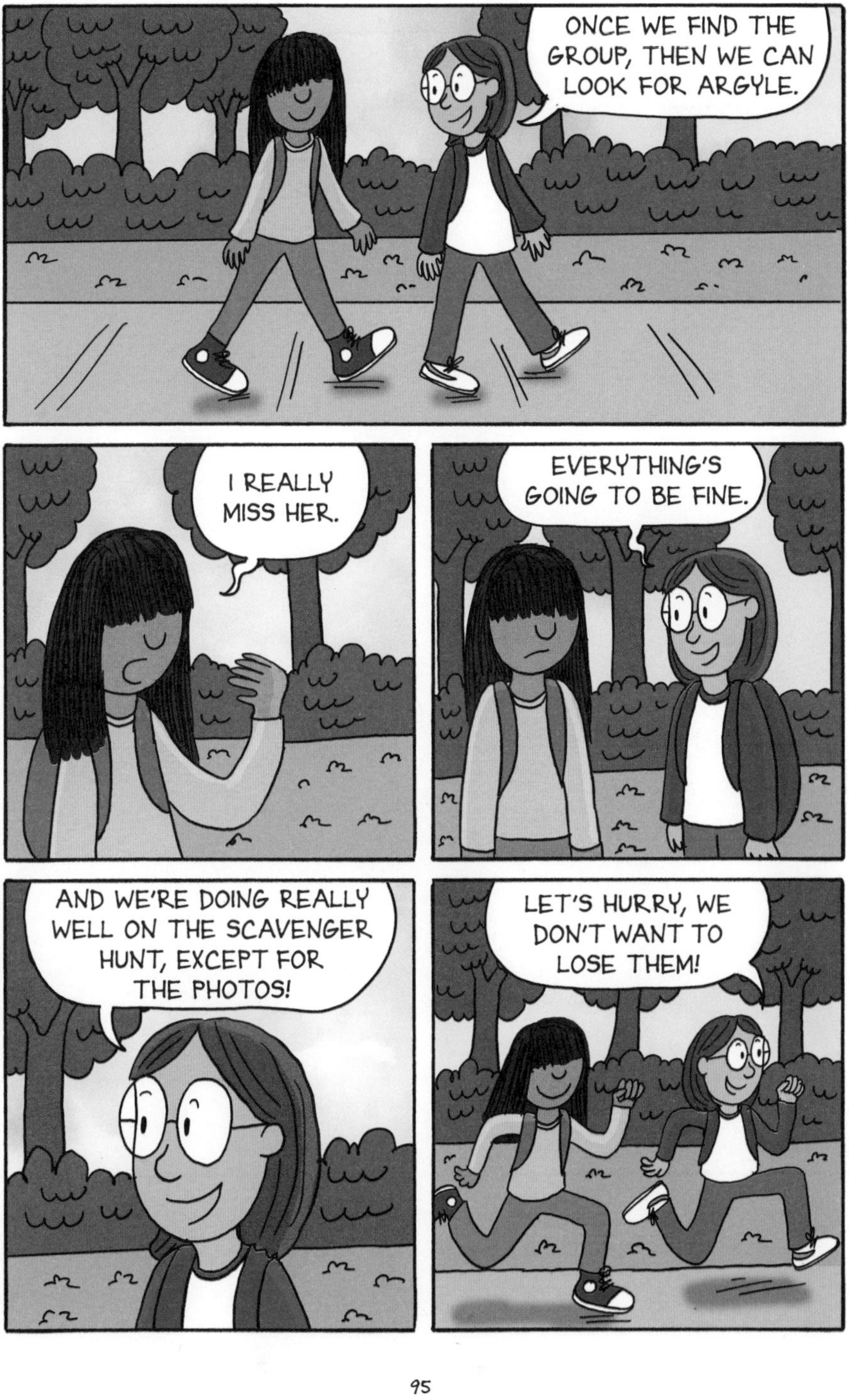
ONCE WE FIND THE GROUP, THEN WE CAN LOOK FOR ARGYLE.
I REALLY MISS HER.
EVERYTHING'S GOING TO BE FINE.
AND WE'RE DOING REALLY WELL ON THE SCAVENGER HUNT, EXCEPT FOR THE PHOTOS!
LET'S HURRY, WE DON'T WANT TO LOSE THEM!

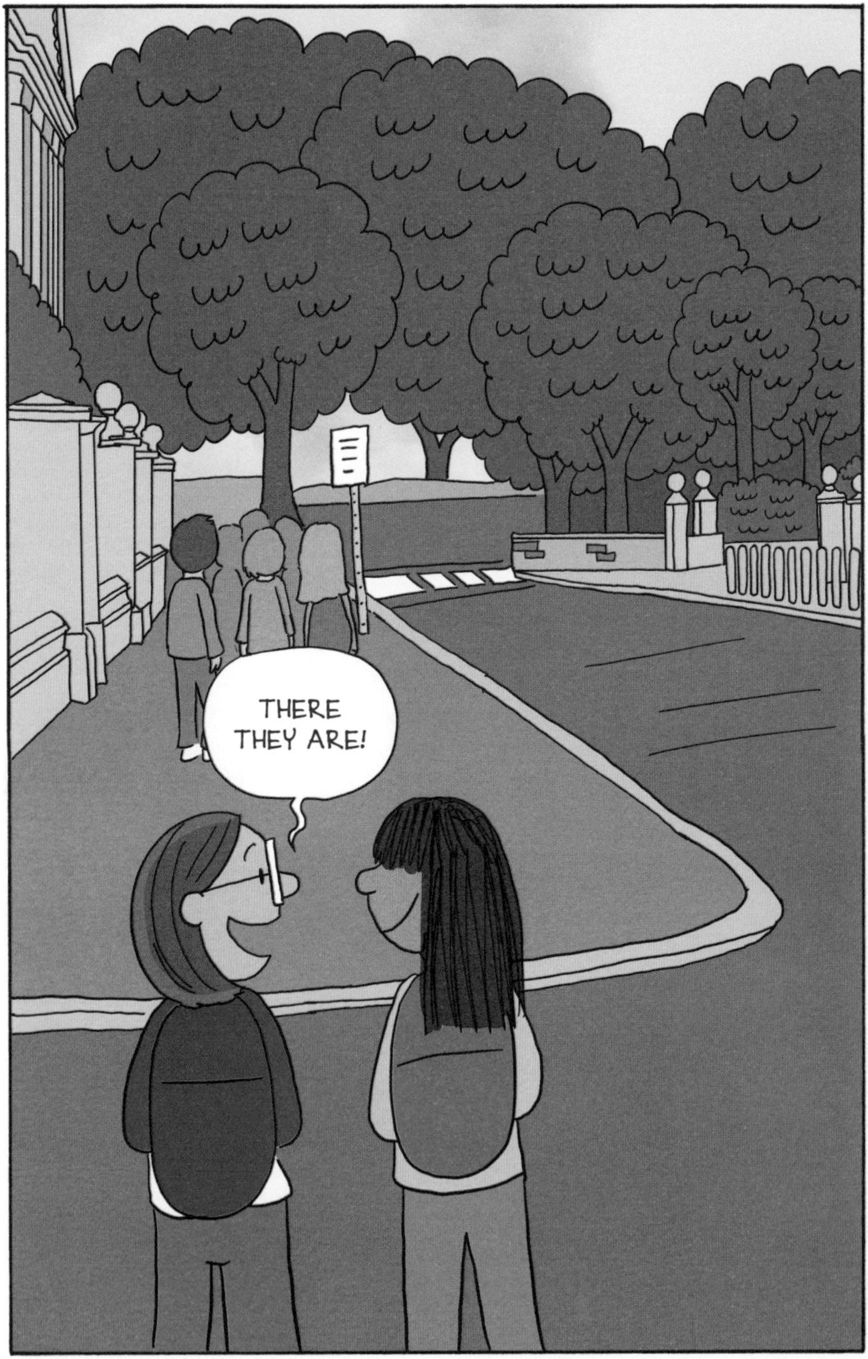
THERE THEY ARE!

CHAPTER 8
QUESTION AND ANSWER

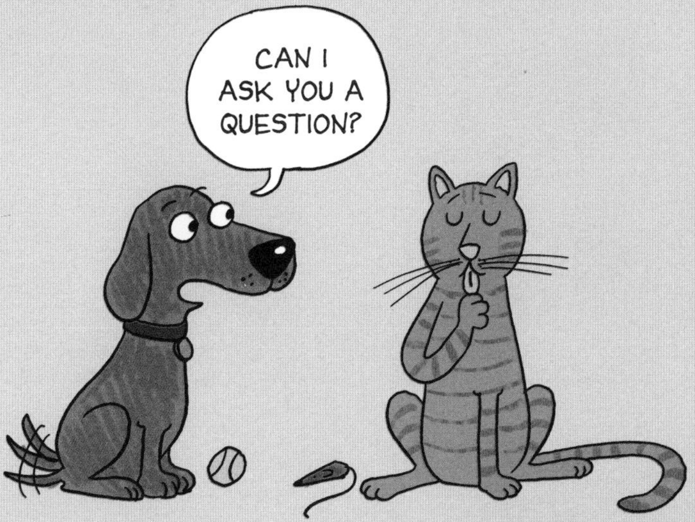
CAN I ASK YOU A QUESTION?

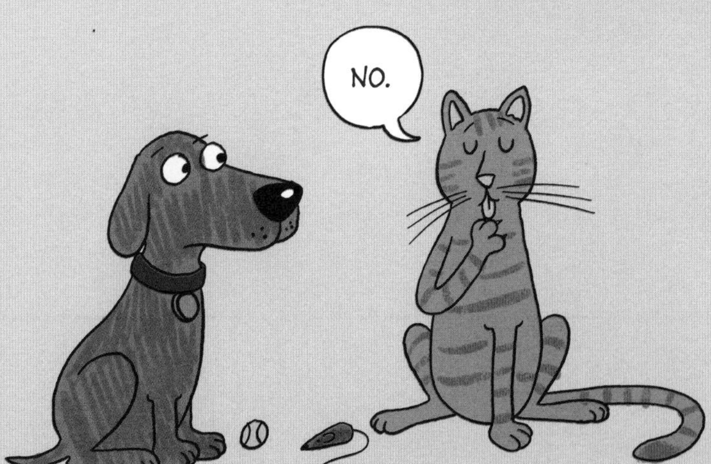
NO.

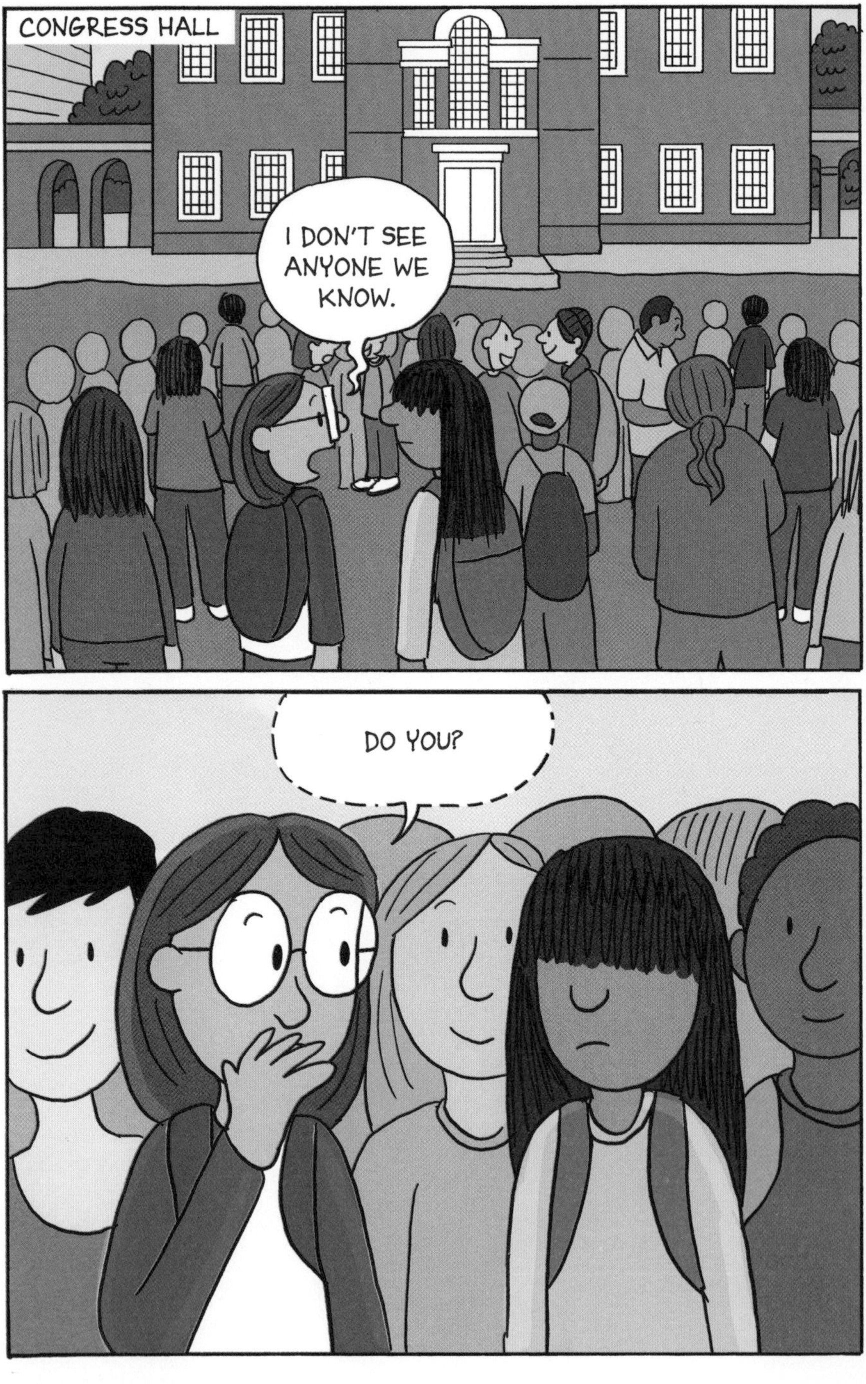
CONGRESS HALL
I DON'T SEE ANYONE WE KNOW.
DO YOU?

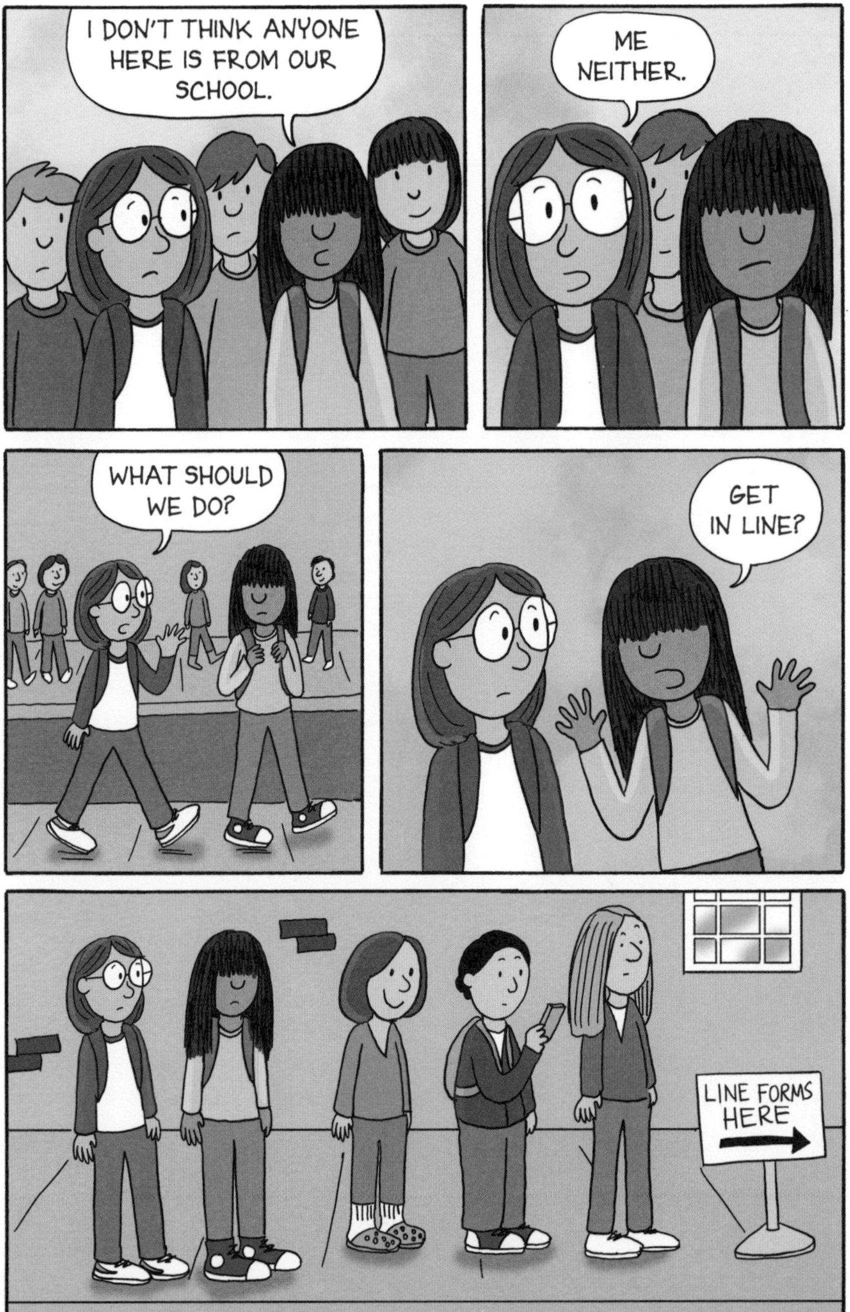
I DON'T THINK ANYONE HERE IS FROM OUR SCHOOL.
ME NEITHER.
WHAT SHOULD WE DO?
GET IN LINE?
LINE FORMS HERE

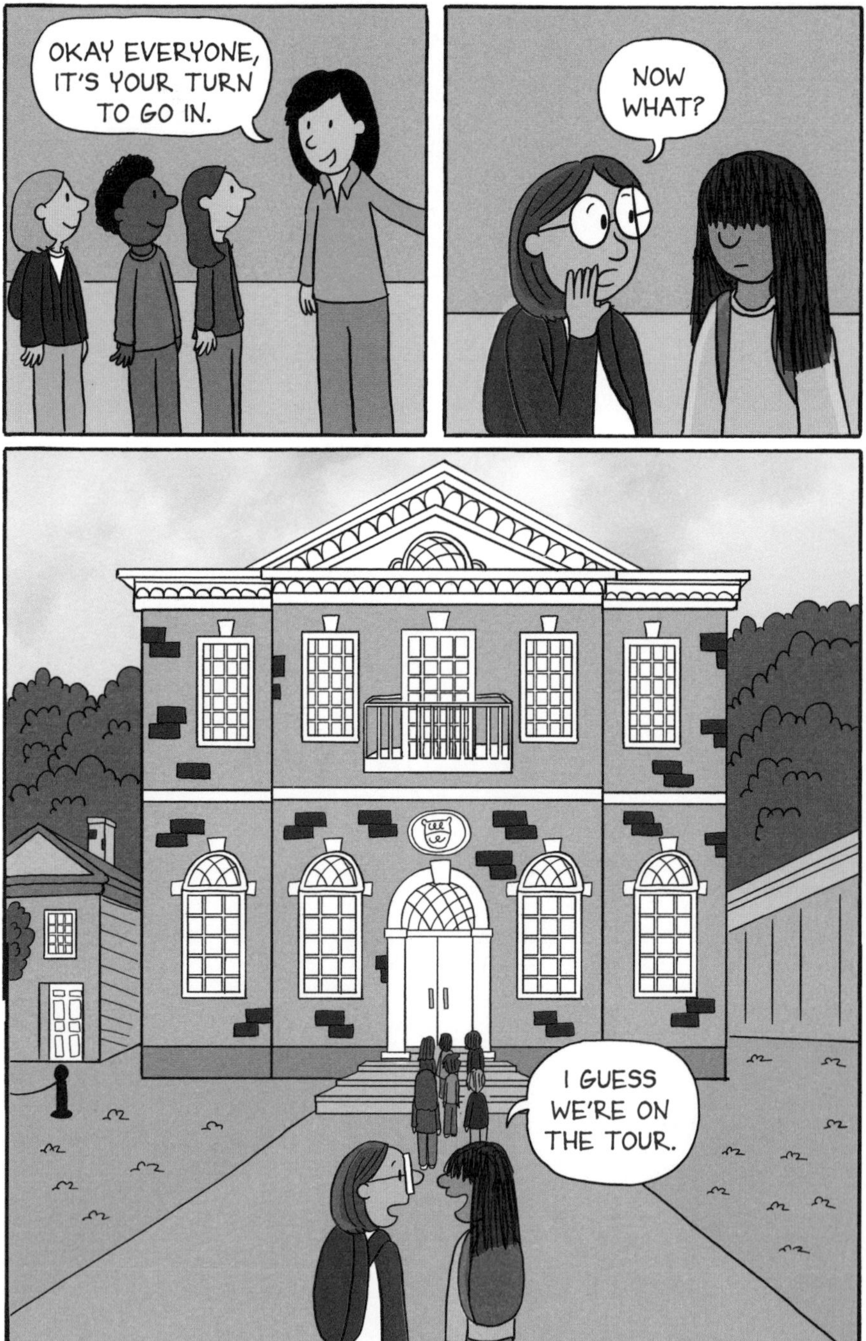
OKAY EVERYONE, IT'S YOUR TURN TO GO IN.
NOW WHAT?
I GUESS WE'RE ON THE TOUR.

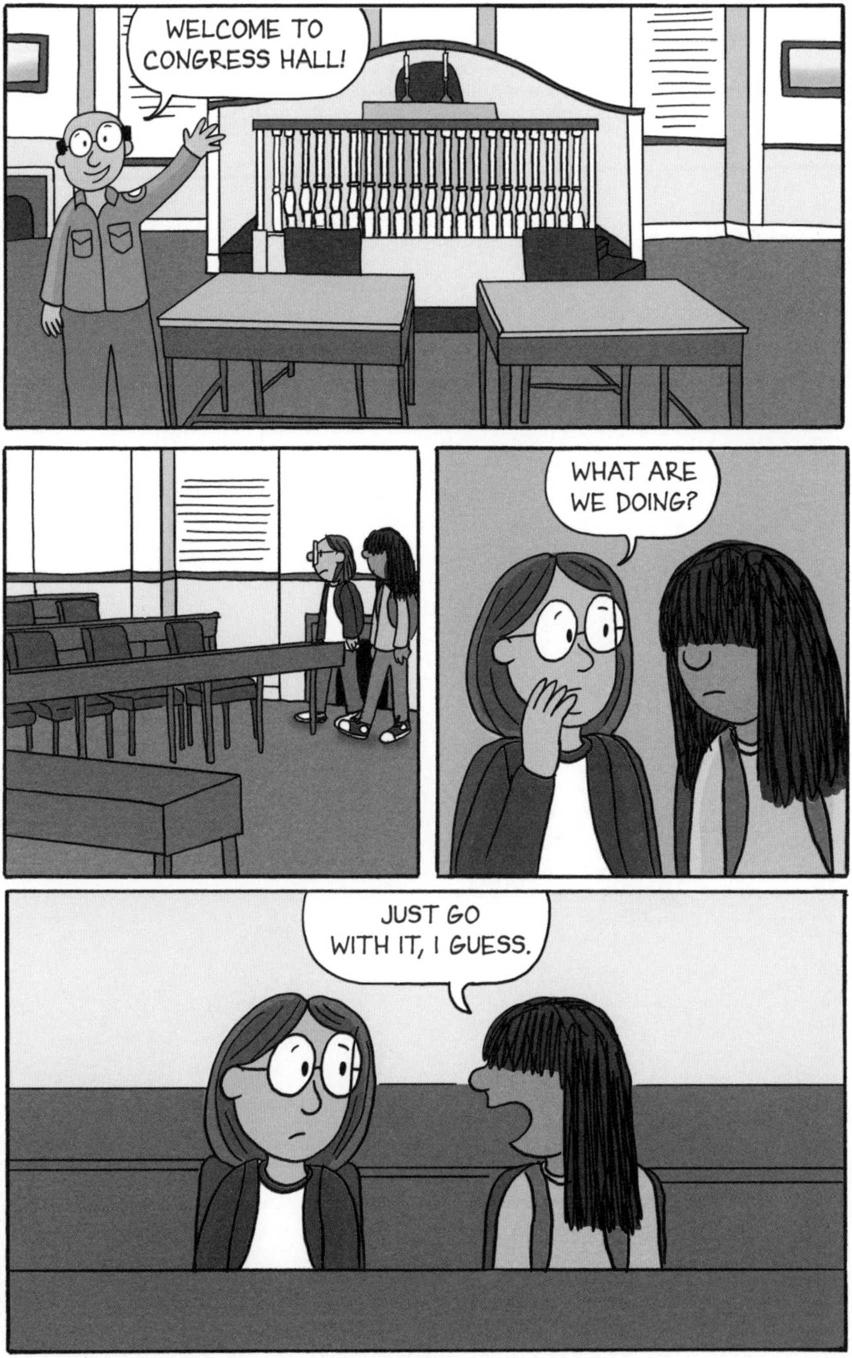
WELCOME TO CONGRESS HALL!
WHAT ARE WE DOING?
JUST GO WITH IT, I GUESS.

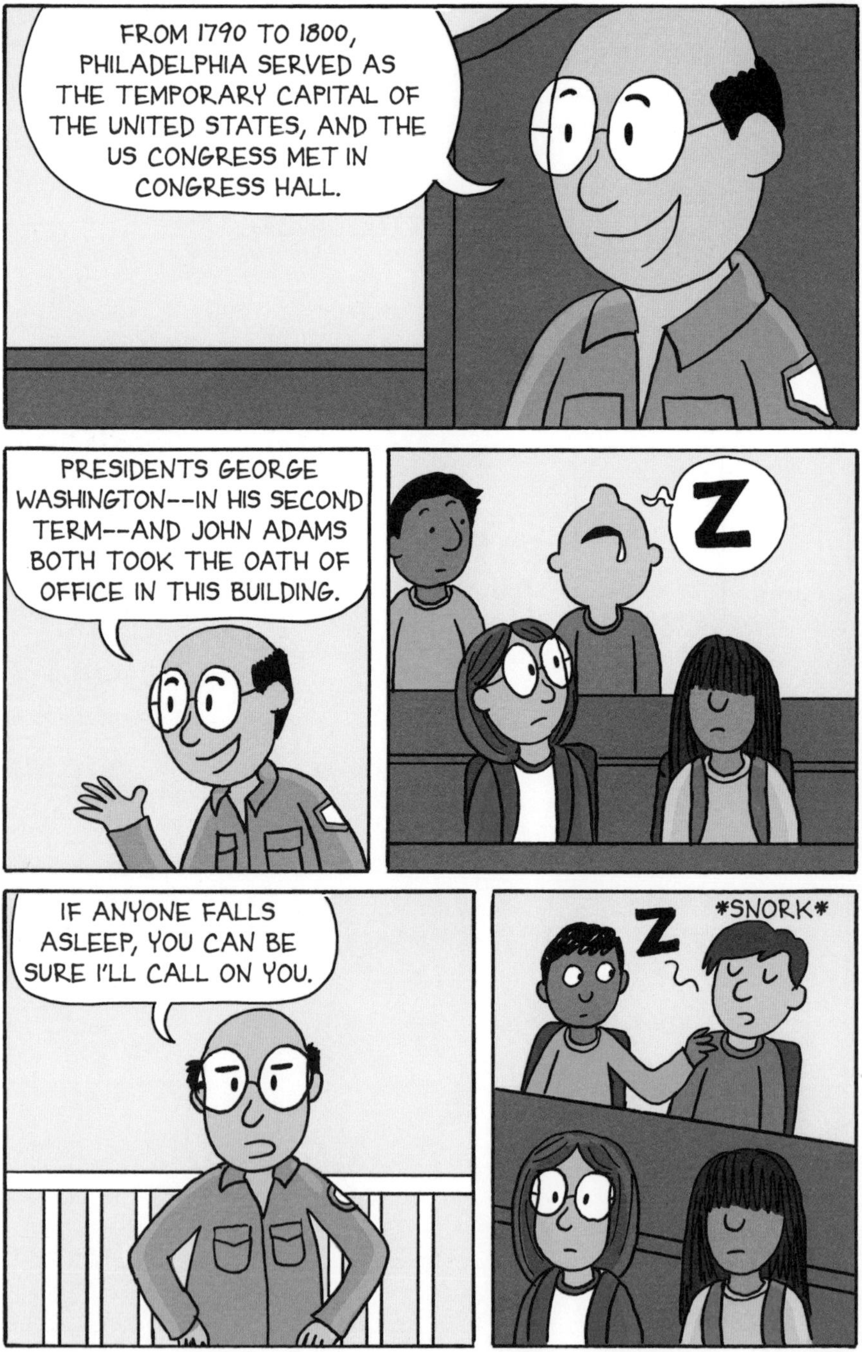
FROM 1790 TO 1800, PHILADELPHIA SERVED AS THE TEMPORARY CAPITAL OF THE UNITED STATES, AND THE US CONGRESS MET IN CONGRESS HALL.
PRESIDENTS GEORGE WASHINGTON--IN HIS SECOND TERM--AND JOHN ADAMS BOTH TOOK THE OATH OF OFFICE IN THIS BUILDING.
Z
IF ANYONE FALLS ASLEEP, YOU CAN BE SURE I'LL CALL ON YOU.
Z
SNORK

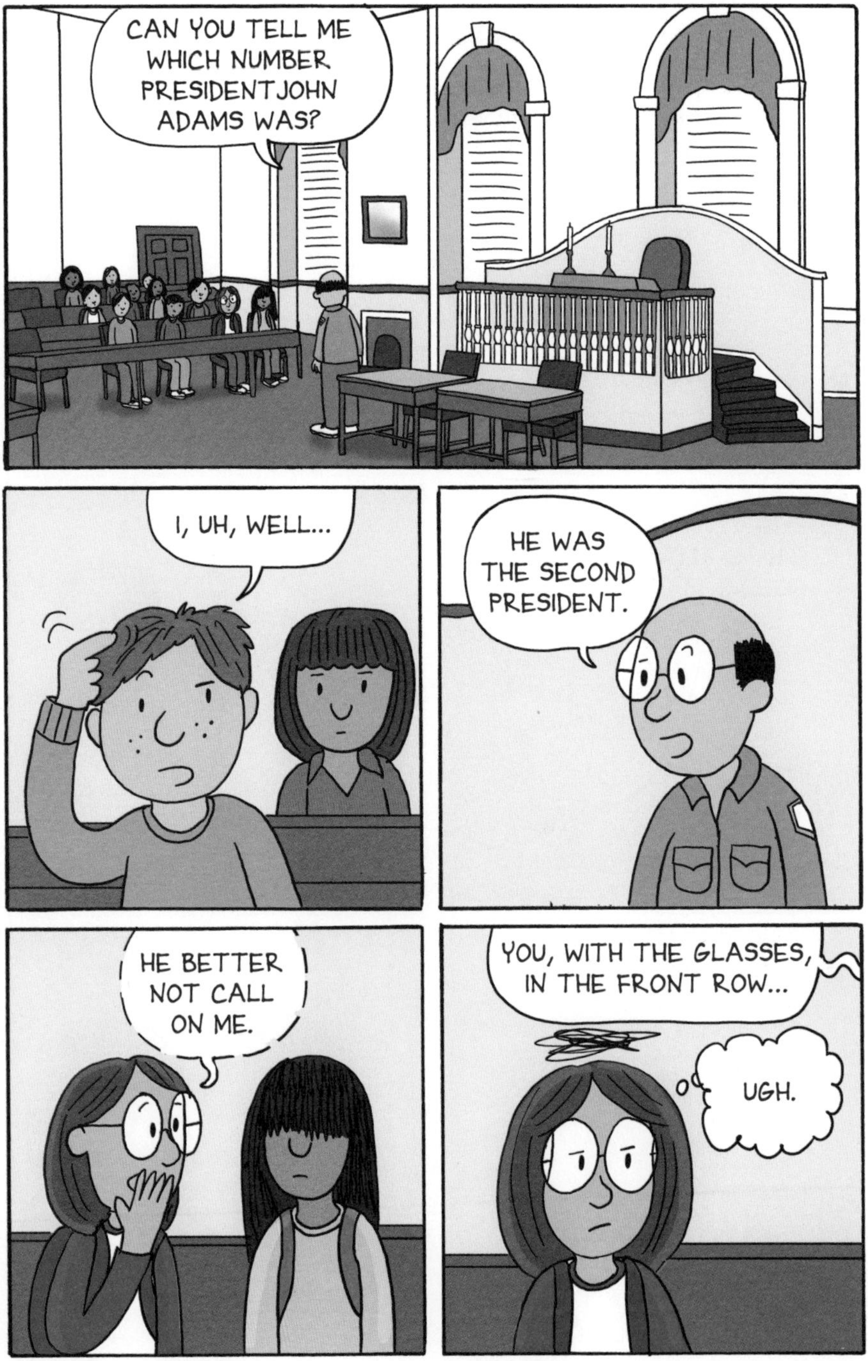
CAN YOU TELL ME WHICH NUMBER PRESIDENTJOHN ADAMS WAS?
I, UH, WELL...
HE WAS THE SECOND PRESIDENT.
HE BETTER NOT CALL ON ME.
YOU, WITH THE GLASSES, IN THE FRONT ROW...
UGH.

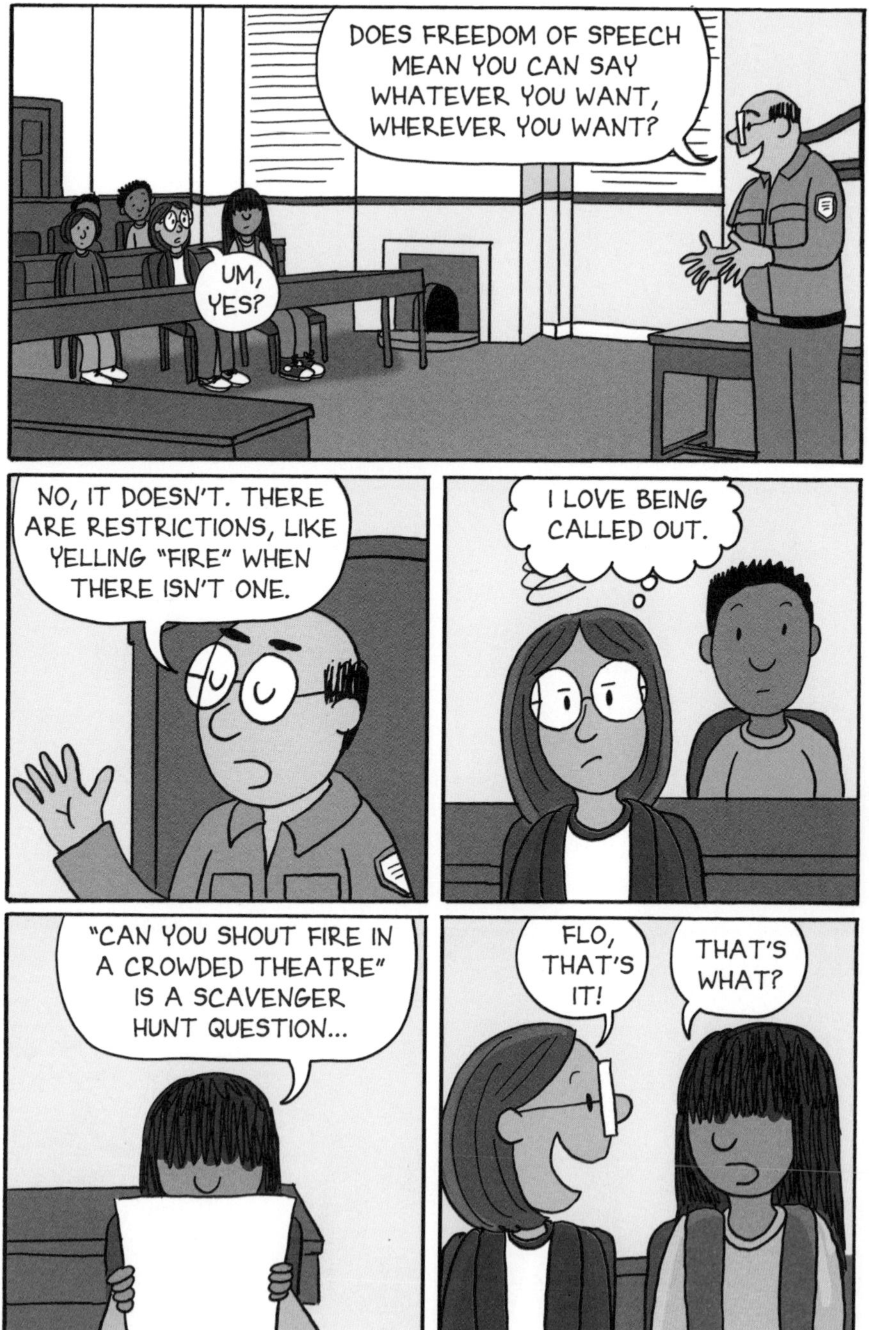
DOES FREEDOM OF SPEECH MEAN YOU CAN SAY WHATEVER YOU WANT, WHEREVER YOU WANT?
UM, YES?
NO, IT DOESN'T. THERE ARE RESTRICTIONS, LIKE YELLING "FIRE" WHEN THERE ISN'T ONE.
I LOVE BEING CALLED OUT.
"CAN YOU SHOUT FIRE IN A CROWDED THEATRE" IS A SCAVENGER HUNT QUESTION...
FLO, THAT'S IT!
THAT'S WHAT?

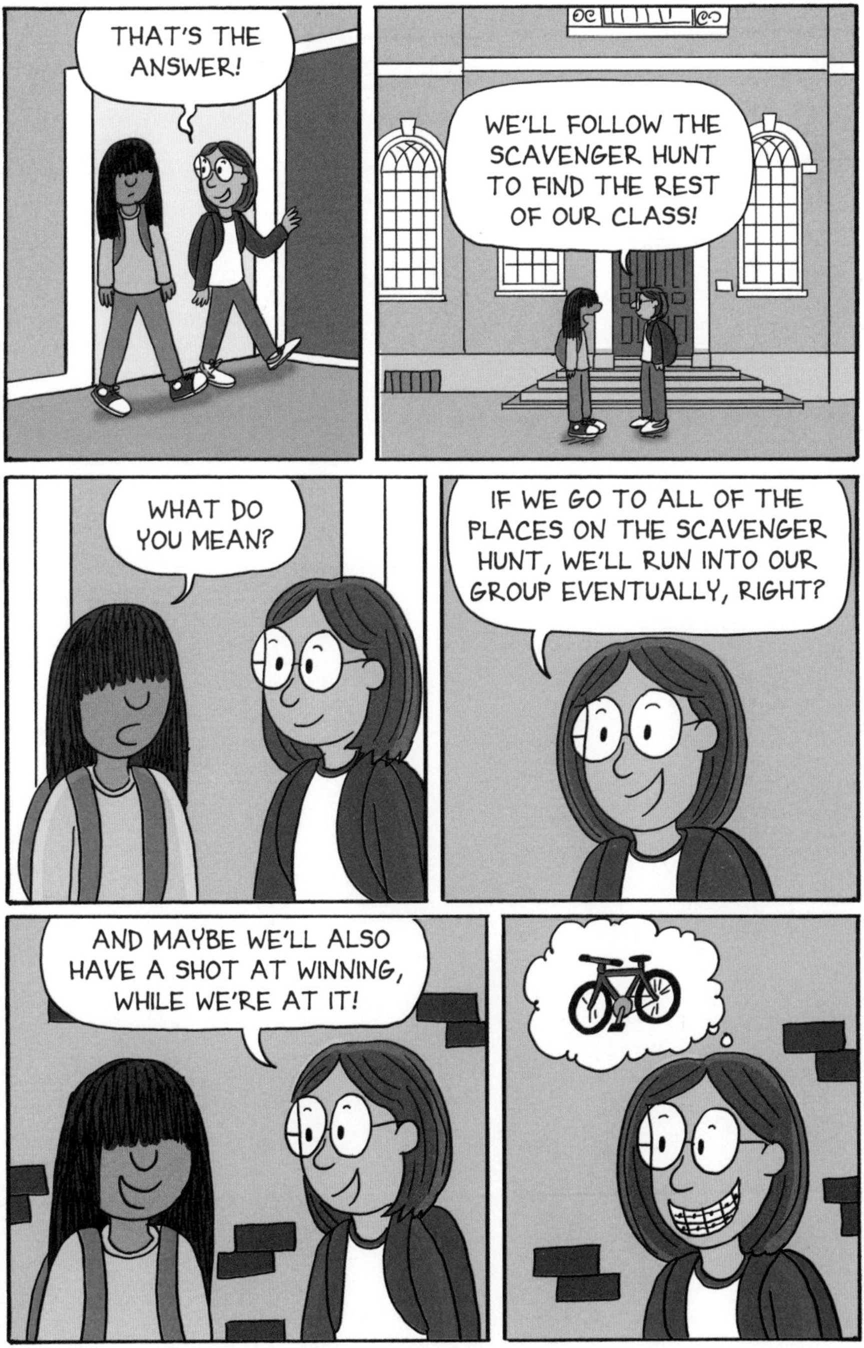
THAT'S THE ANSWER!
WE'LL FOLLOW THE SCAVENGER HUNT TO FIND THE REST OF OUR CLASS!
WHAT DO YOU MEAN?
IF WE GO TO ALL OF THE PLACES ON THE SCAVENGER HUNT, WE'LL RUN INTO OUR GROUP EVENTUALLY, RIGHT?
AND MAYBE WE'LL ALSO HAVE A SHOT AT WINNING, WHILE WE'RE AT IT!

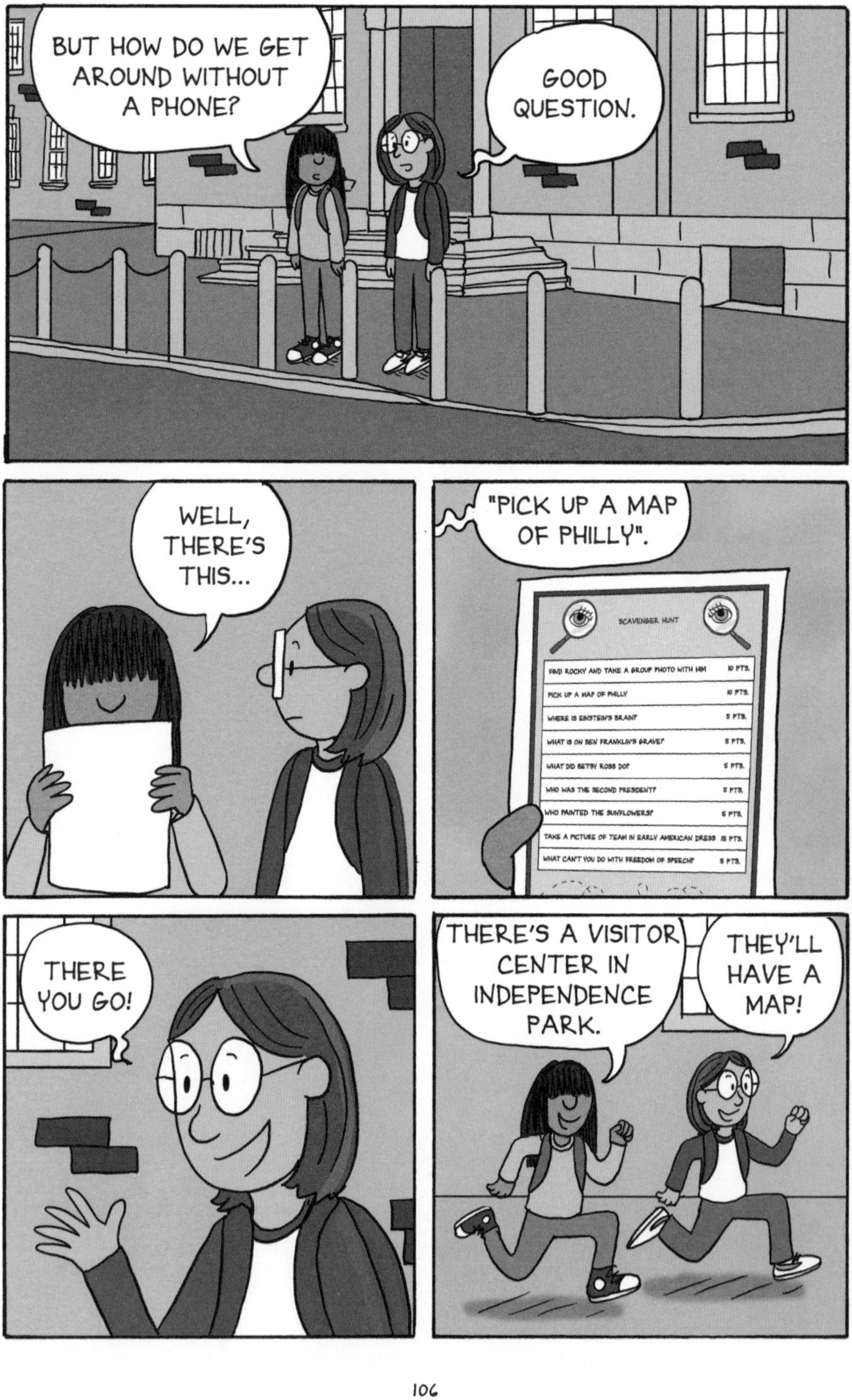
BUT HOW DO WE GET AROUND WITHOUT A PHONE?
GOOD QUESTION.
WELL, THERE'S THIS...
"PICK UP A MAP OF PHILLY".
SCAVENGER HUNT
FIND ROCKY AND TAKE A GROUP PHOTO WITH HIM 10 PTS.
PICK UP A MAP OF PHILLY 10 PTS.
WHERE IS EINSTEIN'S BRAIN? 5 PTS.
WHAT IS ON BEN FRANKLIN'S GRAVE? 5 PTS.
WHAT DID BETSY ROSS DO? 5 PTS.
WHO WAS THE SECOND PRESIDENT? 5 PTS.
WHO PAINTED THE SUNFLOWERS? 5 PTS.
TAKE A PICTURE OF TEAM IN EARLY AMERICAN DRESS 15 PTS.
WHAT CAN'T YOU DO WITH FREEDOM OF SPEECH? 5 PTS.
THERE YOU GO!
THERE'S A VISITOR CENTER IN INDEPENDENCE PARK.
THEY'LL HAVE A MAP!

CHAPTER 9
MAP

MAP OF A DOG'S BRAIN:

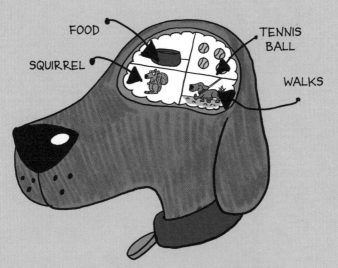

FOOD

SQUIRREL

TENNIS BALL

WALKS

MAP OF A CAT'S BRAIN:

NAPS

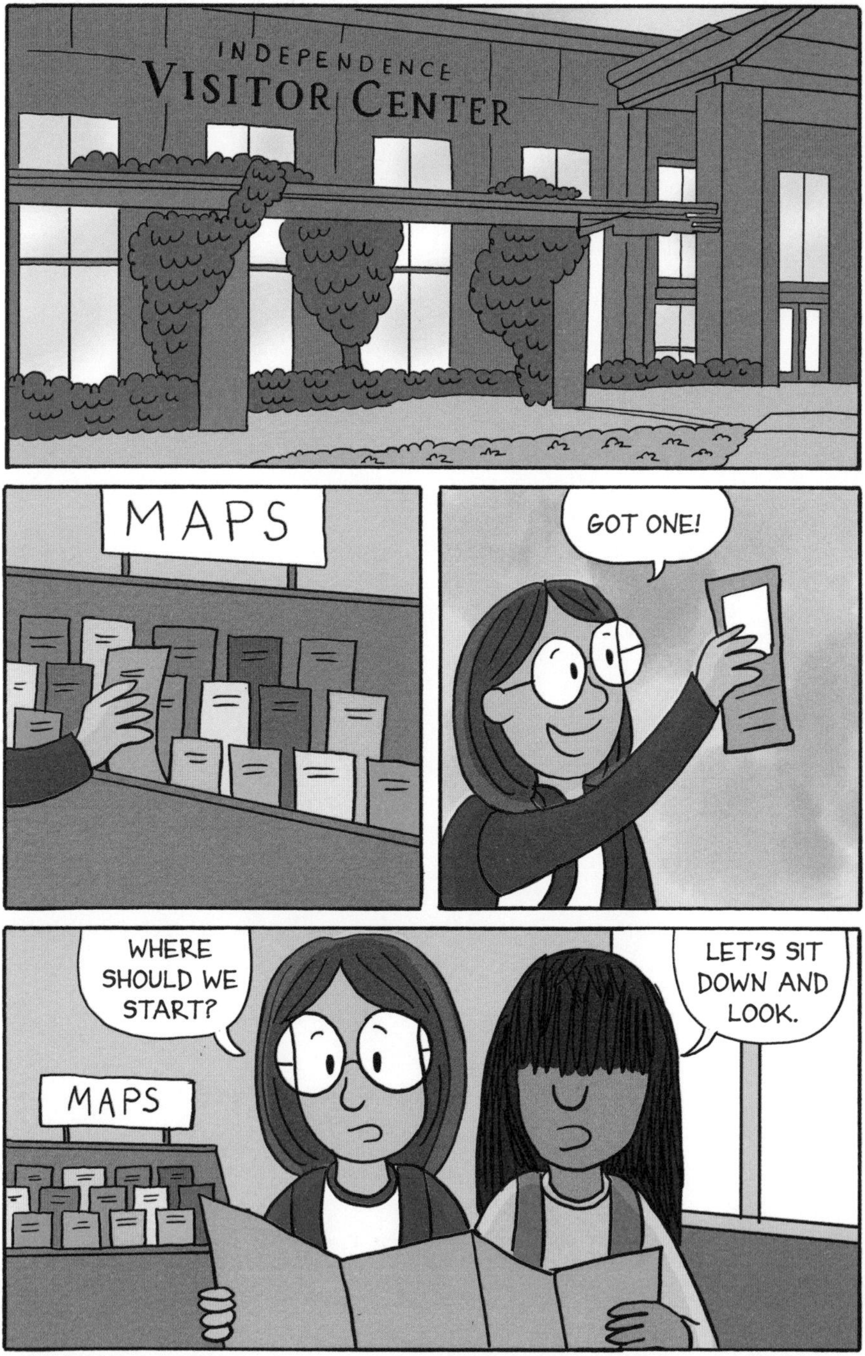
INDEPENDENCE VISITOR CENTER
MAPS
GOT ONE!
WHERE SHOULD WE START?
LET'S SIT DOWN AND LOOK.
MAPS

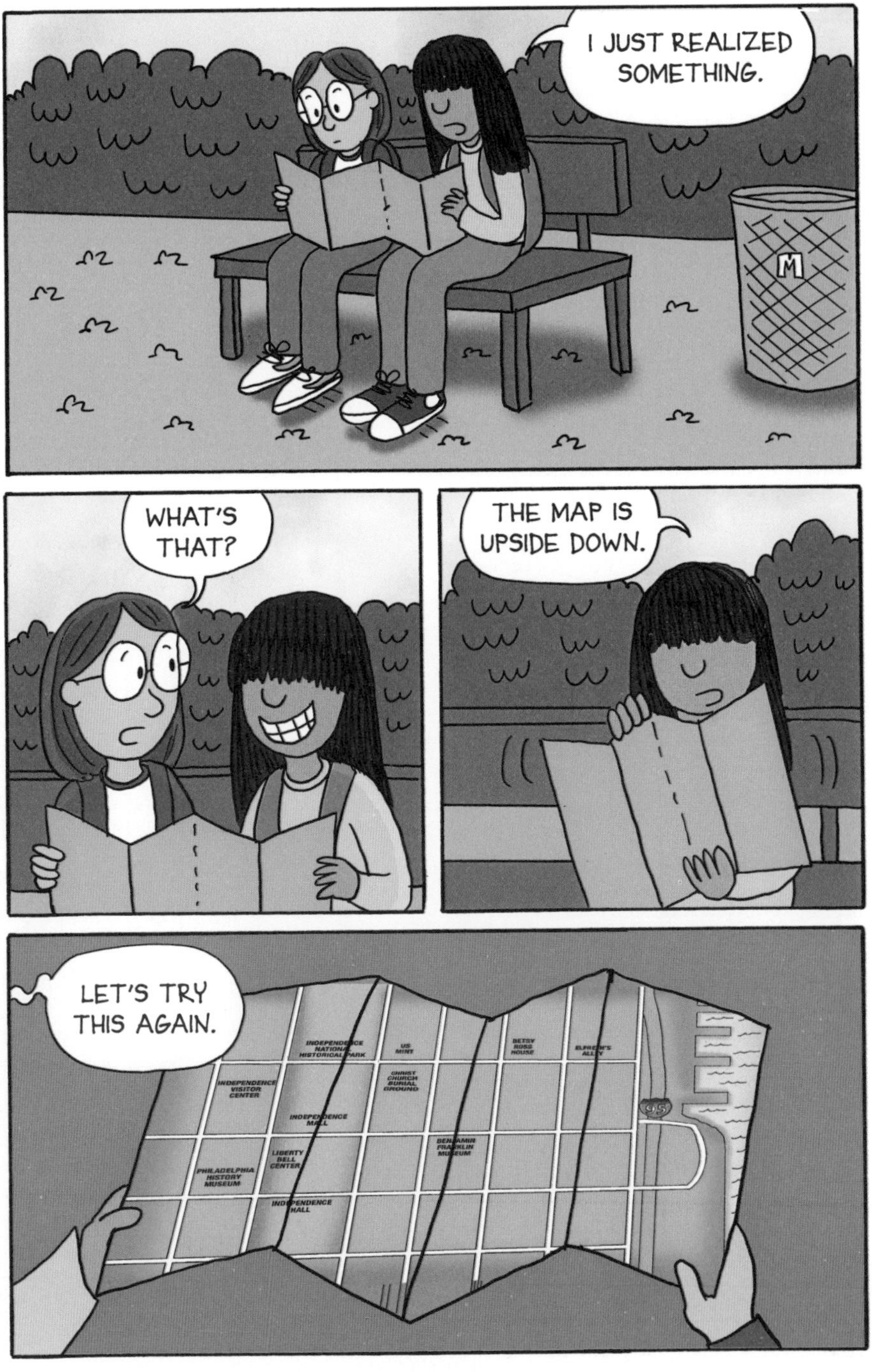
I JUST REALIZED SOMETHING.
WHAT'S THAT?
THE MAP IS UPSIDE DOWN.
LET'S TRY THIS AGAIN.
US MINT
BETSY ROSS HOUSE
INDEPENDENCE VISITOR CENTER
CHRIST CHURCH BURIAL GROUND
95
LIBERTY BELL CENTER
PHILADELPHIA HISTORY MUSEUM

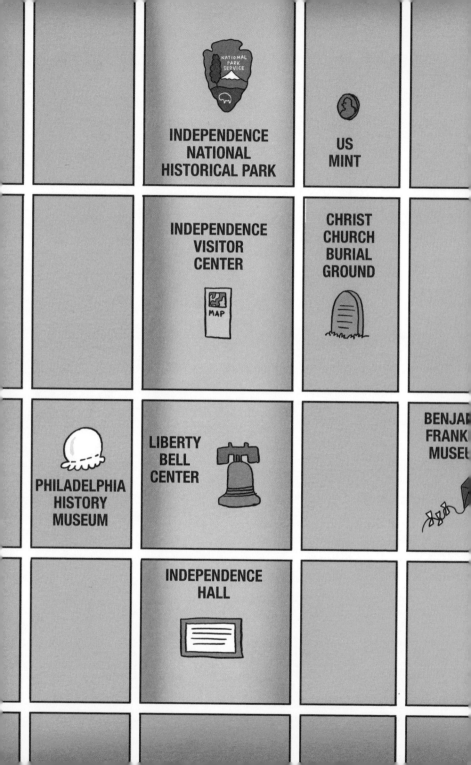

INDEPENDENCE NATIONAL HISTORICAL PARK

US MINT

INDEPENDENCE VISITOR CENTER

MAP

CHRIST CHURCH BURIAL GROUND

PHILADELPHIA HISTORY MUSEUM

LIBERTY BELL CENTER

BENJAMIN FRANKLIN MUSEUM

INDEPENDENCE HALL

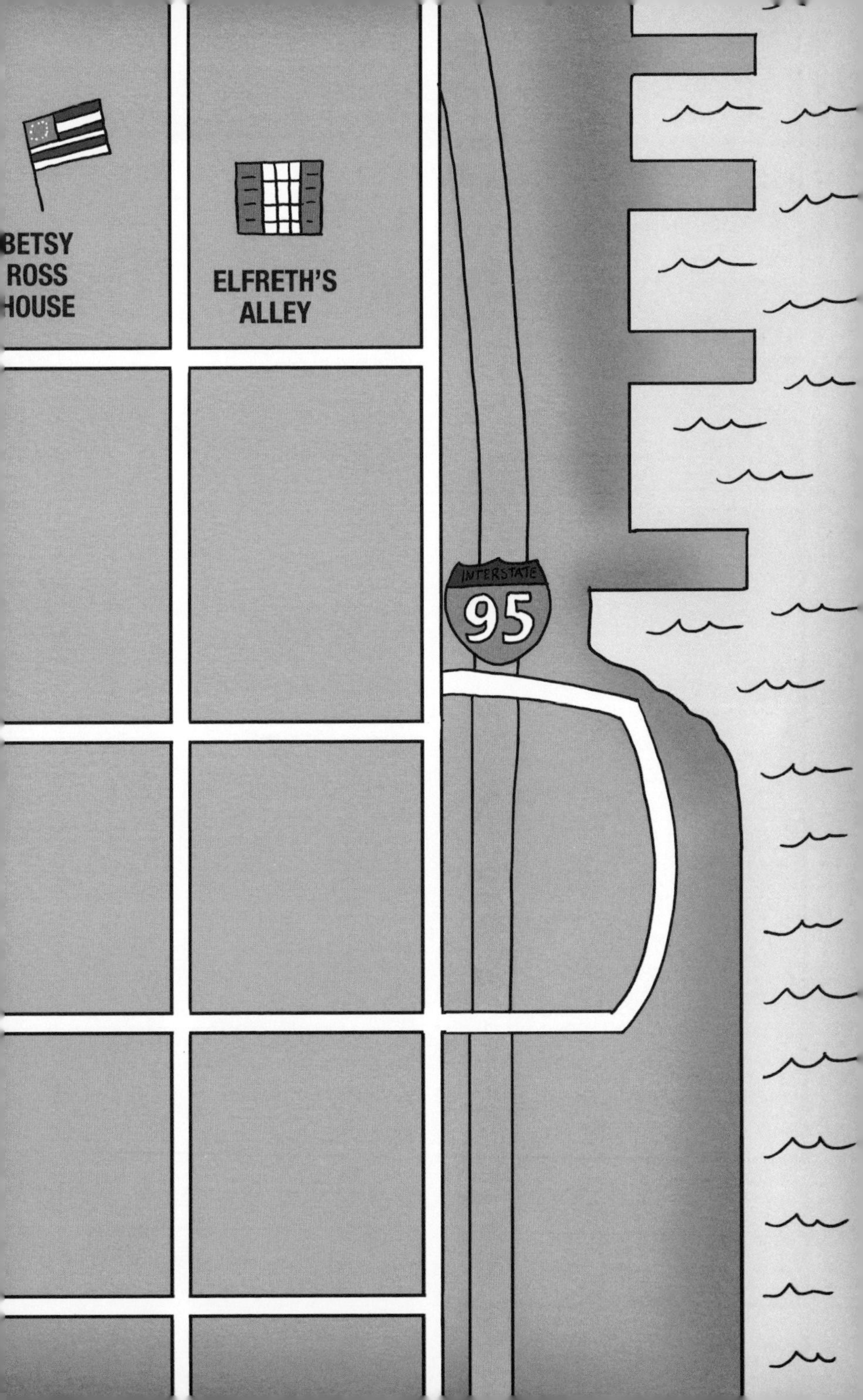
BETSY
ROSS
HOUSE
ELFRETH'S
ALLEY
INTERSTATE
95

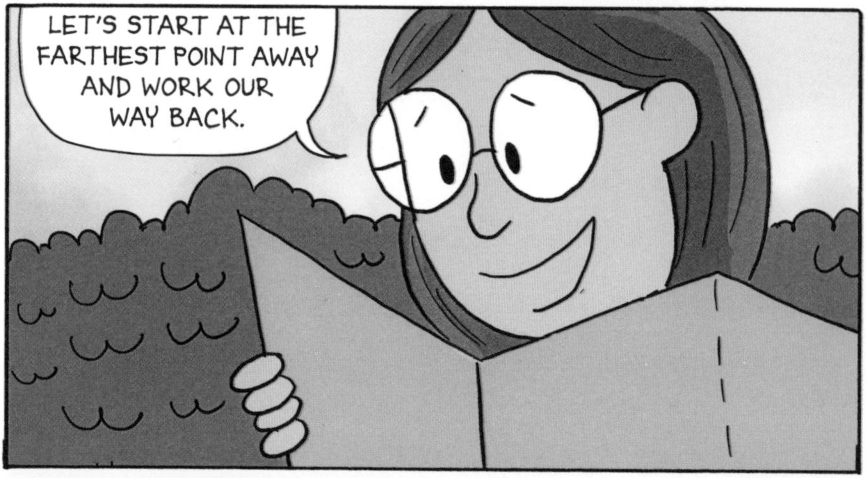
LET'S START AT THE FARTHEST POINT AWAY AND WORK OUR WAY BACK.

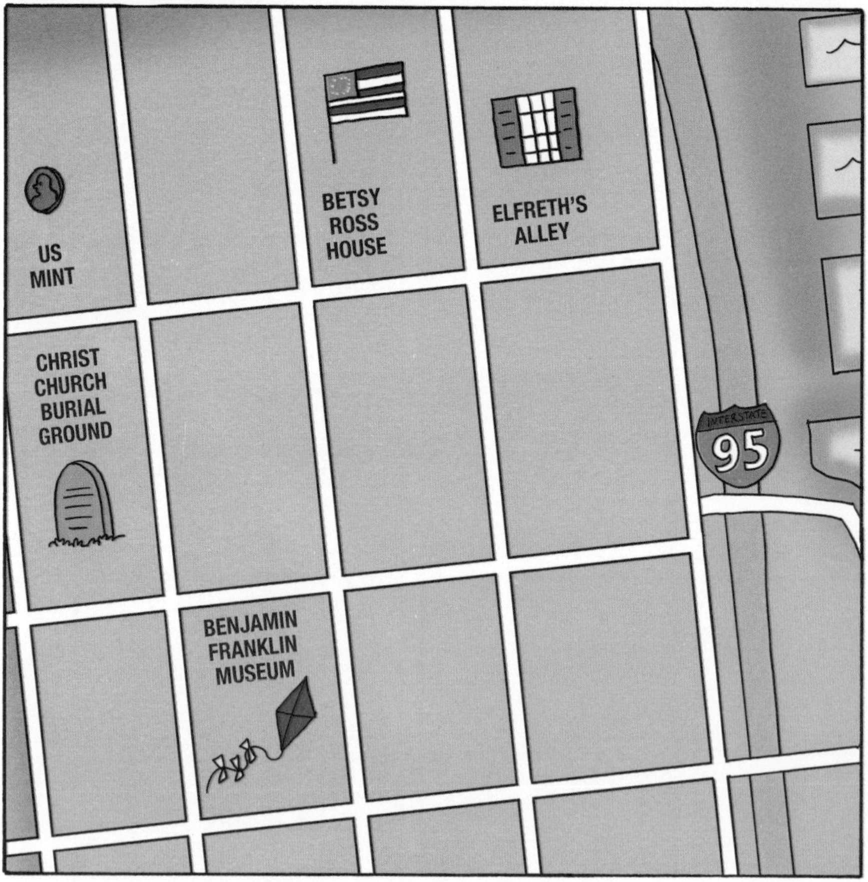
US MINT
BETSY ROSS HOUSE
ELFRETH'S ALLEY
CHRIST CHURCH BURIAL GROUND
INTERSTATE 95
BENJAMIN FRANKLIN MUSEUM

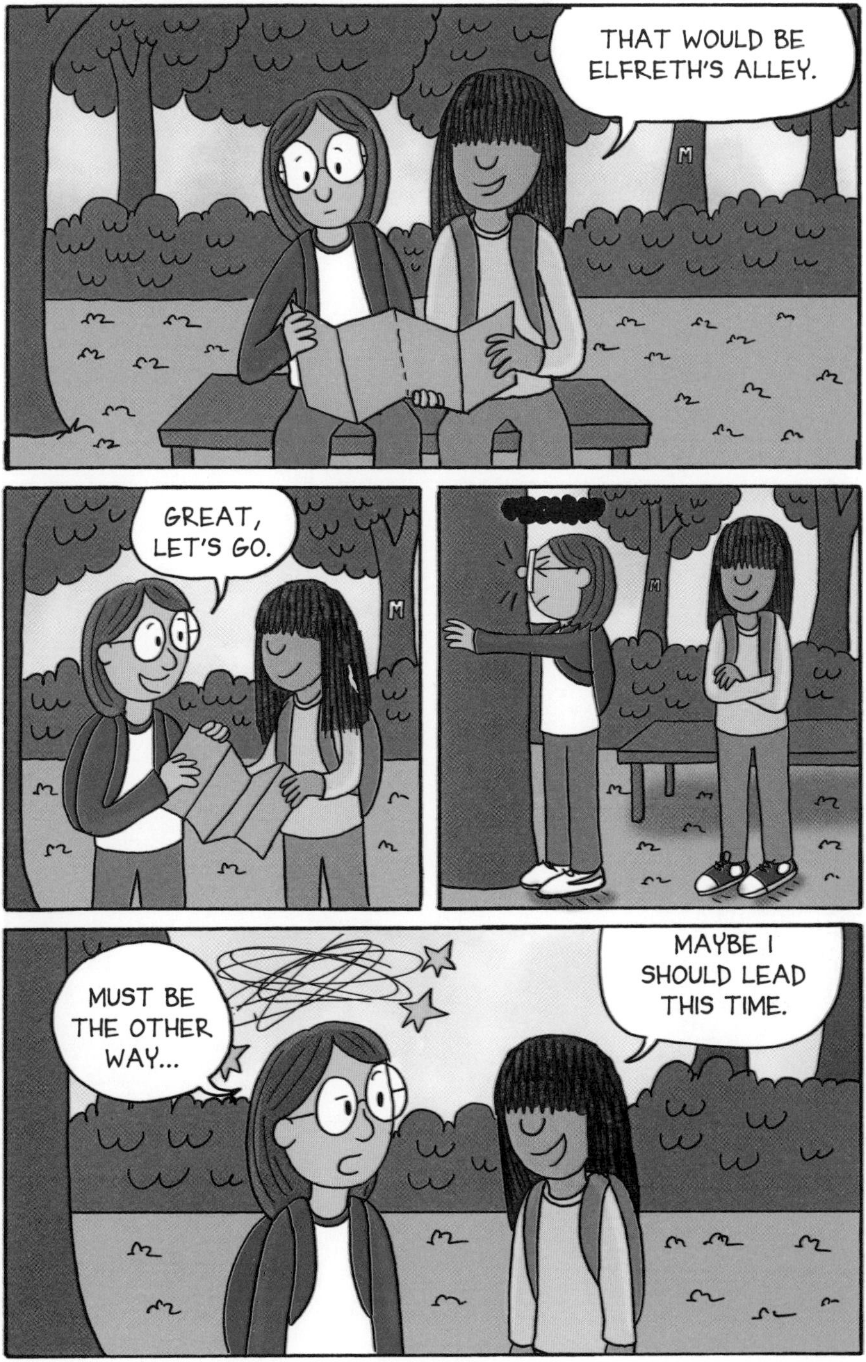
THAT WOULD BE ELFRETH'S ALLEY.
GREAT, LET'S GO.
MUST BE THE OTHER WAY...
MAYBE I SHOULD LEAD THIS TIME.

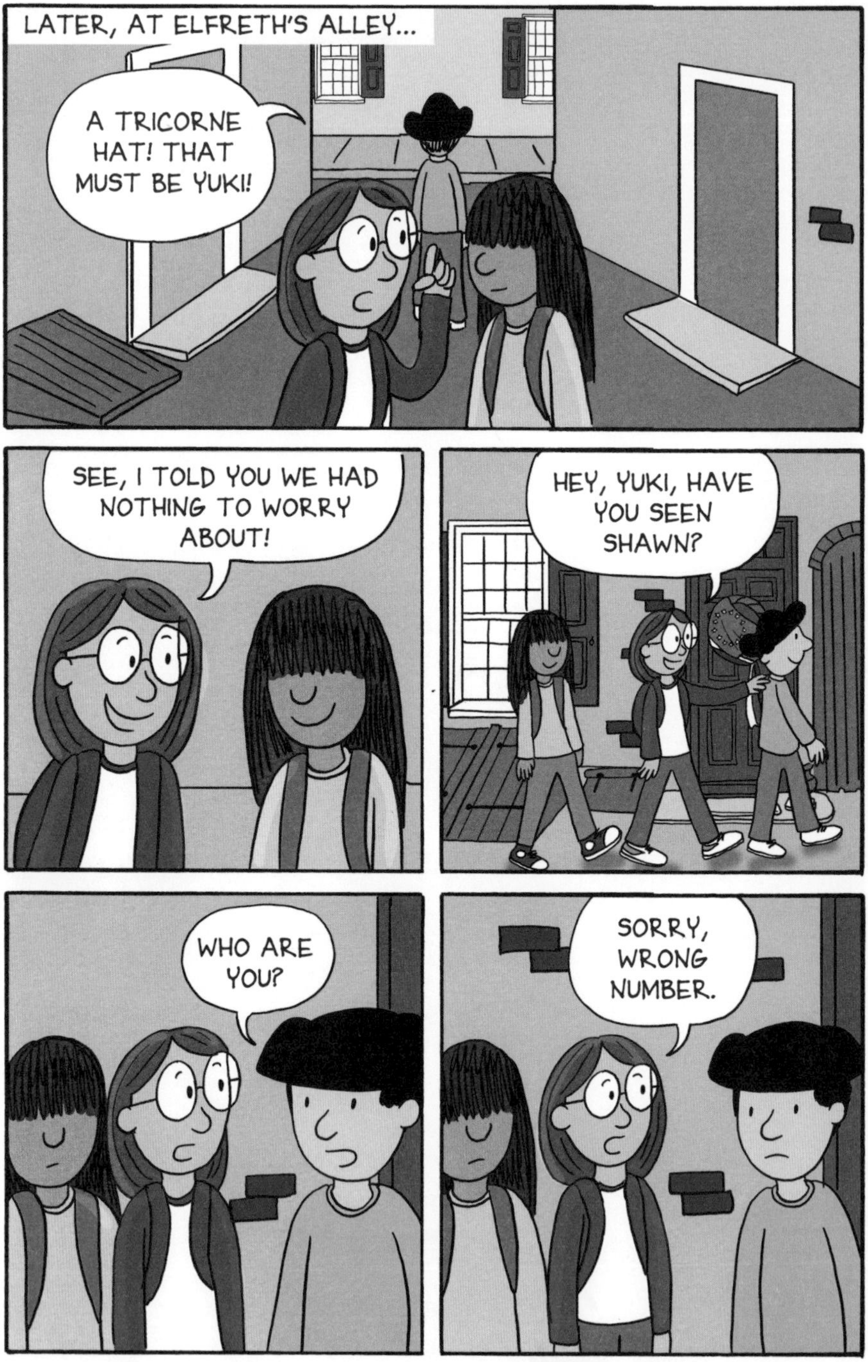
LATER, AT ELFRETH'S ALLEY...
A TRICORNE HAT! THAT MUST BE YUKI!
SEE, I TOLD YOU WE HAD NOTHING TO WORRY ABOUT!
HEY, YUKI, HAVE YOU SEEN SHAWN?
WHO ARE YOU?
SORRY, WRONG NUMBER.

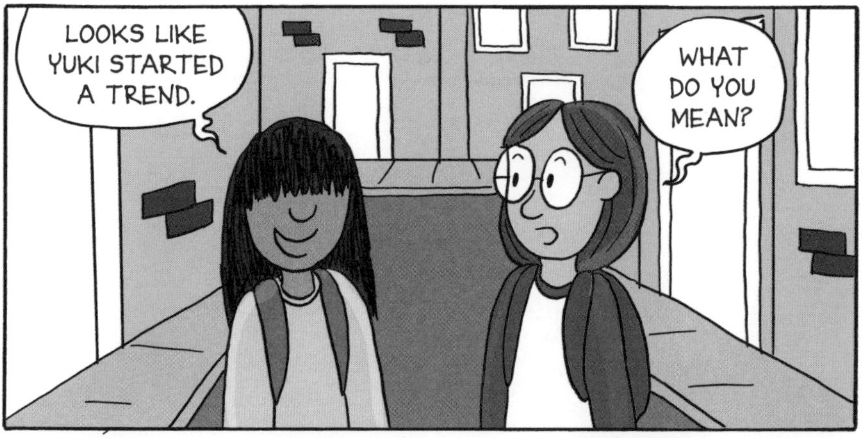
LOOKS LIKE YUKI STARTED A TREND.
WHAT DO YOU MEAN?

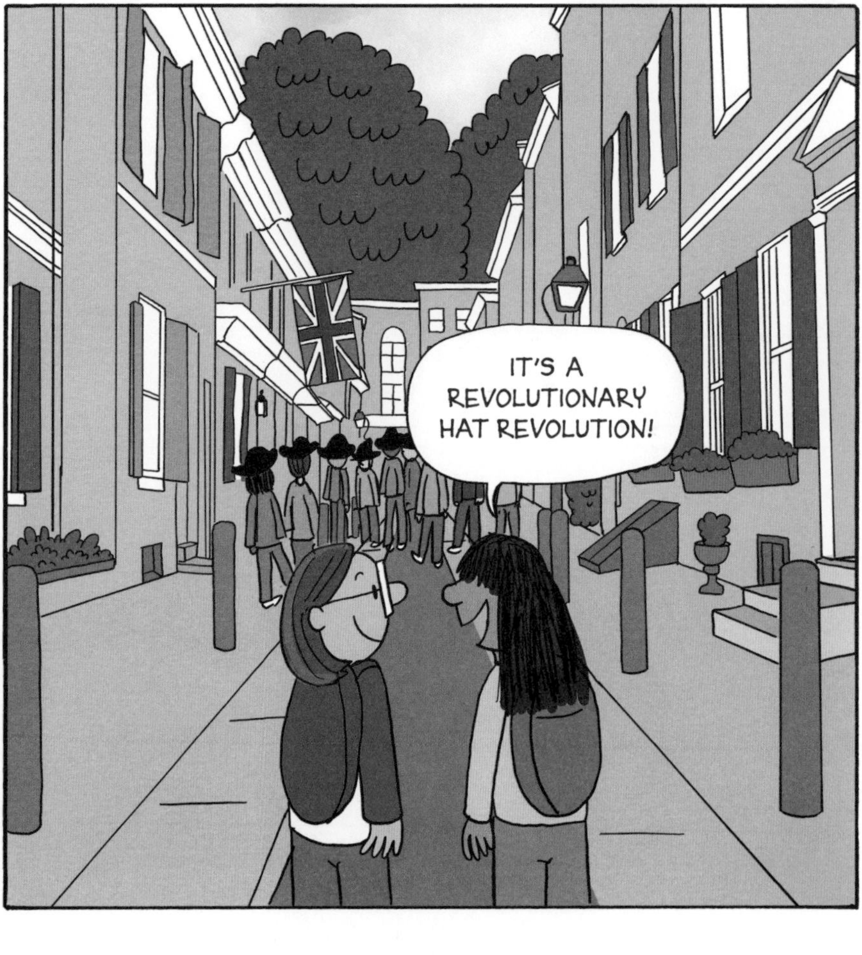
IT'S A REVOLUTIONARY HAT REVOLUTION!

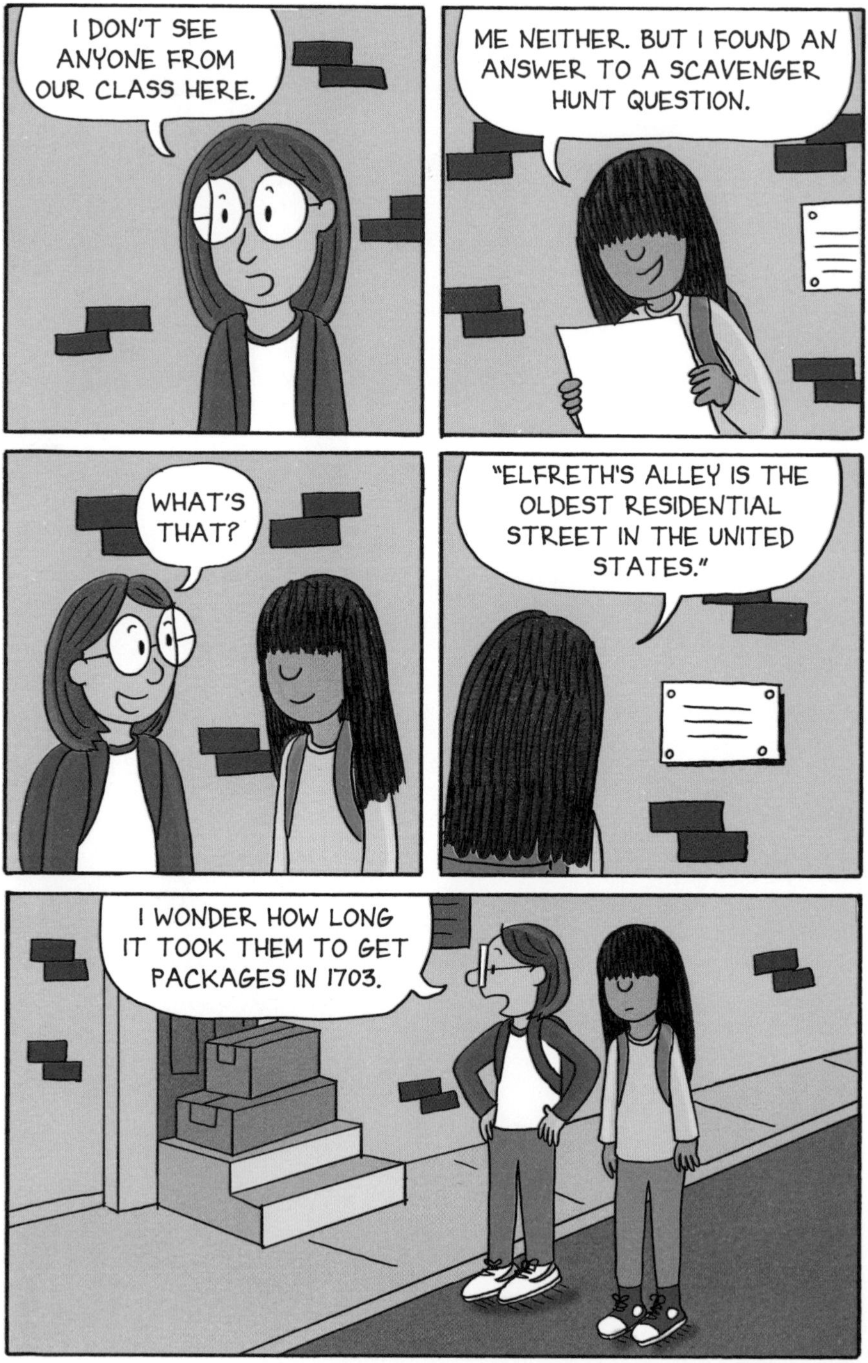
I DON'T SEE ANYONE FROM OUR CLASS HERE.
ME NEITHER. BUT I FOUND AN ANSWER TO A SCAVENGER HUNT QUESTION.
WHAT'S THAT?
"ELFRETH'S ALLEY IS THE OLDEST RESIDENTIAL STREET IN THE UNITED STATES."
I WONDER HOW LONG IT TOOK THEM TO GET PACKAGES IN 1703.

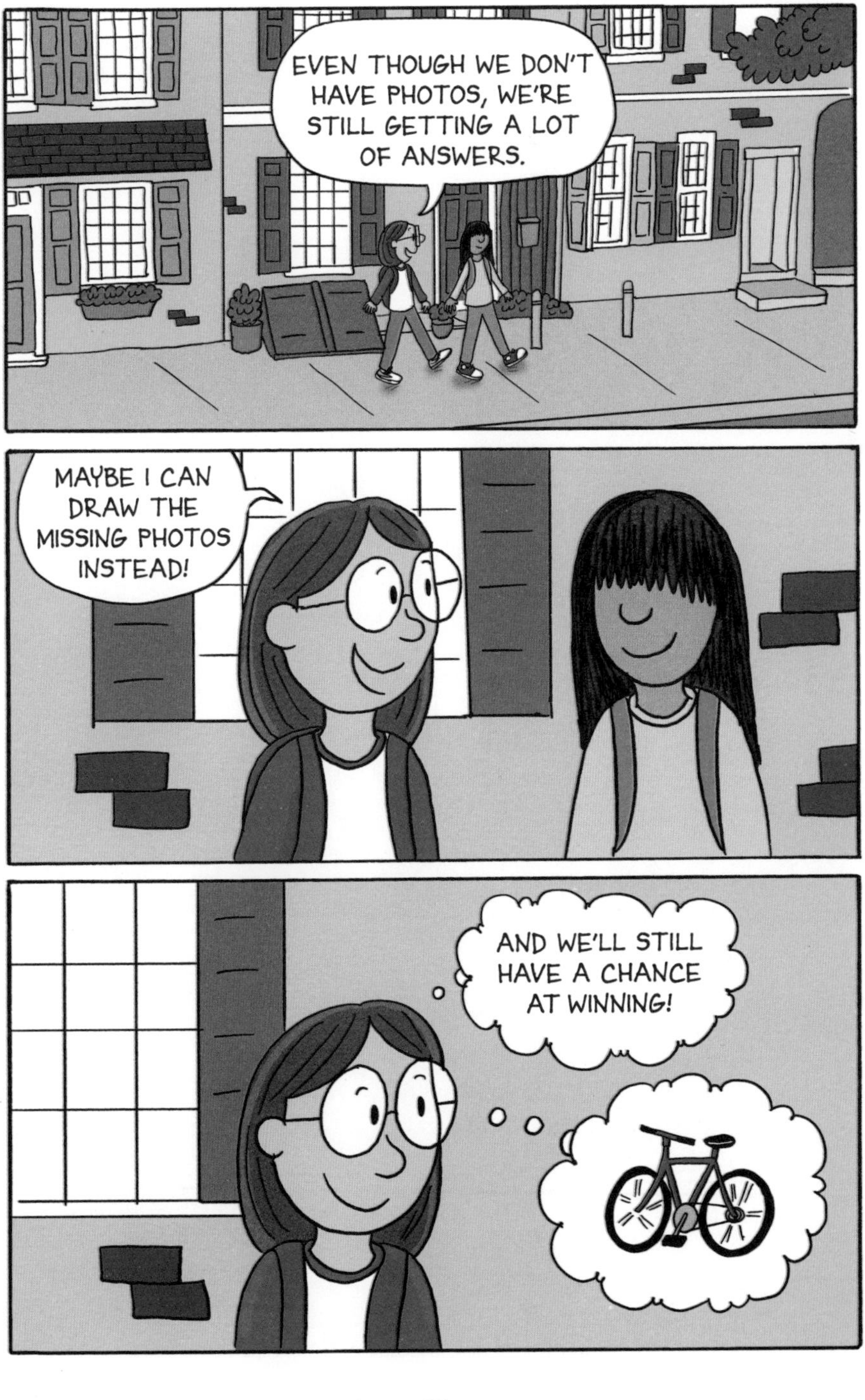
EVEN THOUGH WE DON'T HAVE PHOTOS, WE'RE STILL GETTING A LOT OF ANSWERS.
MAYBE I CAN DRAW THE MISSING PHOTOS INSTEAD!
AND WE'LL STILL HAVE A CHANCE AT WINNING!

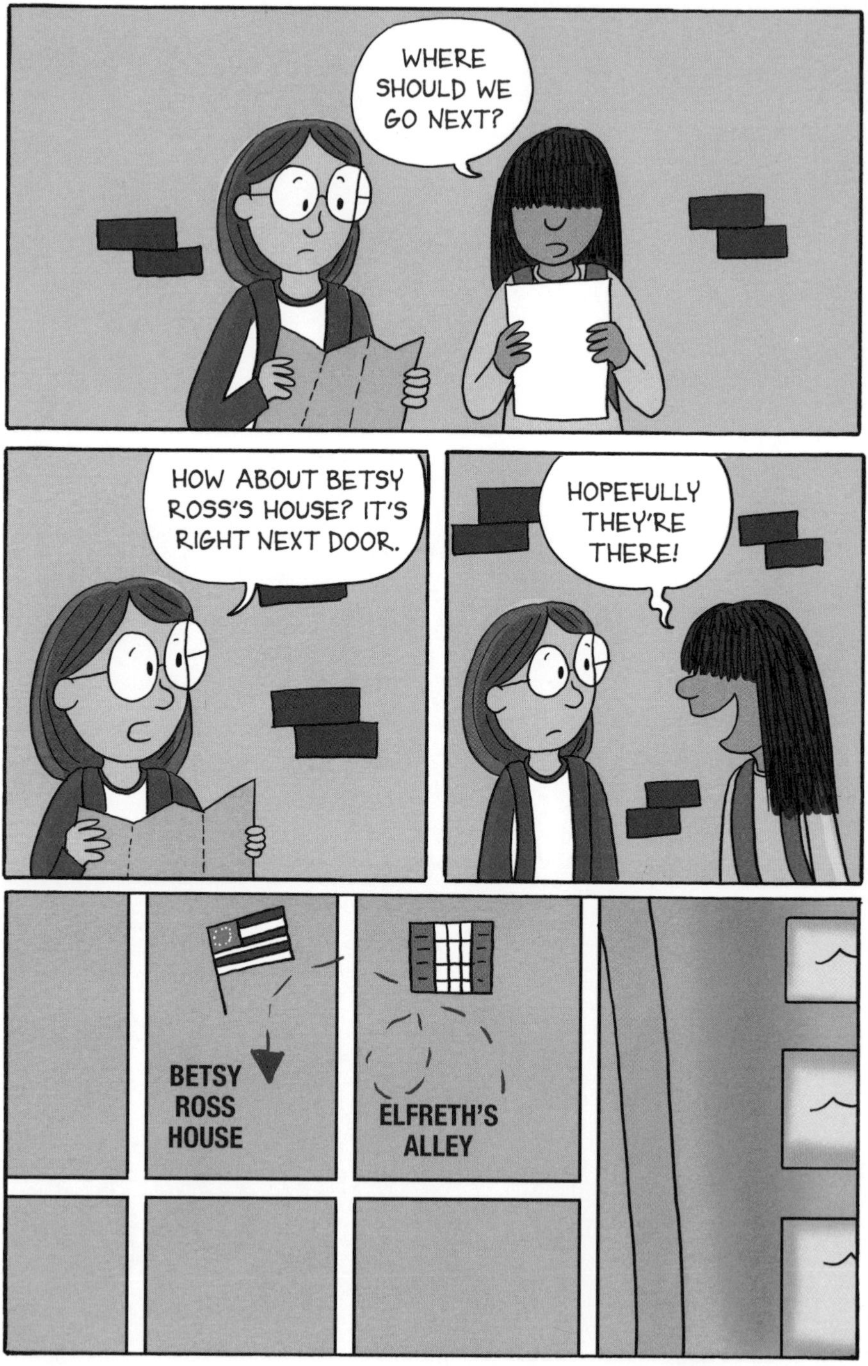
WHERE SHOULD WE GO NEXT?
HOW ABOUT BETSY ROSS'S HOUSE? IT'S RIGHT NEXT DOOR.
HOPEFULLY THEY'RE THERE!
BETSY ROSS HOUSE
ELFRETH'S ALLEY

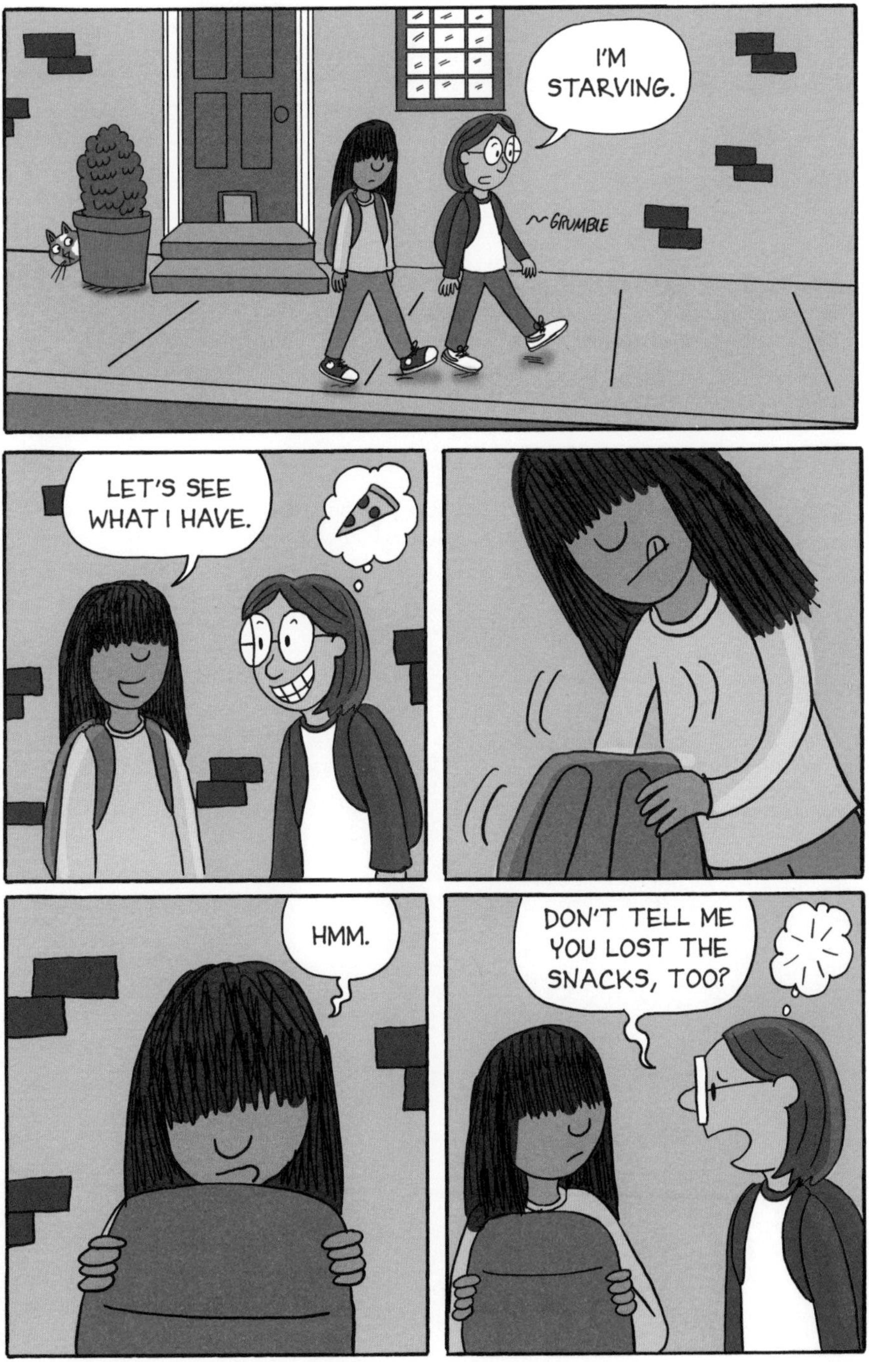
I'M STARVING.
~GRUMBLE
LET'S SEE WHAT I HAVE.
HMM.
DON'T TELL ME YOU LOST THE SNACKS, TOO?

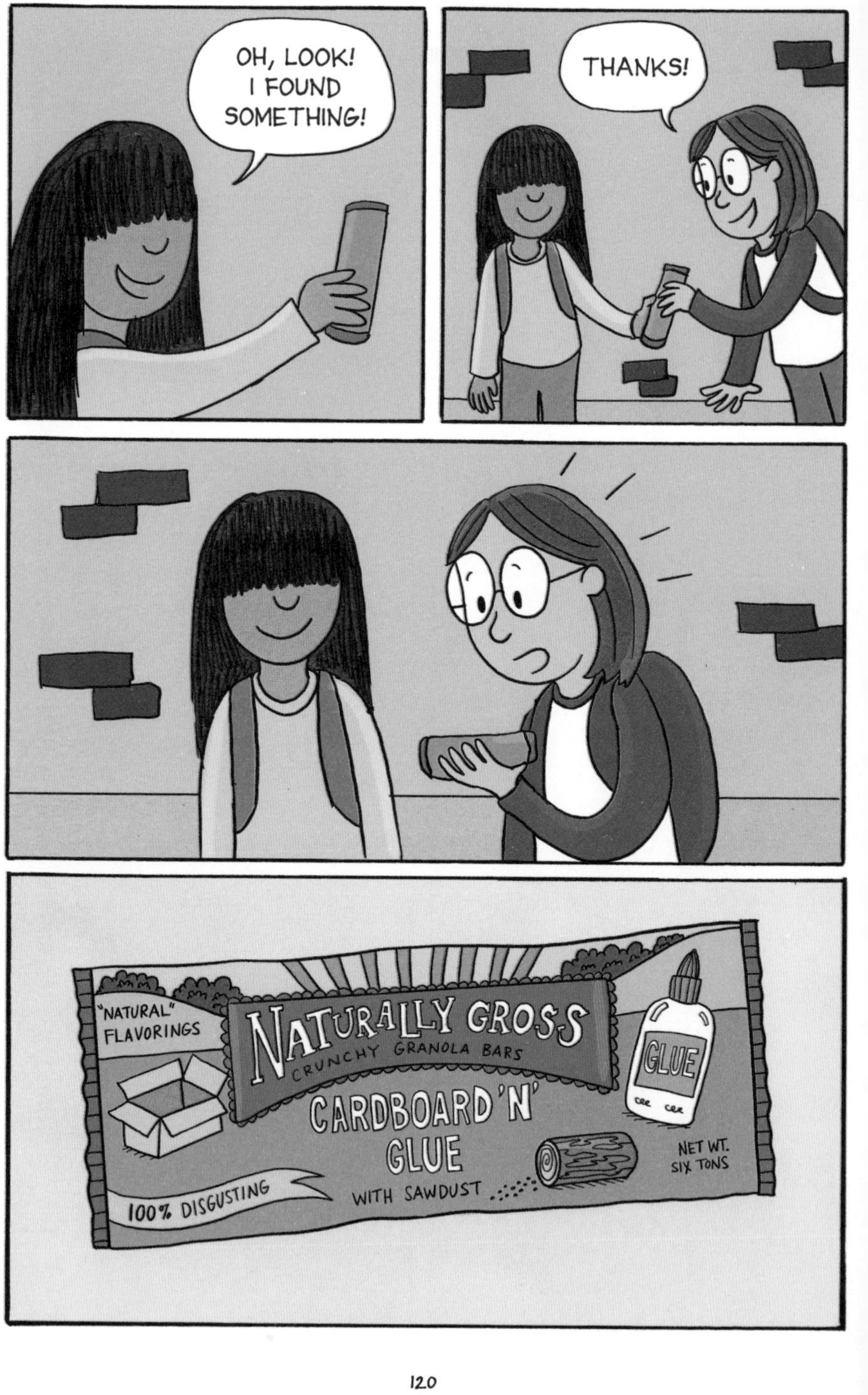
OH, LOOK! I FOUND SOMETHING!
THANKS!
"NATURAL" FLAVORINGS
NATURALLY GROSS
CRUNCHY GRANOLA BARS
GLUE
CARDBOARD 'N' GLUE
WITH SAWDUST
NET WT. SIX TONS
100% DISGUSTING

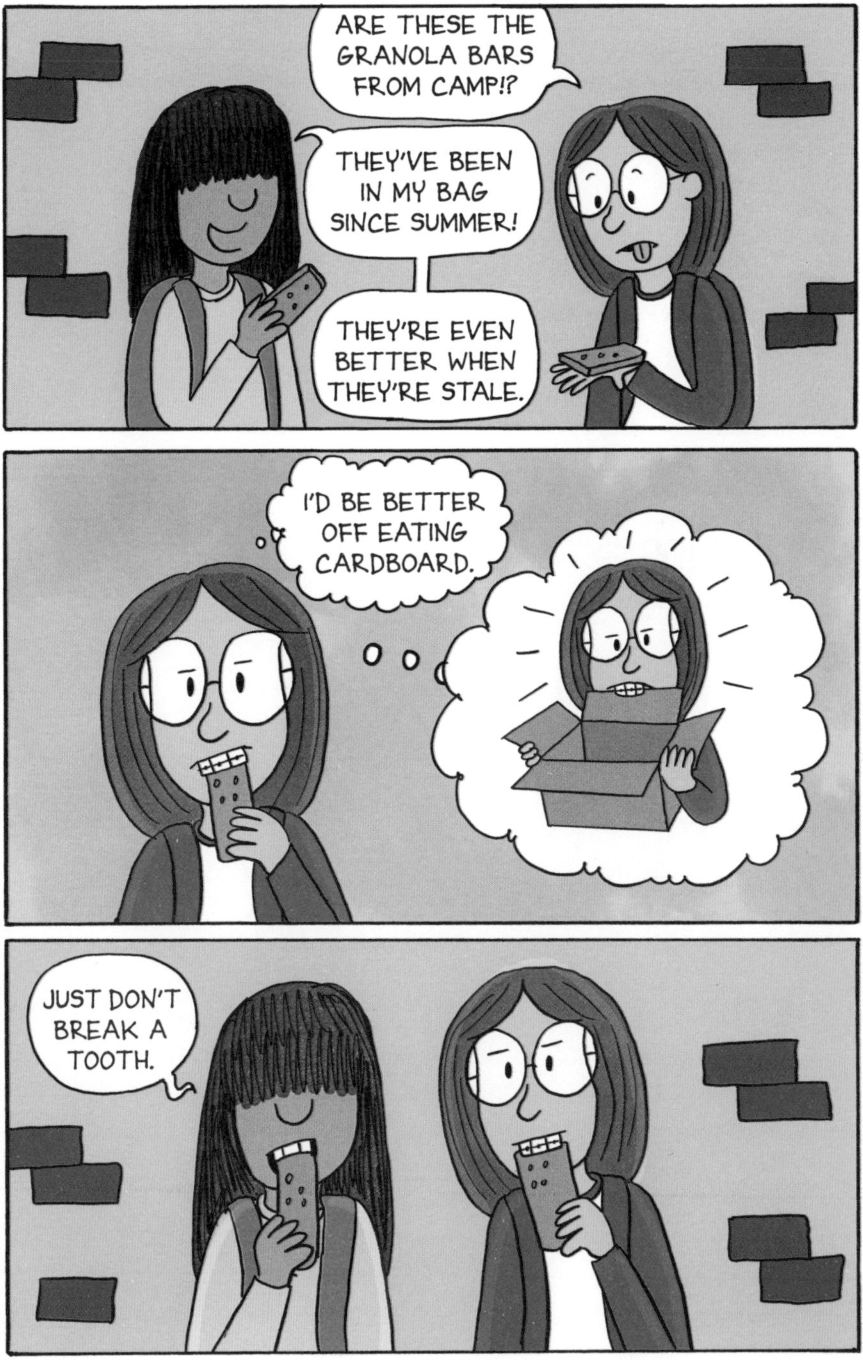
ARE THESE THE GRANOLA BARS FROM CAMP!?
THEY'VE BEEN IN MY BAG SINCE SUMMER!
THEY'RE EVEN BETTER WHEN THEY'RE STALE.
I'D BE BETTER OFF EATING CARDBOARD.
JUST DON'T BREAK A TOOTH.

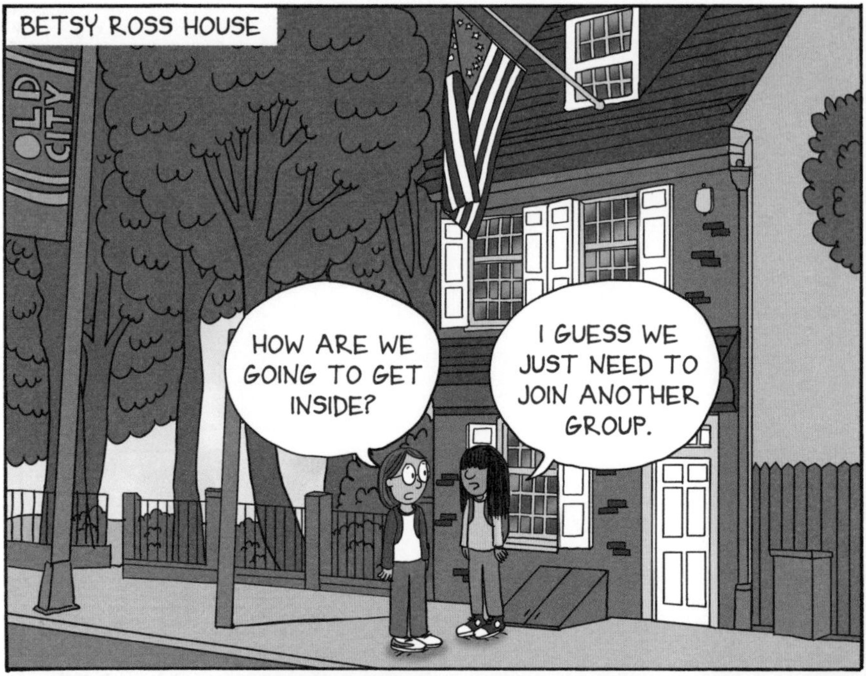
BETSY ROSS HOUSE
OLD CITY
HOW ARE WE GOING TO GET INSIDE?
I GUESS WE JUST NEED TO JOIN ANOTHER GROUP.

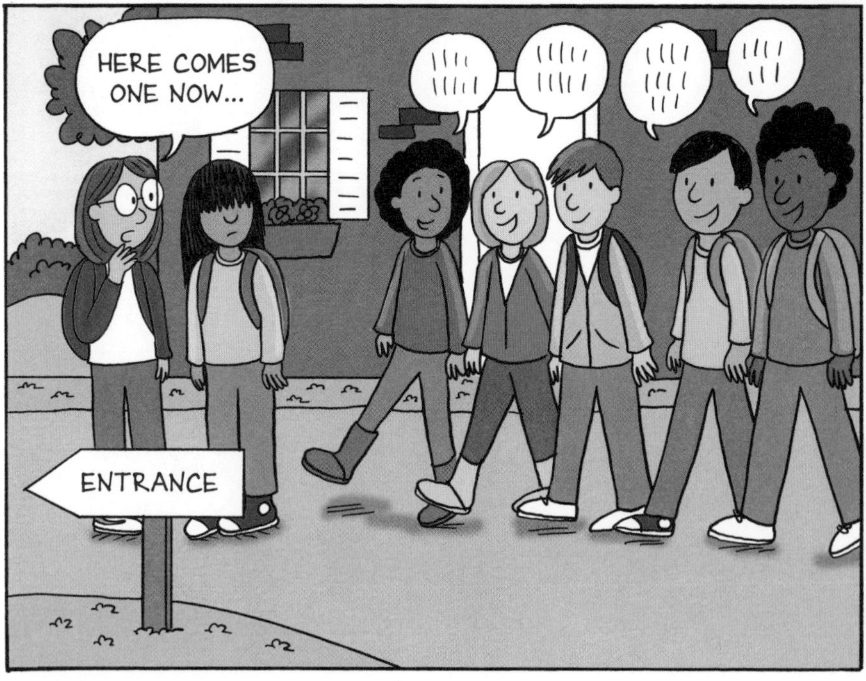
HERE COMES ONE NOW...
ENTRANCE

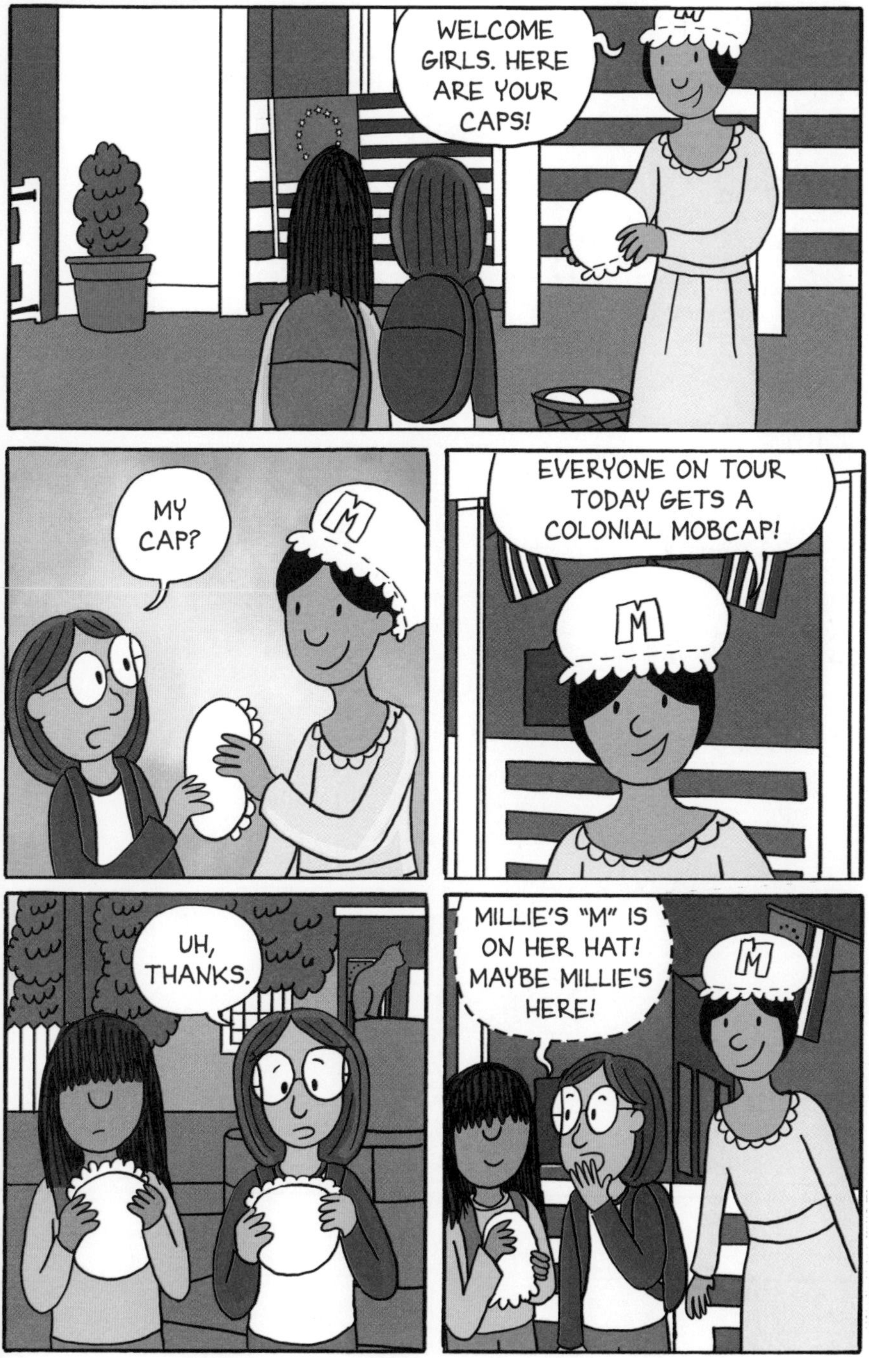
WELCOME GIRLS. HERE ARE YOUR CAPS!
MY CAP?
EVERYONE ON TOUR TODAY GETS A COLONIAL MOBCAP!
UH, THANKS.
MILLIE'S "M" IS ON HER HAT! MAYBE MILLIE'S HERE!

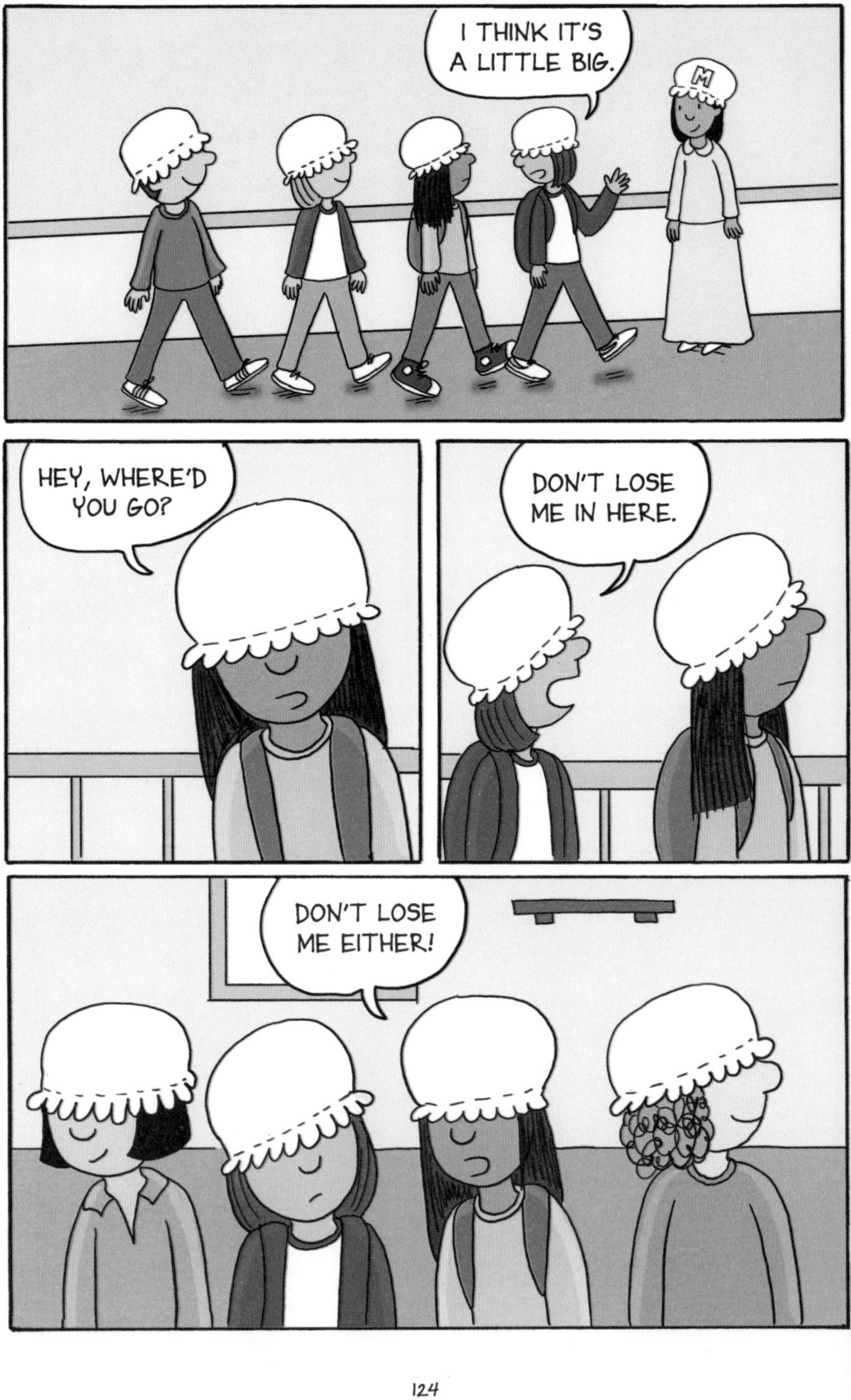

I THINK IT'S A LITTLE BIG.
HEY, WHERE'D YOU GO?
DON'T LOSE ME IN HERE.
DON'T LOSE ME EITHER!

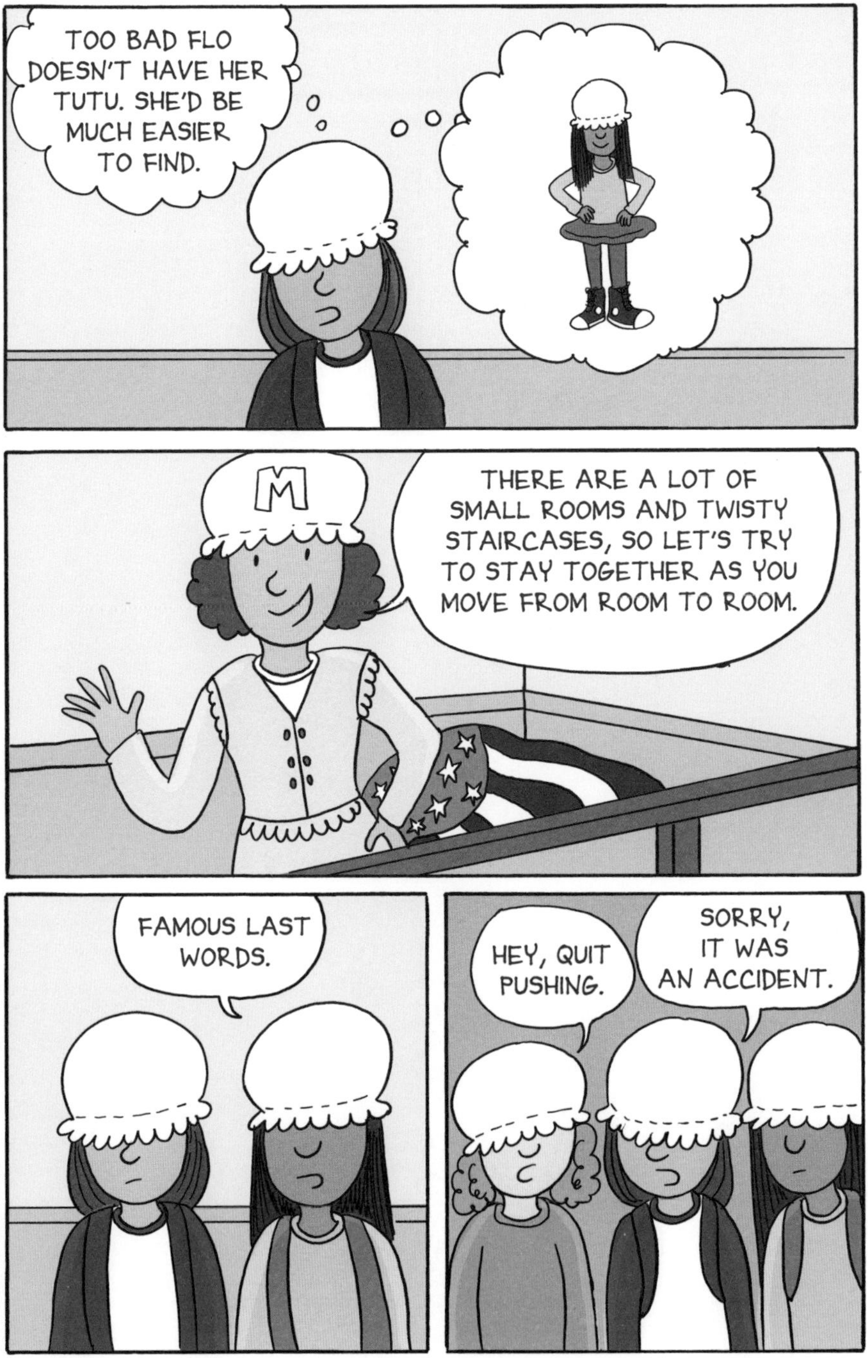
TOO BAD FLO DOESN'T HAVE HER TUTU. SHE'D BE MUCH EASIER TO FIND.
M
THERE ARE A LOT OF SMALL ROOMS AND TWISTY STAIRCASES, SO LET'S TRY TO STAY TOGETHER AS YOU MOVE FROM ROOM TO ROOM.
FAMOUS LAST WORDS.
HEY, QUIT PUSHING.
SORRY, IT WAS AN ACCIDENT.

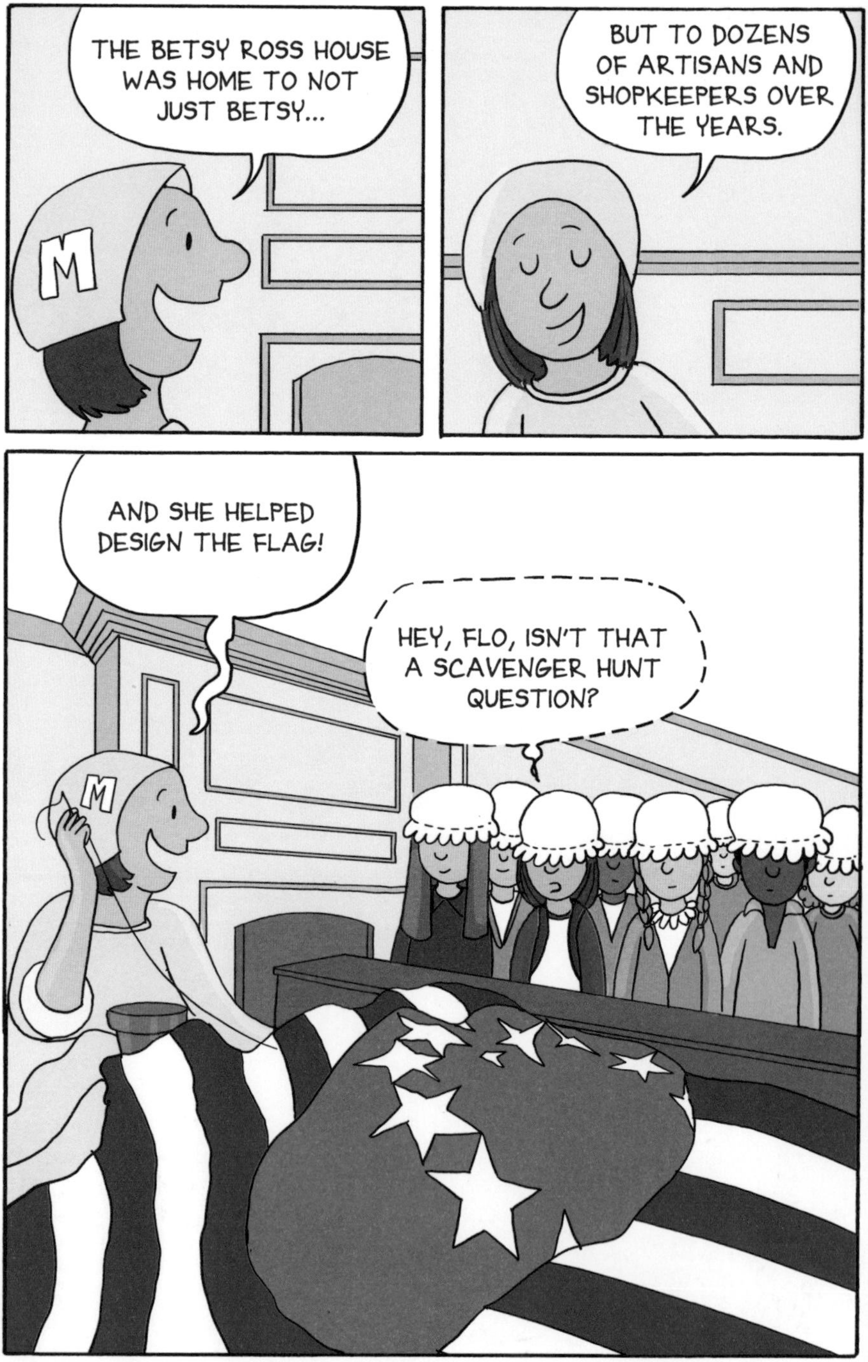
THE BETSY ROSS HOUSE WAS HOME TO NOT JUST BETSY...
BUT TO DOZENS OF ARTISANS AND SHOPKEEPERS OVER THE YEARS.
AND SHE HELPED DESIGN THE FLAG!
HEY, FLO, ISN'T THAT A SCAVENGER HUNT QUESTION?

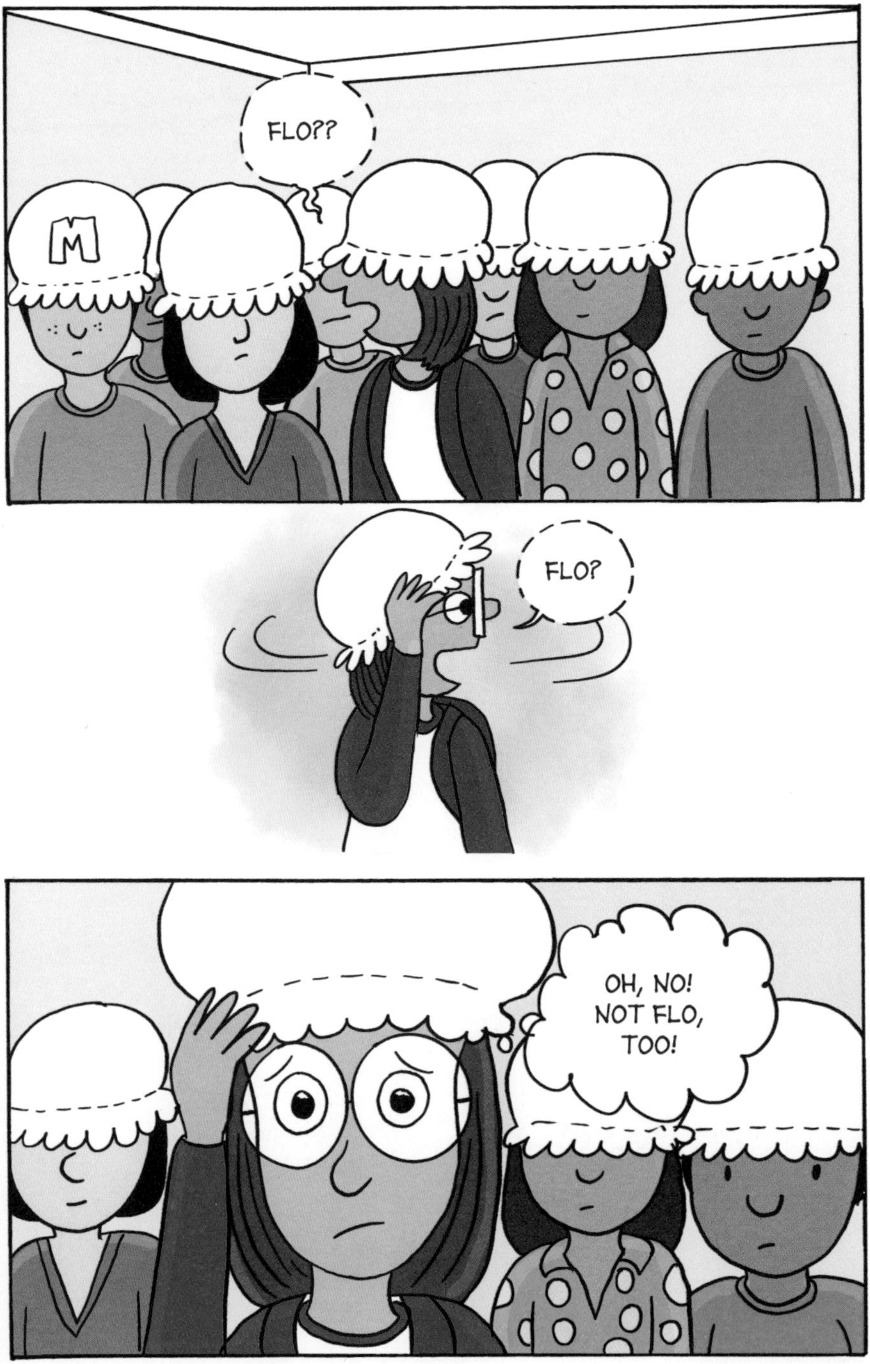
FLO??
FLO?
OH, NO! NOT FLO, TOO!

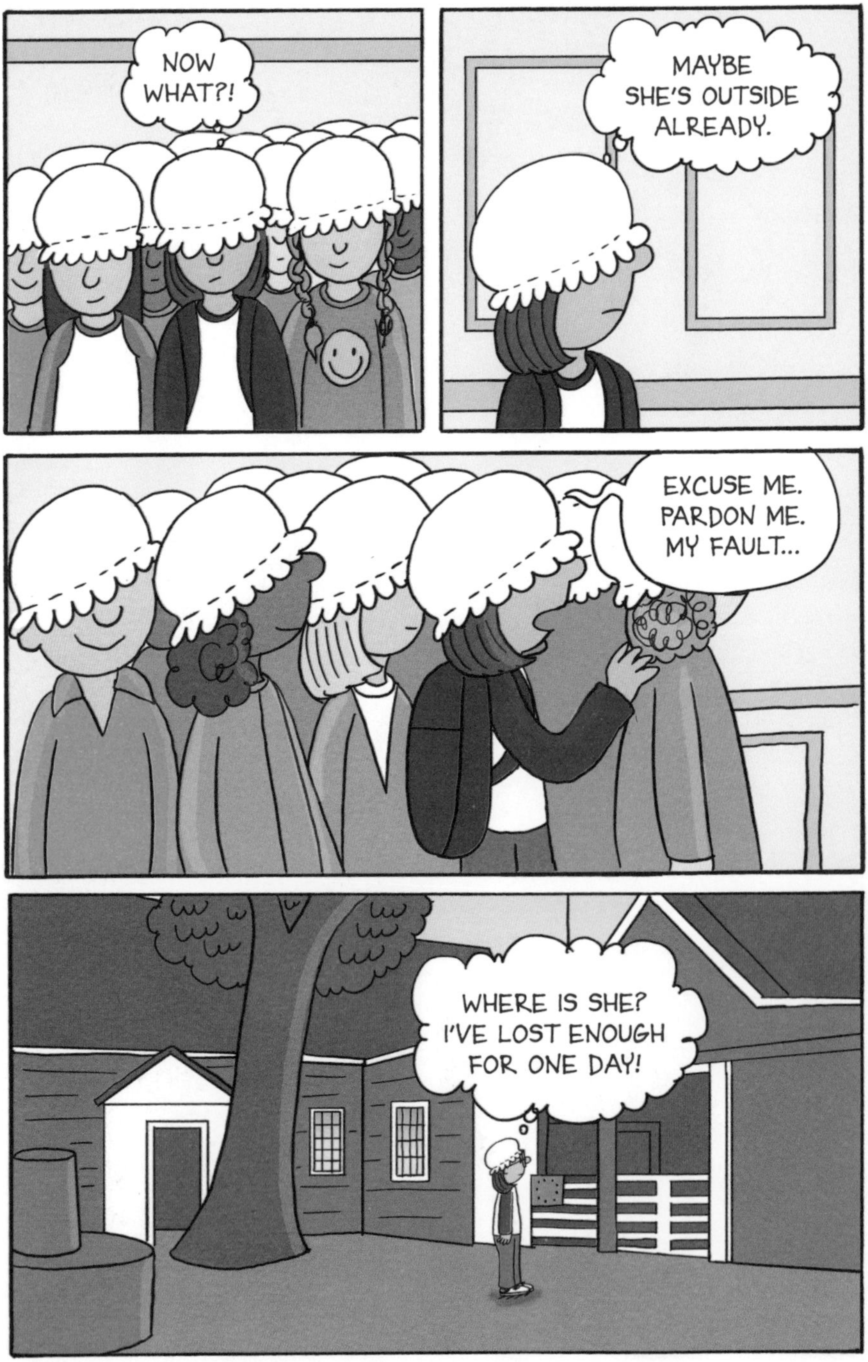
NOW WHAT?!
MAYBE SHE'S OUTSIDE ALREADY.
EXCUSE ME. PARDON ME. MY FAULT...
WHERE IS SHE? I'VE LOST ENOUGH FOR ONE DAY!

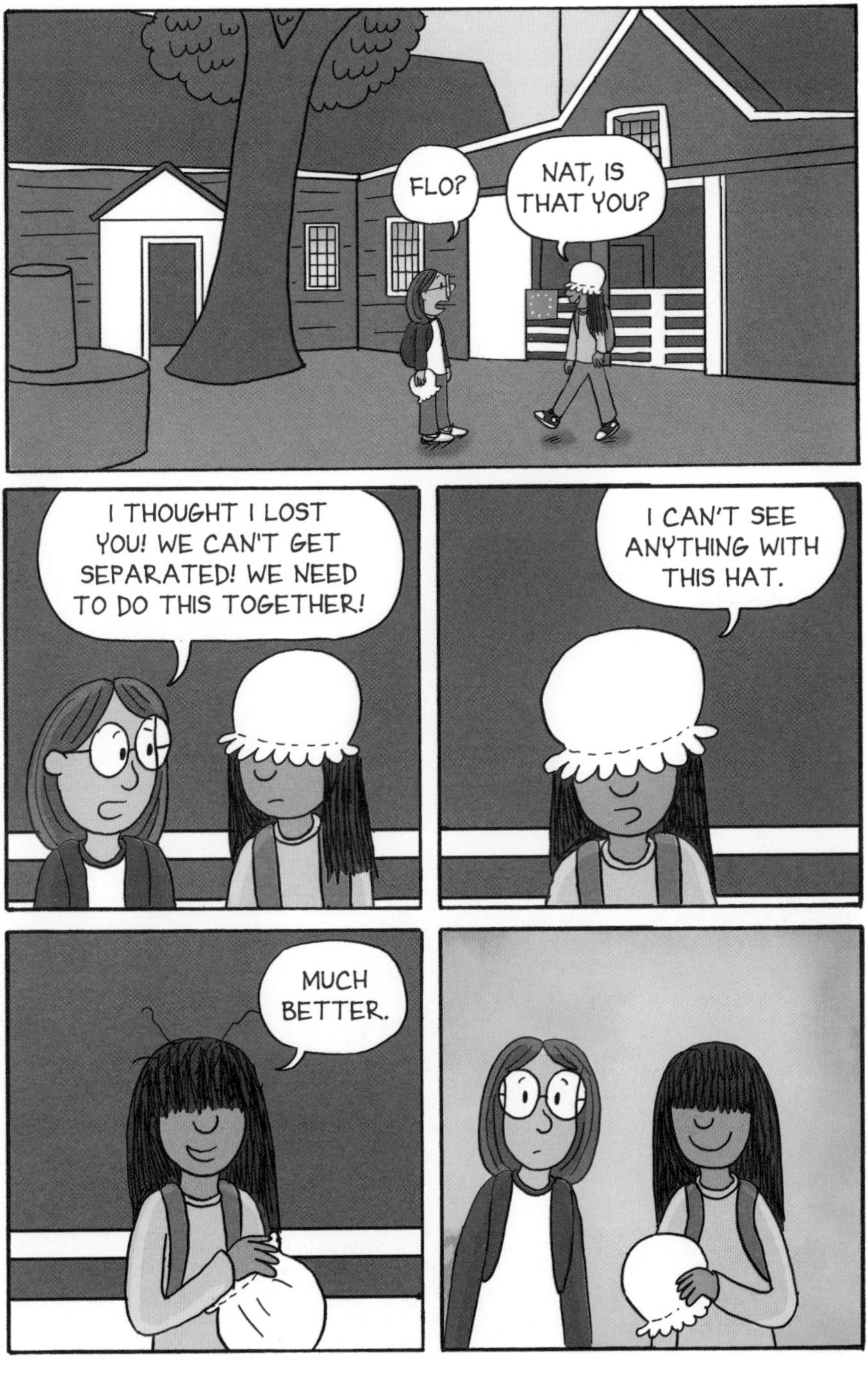
FLO?
NAT, IS THAT YOU?
I THOUGHT I LOST YOU! WE CAN'T GET SEPARATED! WE NEED TO DO THIS TOGETHER!
I CAN'T SEE ANYTHING WITH THIS HAT.
MUCH BETTER.

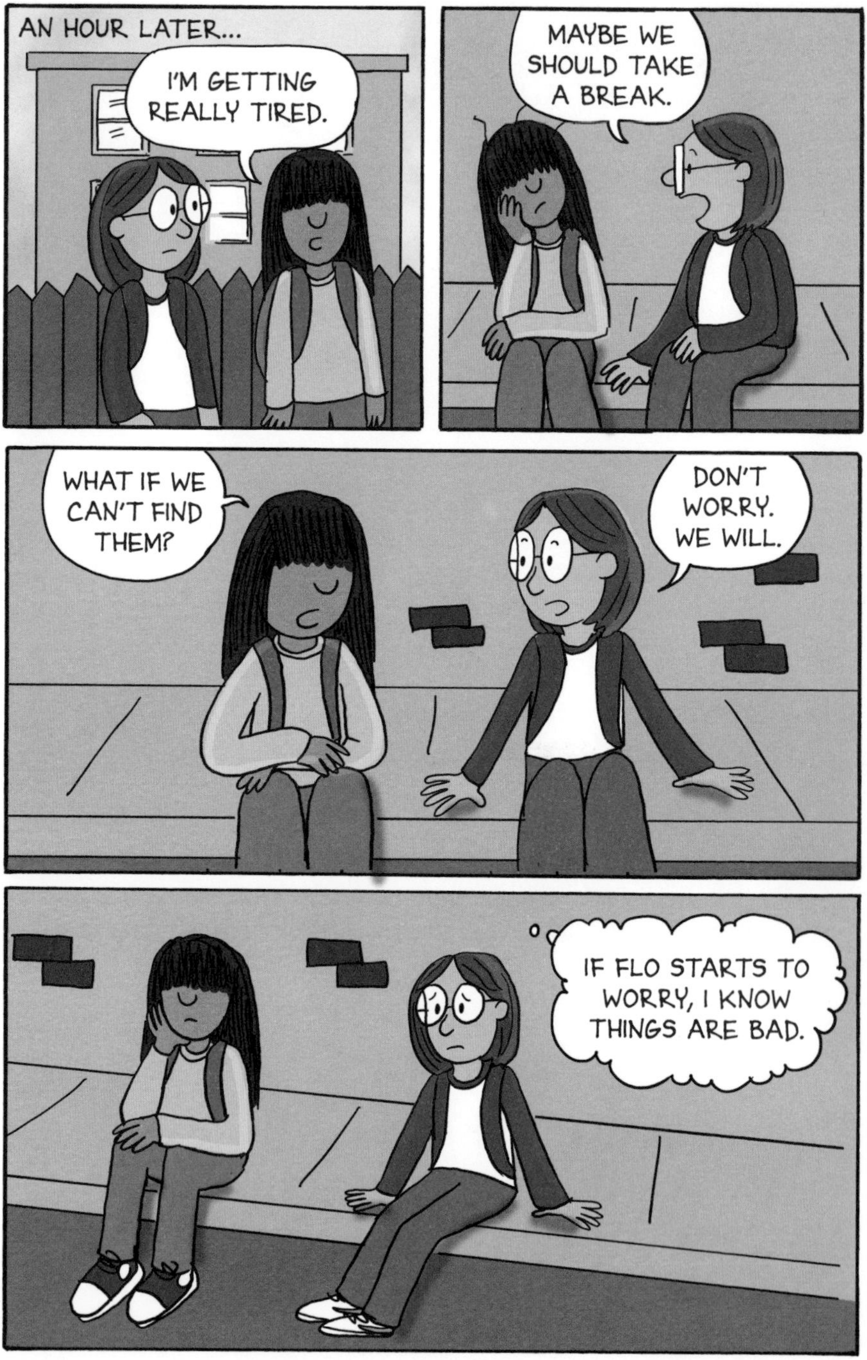
AN HOUR LATER...
I'M GETTING REALLY TIRED.
MAYBE WE SHOULD TAKE A BREAK.
WHAT IF WE CAN'T FIND THEM?
DON'T WORRY. WE WILL.
IF FLO STARTS TO WORRY, I KNOW THINGS ARE BAD.

CHAPTER 10
BEN FRANKLIN

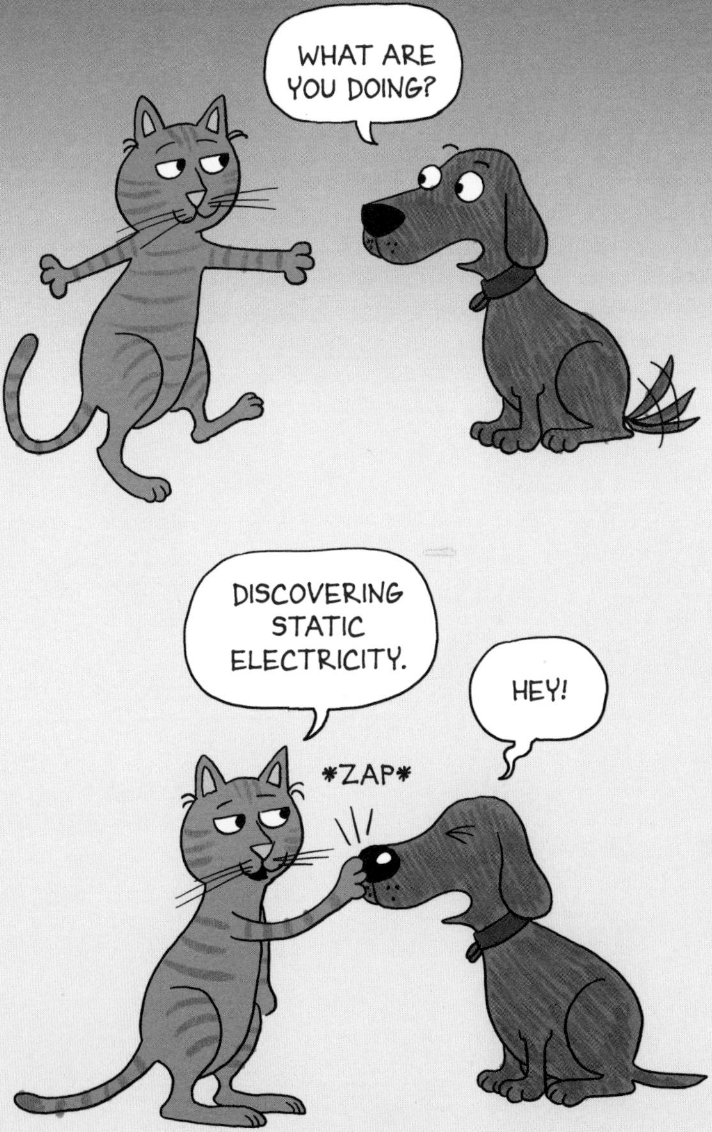

WHAT ARE YOU DOING?
DISCOVERING STATIC ELECTRICITY.
HEY!
ZAP

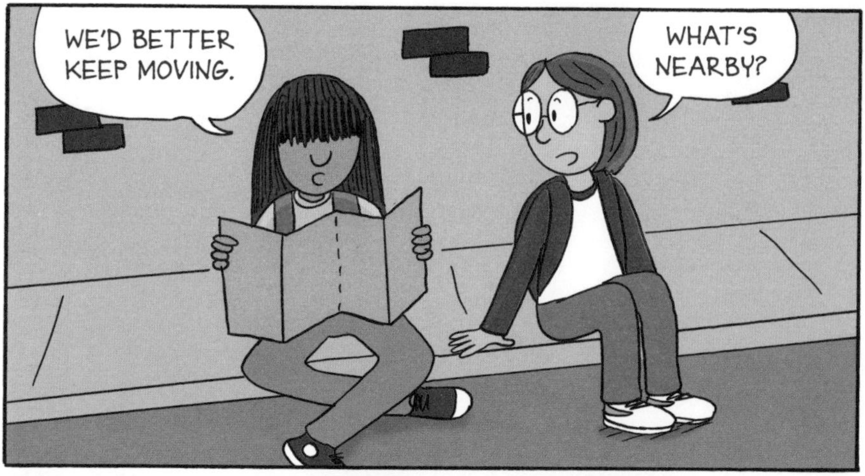
WE'D BETTER KEEP MOVING.
WHAT'S NEARBY?

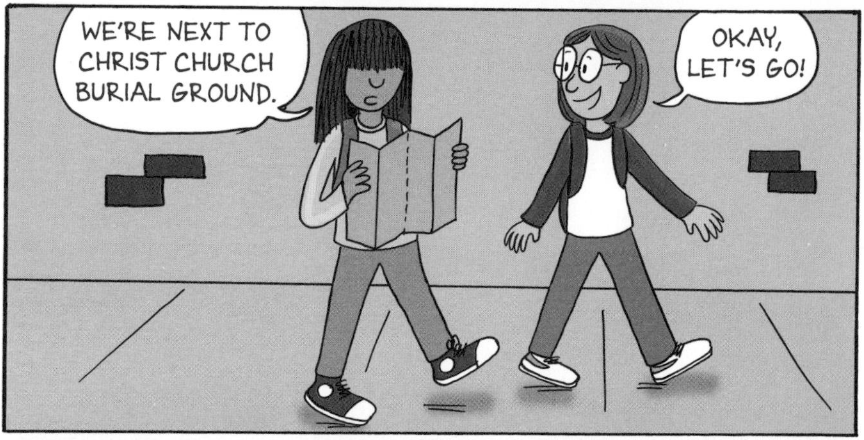
WE'RE NEXT TO CHRIST CHURCH BURIAL GROUND.
OKAY, LET'S GO!

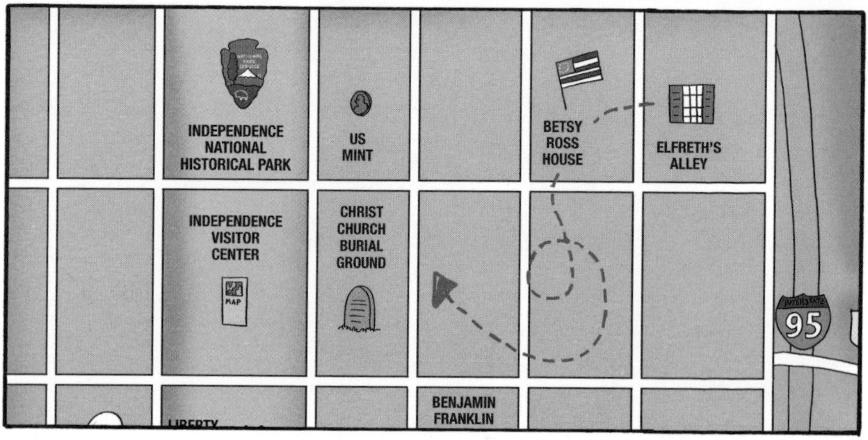
INDEPENDENCE NATIONAL HISTORICAL PARK
US MINT
BETSY ROSS HOUSE
ELFRETH'S ALLEY
INDEPENDENCE VISITOR CENTER
MAP
CHRIST CHURCH BURIAL GROUND
95
BENJAMIN FRANKLIN

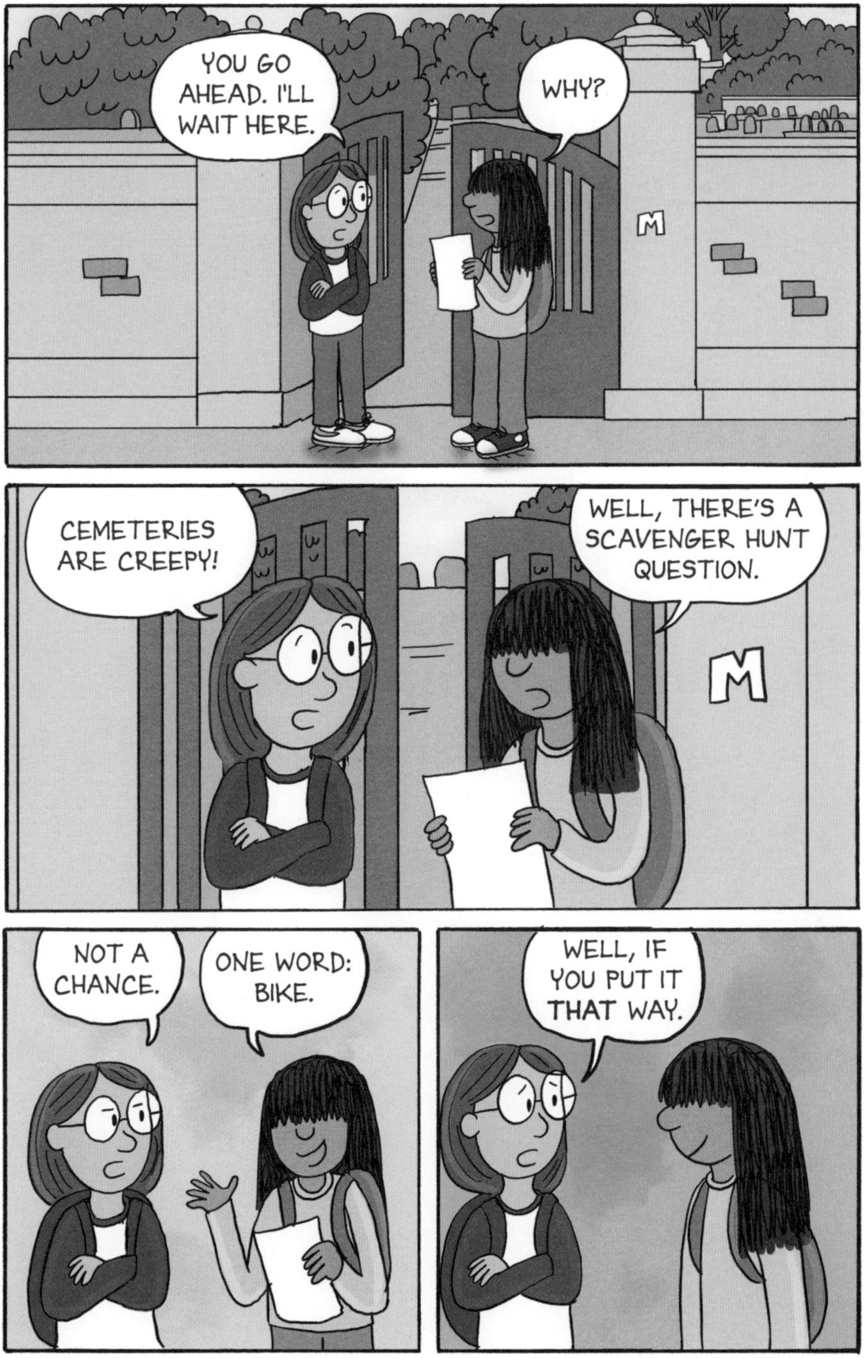
YOU GO AHEAD. I'LL WAIT HERE.
WHY?
CEMETERIES ARE CREEPY!
WELL, THERE'S A SCAVENGER HUNT QUESTION.
NOT A CHANCE.
ONE WORD: BIKE.
WELL, IF YOU PUT IT THAT WAY.

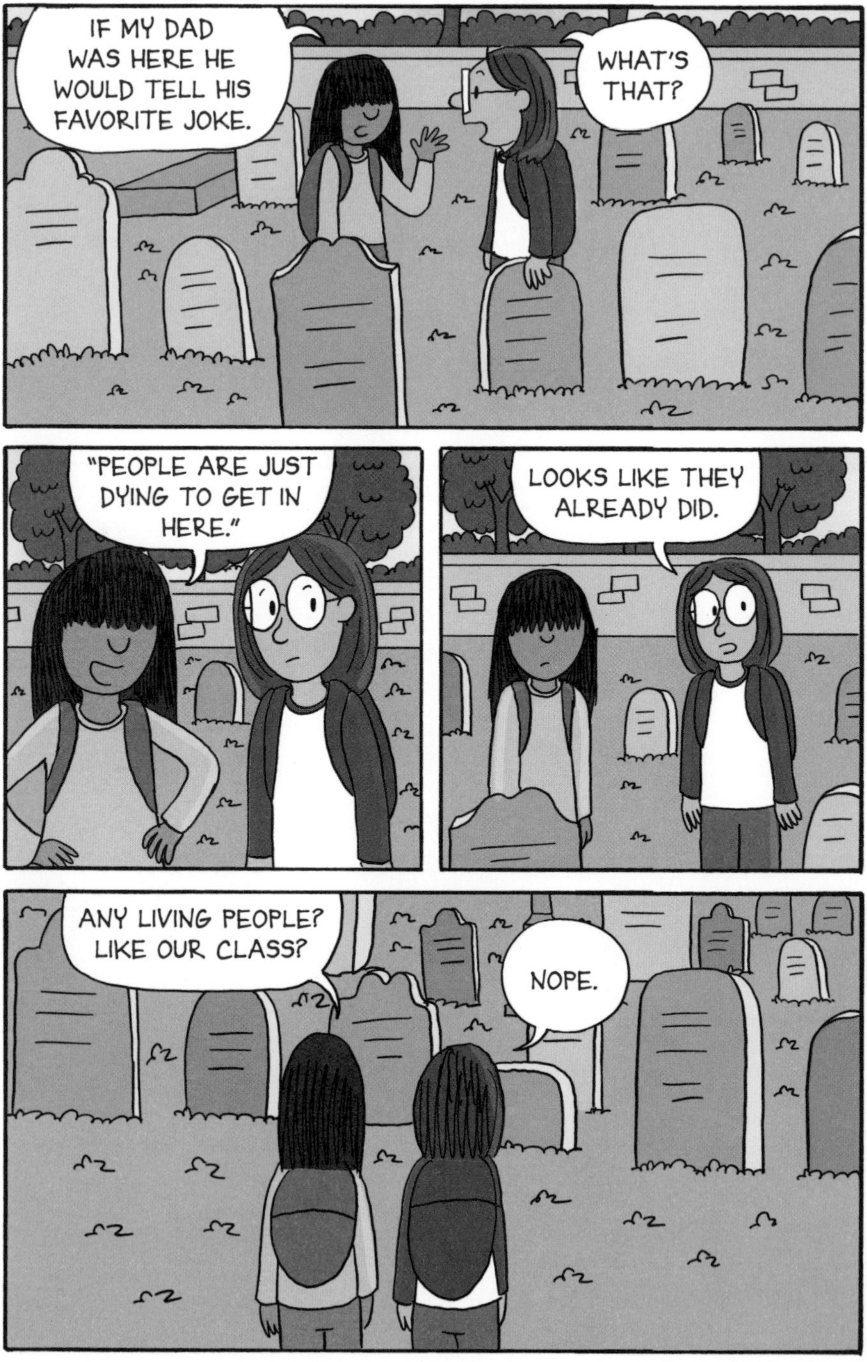
IF MY DAD WAS HERE HE WOULD TELL HIS FAVORITE JOKE.
WHAT'S THAT?
"PEOPLE ARE JUST DYING TO GET IN HERE."
LOOKS LIKE THEY ALREADY DID.
ANY LIVING PEOPLE? LIKE OUR CLASS?
NOPE.

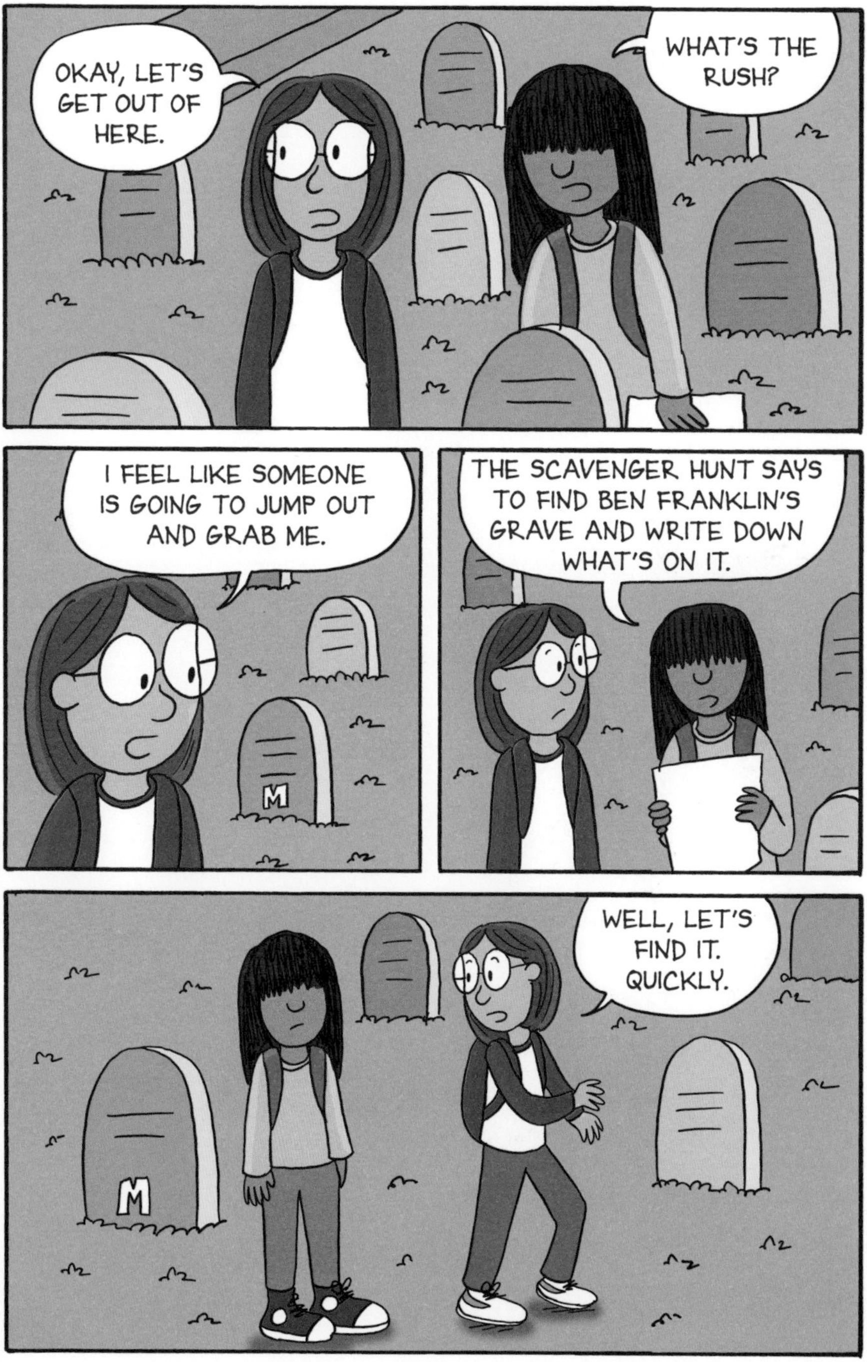
OKAY, LET'S GET OUT OF HERE.
WHAT'S THE RUSH?
I FEEL LIKE SOMEONE IS GOING TO JUMP OUT AND GRAB ME.
M
THE SCAVENGER HUNT SAYS TO FIND BEN FRANKLIN'S GRAVE AND WRITE DOWN WHAT'S ON IT.
WELL, LET'S FIND IT. QUICKLY.
M

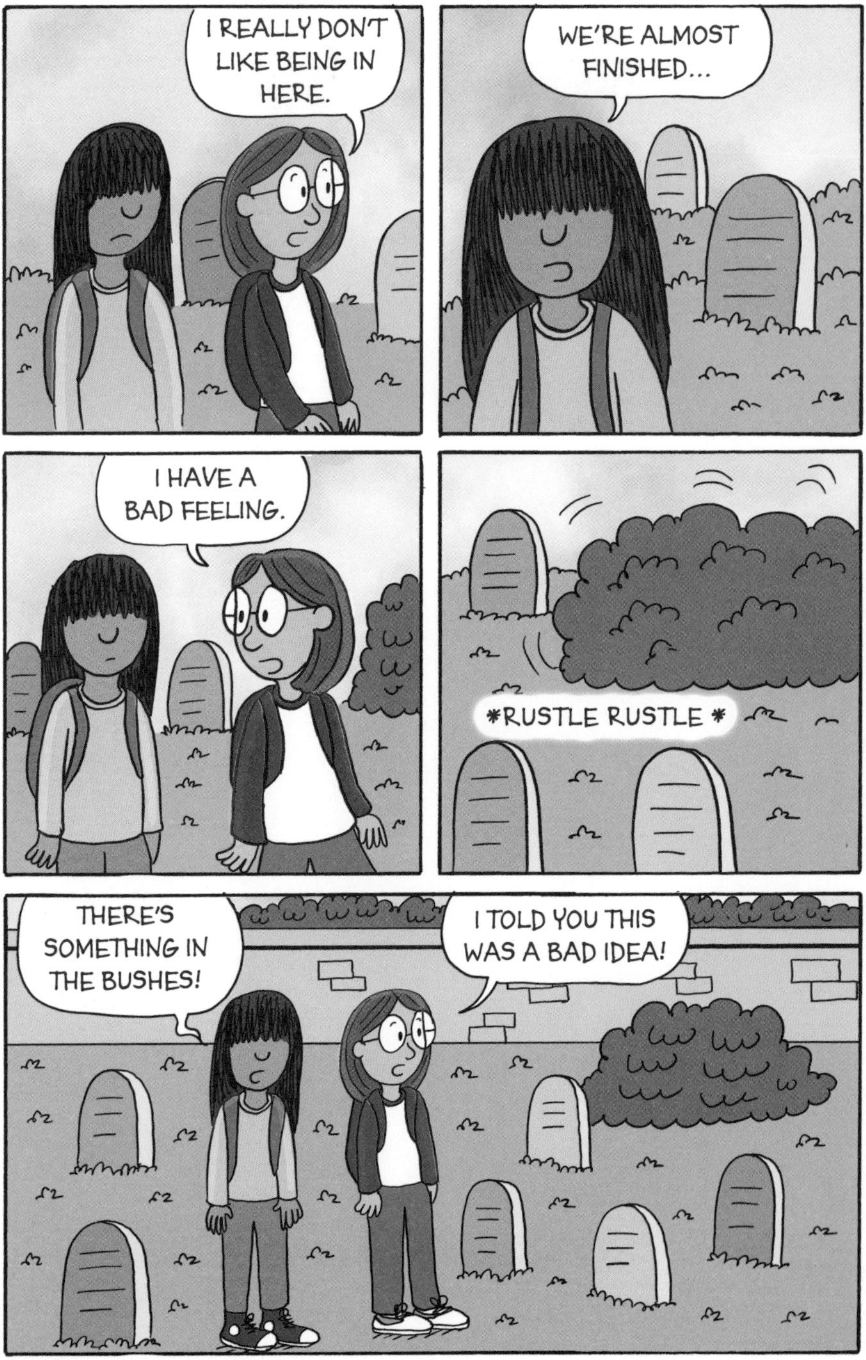

I REALLY DON'T LIKE BEING IN HERE.
WE'RE ALMOST FINISHED...
I HAVE A BAD FEELING.
RUSTLE RUSTLE
THERE'S SOMETHING IN THE BUSHES!
I TOLD YOU THIS WAS A BAD IDEA!

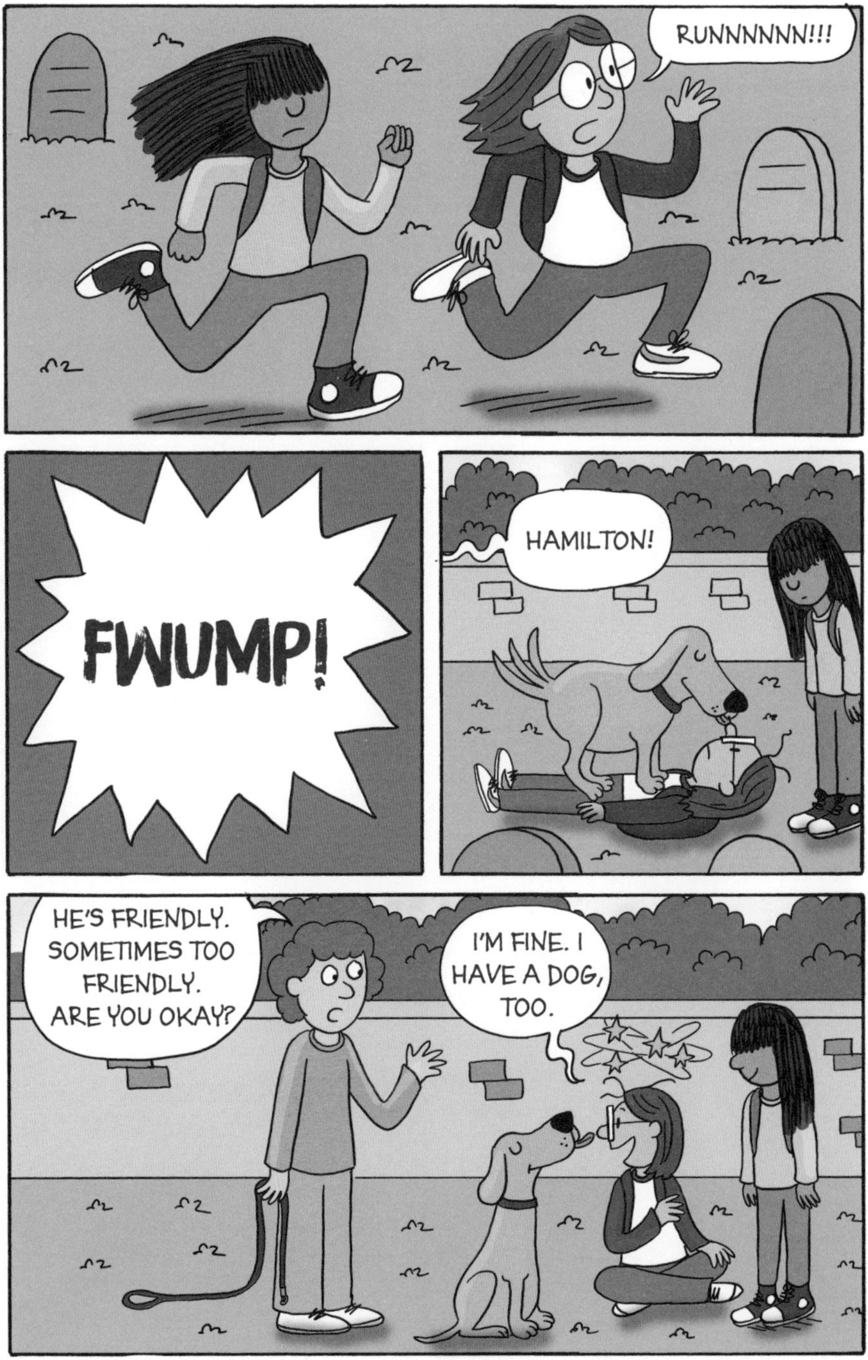
RUNNNNNN!!!
FWUMP!
HAMILTON!
HE'S FRIENDLY. SOMETIMES TOO FRIENDLY. ARE YOU OKAY?
I'M FINE. I HAVE A DOG, TOO.

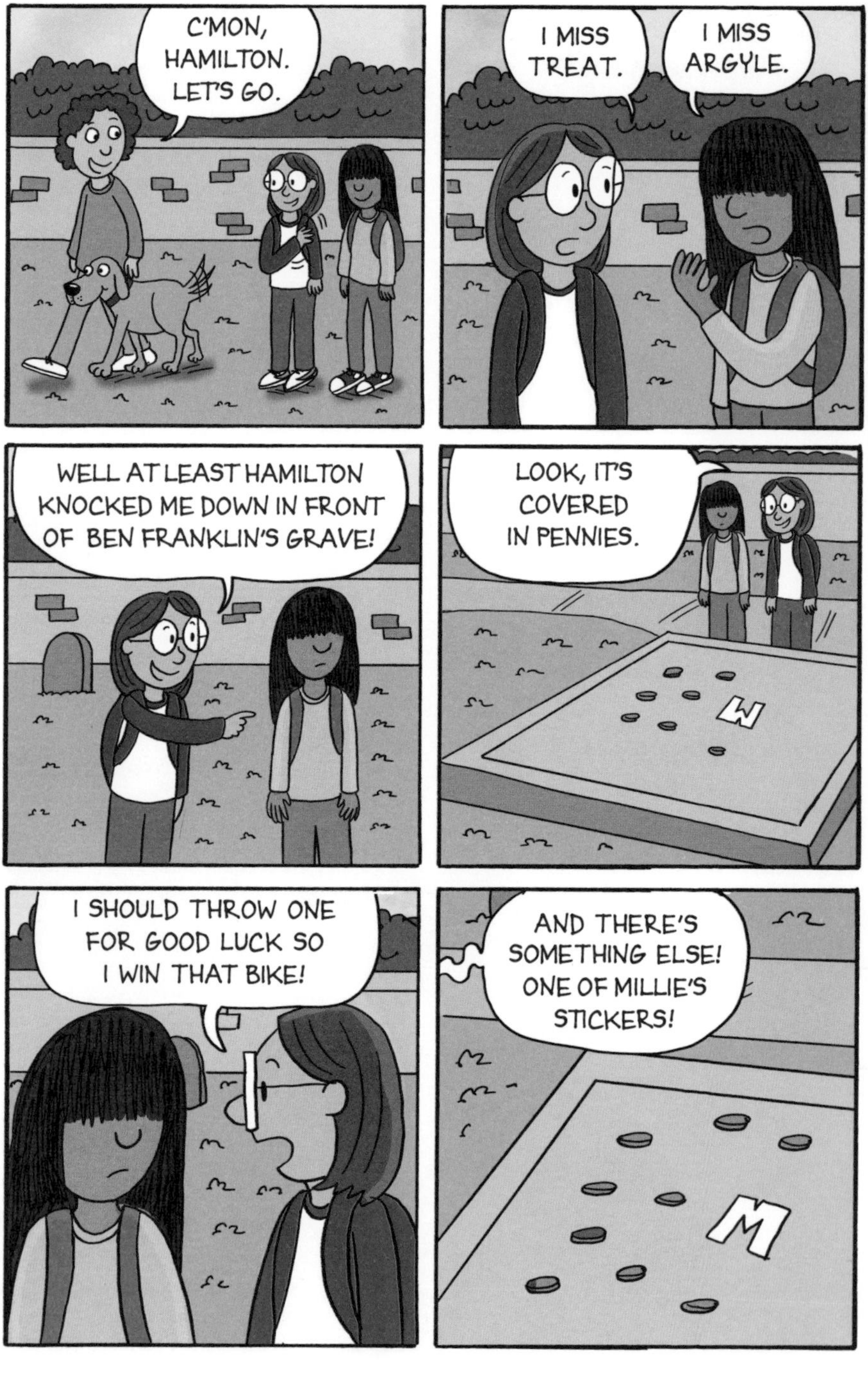
C'MON, HAMILTON. LET'S GO.
I MISS TREAT.
I MISS ARGYLE.
WELL AT LEAST HAMILTON KNOCKED ME DOWN IN FRONT OF BEN FRANKLIN'S GRAVE!
LOOK, IT'S COVERED IN PENNIES.
I SHOULD THROW ONE FOR GOOD LUCK SO I WIN THAT BIKE!
AND THERE'S SOMETHING ELSE! ONE OF MILLIE'S STICKERS!

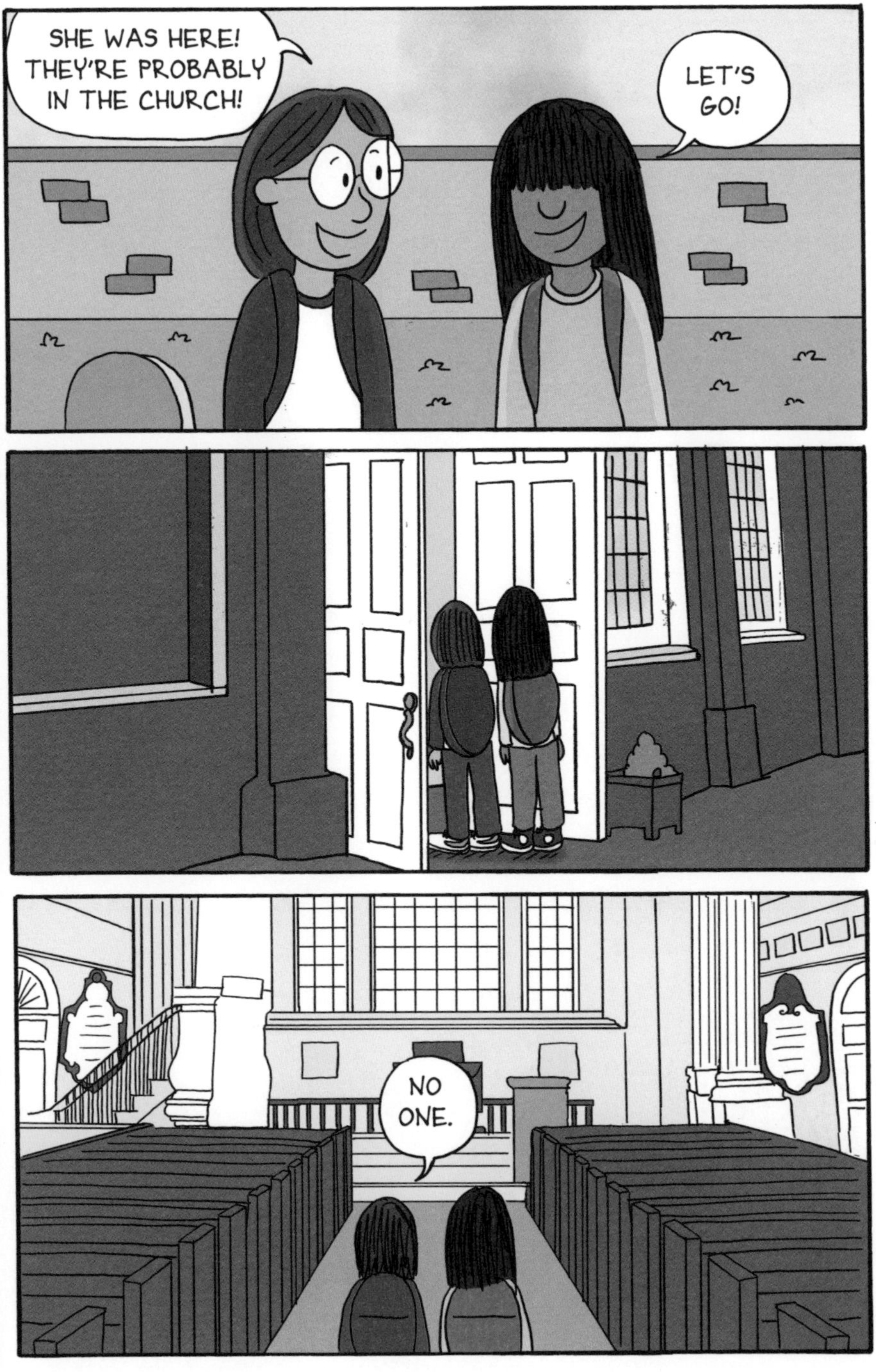
SHE WAS HERE! THEY'RE PROBABLY IN THE CHURCH!
LET'S GO!
NO ONE.

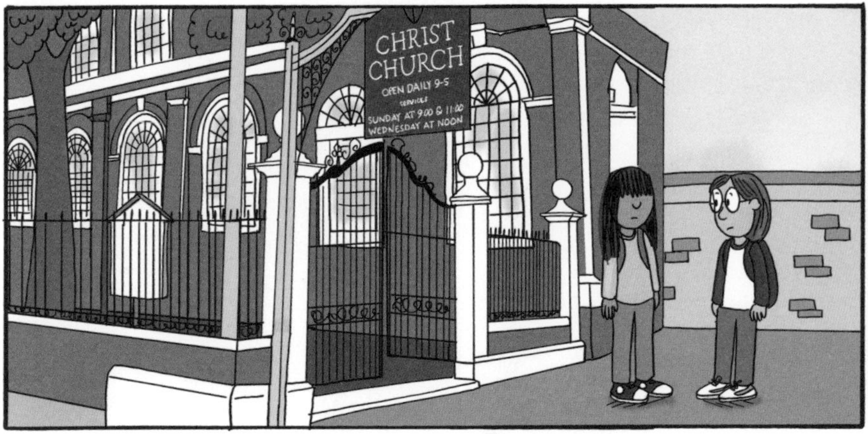
CHRIST CHURCH
OPEN DAILY 9-5
SERVICES
SUNDAY AT 9:00 & 11:00
WEDNESDAY AT NOON

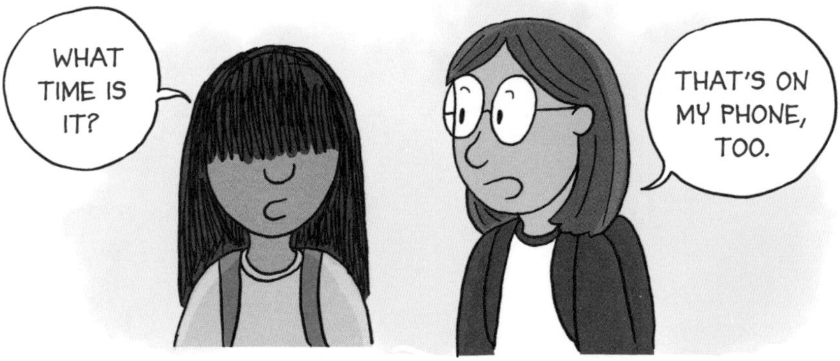
WHAT TIME IS IT?
THAT'S ON MY PHONE, TOO.

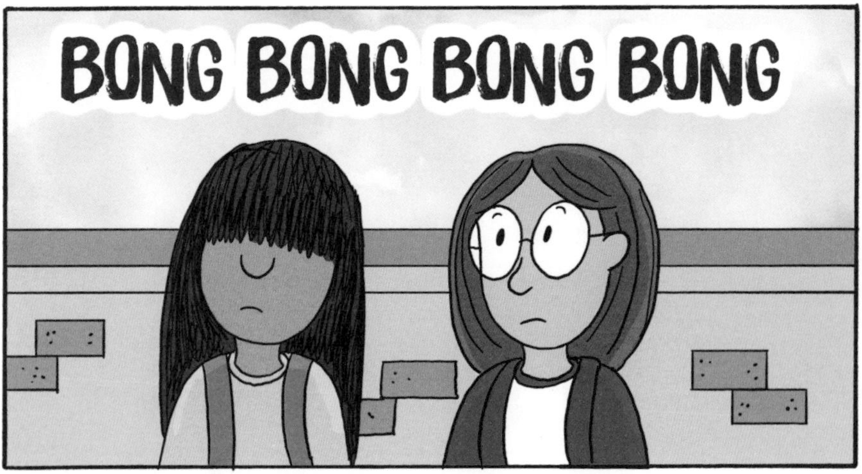
BONG BONG BONG BONG

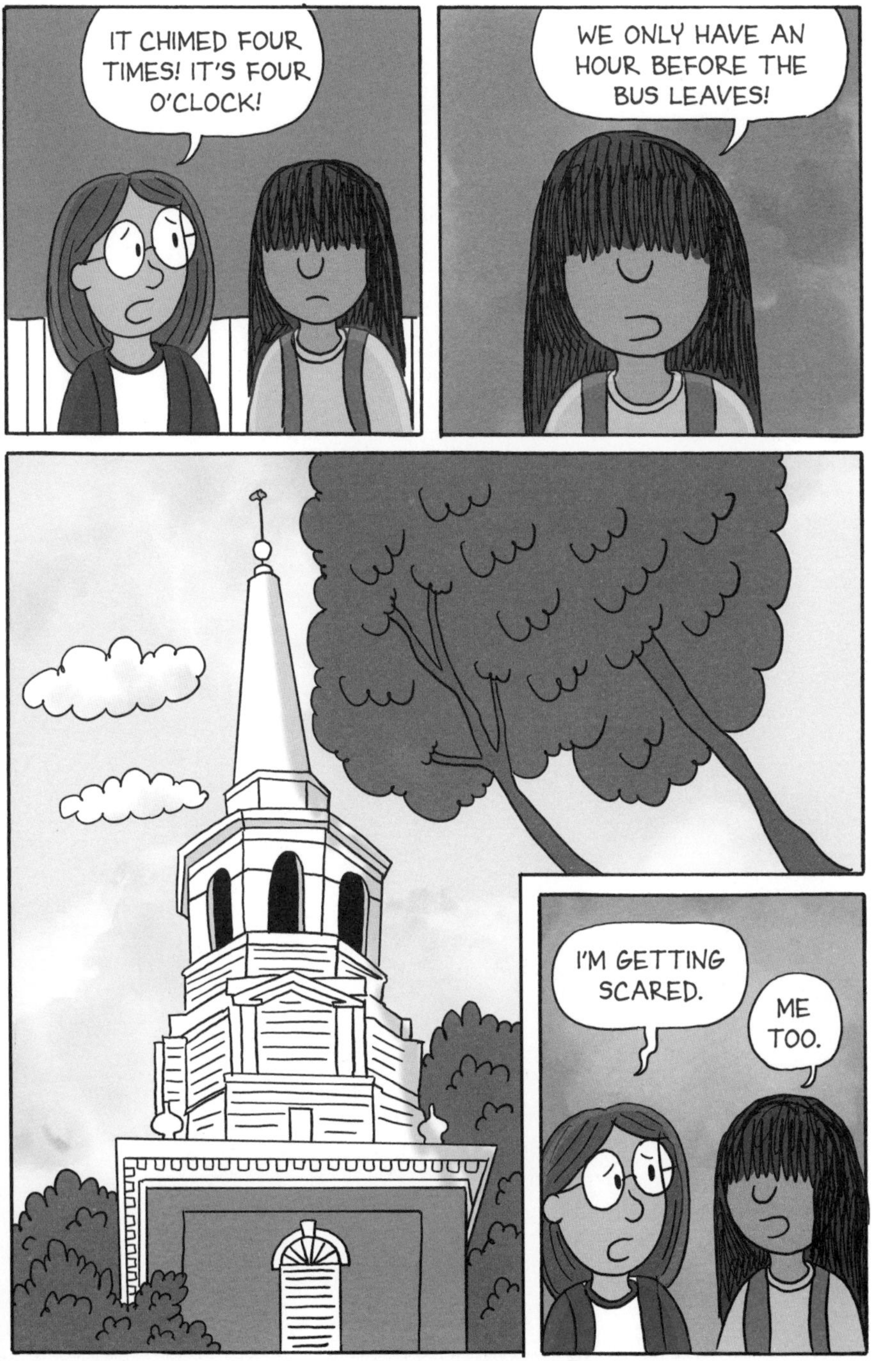
IT CHIMED FOUR TIMES! IT'S FOUR O'CLOCK!
WE ONLY HAVE AN HOUR BEFORE THE BUS LEAVES!
I'M GETTING SCARED.
ME TOO.

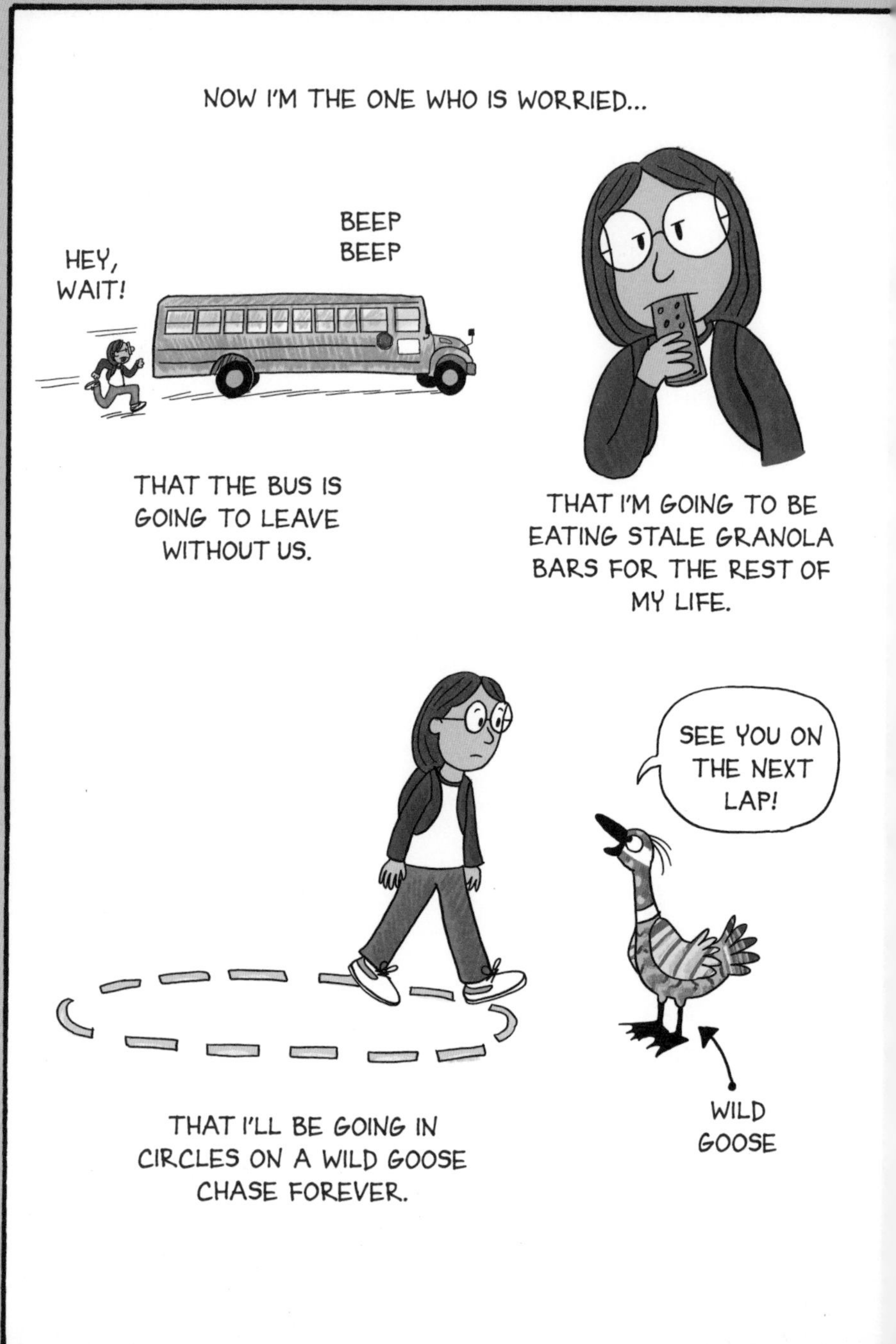
NOW I'M THE ONE WHO IS WORRIED...
HEY, WAIT!
BEEP BEEP
THAT THE BUS IS GOING TO LEAVE WITHOUT US.
THAT I'M GOING TO BE EATING STALE GRANOLA BARS FOR THE REST OF MY LIFE.
SEE YOU ON THE NEXT LAP!
WILD GOOSE
THAT I'LL BE GOING IN CIRCLES ON A WILD GOOSE CHASE FOREVER.

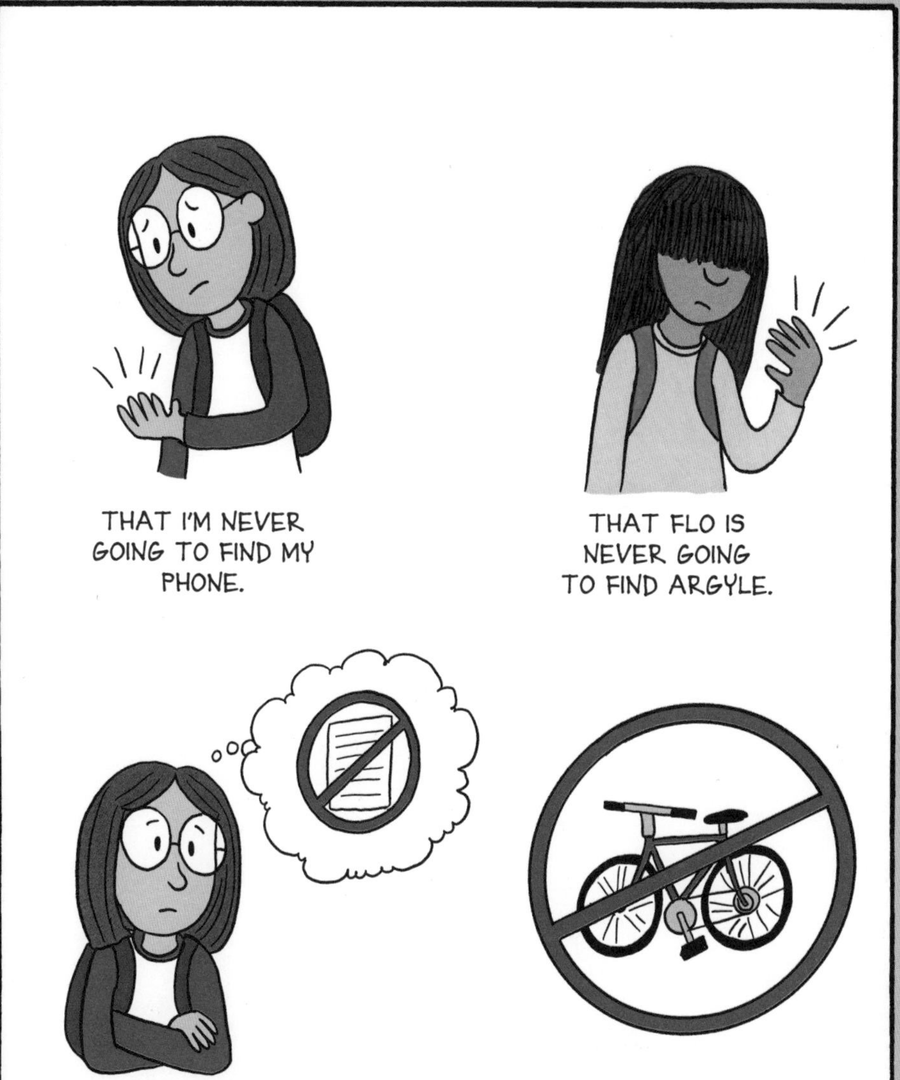
THAT I'M NEVER GOING TO FIND MY PHONE.
THAT FLO IS NEVER GOING TO FIND ARGYLE.
THAT I'LL LOSE THE SCAVENGER HUNT.
THAT I'LL NEVER WIN THAT BIKE!

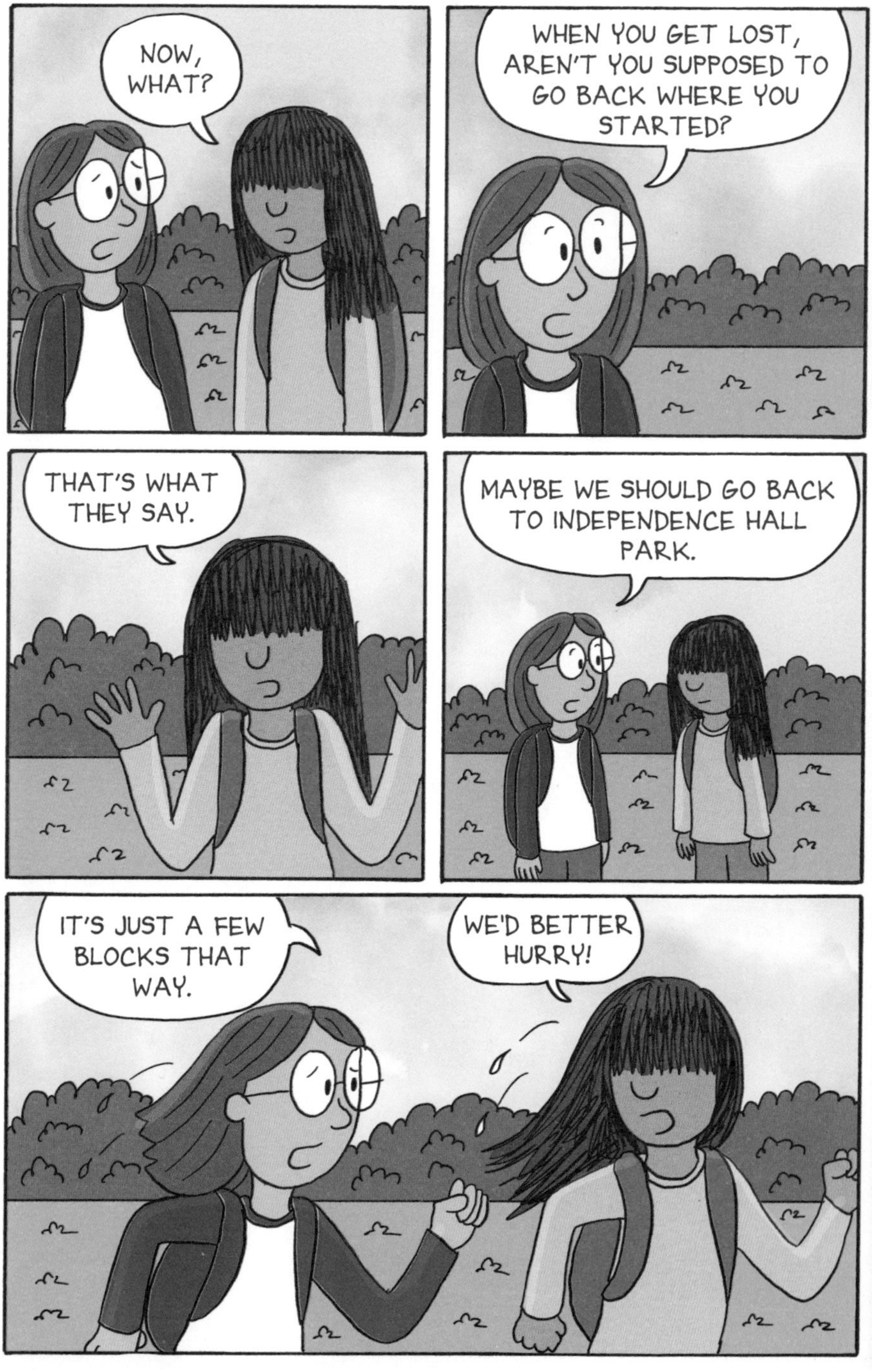
NOW, WHAT?
WHEN YOU GET LOST, AREN'T YOU SUPPOSED TO GO BACK WHERE YOU STARTED?
THAT'S WHAT THEY SAY.
MAYBE WE SHOULD GO BACK TO INDEPENDENCE HALL PARK.
IT'S JUST A FEW BLOCKS THAT WAY.
WE'D BETTER HURRY!

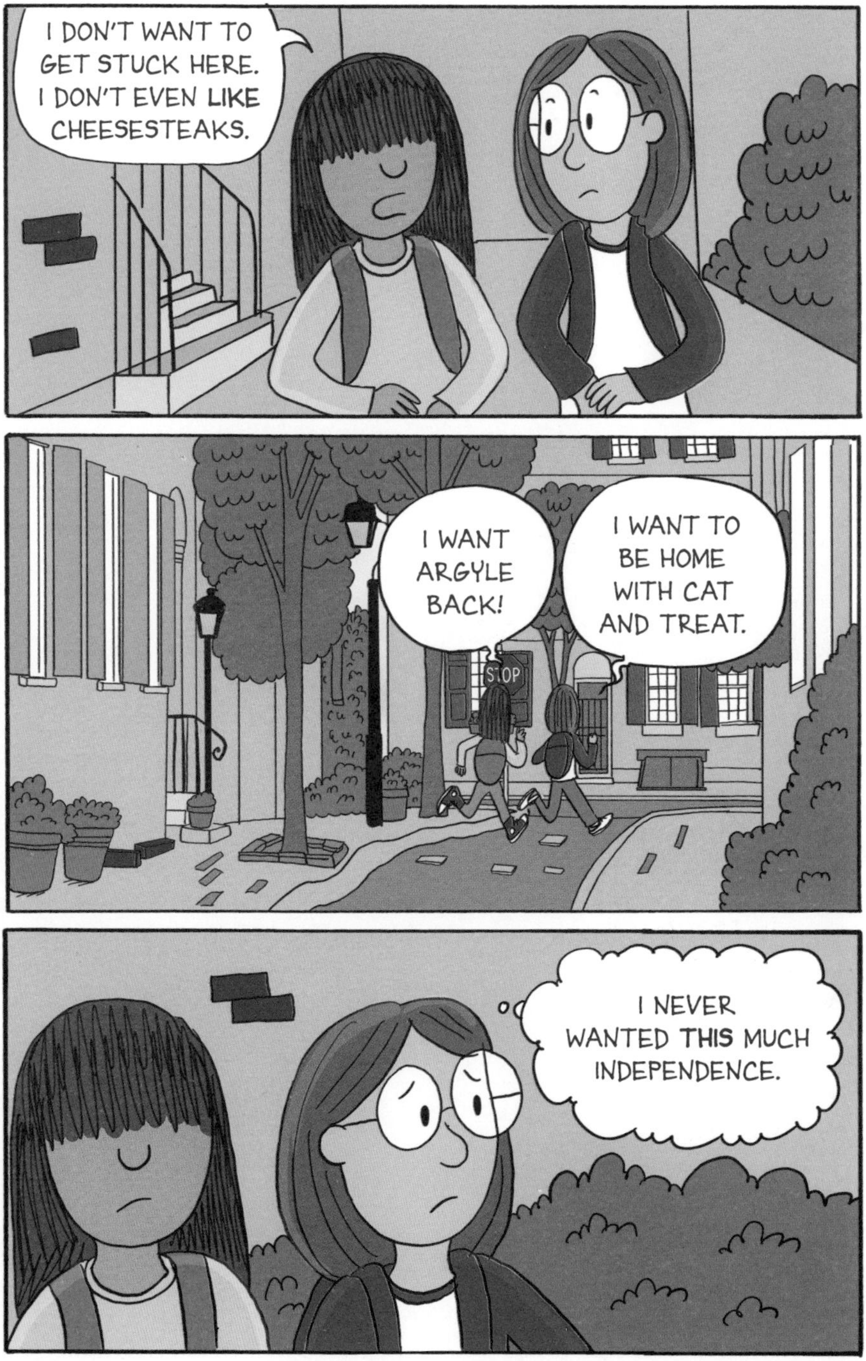
I DON'T WANT TO GET STUCK HERE. I DON'T EVEN **LIKE** CHEESESTEAKS.
I WANT ARGYLE BACK!
I WANT TO BE HOME WITH CAT AND TREAT.
STOP
I NEVER WANTED **THIS** MUCH INDEPENDENCE.

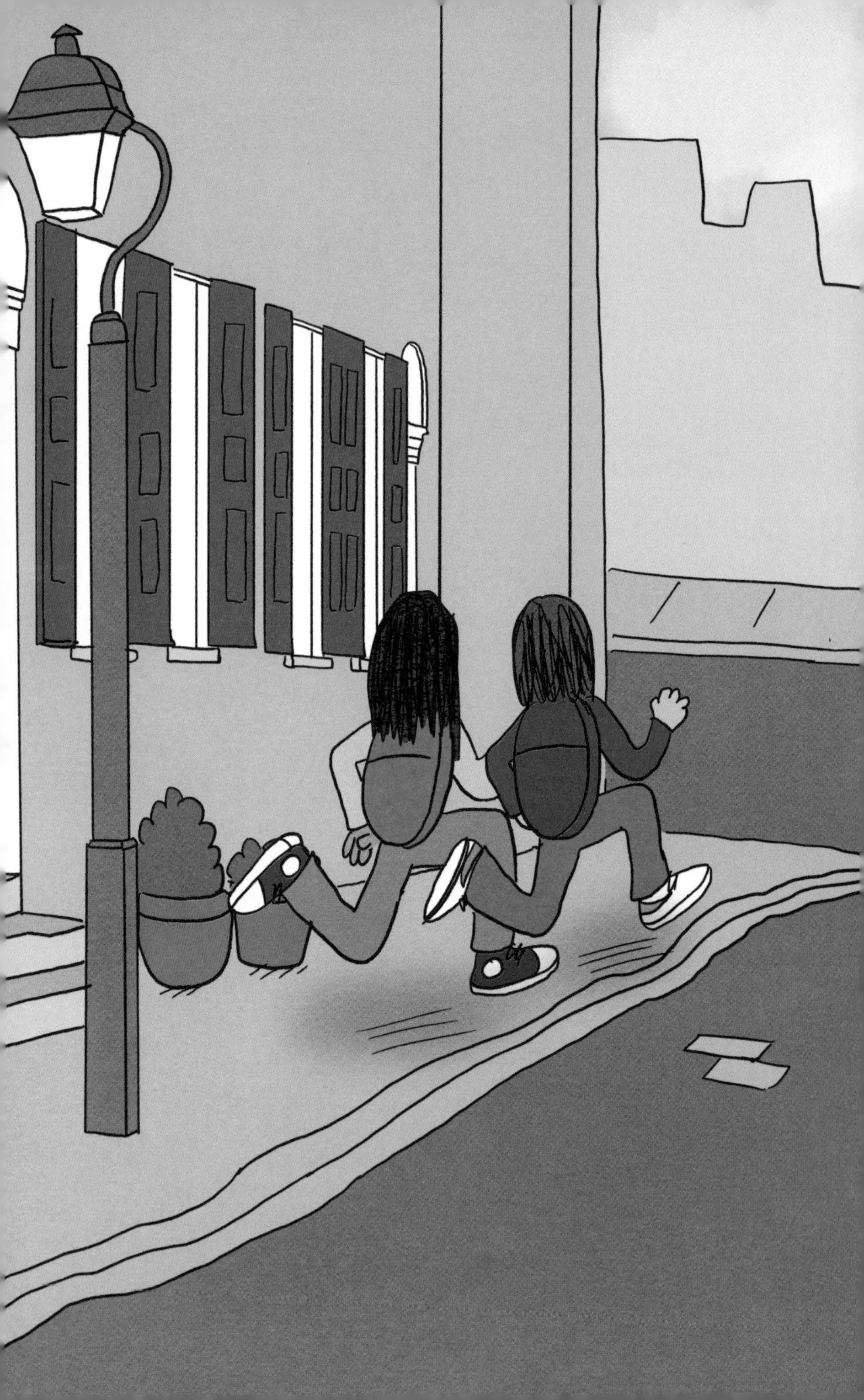

CHAPTER 11
LOST

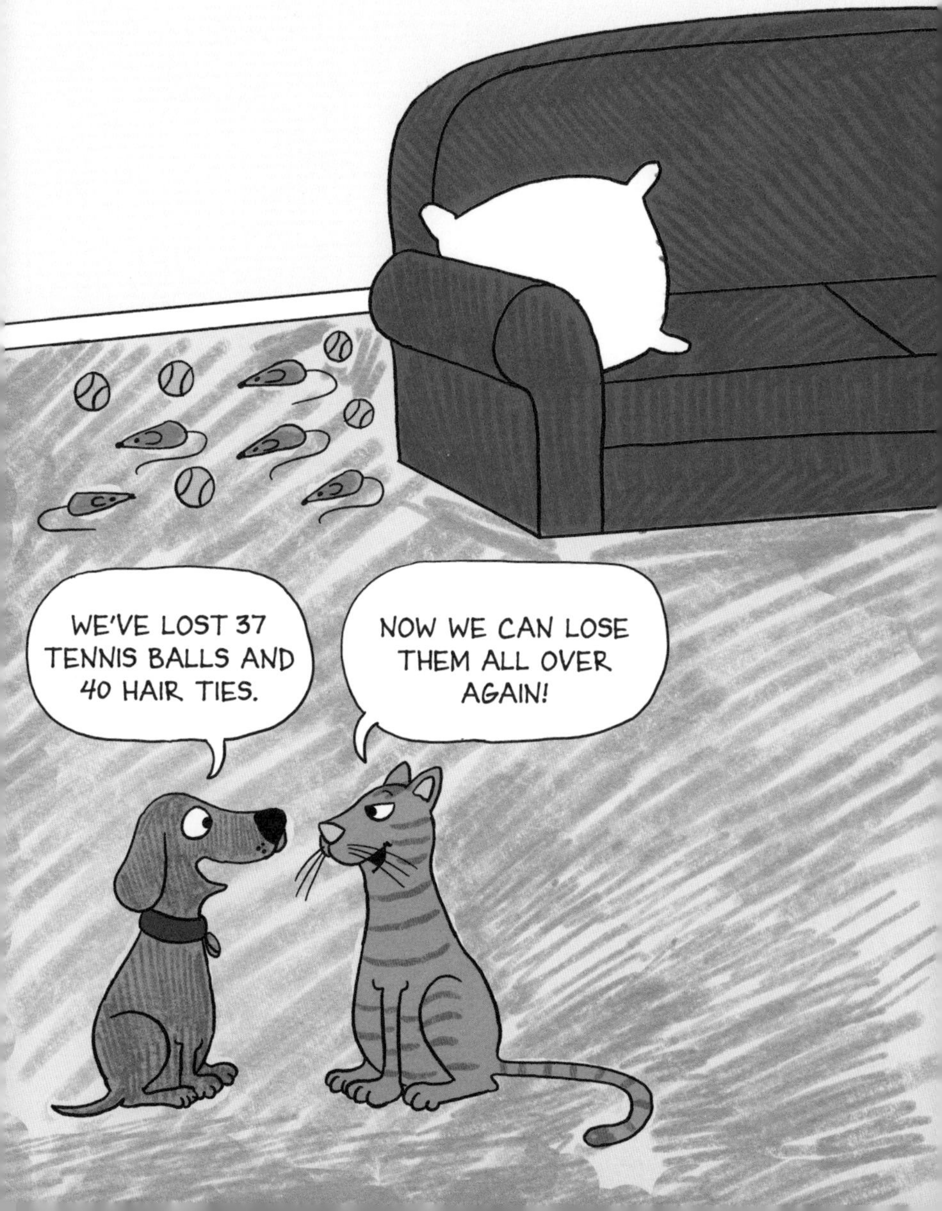
WE'VE LOST 37 TENNIS BALLS AND 40 HAIR TIES.
NOW WE CAN LOSE THEM ALL OVER AGAIN!

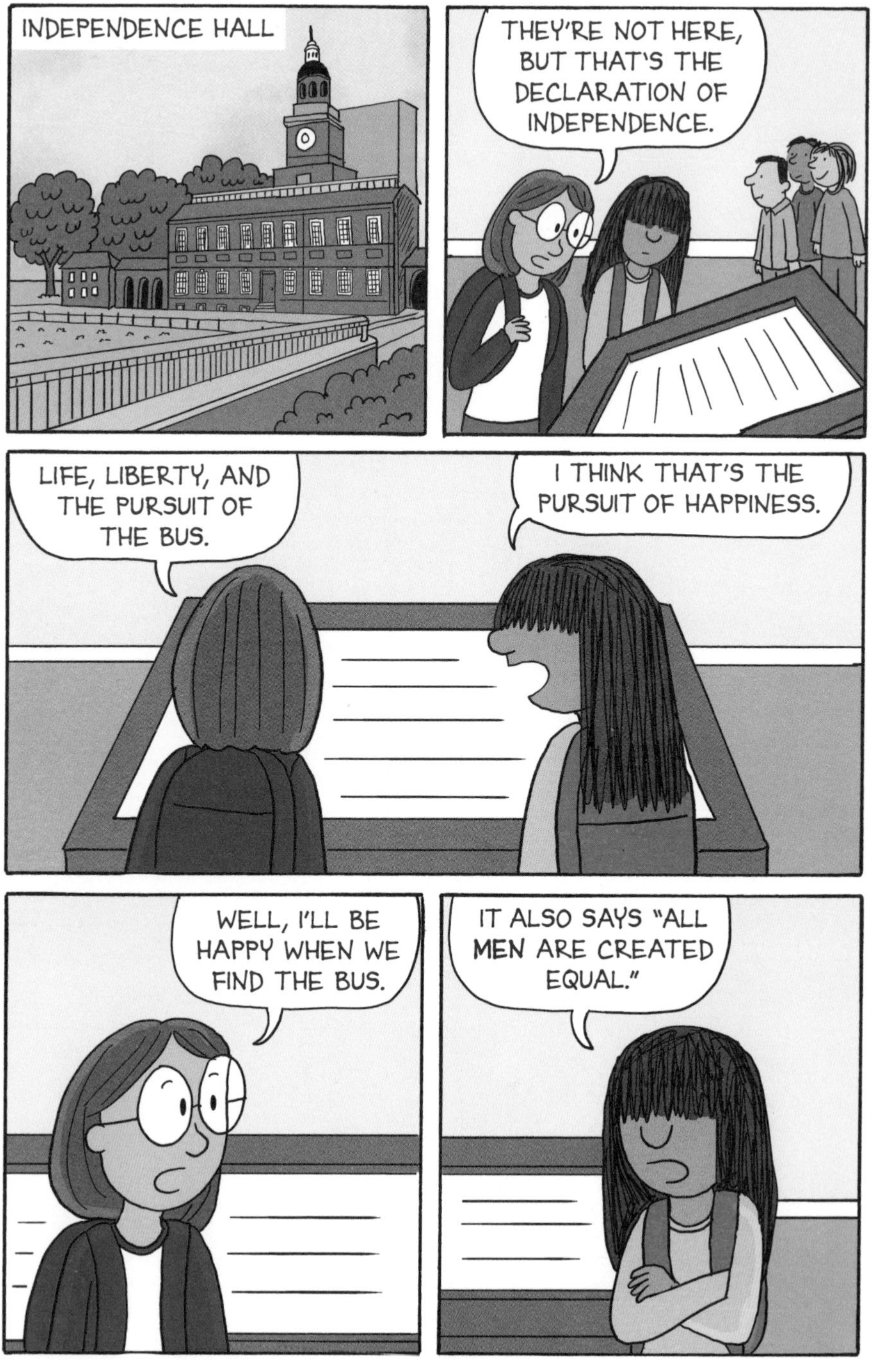
INDEPENDENCE HALL
THEY'RE NOT HERE, BUT THAT'S THE DECLARATION OF INDEPENDENCE.
LIFE, LIBERTY, AND THE PURSUIT OF THE BUS.
I THINK THAT'S THE PURSUIT OF HAPPINESS.
WELL, I'LL BE HAPPY WHEN WE FIND THE BUS.
IT ALSO SAYS "ALL MEN ARE CREATED EQUAL."

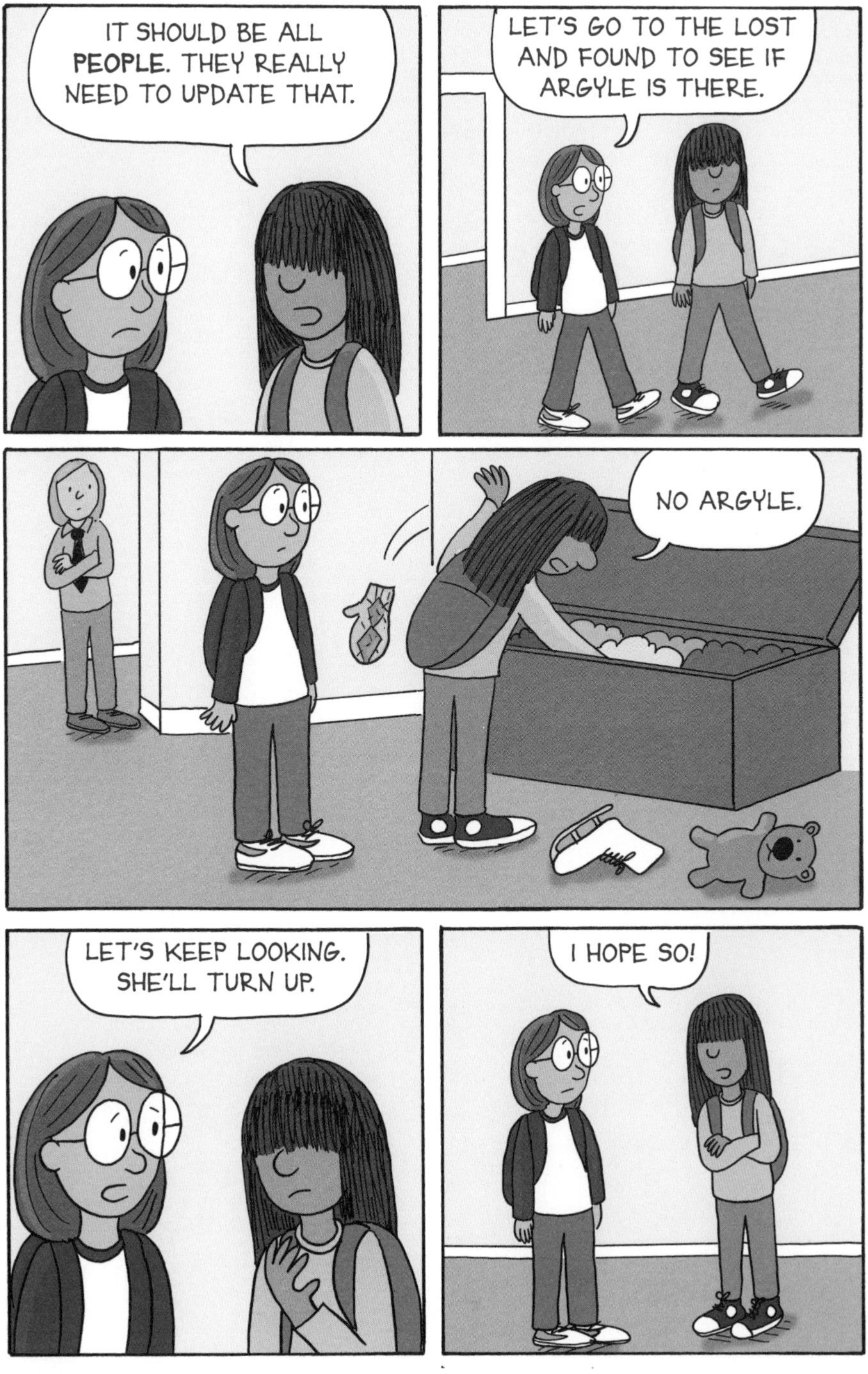
IT SHOULD BE ALL **PEOPLE**. THEY REALLY NEED TO UPDATE THAT.
LET'S GO TO THE LOST AND FOUND TO SEE IF ARGYLE IS THERE.
NO ARGYLE.
LET'S KEEP LOOKING. SHE'LL TURN UP.
I HOPE SO!

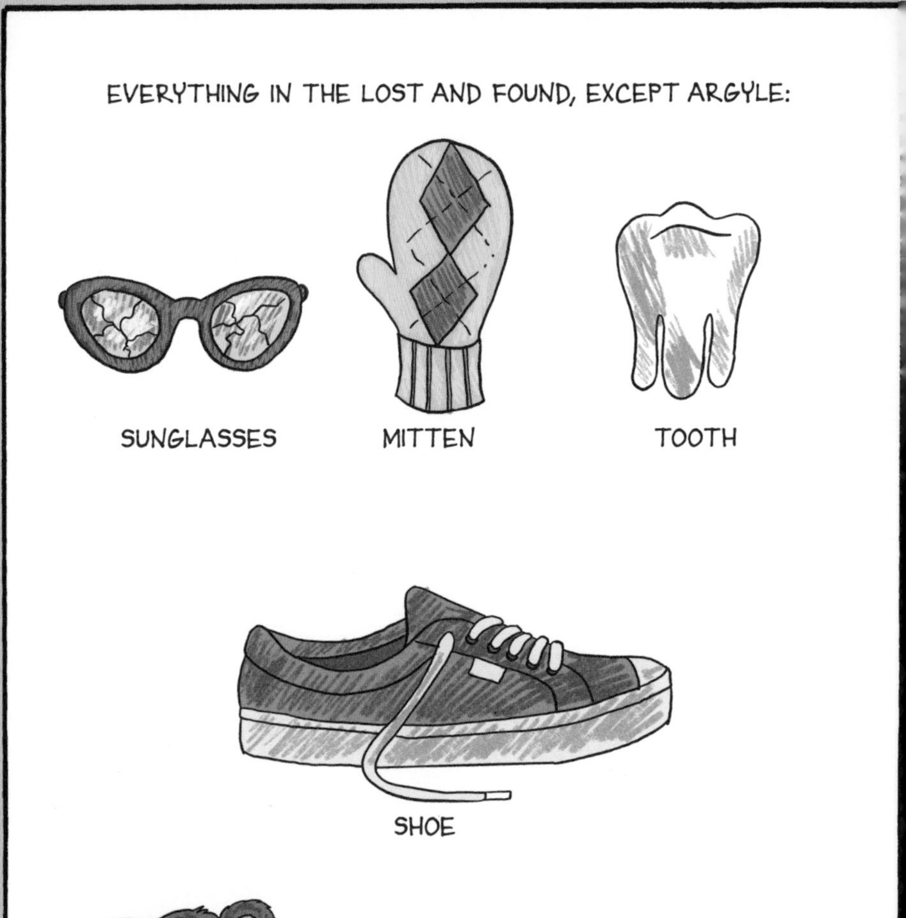

EVERYTHING IN THE LOST AND FOUND, EXCEPT ARGYLE:

SUNGLASSES

MITTEN

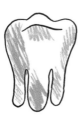
TOOTH

SHOE

TEDDY BEAR

ICE SKATE

SNORKELING GOGGLES

CAR KEYS

TROPHY

PIZZA COSTUME
(PERSON NOT INCLUDED)

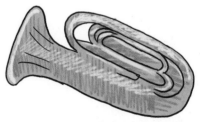

TUBA

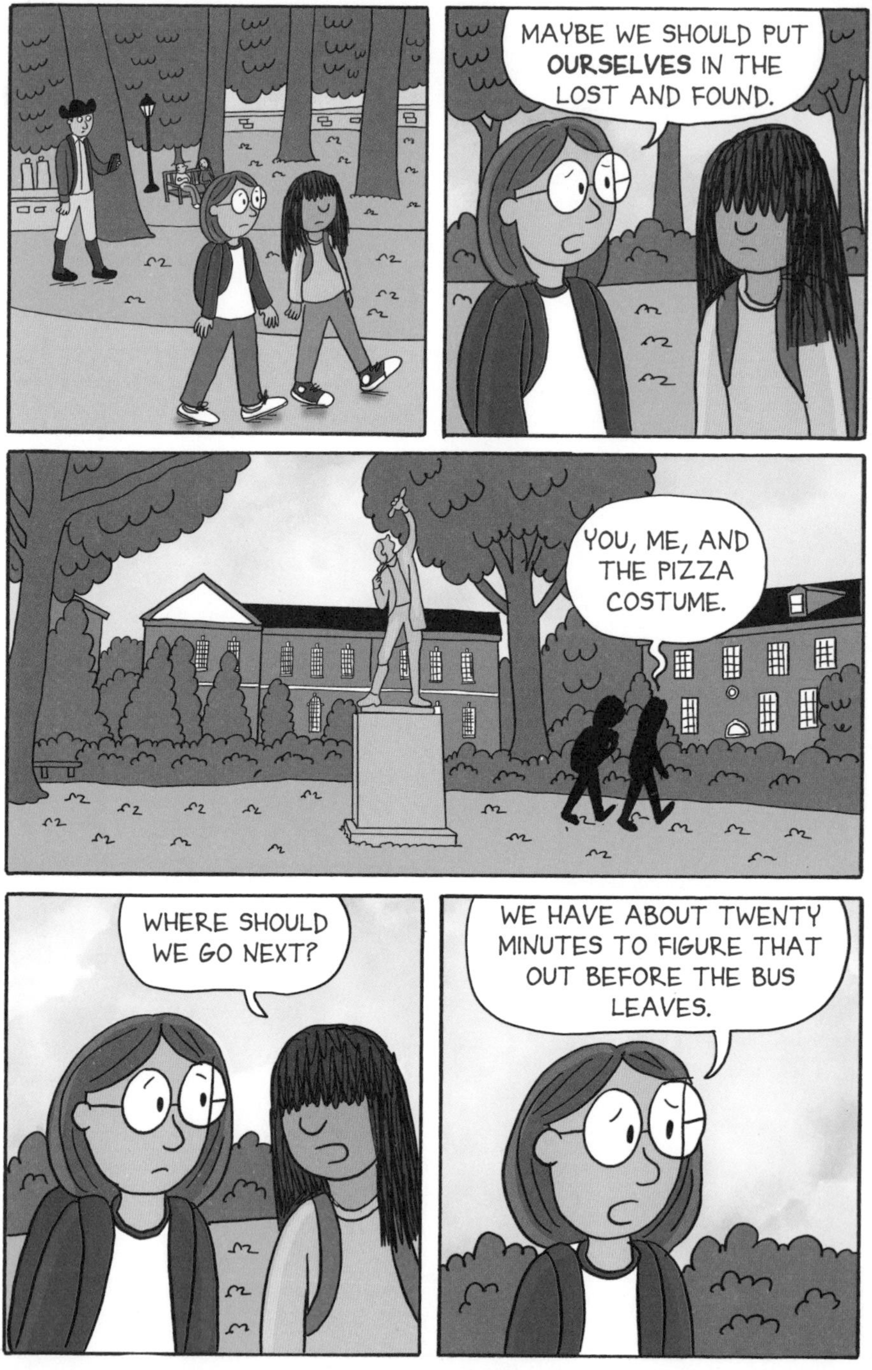
MAYBE WE SHOULD PUT **OURSELVES** IN THE LOST AND FOUND.
YOU, ME, AND THE PIZZA COSTUME.
WHERE SHOULD WE GO NEXT?
WE HAVE ABOUT TWENTY MINUTES TO FIGURE THAT OUT BEFORE THE BUS LEAVES.

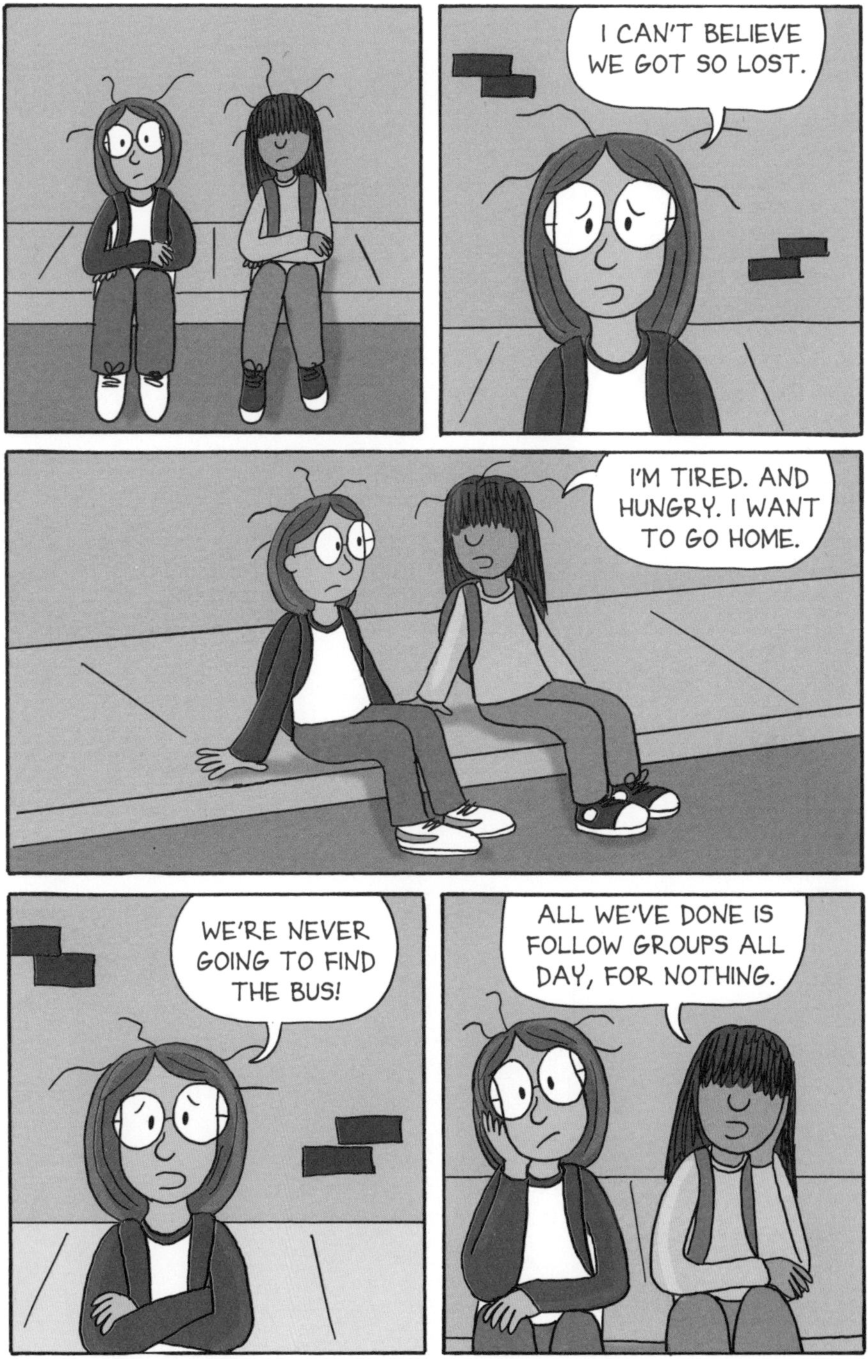
I CAN'T BELIEVE WE GOT SO LOST.
I'M TIRED. AND HUNGRY. I WANT TO GO HOME.
WE'RE NEVER GOING TO FIND THE BUS!
ALL WE'VE DONE IS FOLLOW GROUPS ALL DAY, FOR NOTHING.

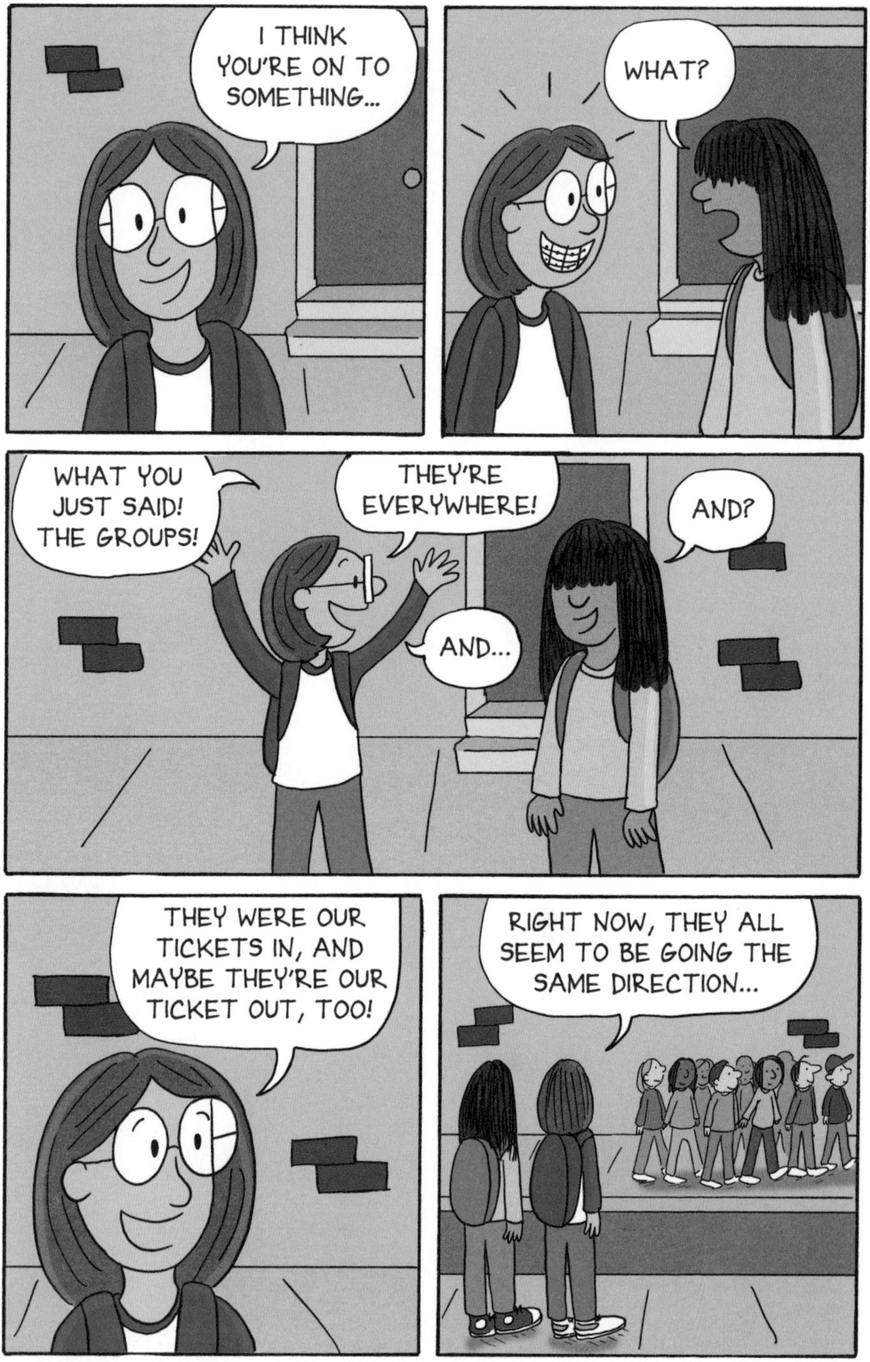
I THINK YOU'RE ON TO SOMETHING...
WHAT?
WHAT YOU JUST SAID! THE GROUPS!
THEY'RE EVERYWHERE!
AND?
AND...
THEY WERE OUR TICKETS IN, AND MAYBE THEY'RE OUR TICKET OUT, TOO!
RIGHT NOW, THEY ALL SEEM TO BE GOING THE SAME DIRECTION...

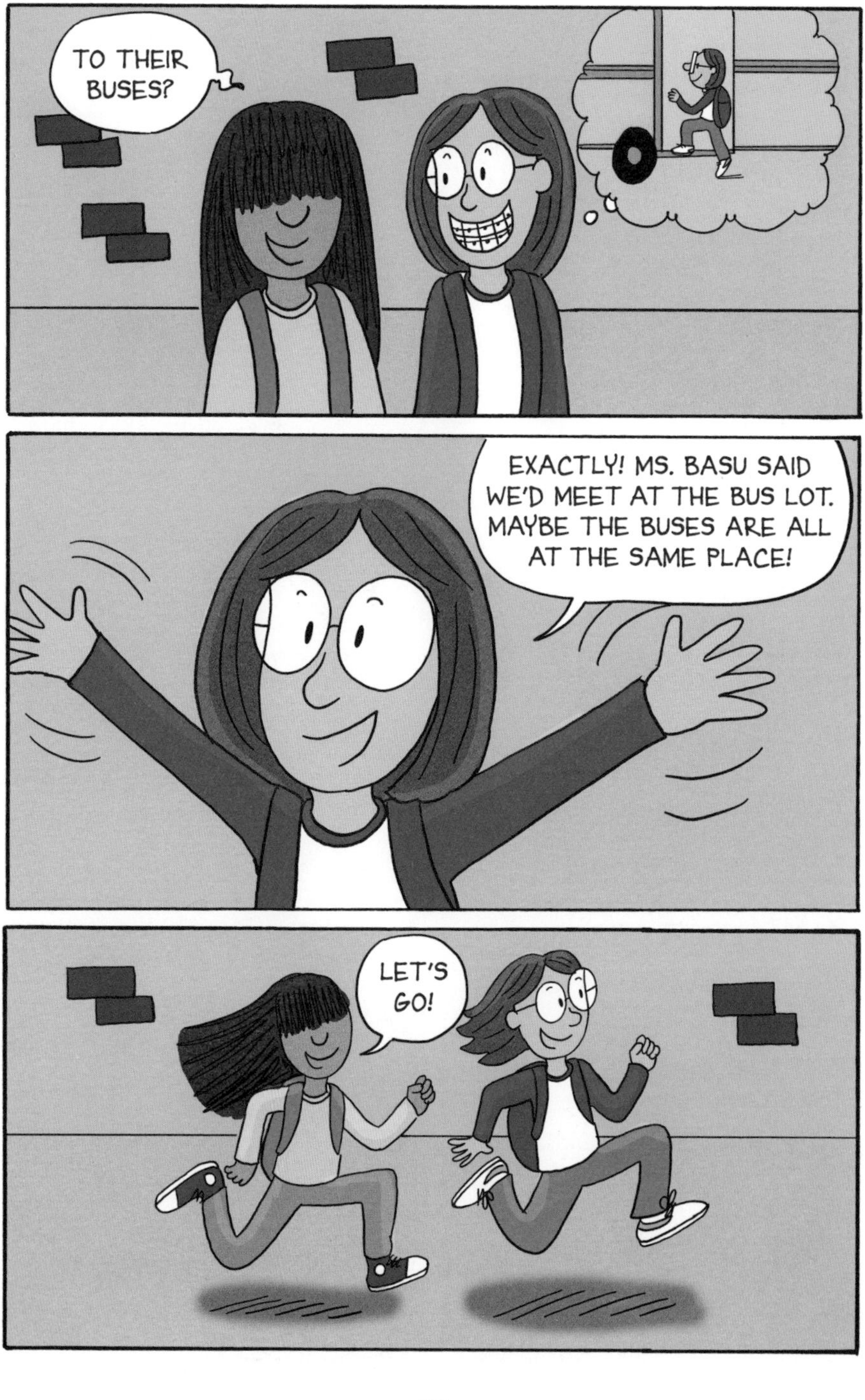
TO THEIR BUSES?
EXACTLY! MS. BASU SAID WE'D MEET AT THE BUS LOT. MAYBE THE BUSES ARE ALL AT THE SAME PLACE!
LET'S GO!

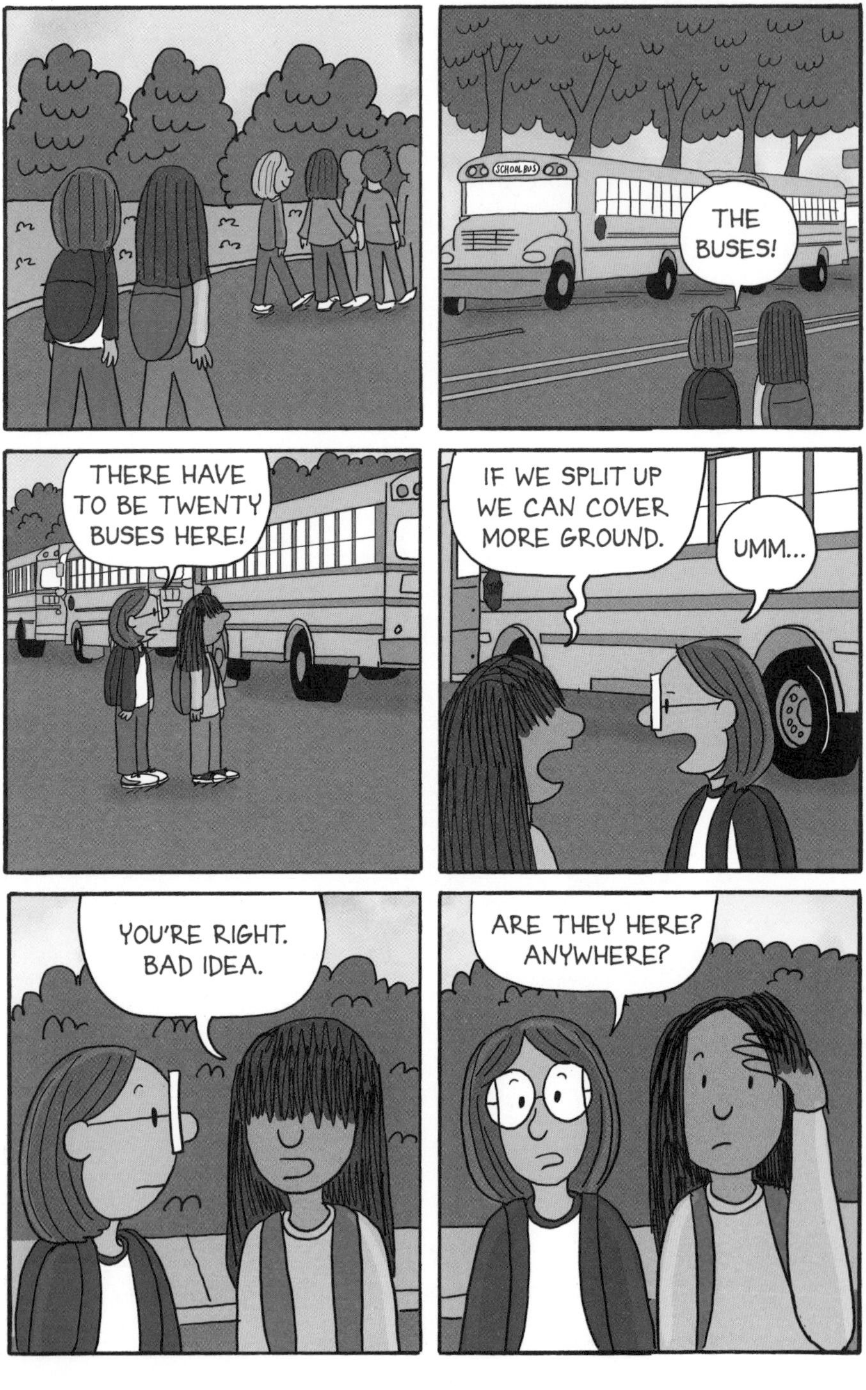
SCHOOL BUS
THE BUSES!
THERE HAVE TO BE TWENTY BUSES HERE!
IF WE SPLIT UP WE CAN COVER MORE GROUND.
UMM...
YOU'RE RIGHT. BAD IDEA.
ARE THEY HERE? ANYWHERE?

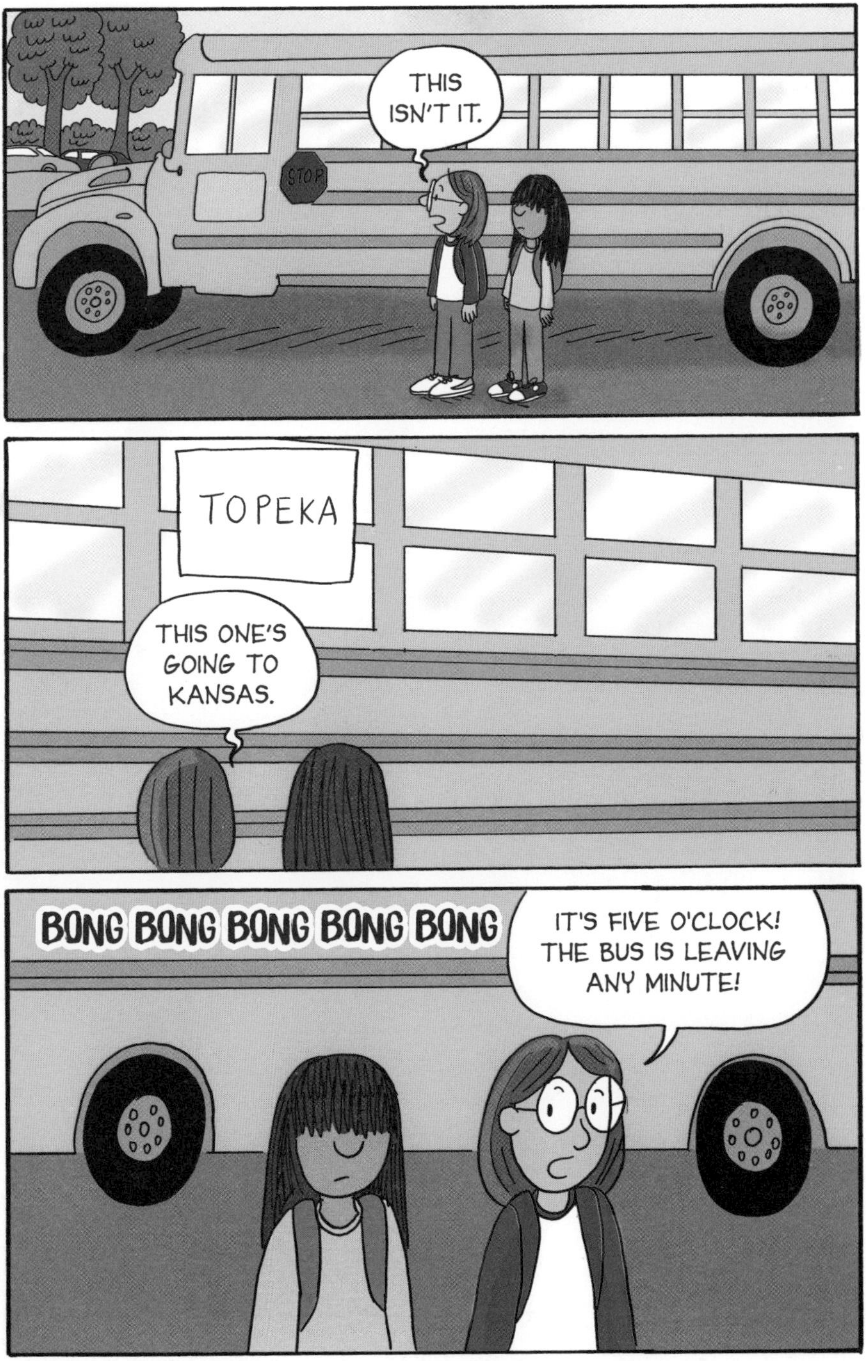
THIS ISN'T IT.
STOP
TOPEKA
THIS ONE'S GOING TO KANSAS.
BONG BONG BONG BONG BONG
IT'S FIVE O'CLOCK! THE BUS IS LEAVING ANY MINUTE!

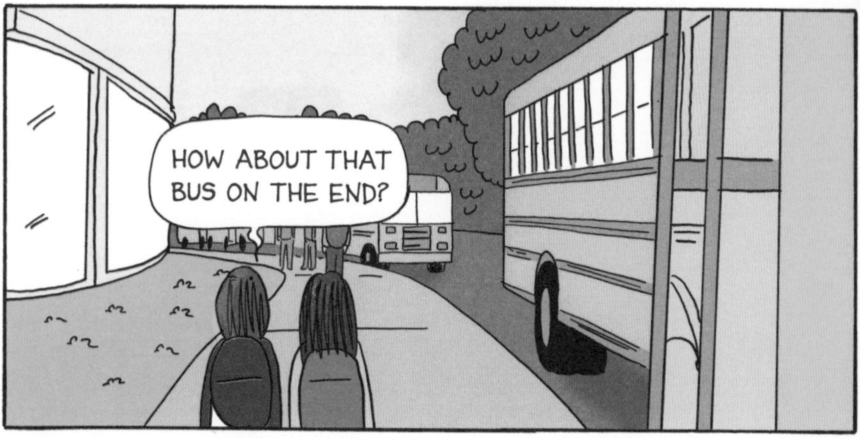
HOW ABOUT THAT BUS ON THE END?

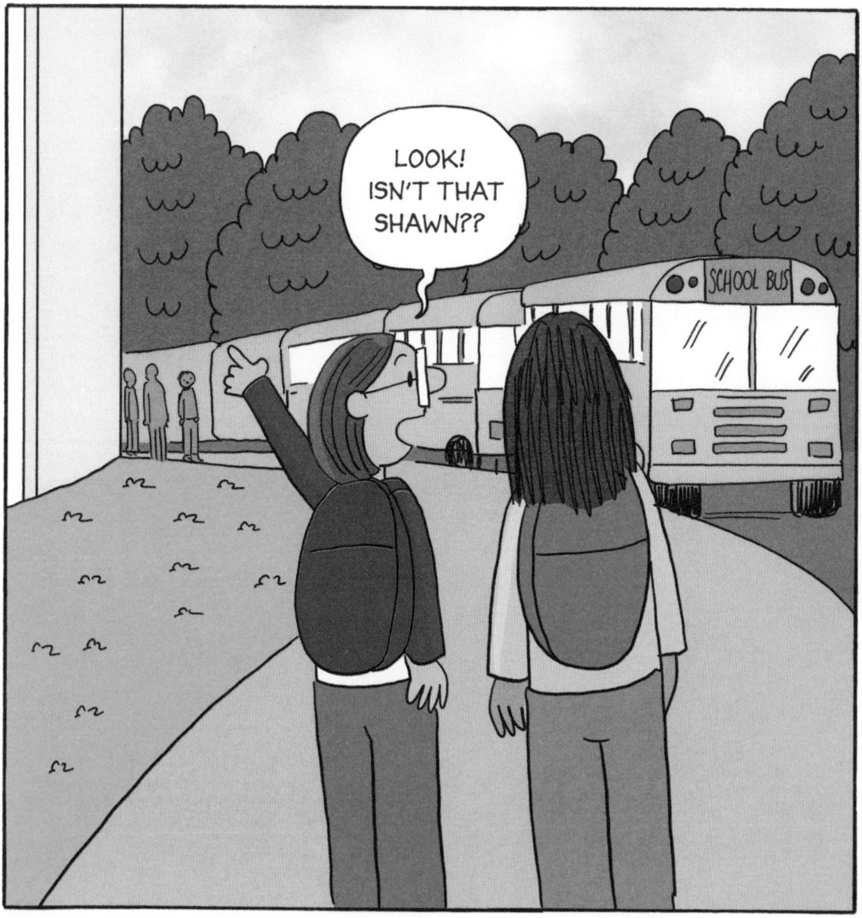
LOOK! ISN'T THAT SHAWN??
SCHOOL BUS

CHAPTER 12
FOUND

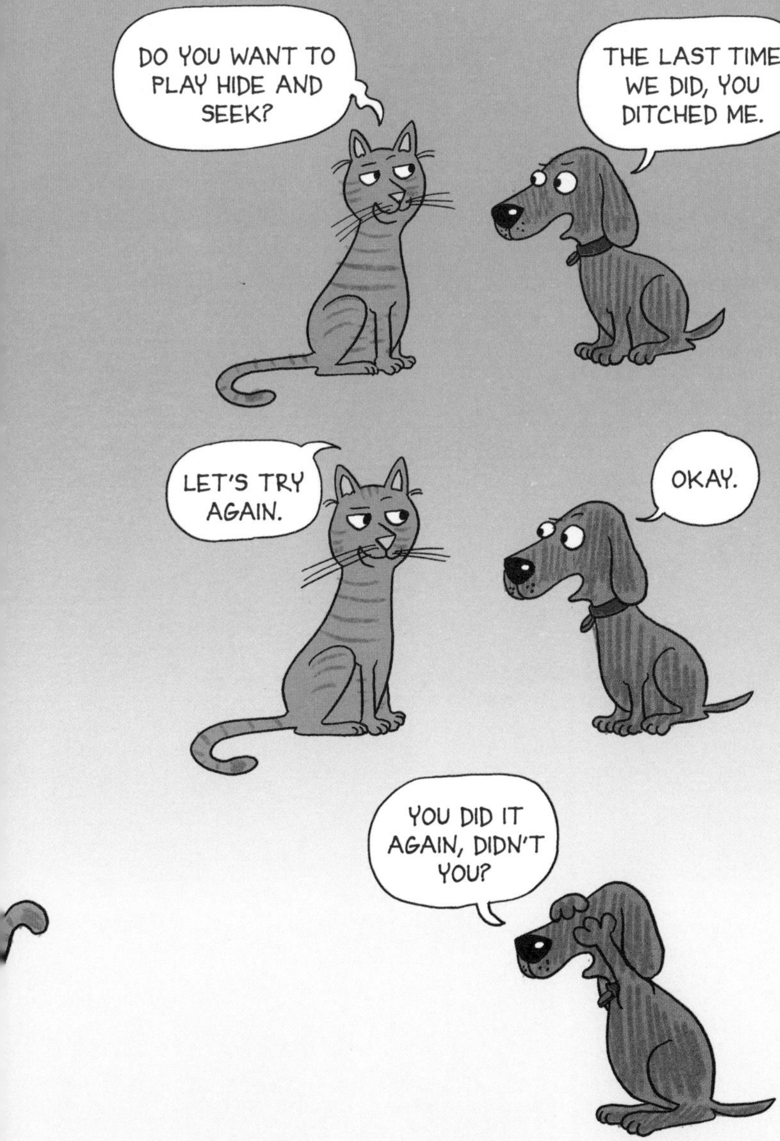
DO YOU WANT TO PLAY HIDE AND SEEK?
THE LAST TIME WE DID, YOU DITCHED ME.
LET'S TRY AGAIN.
OKAY.
YOU DID IT AGAIN, DIDN'T YOU?

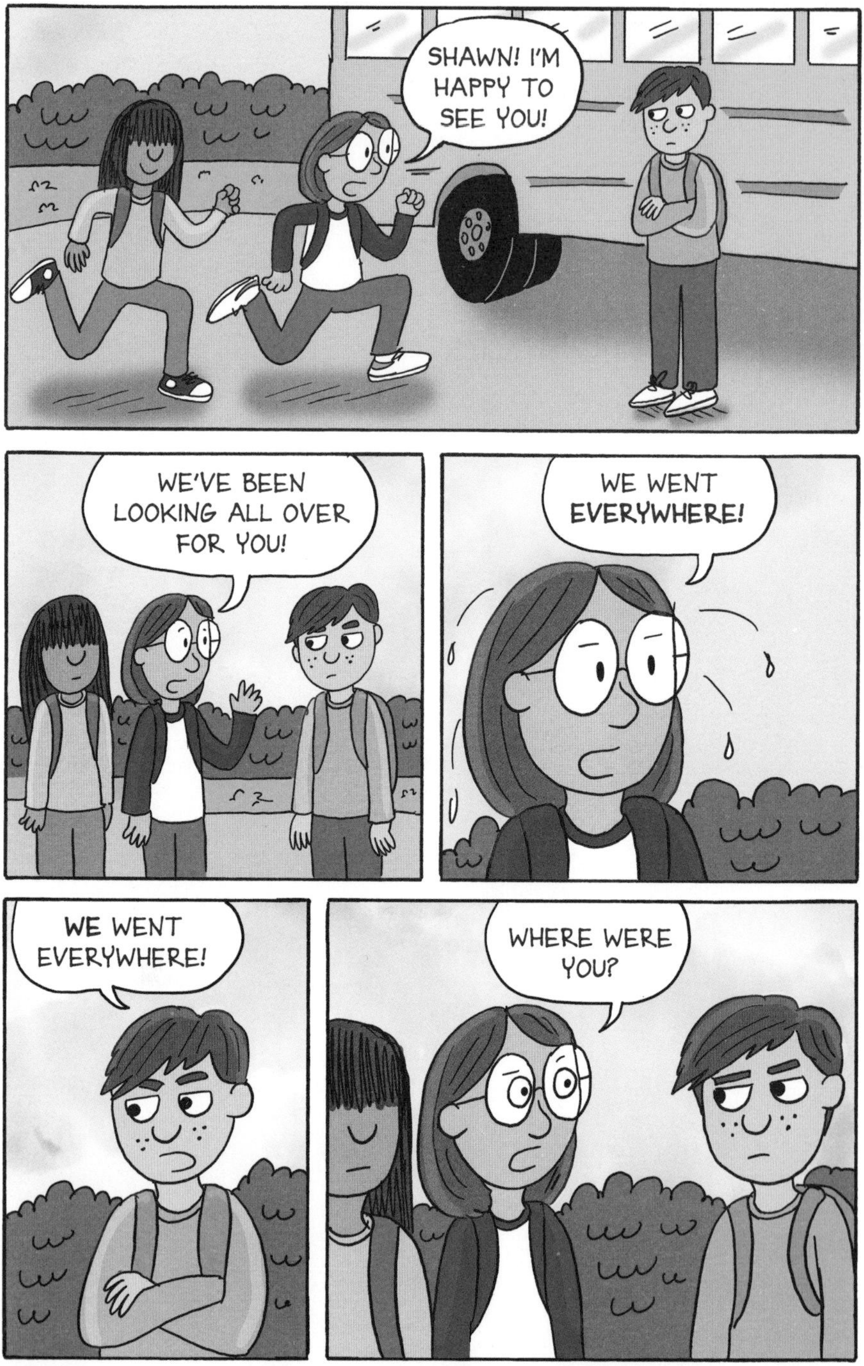
SHAWN! I'M HAPPY TO SEE YOU!
WE'VE BEEN LOOKING ALL OVER FOR YOU!
WE WENT EVERYWHERE!
WE WENT EVERYWHERE!
WHERE WERE YOU?

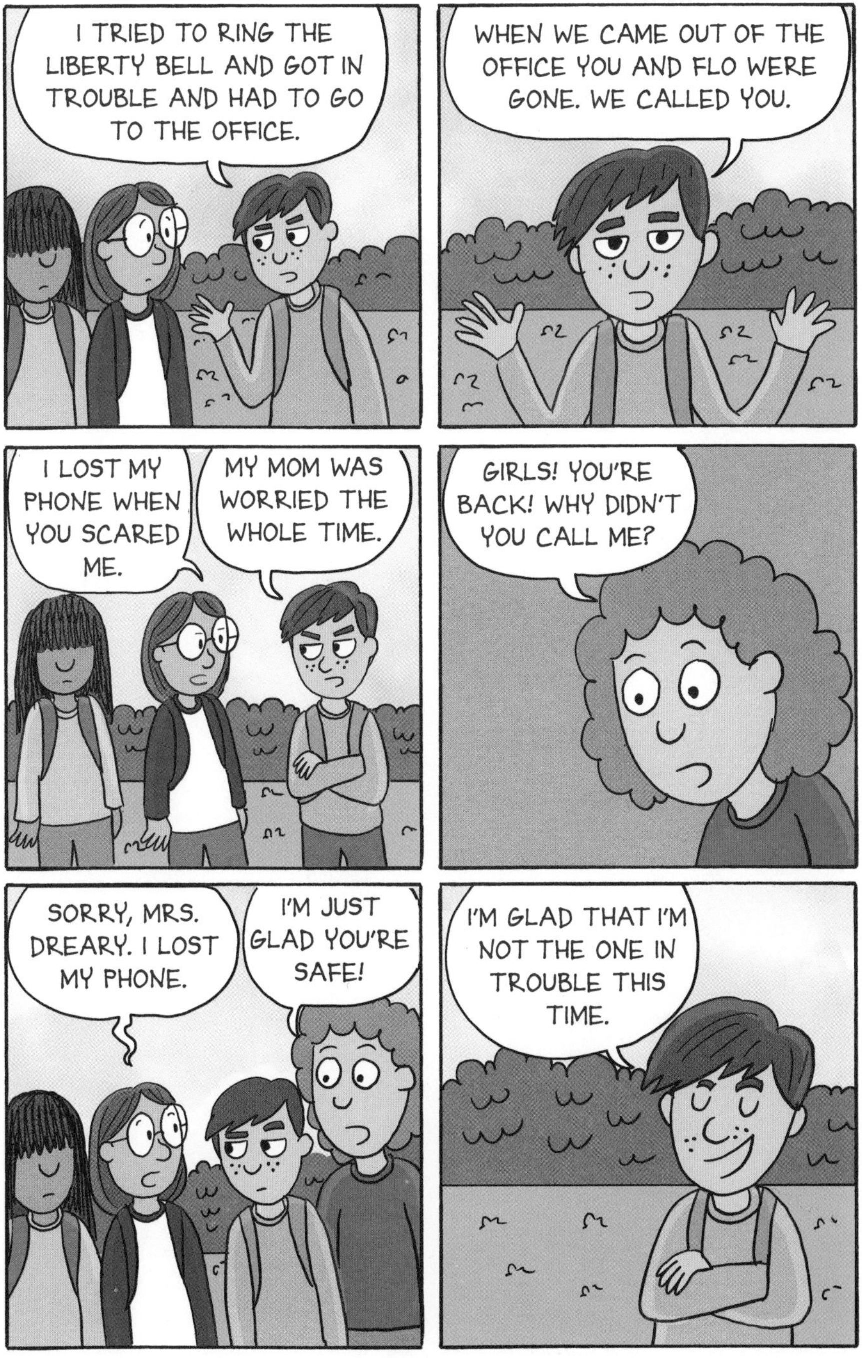
I TRIED TO RING THE LIBERTY BELL AND GOT IN TROUBLE AND HAD TO GO TO THE OFFICE.
WHEN WE CAME OUT OF THE OFFICE YOU AND FLO WERE GONE. WE CALLED YOU.
I LOST MY PHONE WHEN YOU SCARED ME.
MY MOM WAS WORRIED THE WHOLE TIME.
GIRLS! YOU'RE BACK! WHY DIDN'T YOU CALL ME?
SORRY, MRS. DREARY. I LOST MY PHONE.
I'M JUST GLAD YOU'RE SAFE!
I'M GLAD THAT I'M NOT THE ONE IN TROUBLE THIS TIME.

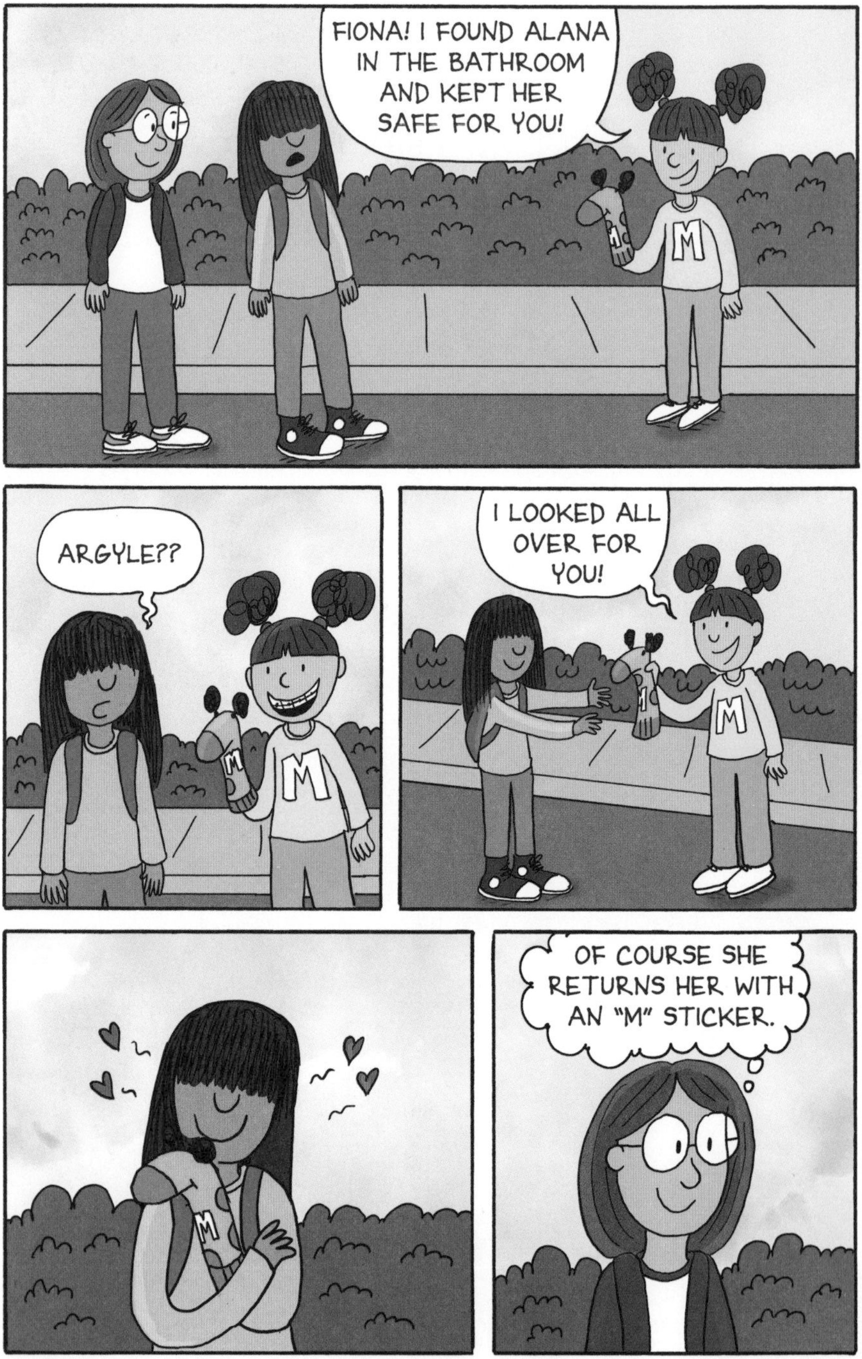
FIONA! I FOUND ALANA IN THE BATHROOM AND KEPT HER SAFE FOR YOU!
ARGYLE??
I LOOKED ALL OVER FOR YOU!
OF COURSE SHE RETURNS HER WITH AN "M" STICKER.

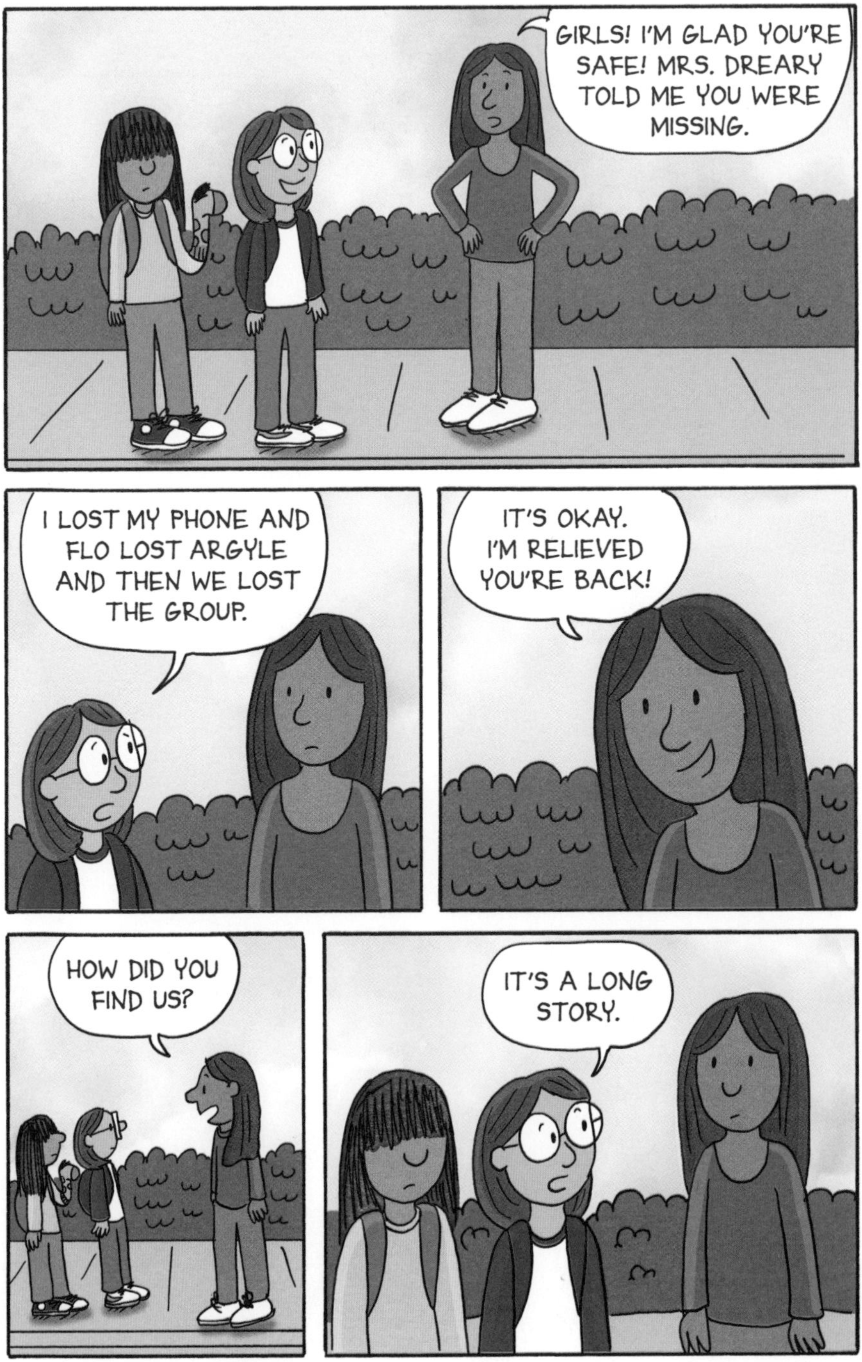
GIRLS! I'M GLAD YOU'RE SAFE! MRS. DREARY TOLD ME YOU WERE MISSING.
I LOST MY PHONE AND FLO LOST ARGYLE AND THEN WE LOST THE GROUP.
IT'S OKAY. I'M RELIEVED YOU'RE BACK!
HOW DID YOU FIND US?
IT'S A LONG STORY.

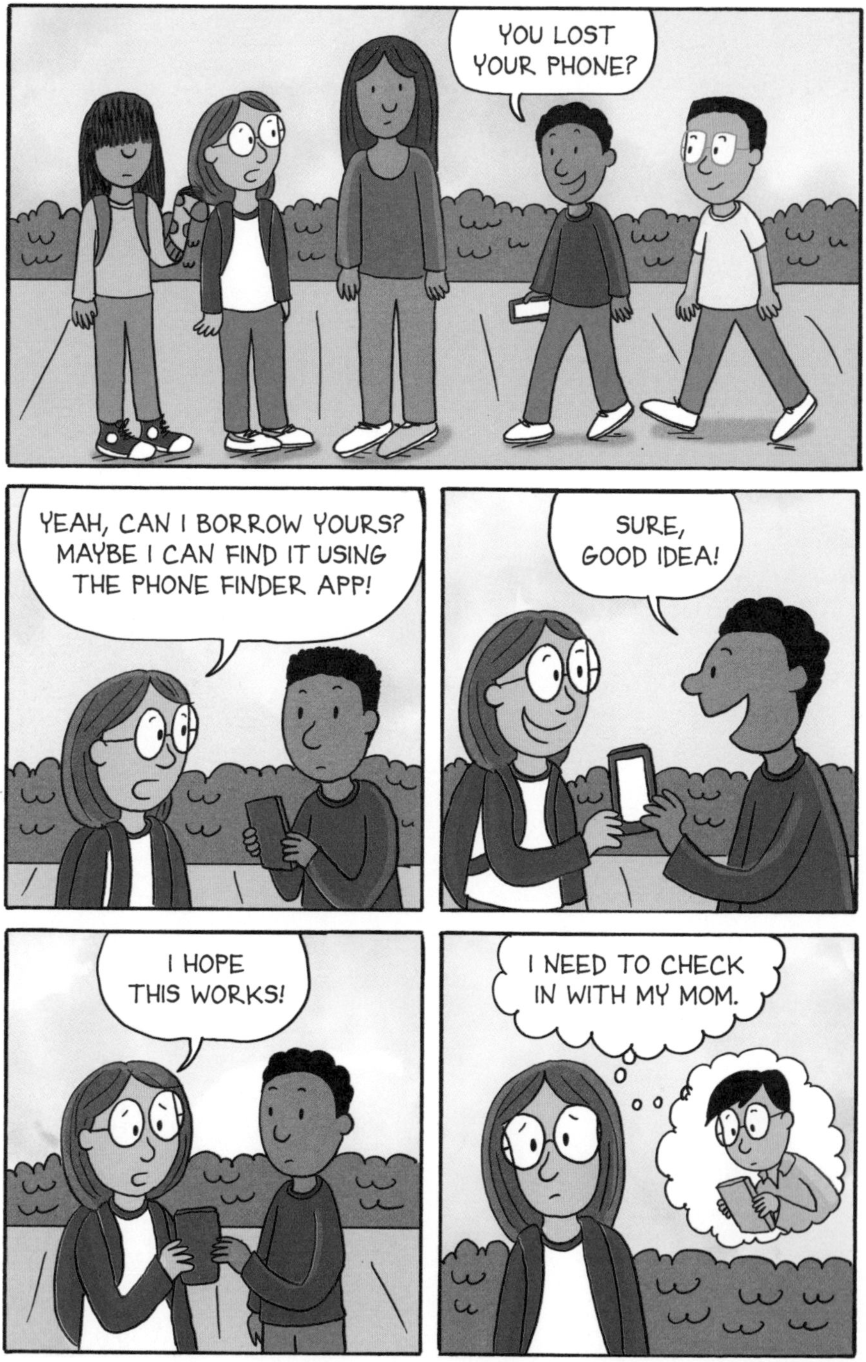
YOU LOST YOUR PHONE?
YEAH, CAN I BORROW YOURS? MAYBE I CAN FIND IT USING THE PHONE FINDER APP!
SURE, GOOD IDEA!
I HOPE THIS WORKS!
I NEED TO CHECK IN WITH MY MOM.

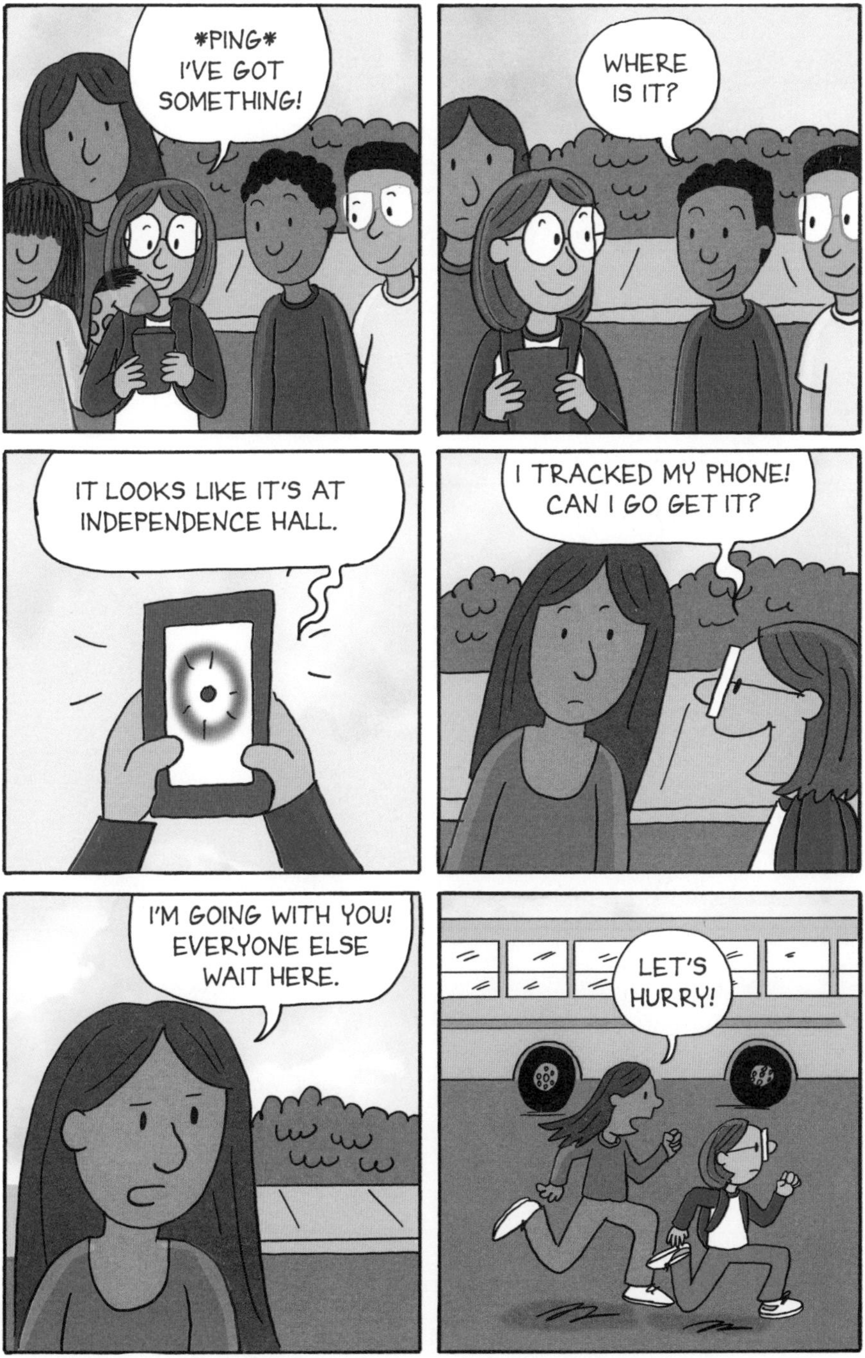
PING
I'VE GOT SOMETHING!
WHERE IS IT?
IT LOOKS LIKE IT'S AT INDEPENDENCE HALL.
I TRACKED MY PHONE! CAN I GO GET IT?
I'M GOING WITH YOU! EVERYONE ELSE WAIT HERE.
LET'S HURRY!

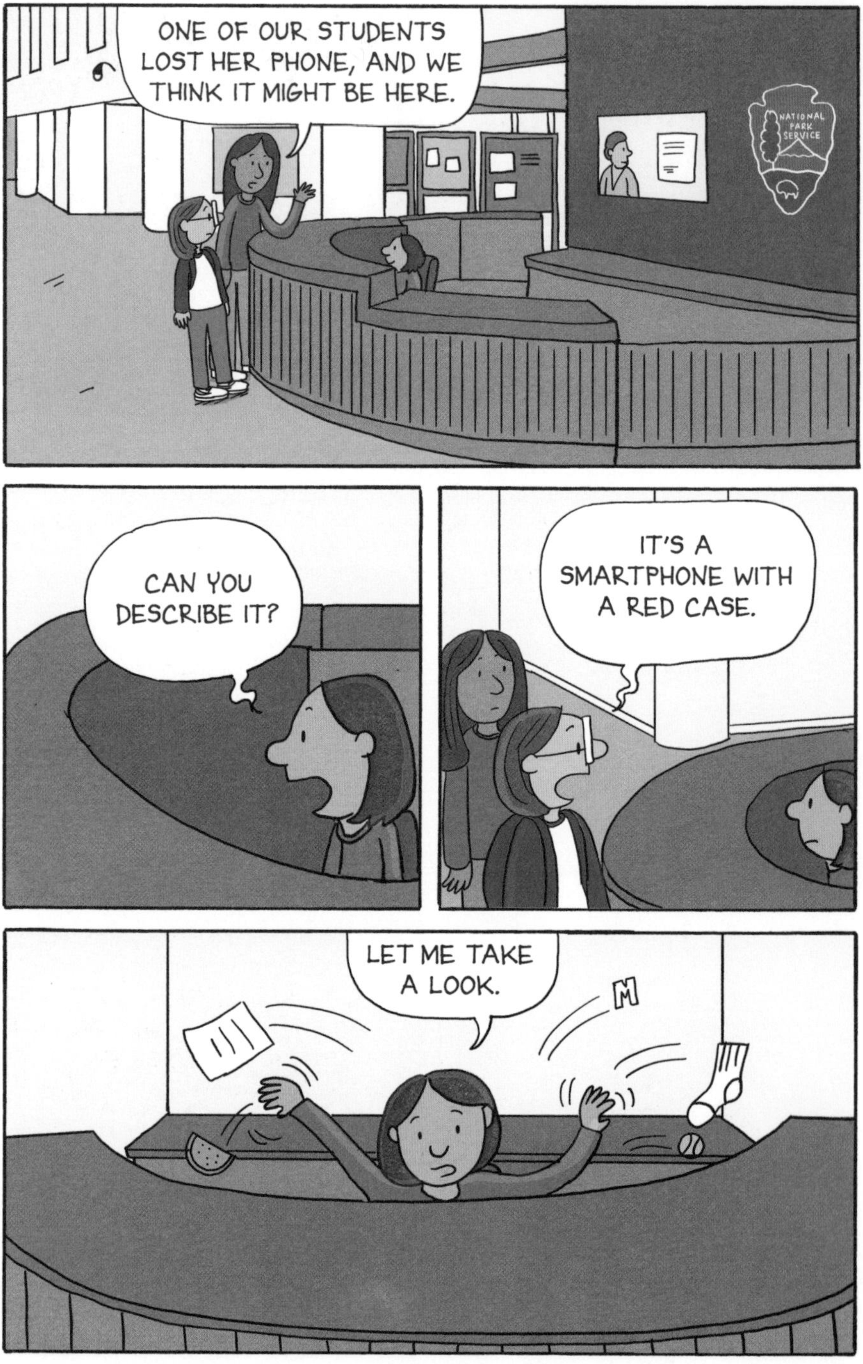
ONE OF OUR STUDENTS LOST HER PHONE, AND WE THINK IT MIGHT BE HERE.
NATIONAL PARK SERVICE
CAN YOU DESCRIBE IT?
IT'S A SMARTPHONE WITH A RED CASE.
LET ME TAKE A LOOK.
M

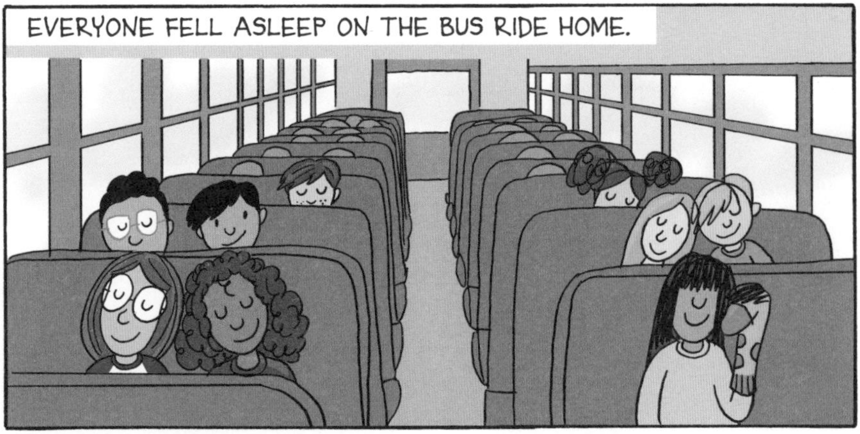
EVERYONE FELL ASLEEP ON THE BUS RIDE HOME.

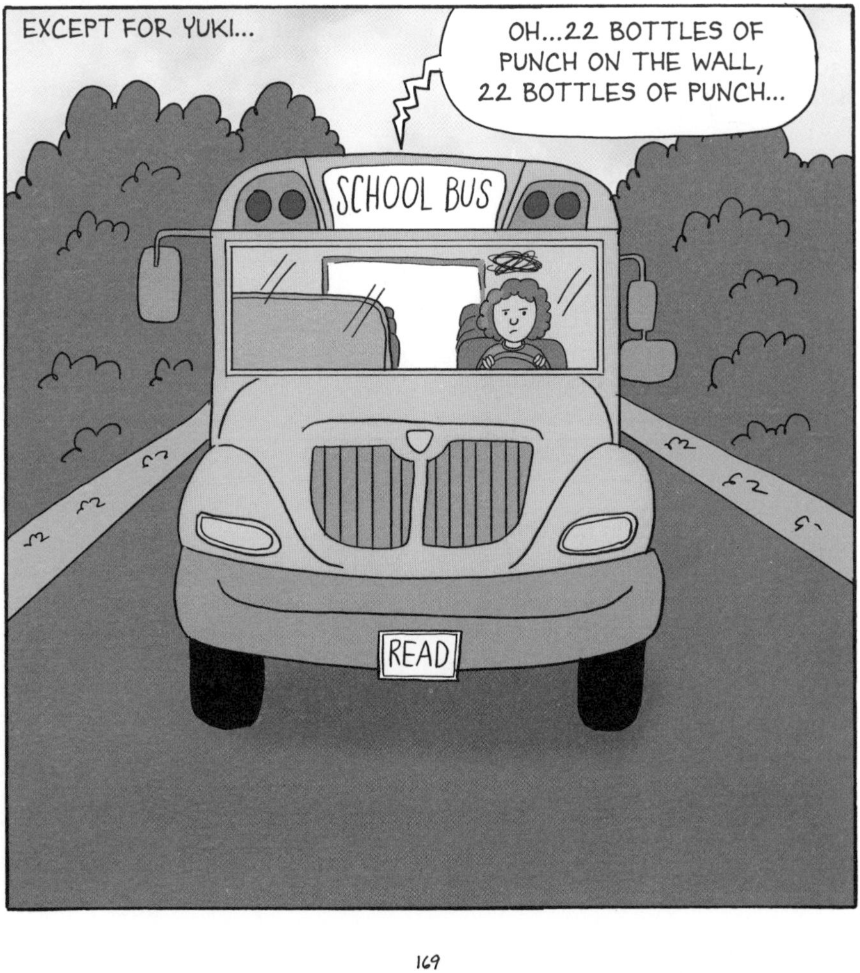
EXCEPT FOR YUKI...
OH...22 BOTTLES OF PUNCH ON THE WALL, 22 BOTTLES OF PUNCH...
SCHOOL BUS
READ

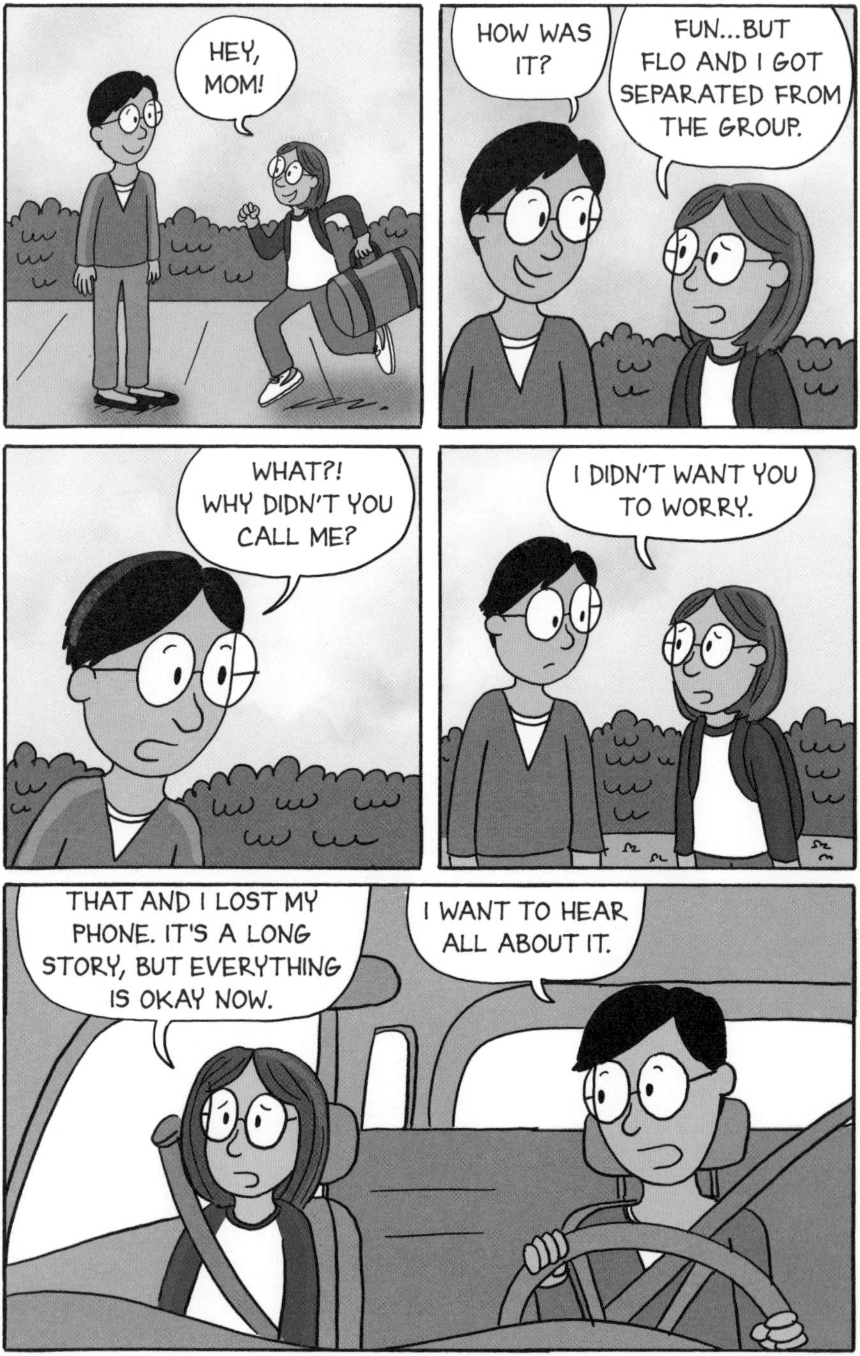
HEY, MOM!
HOW WAS IT?
FUN...BUT FLO AND I GOT SEPARATED FROM THE GROUP.
WHAT?! WHY DIDN'T YOU CALL ME?
I DIDN'T WANT YOU TO WORRY.
THAT AND I LOST MY PHONE. IT'S A LONG STORY, BUT EVERYTHING IS OKAY NOW.
I WANT TO HEAR ALL ABOUT IT.

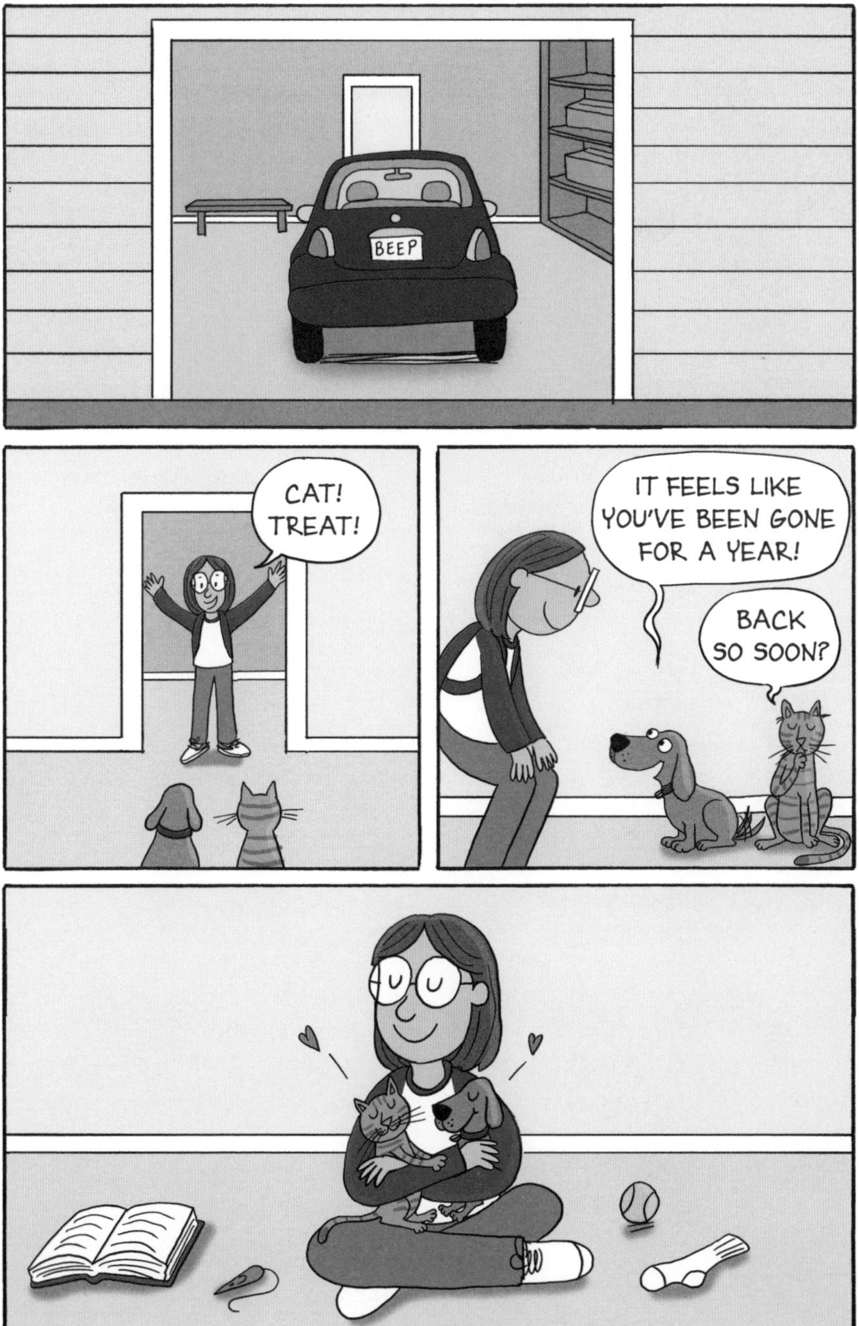
BEEP
CAT! TREAT!
IT FEELS LIKE YOU'VE BEEN GONE FOR A YEAR!
BACK SO SOON?

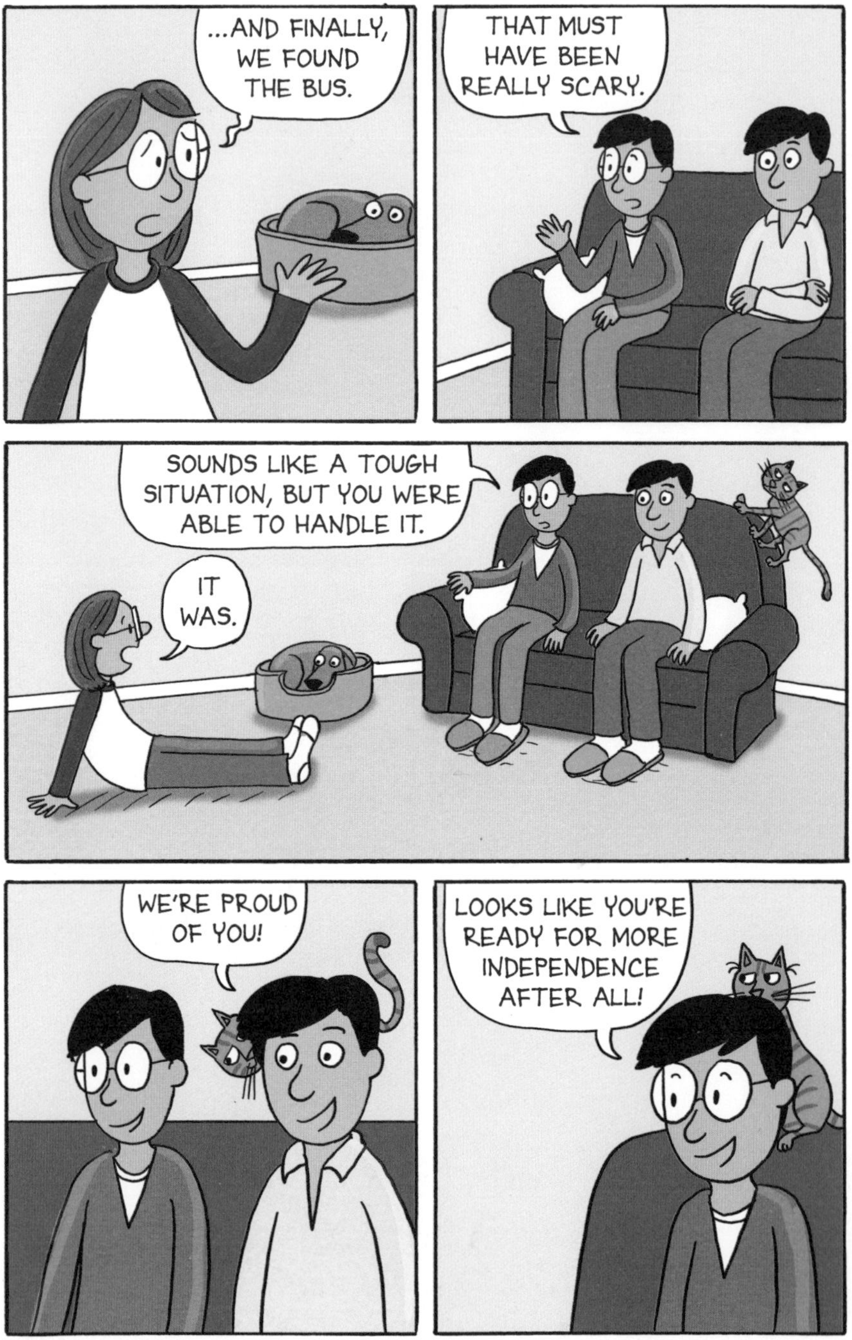
...AND FINALLY, WE FOUND THE BUS.
THAT MUST HAVE BEEN REALLY SCARY.
SOUNDS LIKE A TOUGH SITUATION, BUT YOU WERE ABLE TO HANDLE IT.
IT WAS.
WE'RE PROUD OF YOU!
LOOKS LIKE YOU'RE READY FOR MORE INDEPENDENCE AFTER ALL!

CHAPTER 13
SCAVENGER HUNT

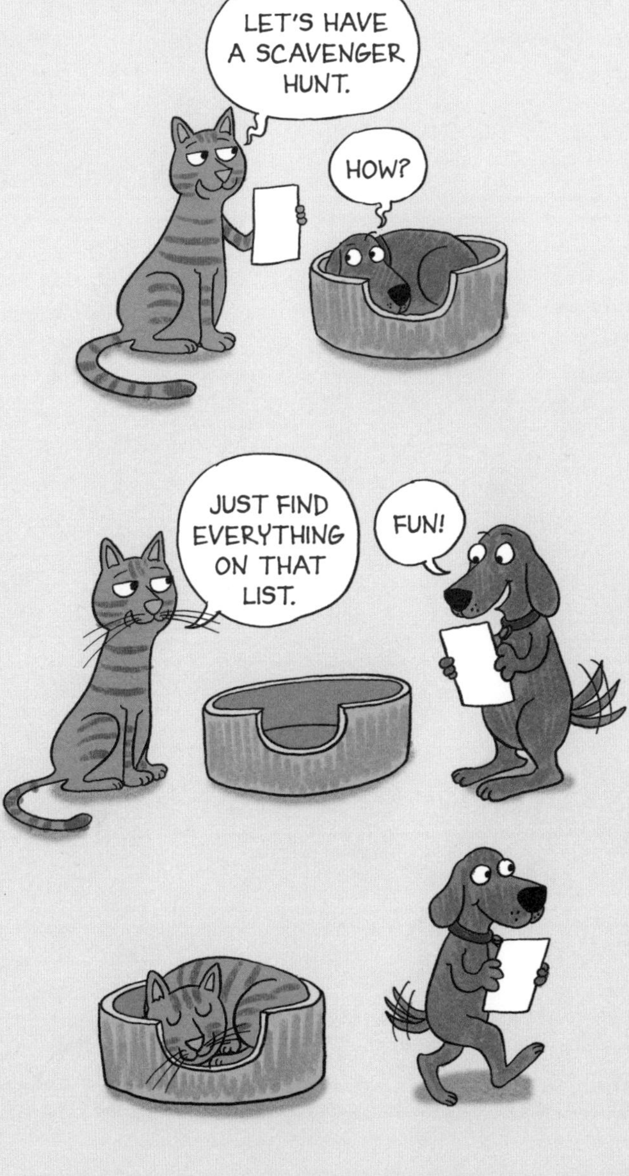

LET'S HAVE A SCAVENGER HUNT.
HOW?
JUST FIND EVERYTHING ON THAT LIST.
FUN!

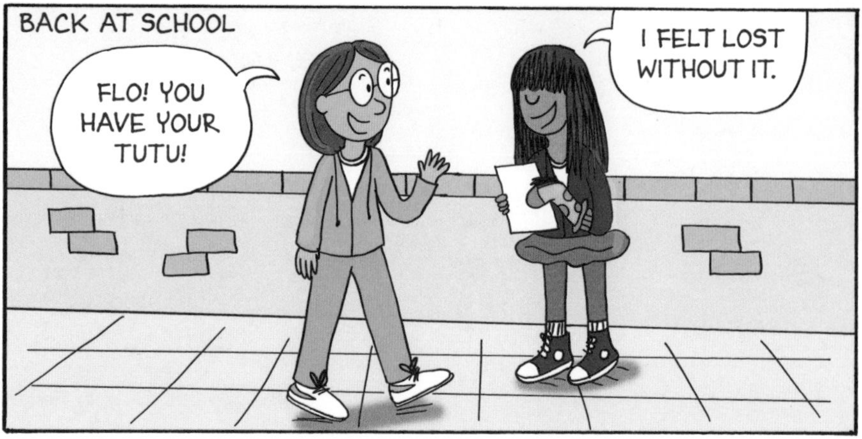
BACK AT SCHOOL
FLO! YOU HAVE YOUR TUTU!
I FELT LOST WITHOUT IT.

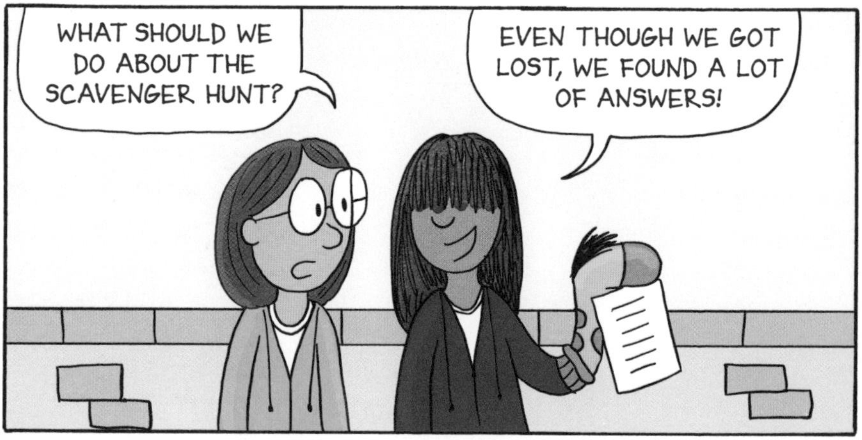
WHAT SHOULD WE DO ABOUT THE SCAVENGER HUNT?
EVEN THOUGH WE GOT LOST, WE FOUND A LOT OF ANSWERS!

FIND ROCKY AND TAKE A GROUP PHOTO WITH HIM	10 PTS.
PICK UP A MAP OF PHILLY	10 PTS.
WHERE IS EINSTEIN'S BRAIN?	5 PTS.
WHAT IS ON BEN FRANKLIN'S GRAVE?	5 PTS.
WHAT DID BETSY ROSS DO?	5 PTS.

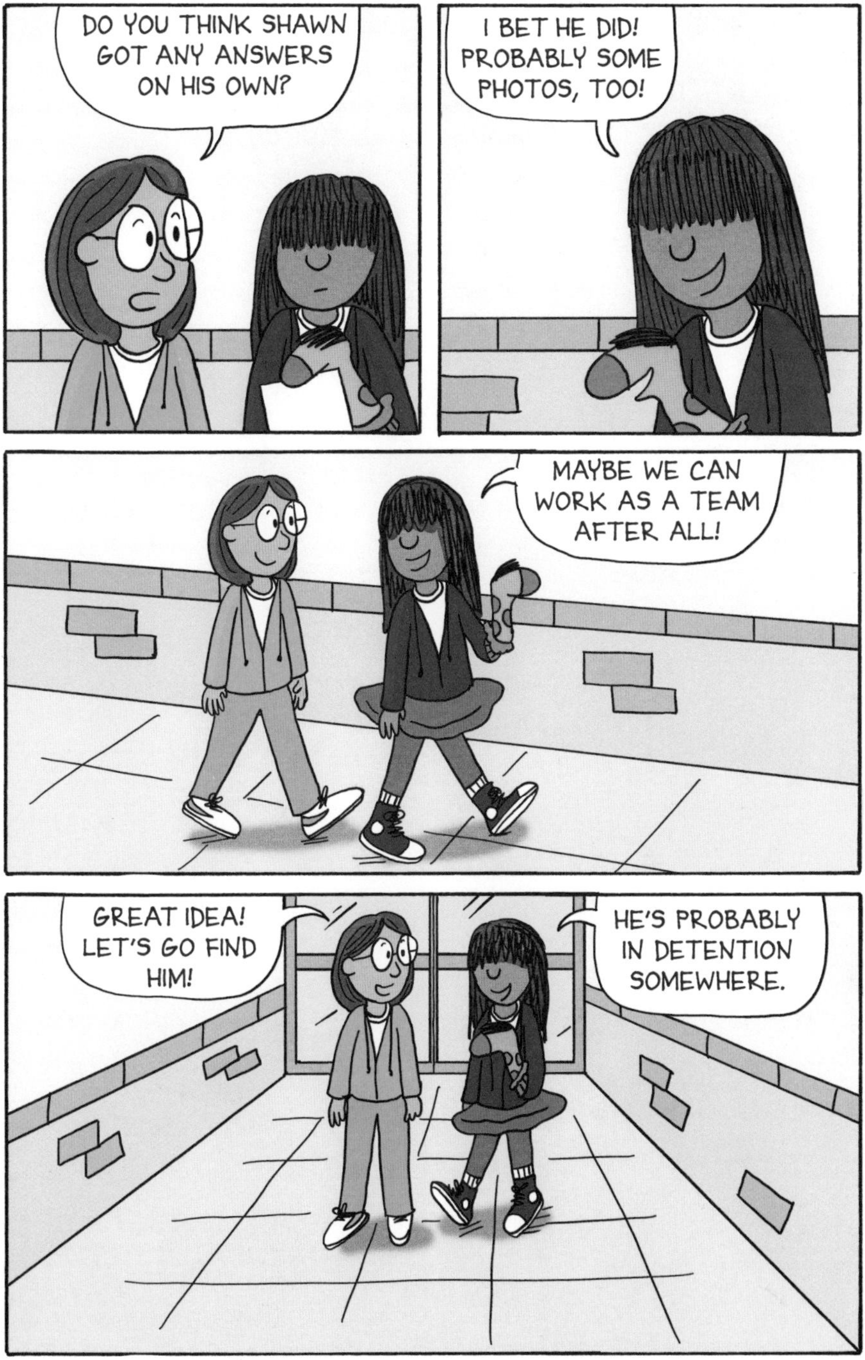
DO YOU THINK SHAWN GOT ANY ANSWERS ON HIS OWN?
I BET HE DID! PROBABLY SOME PHOTOS, TOO!
MAYBE WE CAN WORK AS A TEAM AFTER ALL!
GREAT IDEA! LET'S GO FIND HIM!
HE'S PROBABLY IN DETENTION SOMEWHERE.

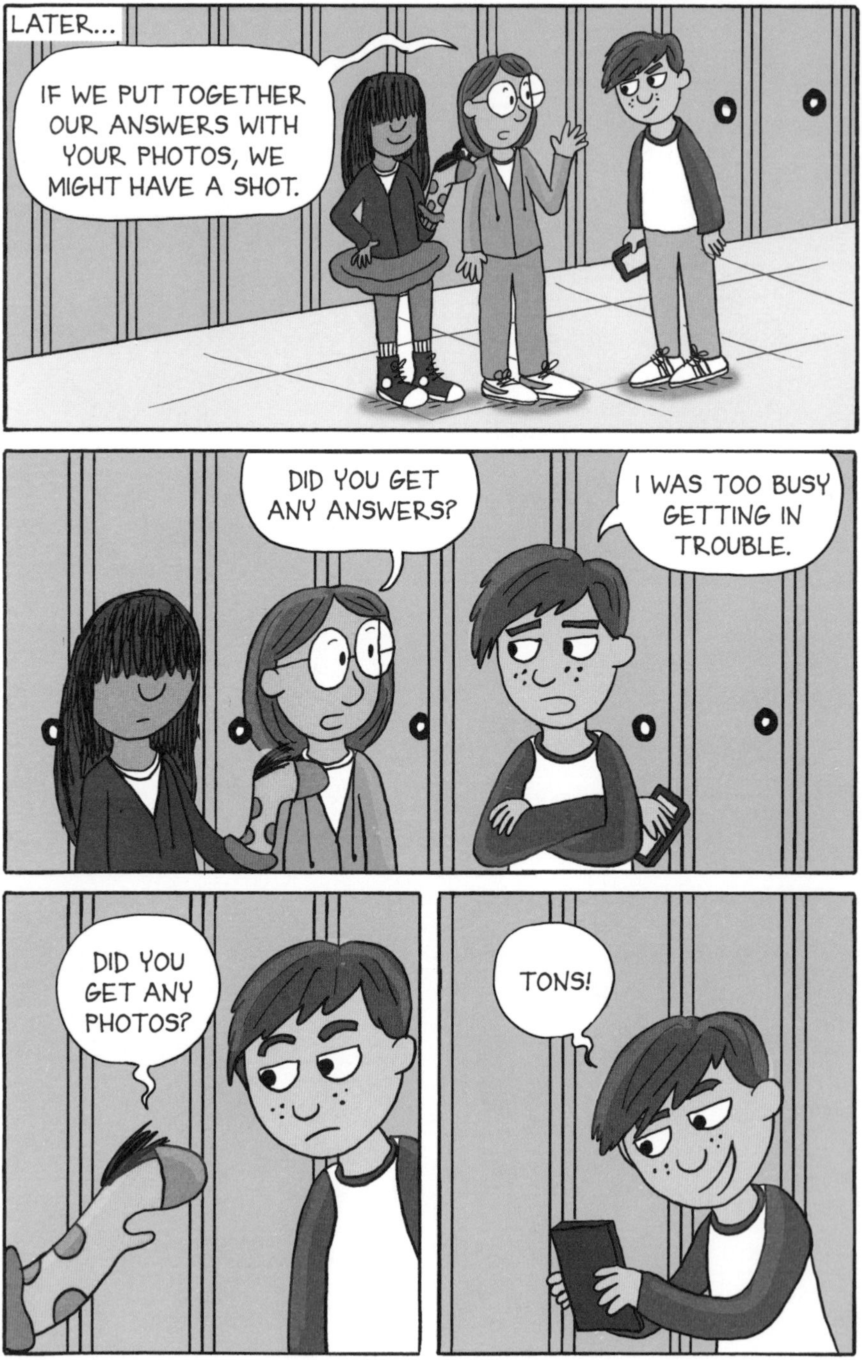
LATER...
IF WE PUT TOGETHER OUR ANSWERS WITH YOUR PHOTOS, WE MIGHT HAVE A SHOT.
DID YOU GET ANY ANSWERS?
I WAS TOO BUSY GETTING IN TROUBLE.
DID YOU GET ANY PHOTOS?
TONS!

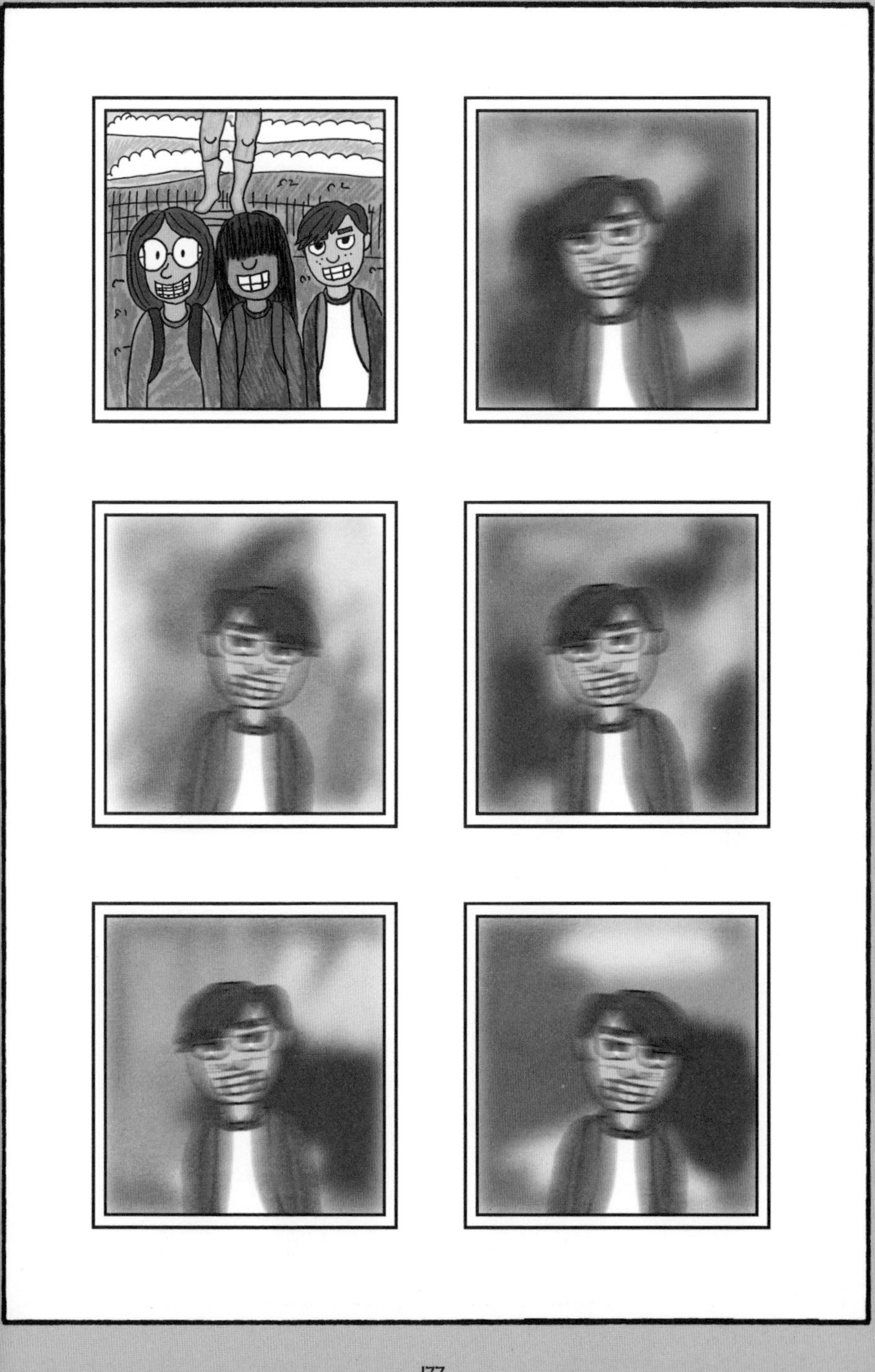

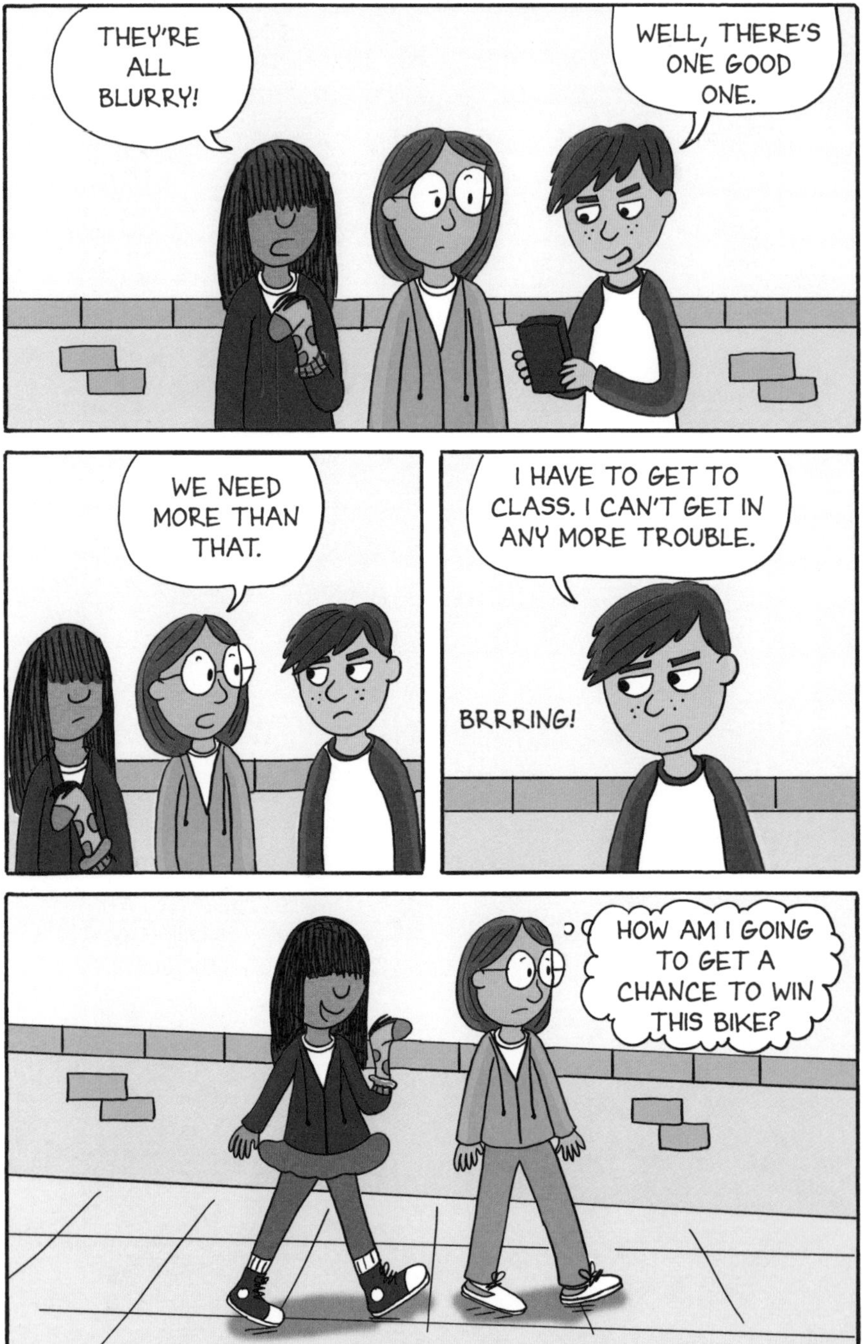
THEY'RE ALL BLURRY!
WELL, THERE'S ONE GOOD ONE.
WE NEED MORE THAN THAT.
I HAVE TO GET TO CLASS. I CAN'T GET IN ANY MORE TROUBLE.
BRRRING!
HOW AM I GOING TO GET A CHANCE TO WIN THIS BIKE?

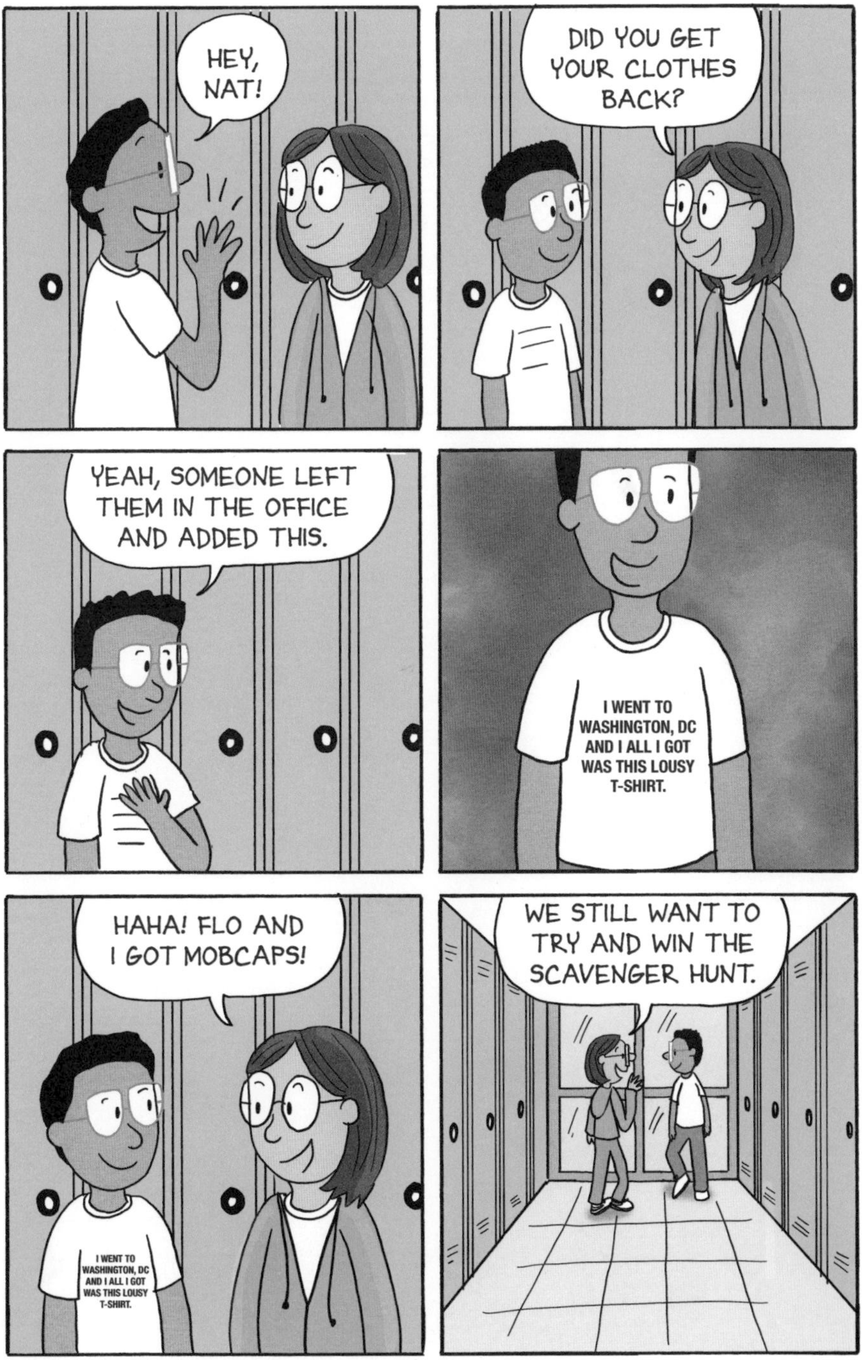
HEY, NAT!
DID YOU GET YOUR CLOTHES BACK?
YEAH, SOMEONE LEFT THEM IN THE OFFICE AND ADDED THIS.
I WENT TO WASHINGTON, DC AND I ALL I GOT WAS THIS LOUSY T-SHIRT.
HAHA! FLO AND I GOT MOBCAPS!
I WENT TO WASHINGTON, DC AND I ALL I GOT WAS THIS LOUSY T-SHIRT.
WE STILL WANT TO TRY AND WIN THE SCAVENGER HUNT.

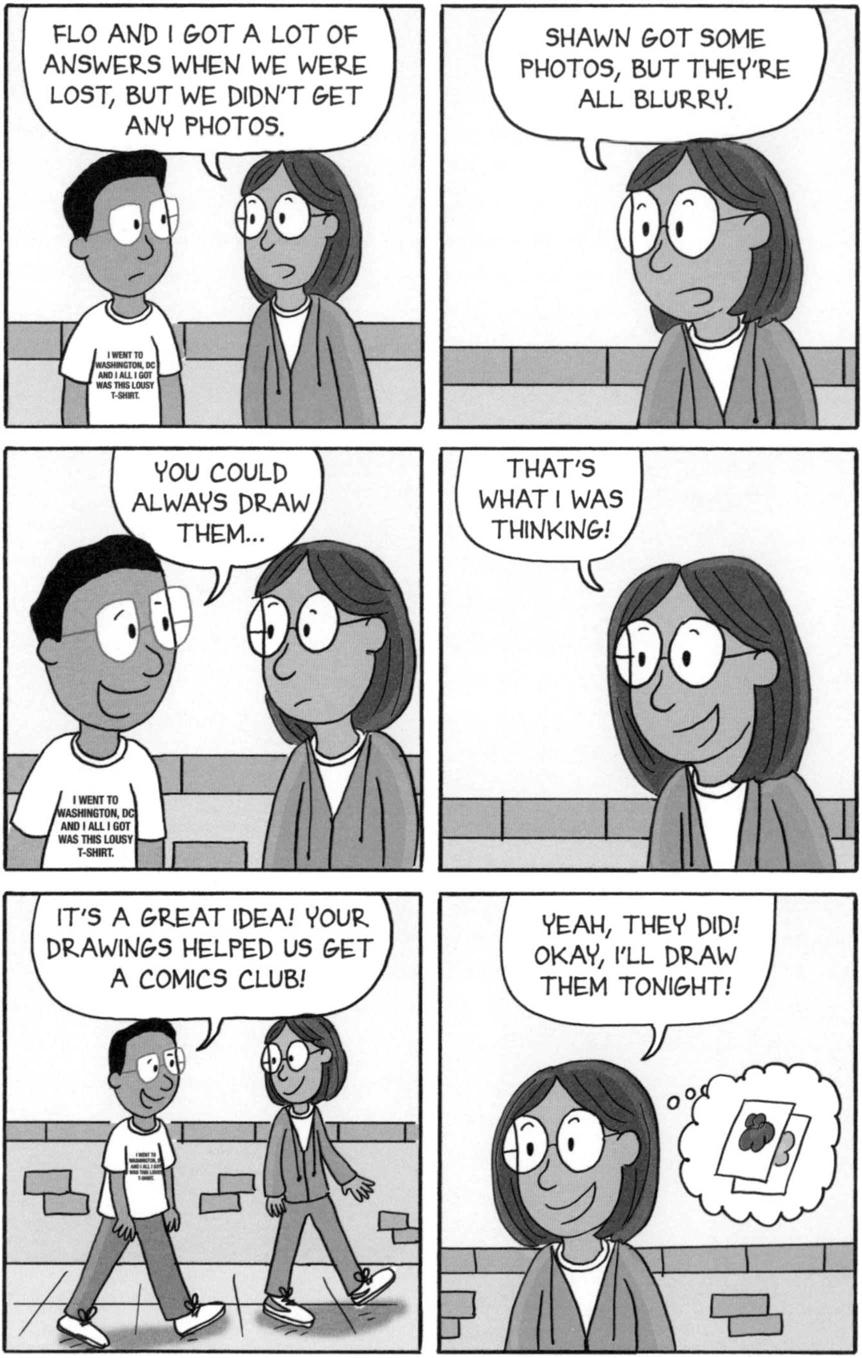
FLO AND I GOT A LOT OF ANSWERS WHEN WE WERE LOST, BUT WE DIDN'T GET ANY PHOTOS.
I WENT TO WASHINGTON, DC AND I ALL I GOT WAS THIS LOUSY T-SHIRT.
SHAWN GOT SOME PHOTOS, BUT THEY'RE ALL BLURRY.
YOU COULD ALWAYS DRAW THEM...
I WENT TO WASHINGTON, DC AND I ALL I GOT WAS THIS LOUSY T-SHIRT.
THAT'S WHAT I WAS THINKING!
IT'S A GREAT IDEA! YOUR DRAWINGS HELPED US GET A COMICS CLUB!
YEAH, THEY DID! OKAY, I'LL DRAW THEM TONIGHT!

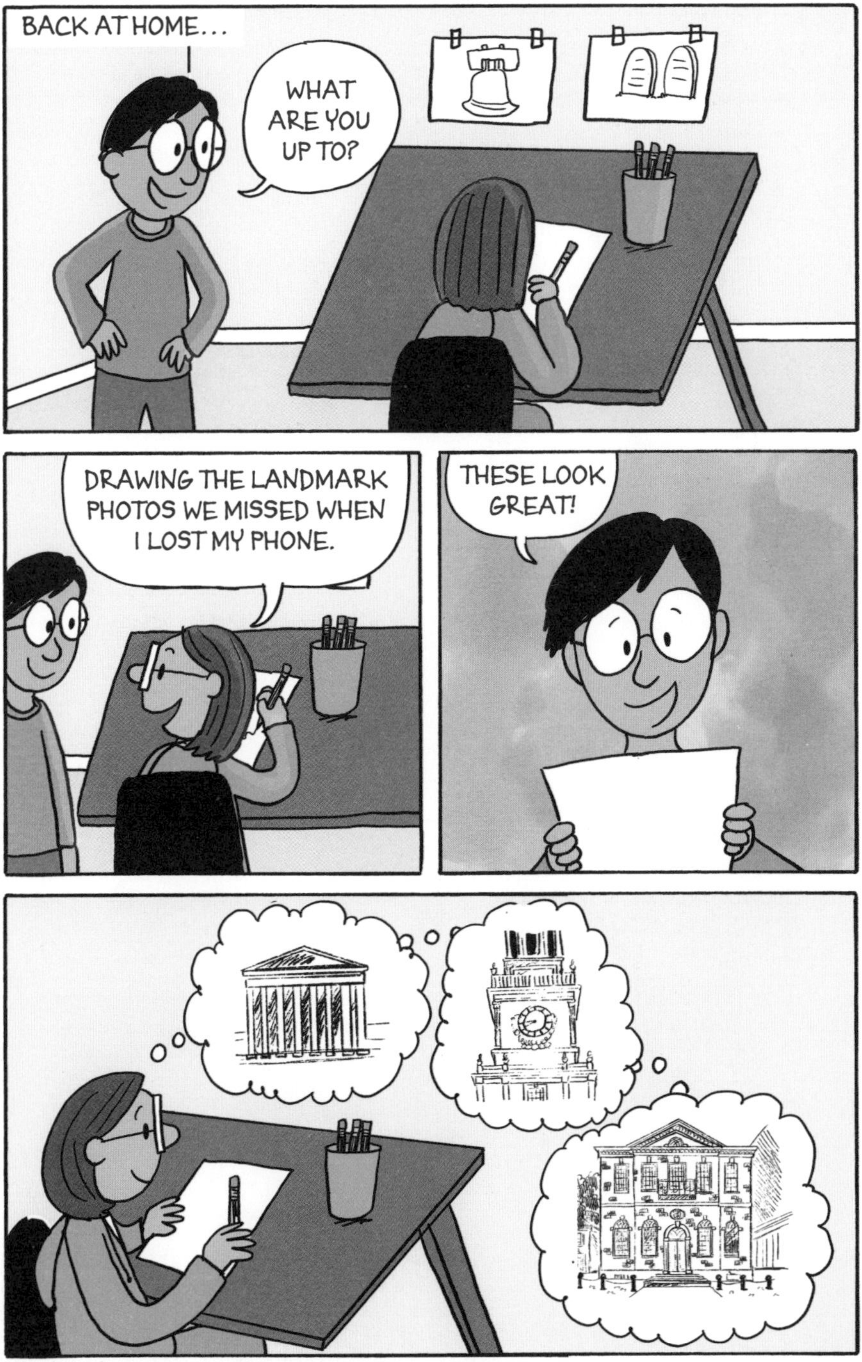
BACK AT HOME...
WHAT ARE YOU UP TO?
DRAWING THE LANDMARK PHOTOS WE MISSED WHEN I LOST MY PHONE.
THESE LOOK GREAT!

PHILADELPHIA LANDMARKS

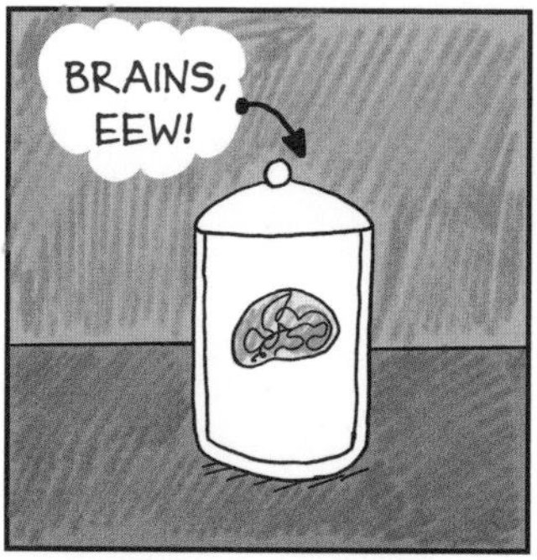
BRAINS, EEW!

MÜTTER MUSEUM

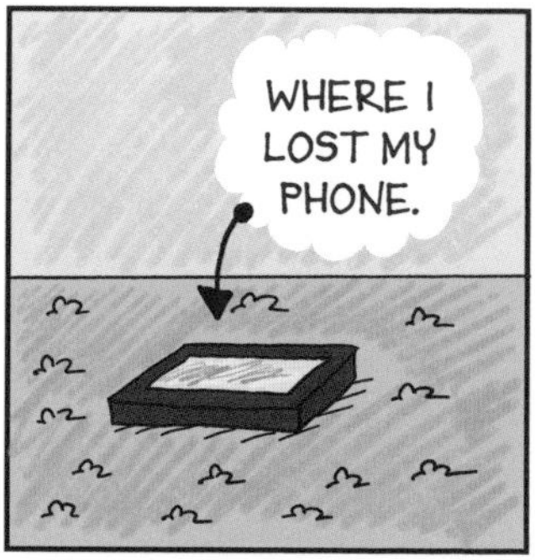
WHERE I LOST MY PHONE.

WASHINGTON PARK

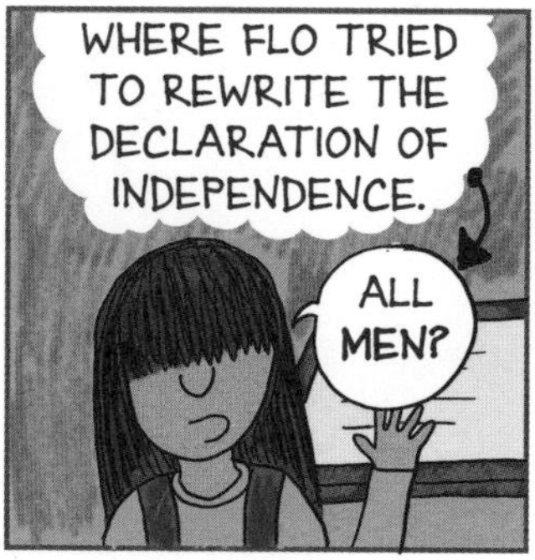
WHERE FLO TRIED TO REWRITE THE DECLARATION OF INDEPENDENCE.
ALL MEN?

INDEPENDENCE HALL

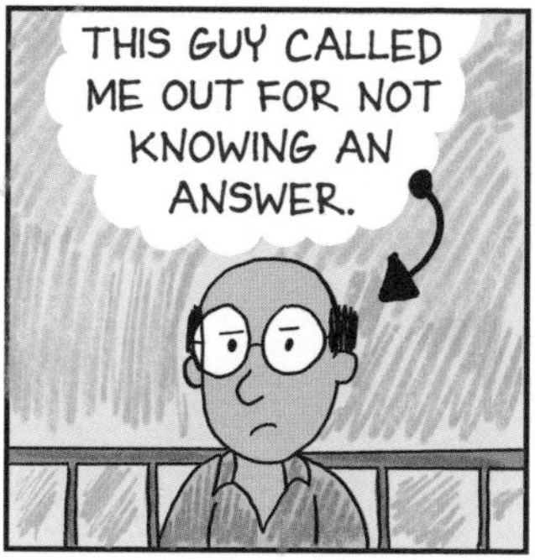
THIS GUY CALLED ME OUT FOR NOT KNOWING AN ANSWER.

CONGRESS HALL

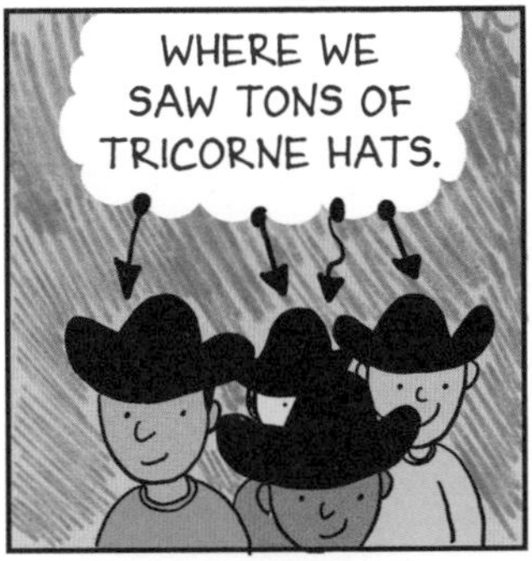
WHERE WE SAW TONS OF TRICORNE HATS.

ELFRETH'S ALLEY

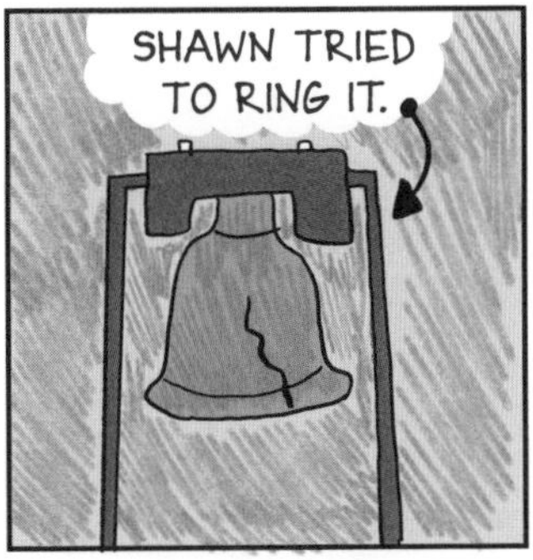
SHAWN TRIED TO RING IT.

LIBERTY BELL

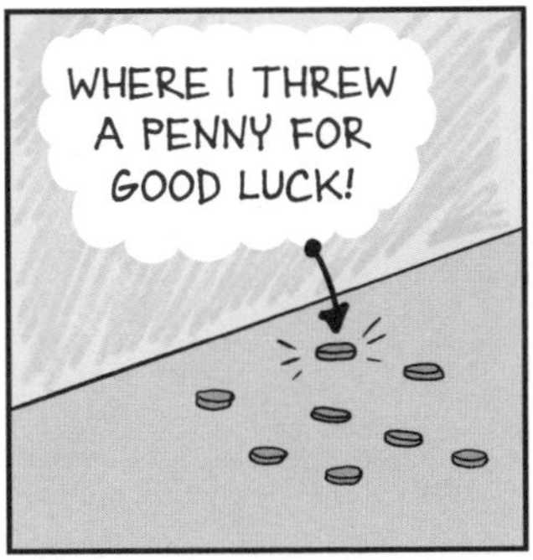
WHERE I THREW A PENNY FOR GOOD LUCK!

BEN FRANKLIN'S GRAVE

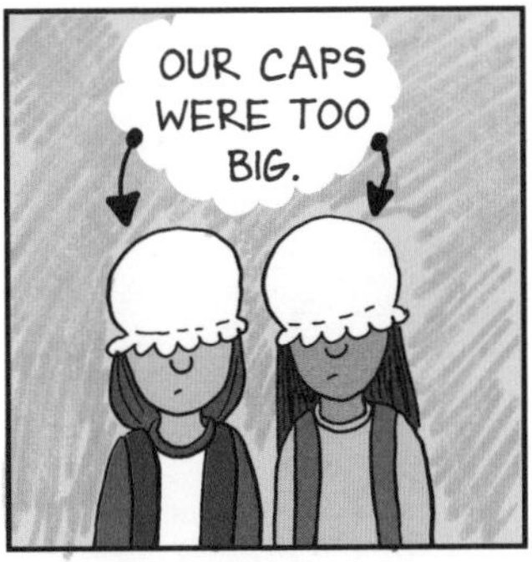
OUR CAPS WERE TOO BIG.

BETSY ROSS HOUSE

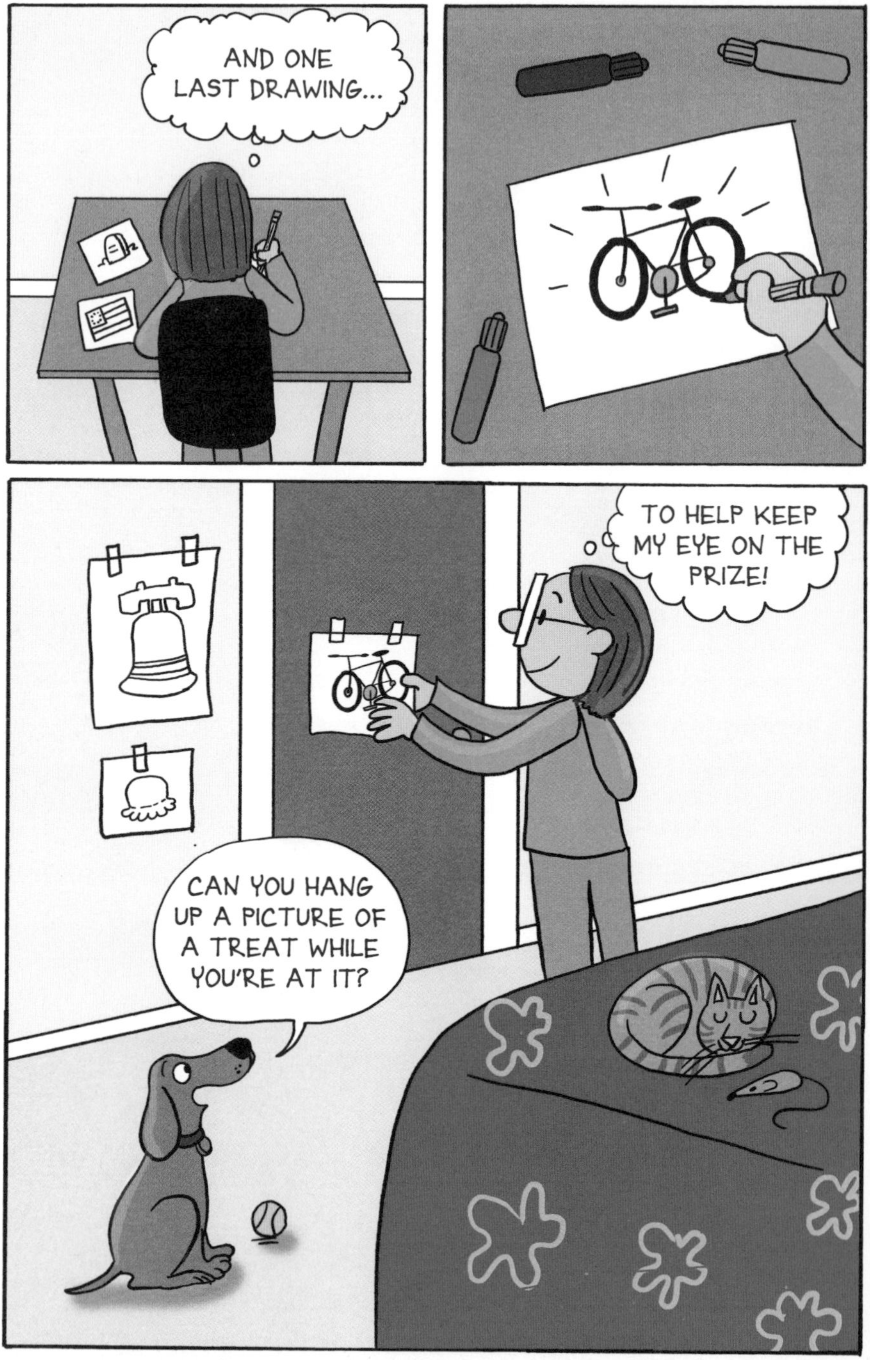
AND ONE LAST DRAWING...
TO HELP KEEP MY EYE ON THE PRIZE!
CAN YOU HANG UP A PICTURE OF A TREAT WHILE YOU'RE AT IT?

CHAPTER 14
TICKETS, PLEASE

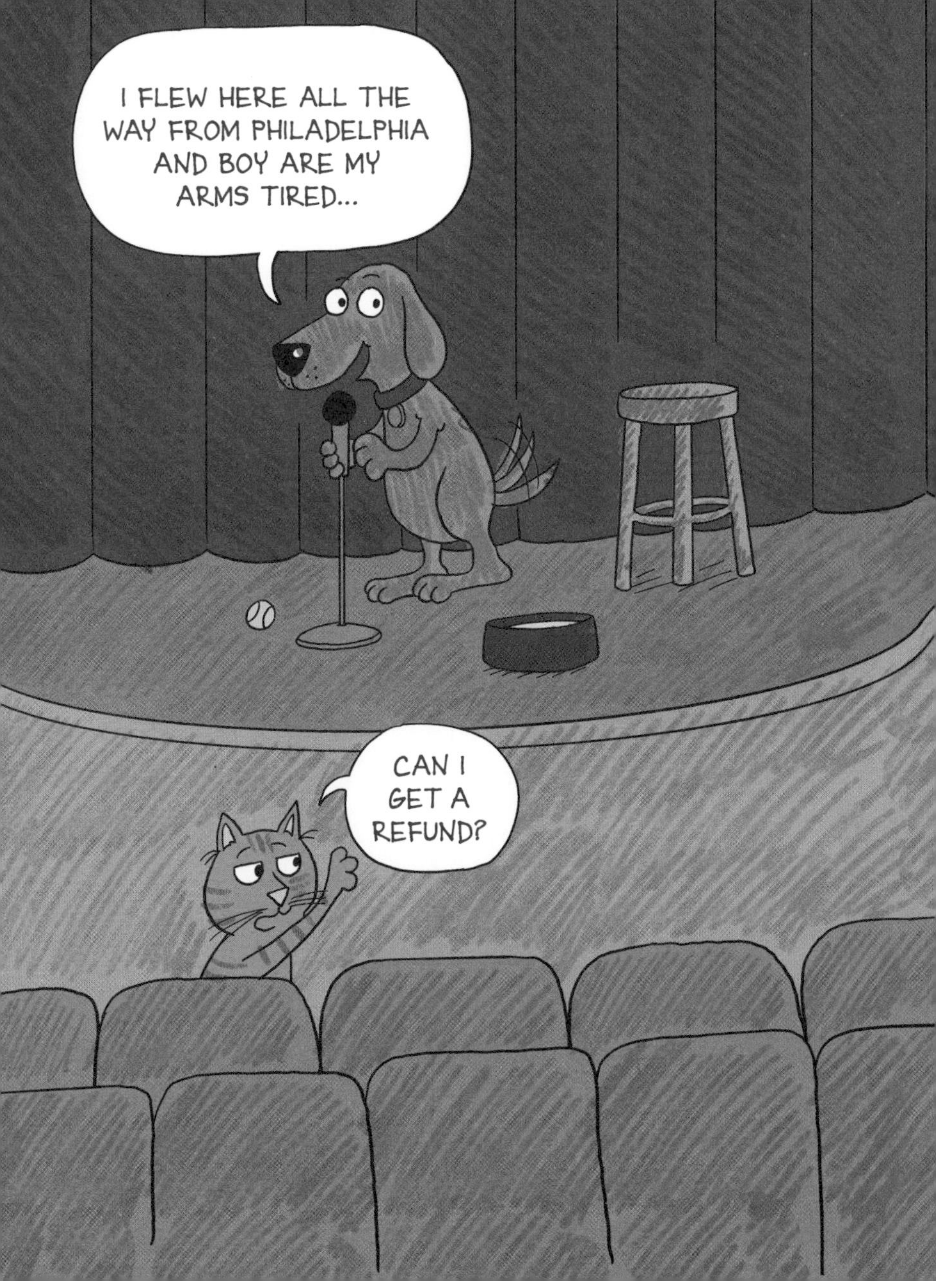
I FLEW HERE ALL THE WAY FROM PHILADELPHIA AND BOY ARE MY ARMS TIRED...
CAN I GET A REFUND?

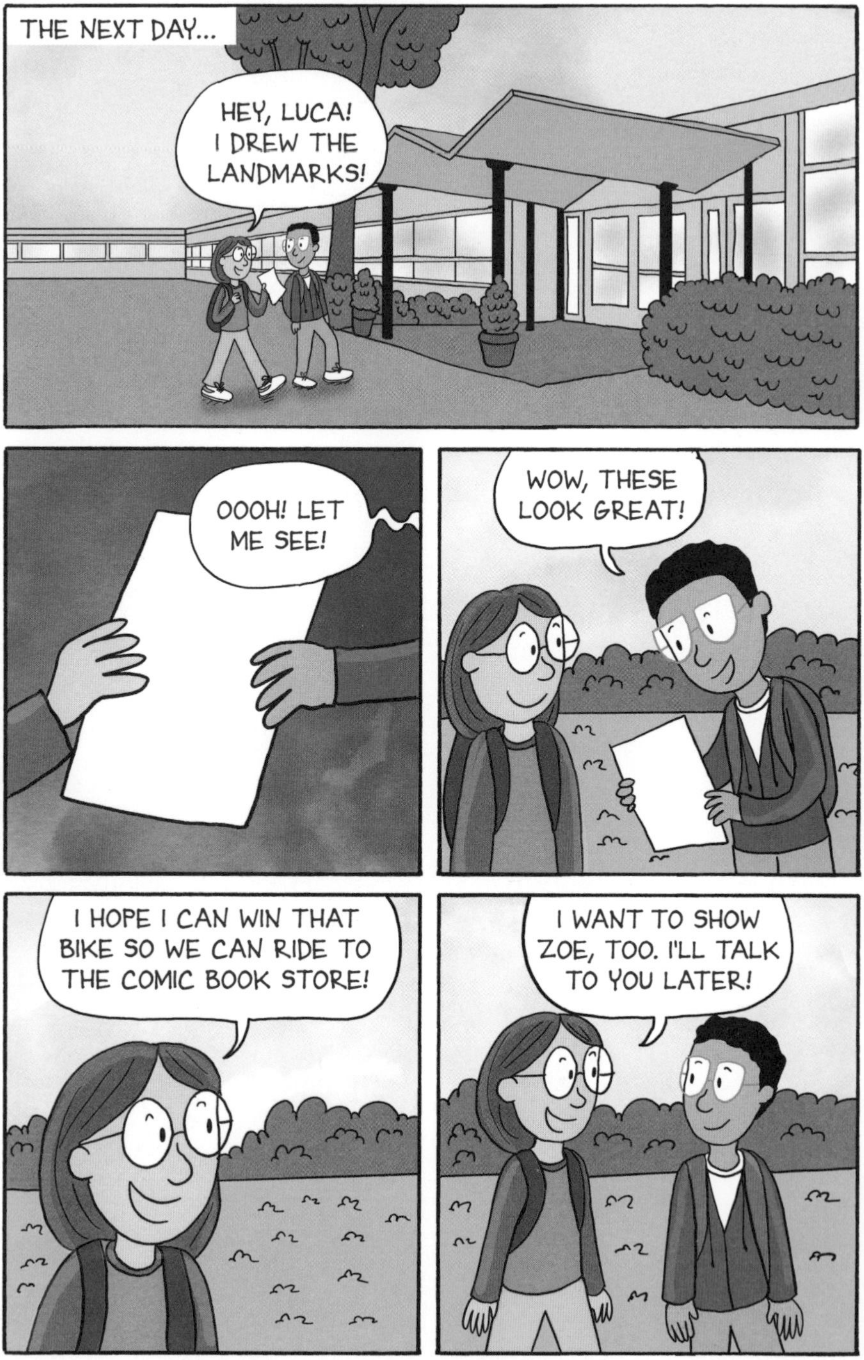
THE NEXT DAY...
HEY, LUCA! I DREW THE LANDMARKS!
OOOH! LET ME SEE!
WOW, THESE LOOK GREAT!
I HOPE I CAN WIN THAT BIKE SO WE CAN RIDE TO THE COMIC BOOK STORE!
I WANT TO SHOW ZOE, TOO. I'LL TALK TO YOU LATER!

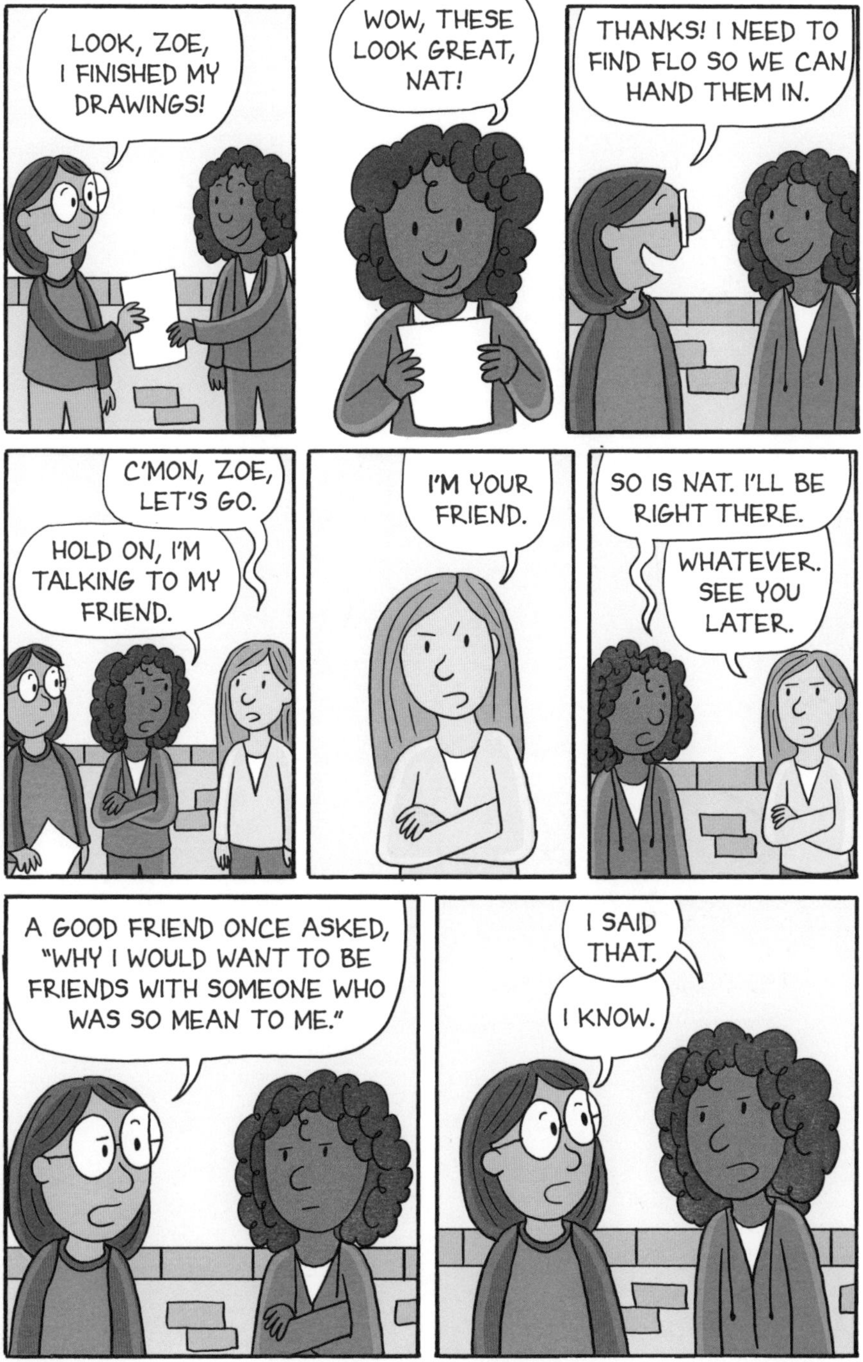

LOOK, ZOE, I FINISHED MY DRAWINGS!
WOW, THESE LOOK GREAT, NAT!
THANKS! I NEED TO FIND FLO SO WE CAN HAND THEM IN.
C'MON, ZOE, LET'S GO.
HOLD ON, I'M TALKING TO MY FRIEND.
I'M YOUR FRIEND.
SO IS NAT. I'LL BE RIGHT THERE.
WHATEVER. SEE YOU LATER.
A GOOD FRIEND ONCE ASKED, "WHY I WOULD WANT TO BE FRIENDS WITH SOMEONE WHO WAS SO MEAN TO ME."
I SAID THAT.
I KNOW.

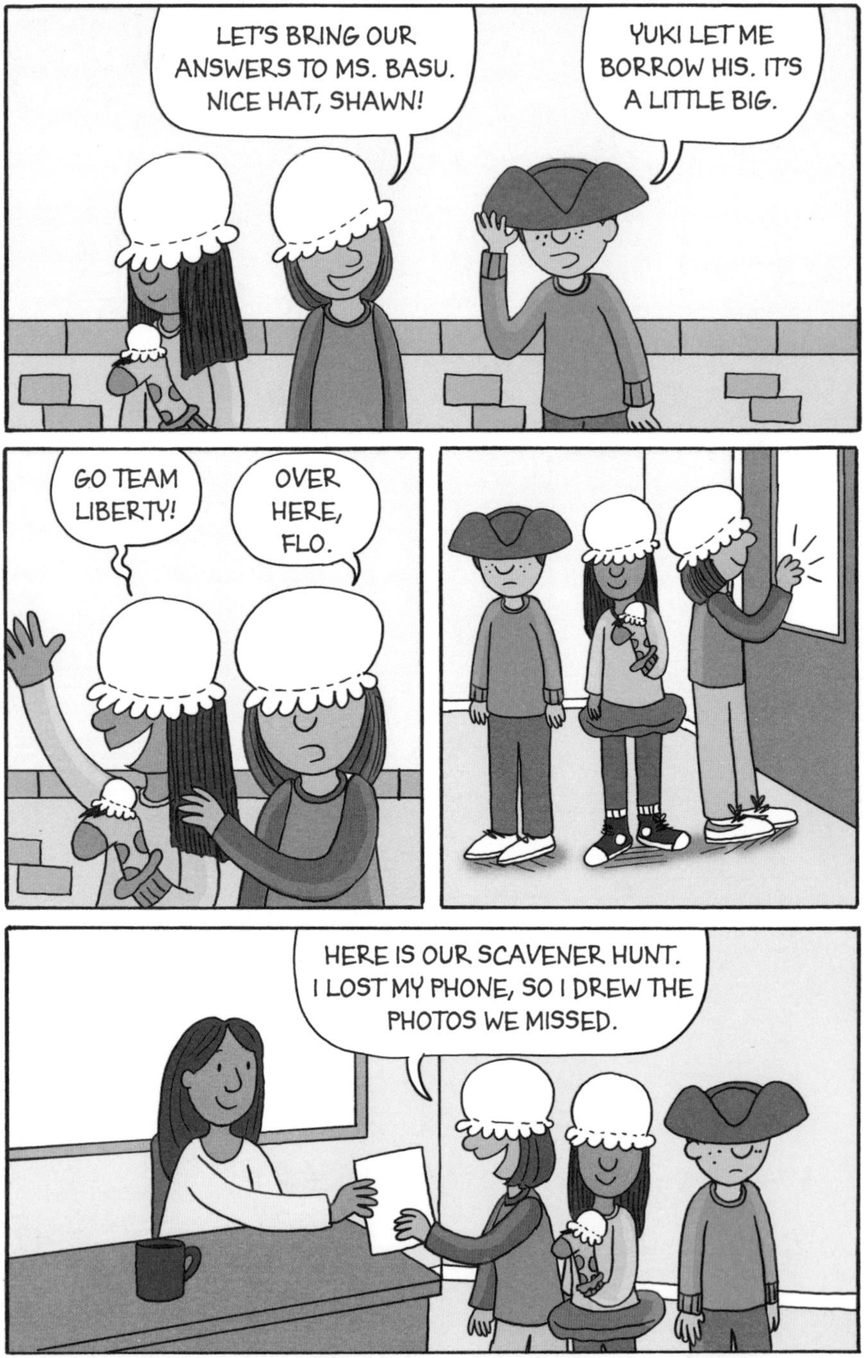
LET'S BRING OUR ANSWERS TO MS. BASU. NICE HAT, SHAWN!
YUKI LET ME BORROW HIS. IT'S A LITTLE BIG.
GO TEAM LIBERTY!
OVER HERE, FLO.
HERE IS OUR SCAVENER HUNT. I LOST MY PHONE, SO I DREW THE PHOTOS WE MISSED.

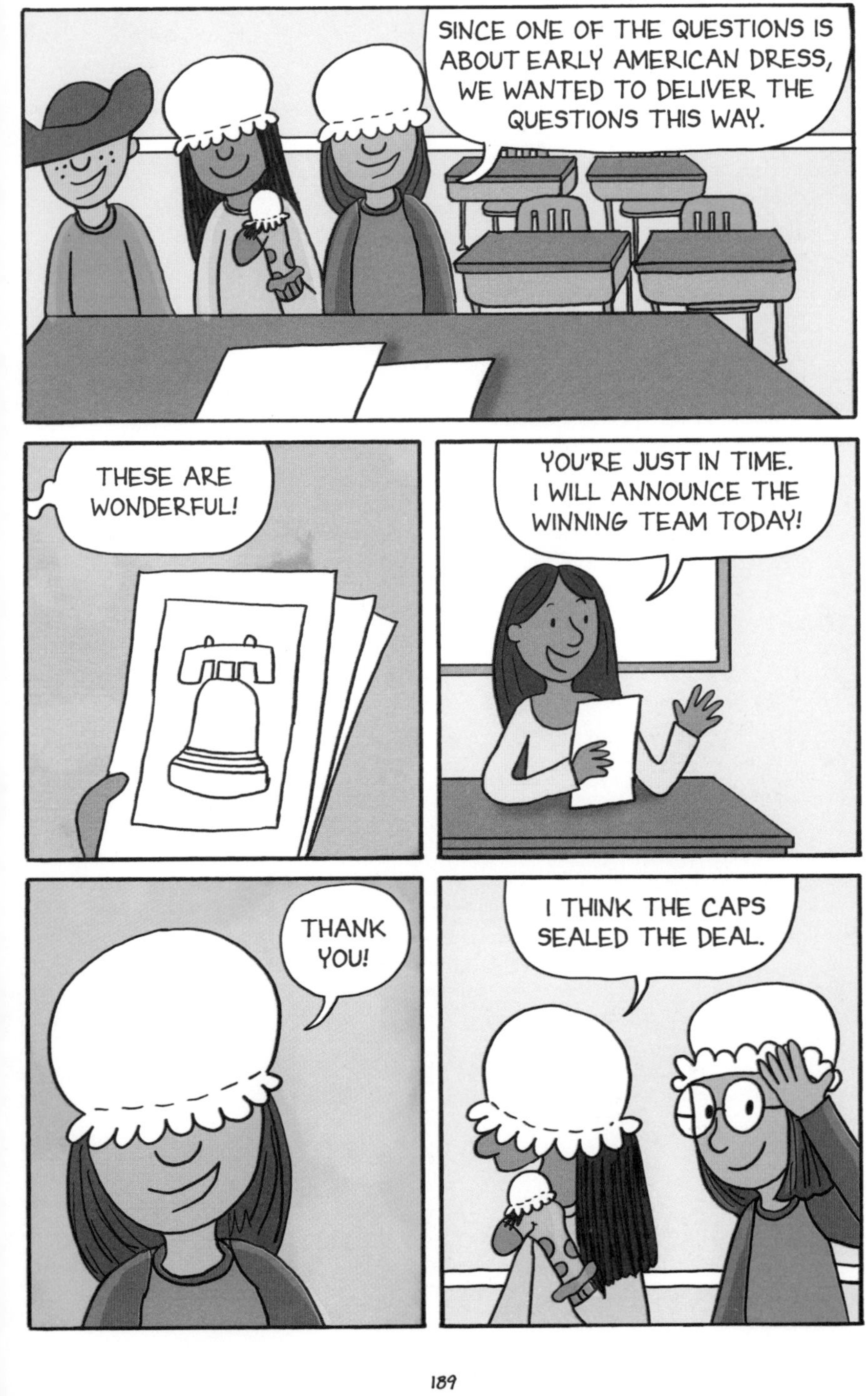
SINCE ONE OF THE QUESTIONS IS ABOUT EARLY AMERICAN DRESS, WE WANTED TO DELIVER THE QUESTIONS THIS WAY.
THESE ARE WONDERFUL!
YOU'RE JUST IN TIME. I WILL ANNOUNCE THE WINNING TEAM TODAY!
THANK YOU!
I THINK THE CAPS SEALED THE DEAL.

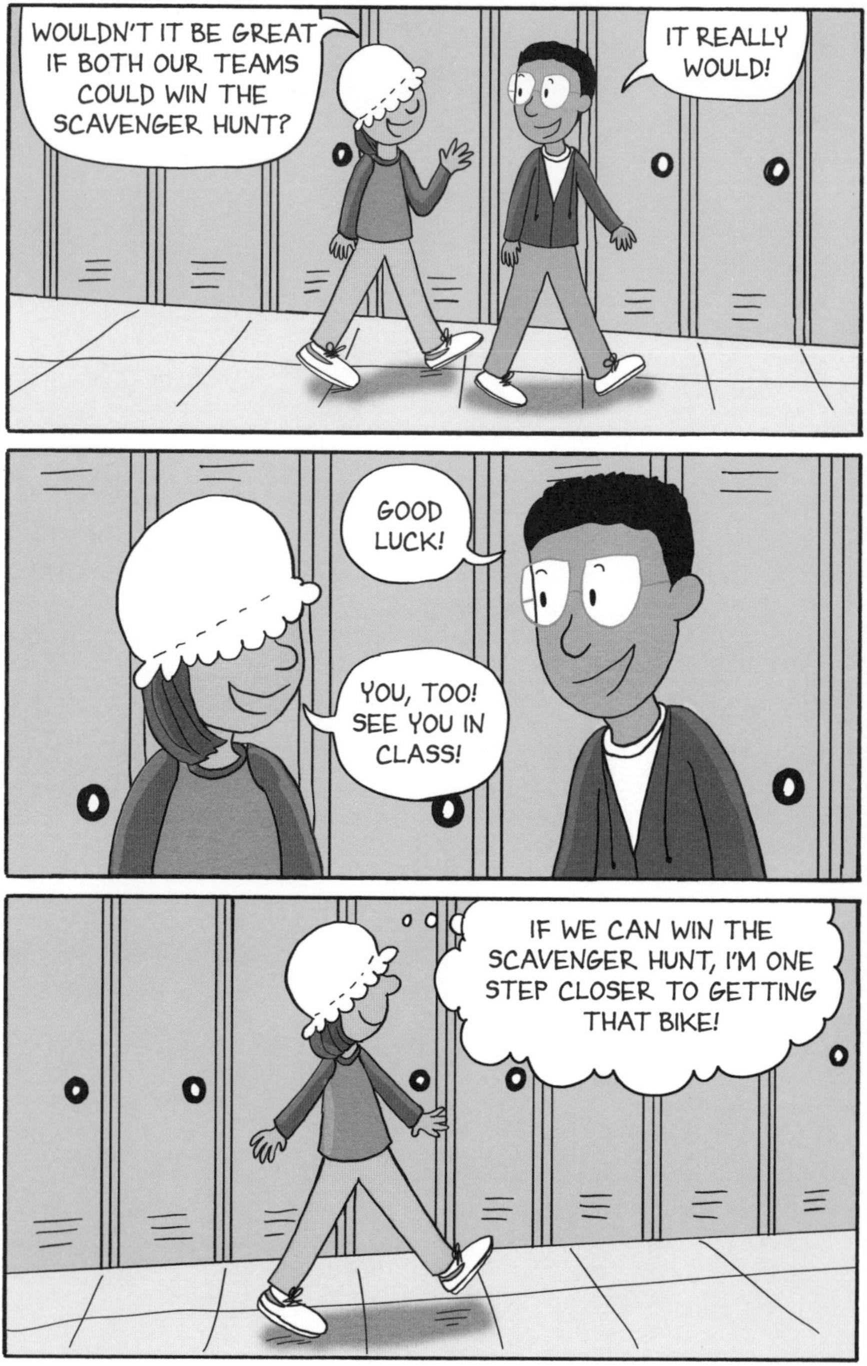
WOULDN'T IT BE GREAT IF BOTH OUR TEAMS COULD WIN THE SCAVENGER HUNT?
IT REALLY WOULD!
GOOD LUCK!
YOU, TOO! SEE YOU IN CLASS!
IF WE CAN WIN THE SCAVENGER HUNT, I'M ONE STEP CLOSER TO GETTING THAT BIKE!

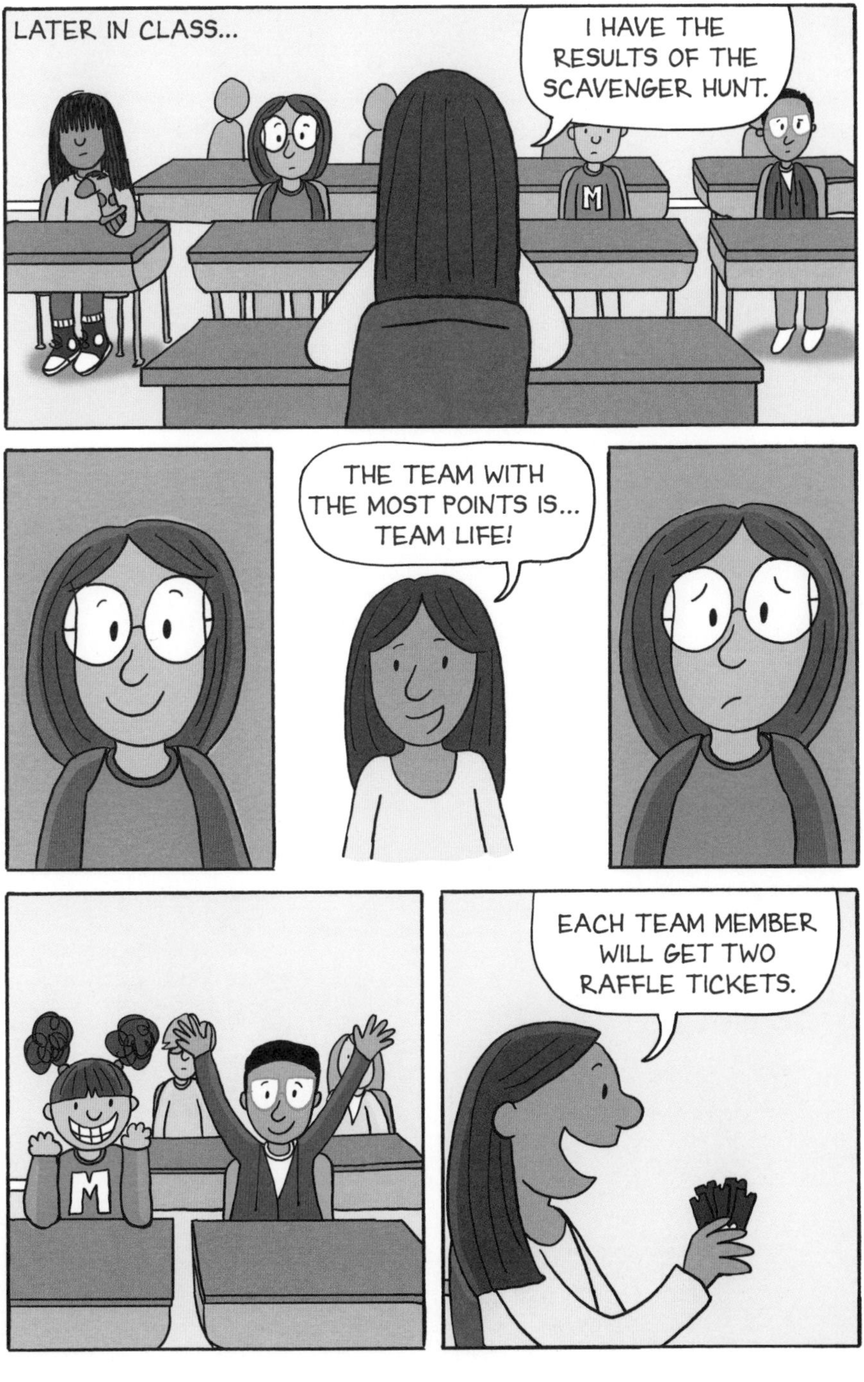
LATER IN CLASS...
I HAVE THE RESULTS OF THE SCAVENGER HUNT.
THE TEAM WITH THE MOST POINTS IS... TEAM LIFE!
EACH TEAM MEMBER WILL GET TWO RAFFLE TICKETS.

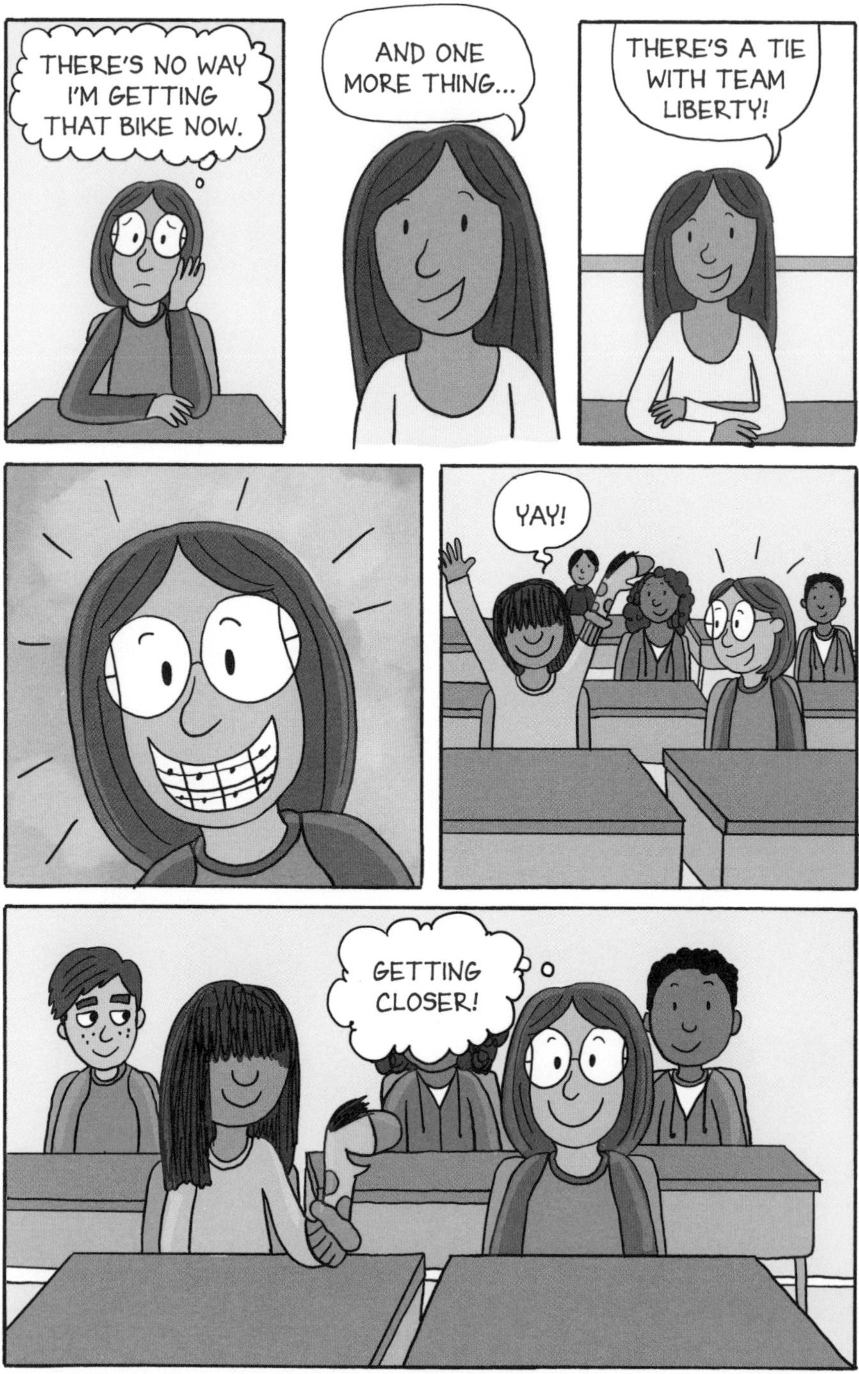
THERE'S NO WAY I'M GETTING THAT BIKE NOW.
AND ONE MORE THING...
THERE'S A TIE WITH TEAM LIBERTY!
YAY!
GETTING CLOSER!

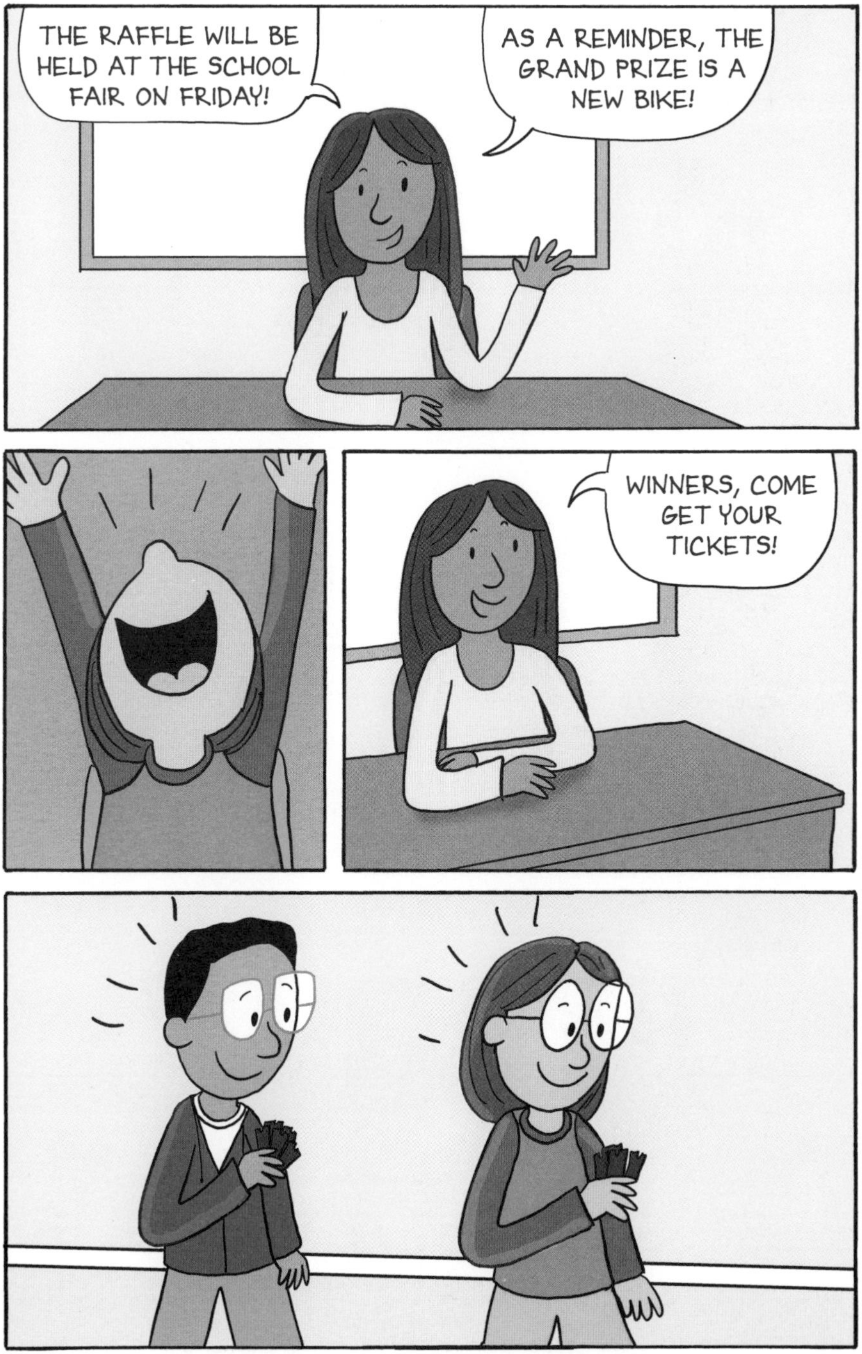
THE RAFFLE WILL BE HELD AT THE SCHOOL FAIR ON FRIDAY!
AS A REMINDER, THE GRAND PRIZE IS A NEW BIKE!
WINNERS, COME GET YOUR TICKETS!

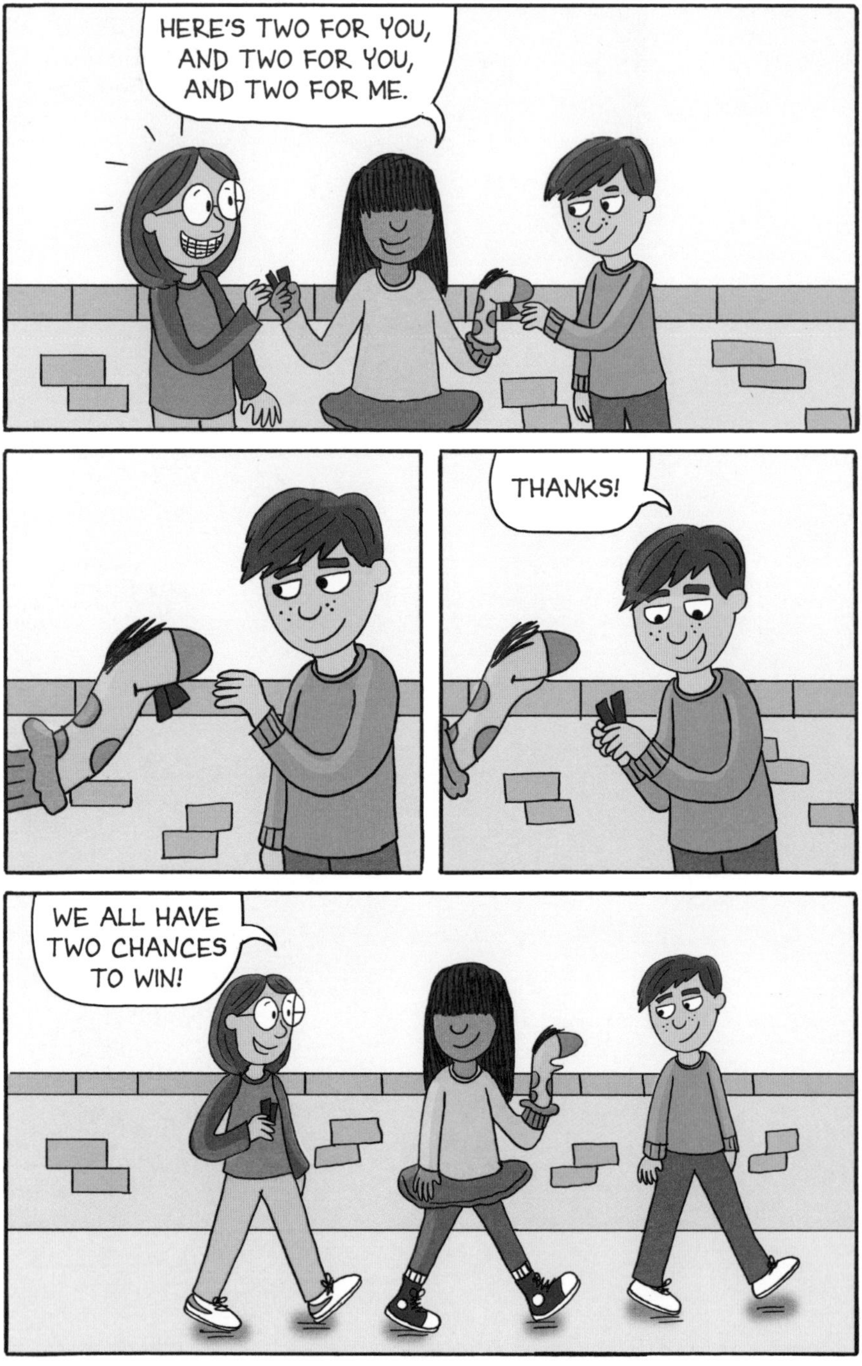
HERE'S TWO FOR YOU, AND TWO FOR YOU, AND TWO FOR ME.
THANKS!
WE ALL HAVE TWO CHANCES TO WIN!

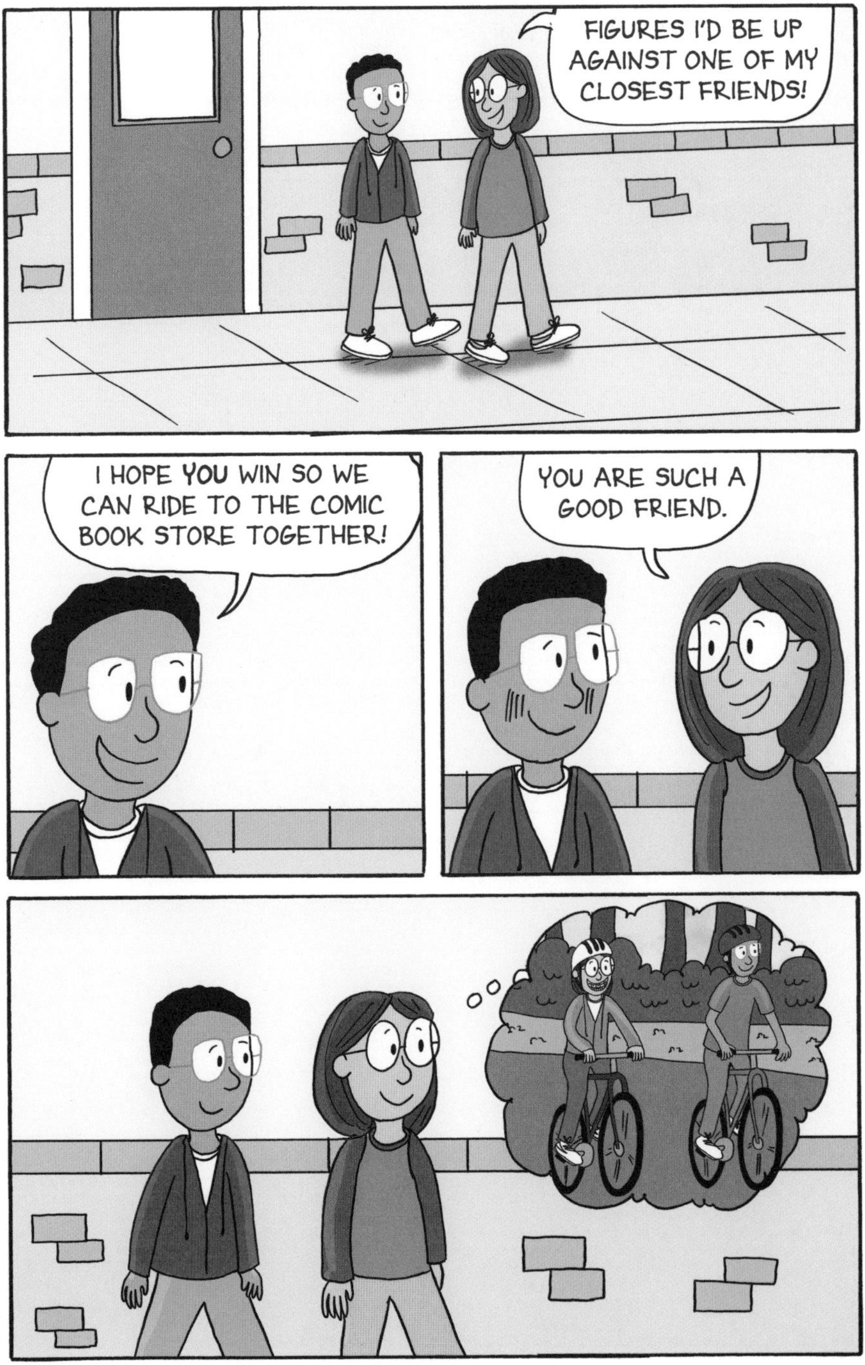
FIGURES I'D BE UP AGAINST ONE OF MY CLOSEST FRIENDS!
I HOPE YOU WIN SO WE CAN RIDE TO THE COMIC BOOK STORE TOGETHER!
YOU ARE SUCH A GOOD FRIEND.

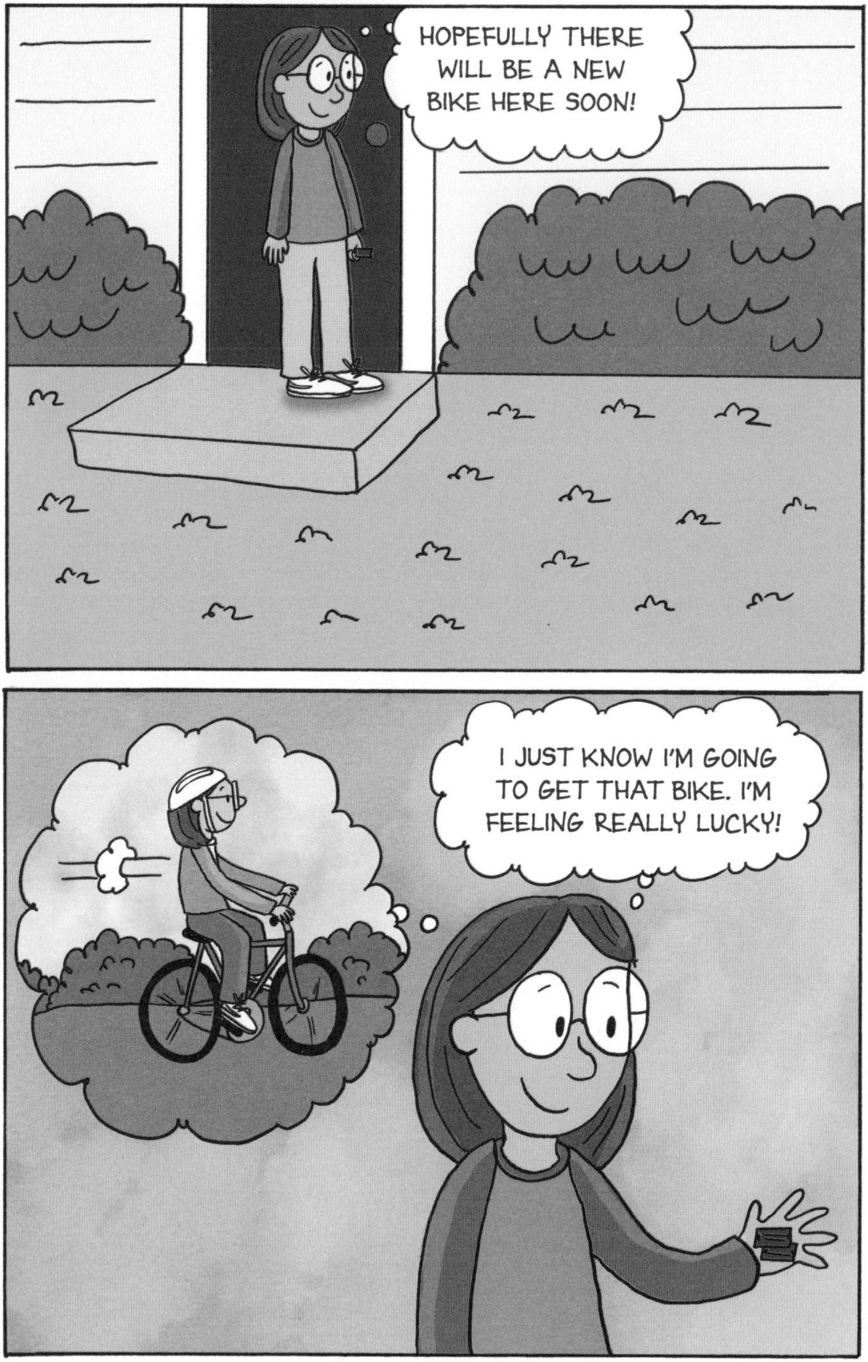
HOPEFULLY THERE WILL BE A NEW BIKE HERE SOON!
I JUST KNOW I'M GOING TO GET THAT BIKE. I'M FEELING REALLY LUCKY!

CHAPTER 15
FAIR IS FAIR

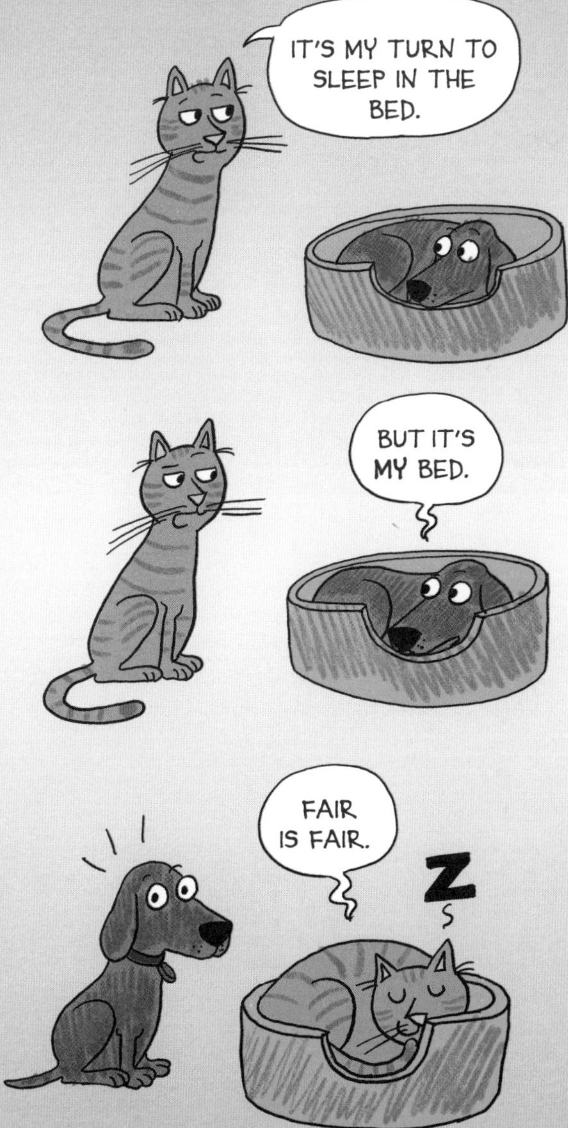
IT'S MY TURN TO SLEEP IN THE BED.
BUT IT'S MY BED.
FAIR IS FAIR.
Z

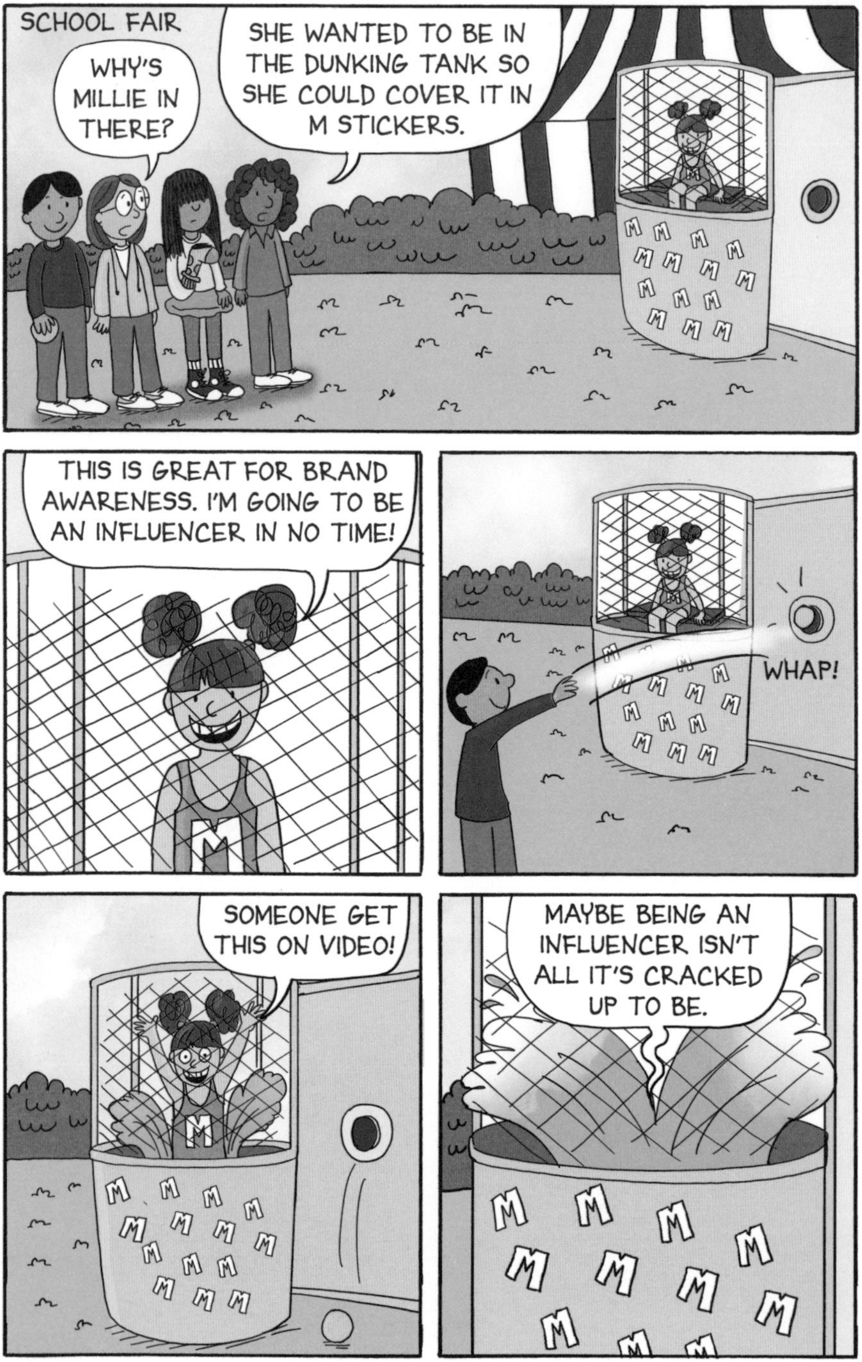
SCHOOL FAIR
WHY'S MILLIE IN THERE?
SHE WANTED TO BE IN THE DUNKING TANK SO SHE COULD COVER IT IN M STICKERS.
THIS IS GREAT FOR BRAND AWARENESS. I'M GOING TO BE AN INFLUENCER IN NO TIME!
WHAP!
SOMEONE GET THIS ON VIDEO!
MAYBE BEING AN INFLUENCER ISN'T ALL IT'S CRACKED UP TO BE.

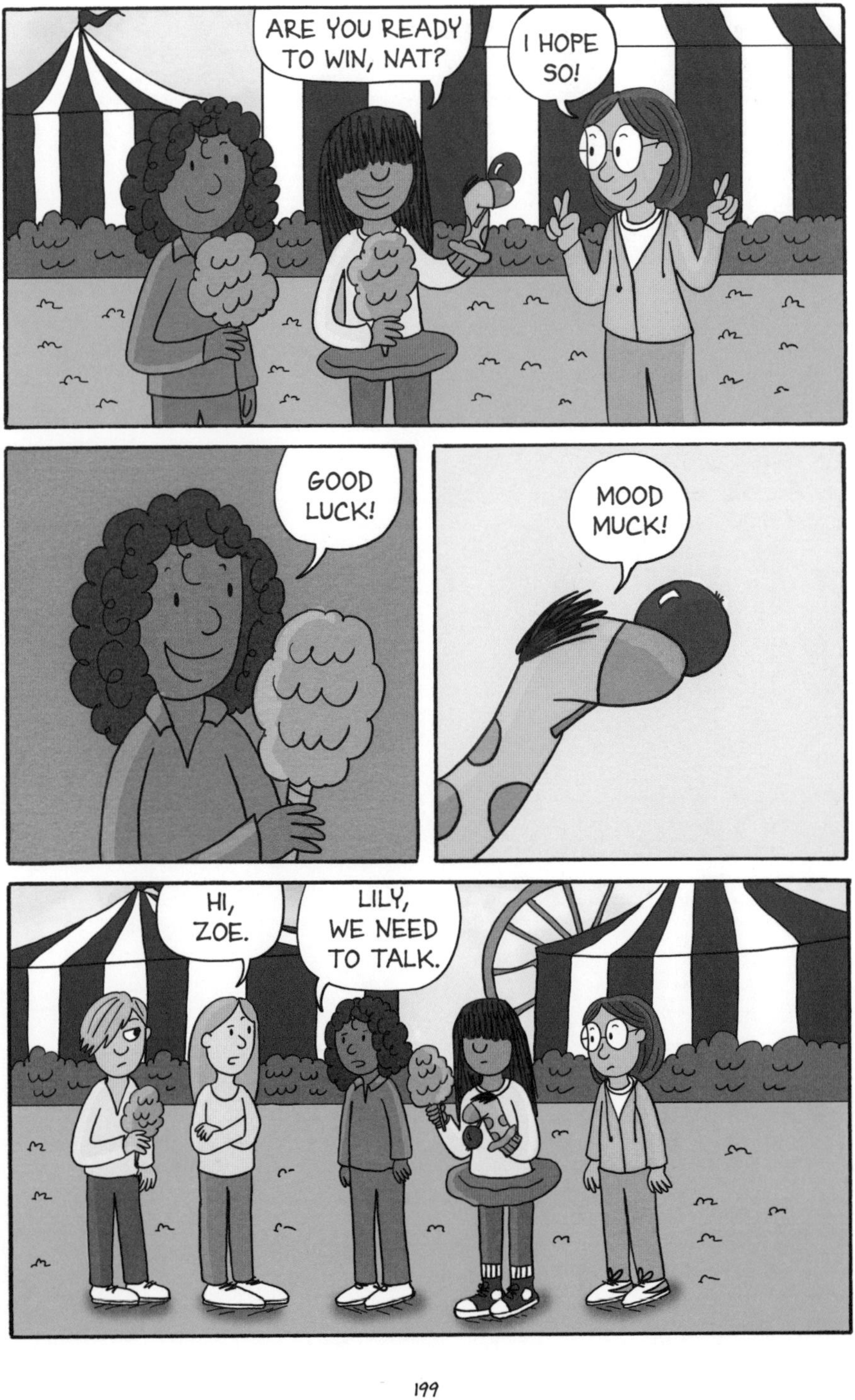
ARE YOU READY TO WIN, NAT?
I HOPE SO!
GOOD LUCK!
MOOD MUCK!
HI, ZOE.
LILY, WE NEED TO TALK.

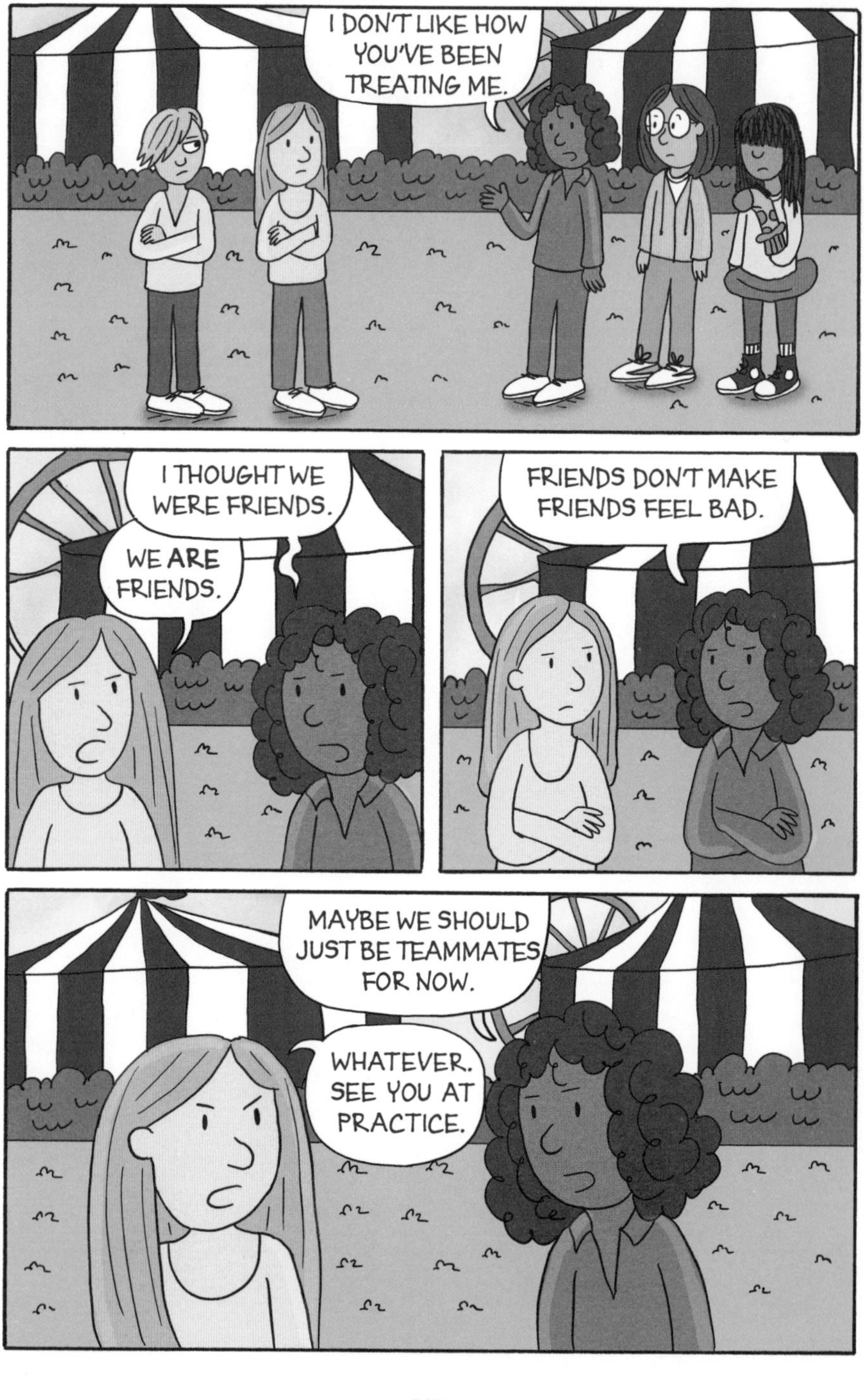
I DON'T LIKE HOW YOU'VE BEEN TREATING ME.
I THOUGHT WE WERE FRIENDS.
WE ARE FRIENDS.
FRIENDS DON'T MAKE FRIENDS FEEL BAD.
MAYBE WE SHOULD JUST BE TEAMMATES FOR NOW.
WHATEVER. SEE YOU AT PRACTICE.

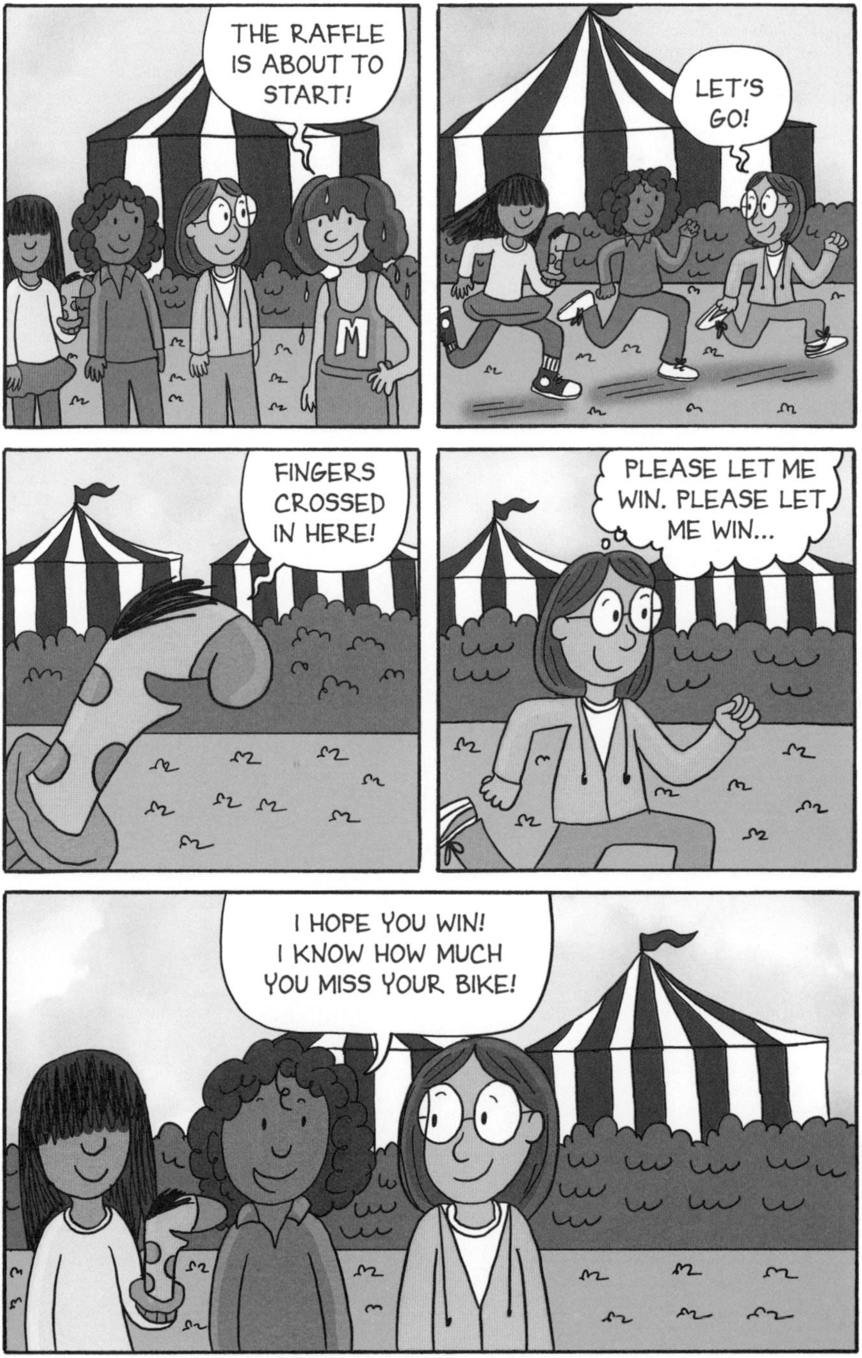
THE RAFFLE IS ABOUT TO START!
M
LET'S GO!
FINGERS CROSSED IN HERE!
PLEASE LET ME WIN. PLEASE LET ME WIN...
I HOPE YOU WIN! I KNOW HOW MUCH YOU MISS YOUR BIKE!

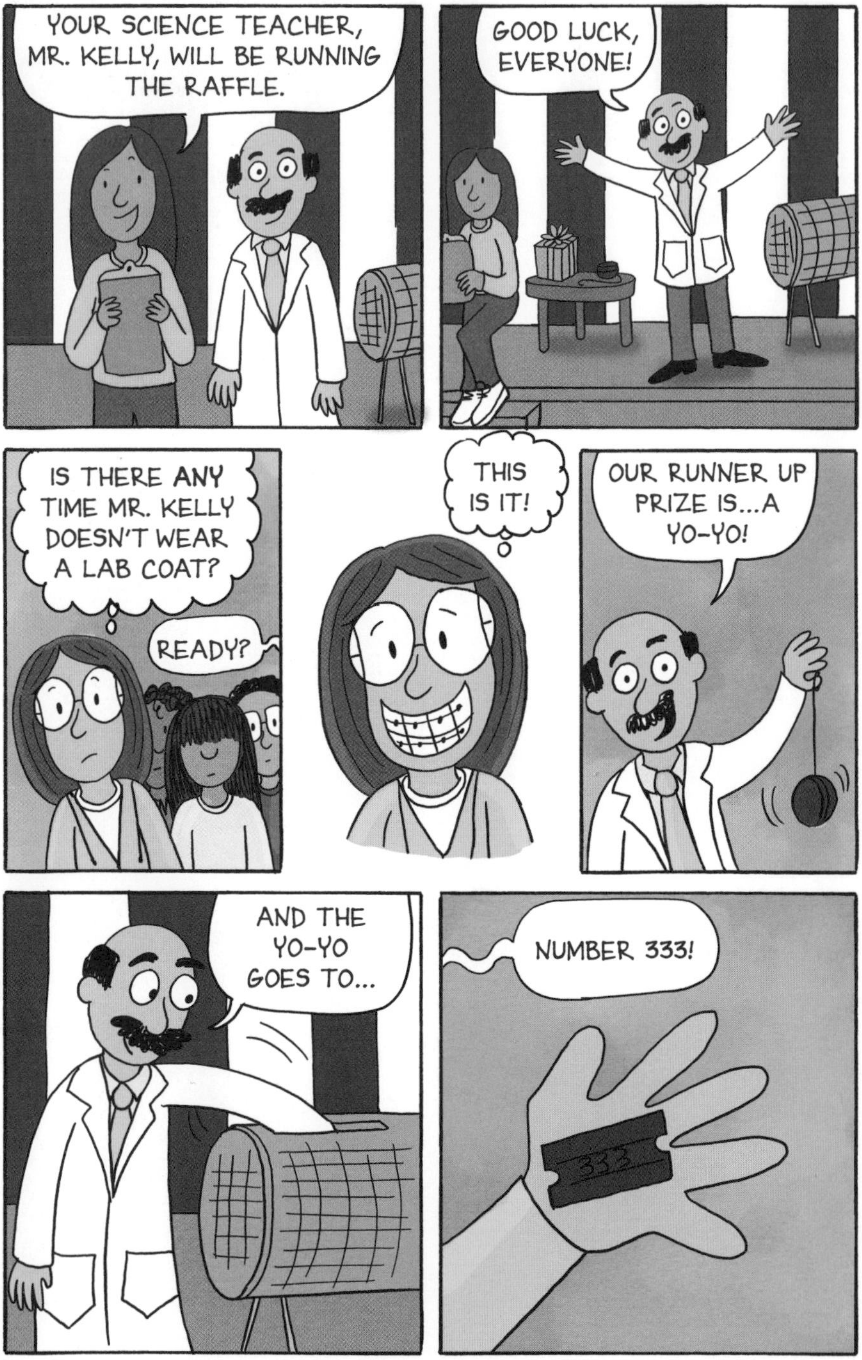
YOUR SCIENCE TEACHER, MR. KELLY, WILL BE RUNNING THE RAFFLE.
GOOD LUCK, EVERYONE!
IS THERE ANY TIME MR. KELLY DOESN'T WEAR A LAB COAT?
READY?
THIS IS IT!
OUR RUNNER UP PRIZE IS...A YO-YO!
AND THE YO-YO GOES TO...
NUMBER 333!
333

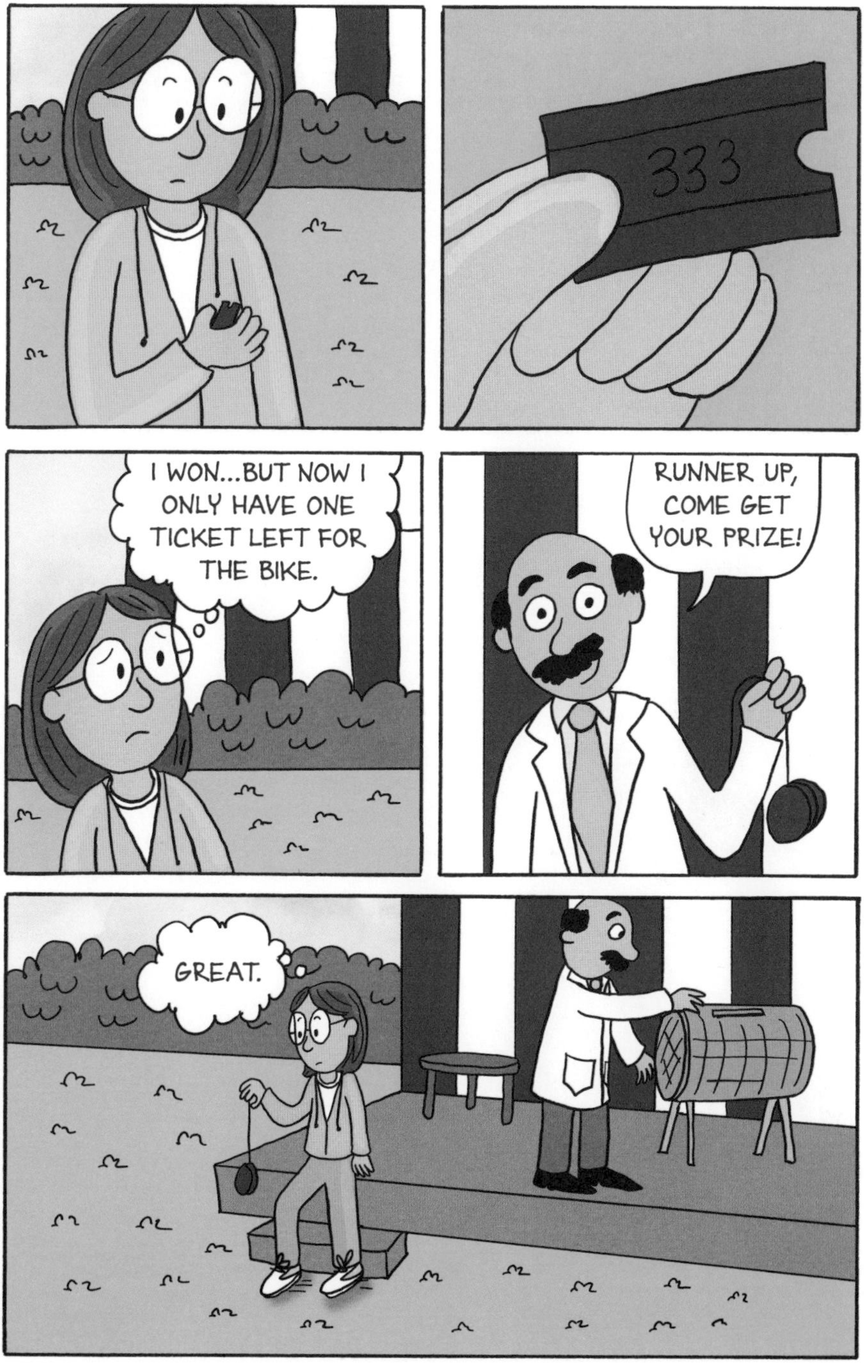
333
I WON...BUT NOW I ONLY HAVE ONE TICKET LEFT FOR THE BIKE.
RUNNER UP, COME GET YOUR PRIZE!
GREAT.

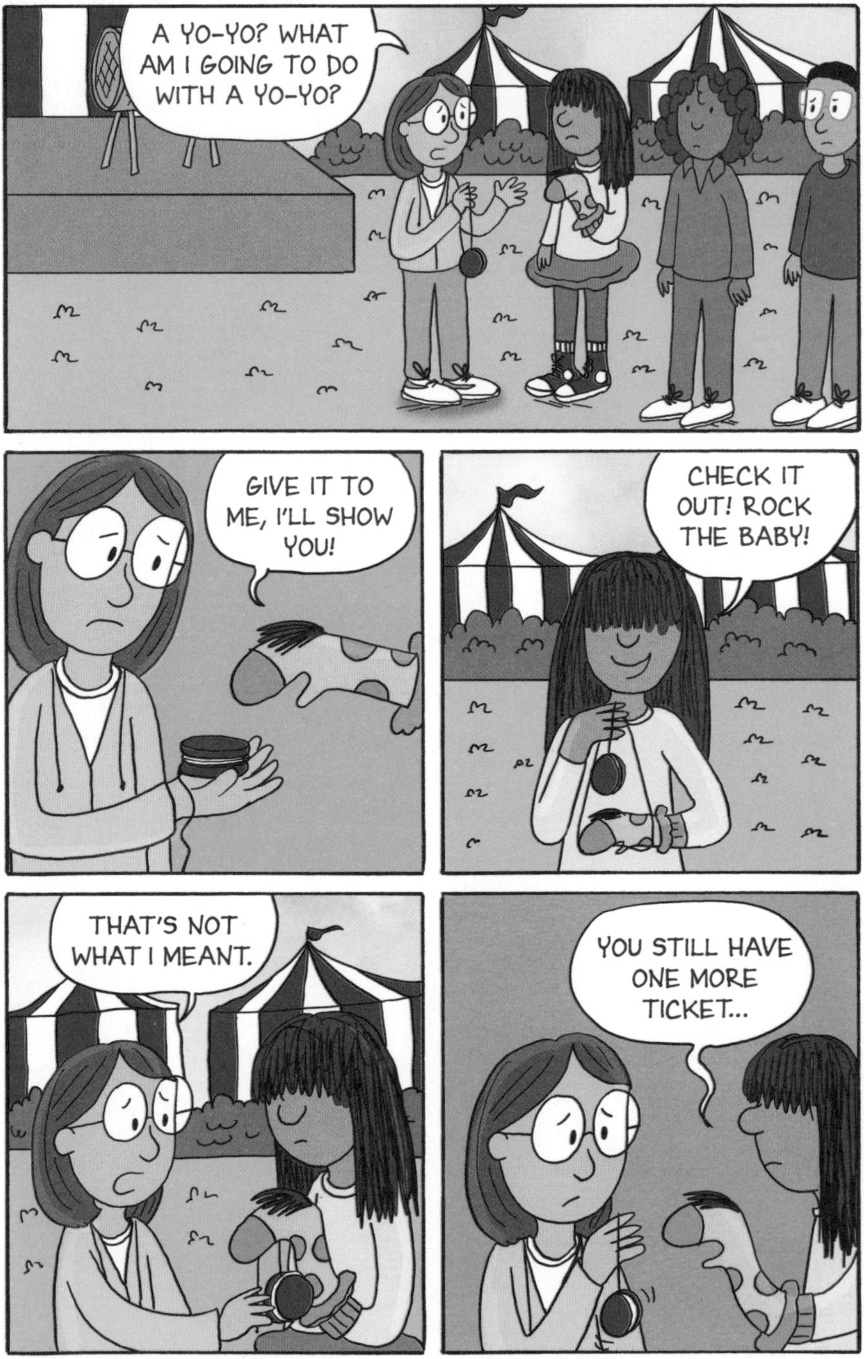
A YO-YO? WHAT AM I GOING TO DO WITH A YO-YO?
GIVE IT TO ME, I'LL SHOW YOU!
CHECK IT OUT! ROCK THE BABY!
THAT'S NOT WHAT I MEANT.
YOU STILL HAVE ONE MORE TICKET...

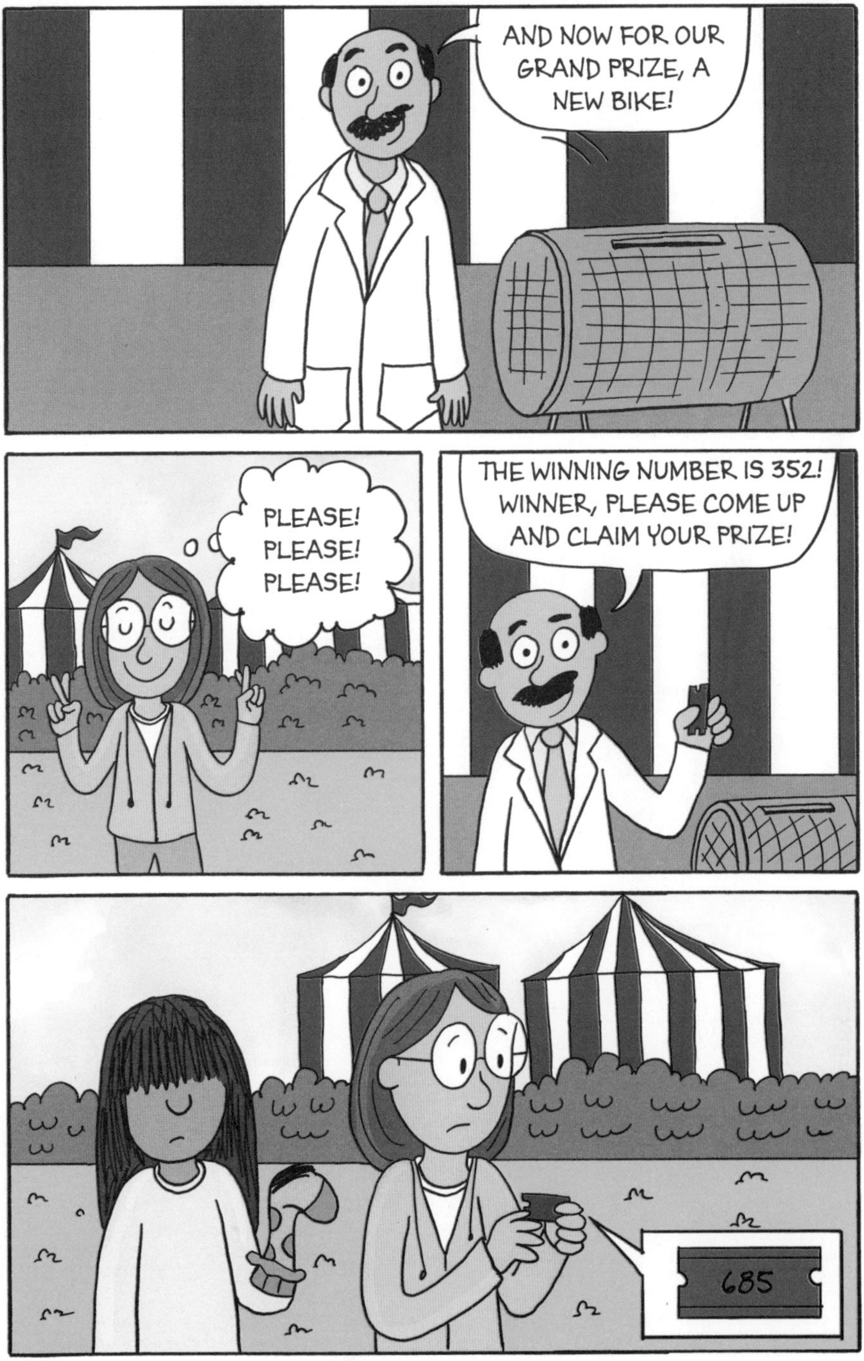
AND NOW FOR OUR GRAND PRIZE, A NEW BIKE!
PLEASE! PLEASE! PLEASE!
THE WINNING NUMBER IS 352! WINNER, PLEASE COME UP AND CLAIM YOUR PRIZE!
685

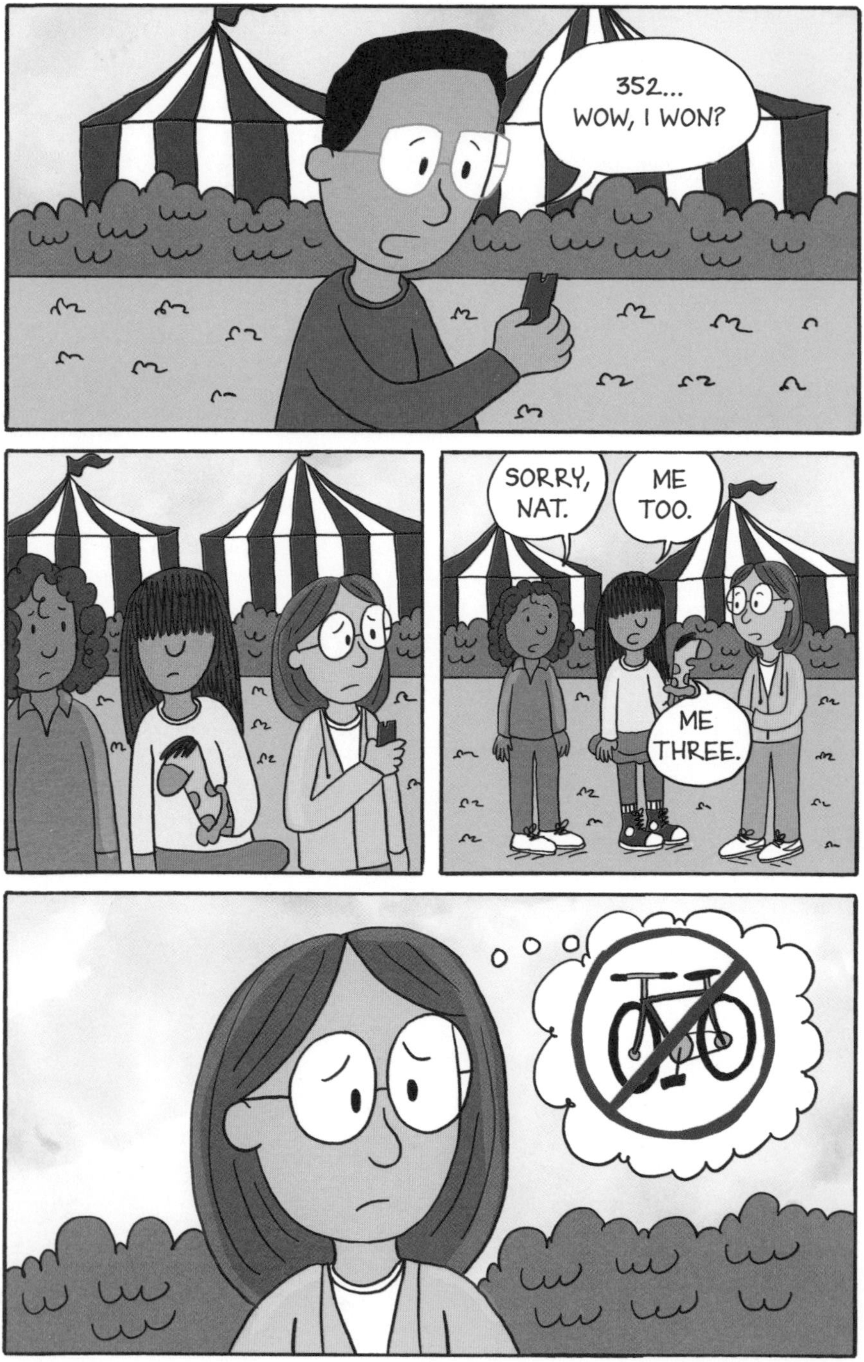
352...
WOW, I WON?
SORRY, NAT.
ME TOO.
ME THREE.

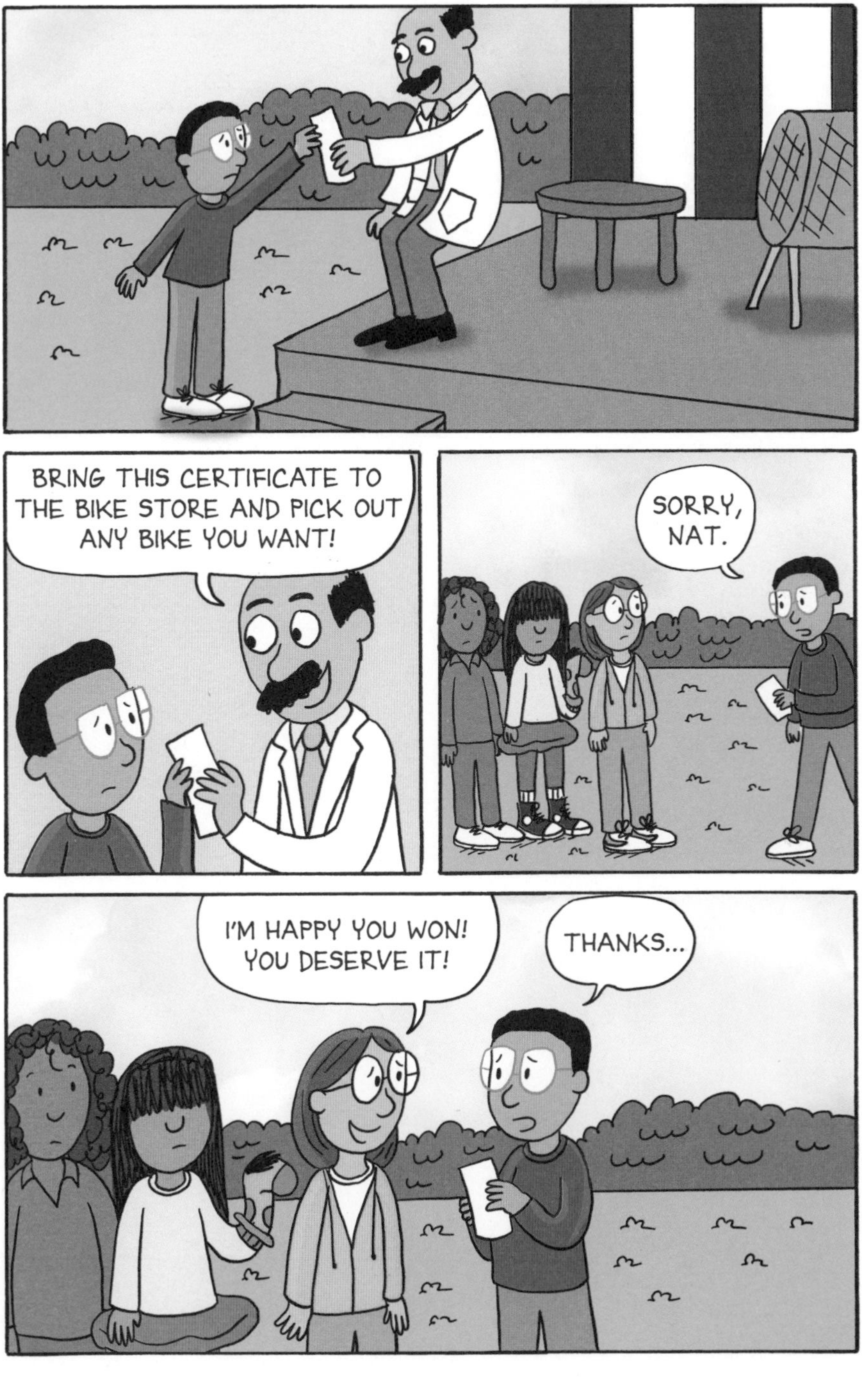
BRING THIS CERTIFICATE TO THE BIKE STORE AND PICK OUT ANY BIKE YOU WANT!
SORRY, NAT.
I'M HAPPY YOU WON! YOU DESERVE IT!
THANKS...

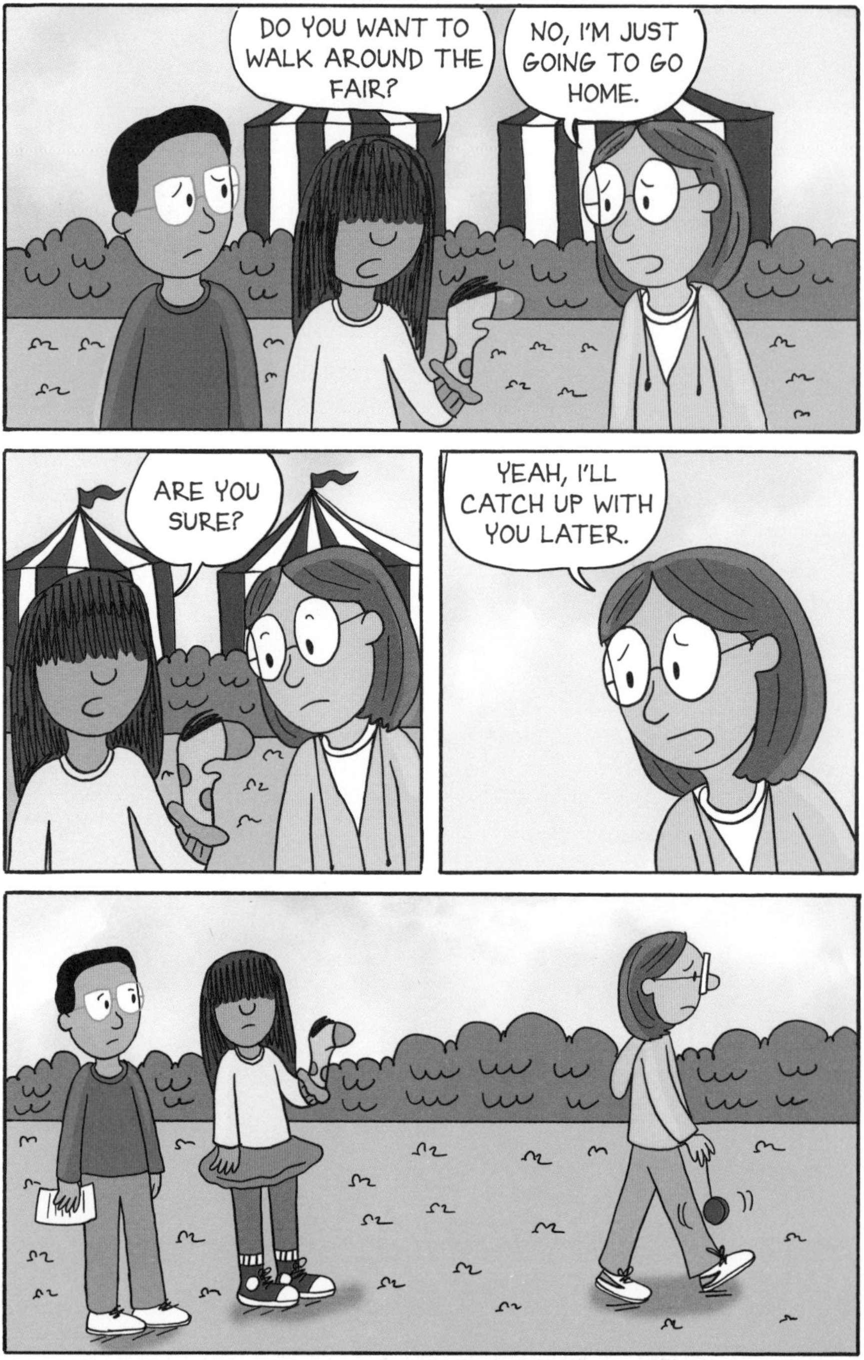
DO YOU WANT TO WALK AROUND THE FAIR?
NO, I'M JUST GOING TO GO HOME.
ARE YOU SURE?
YEAH, I'LL CATCH UP WITH YOU LATER.

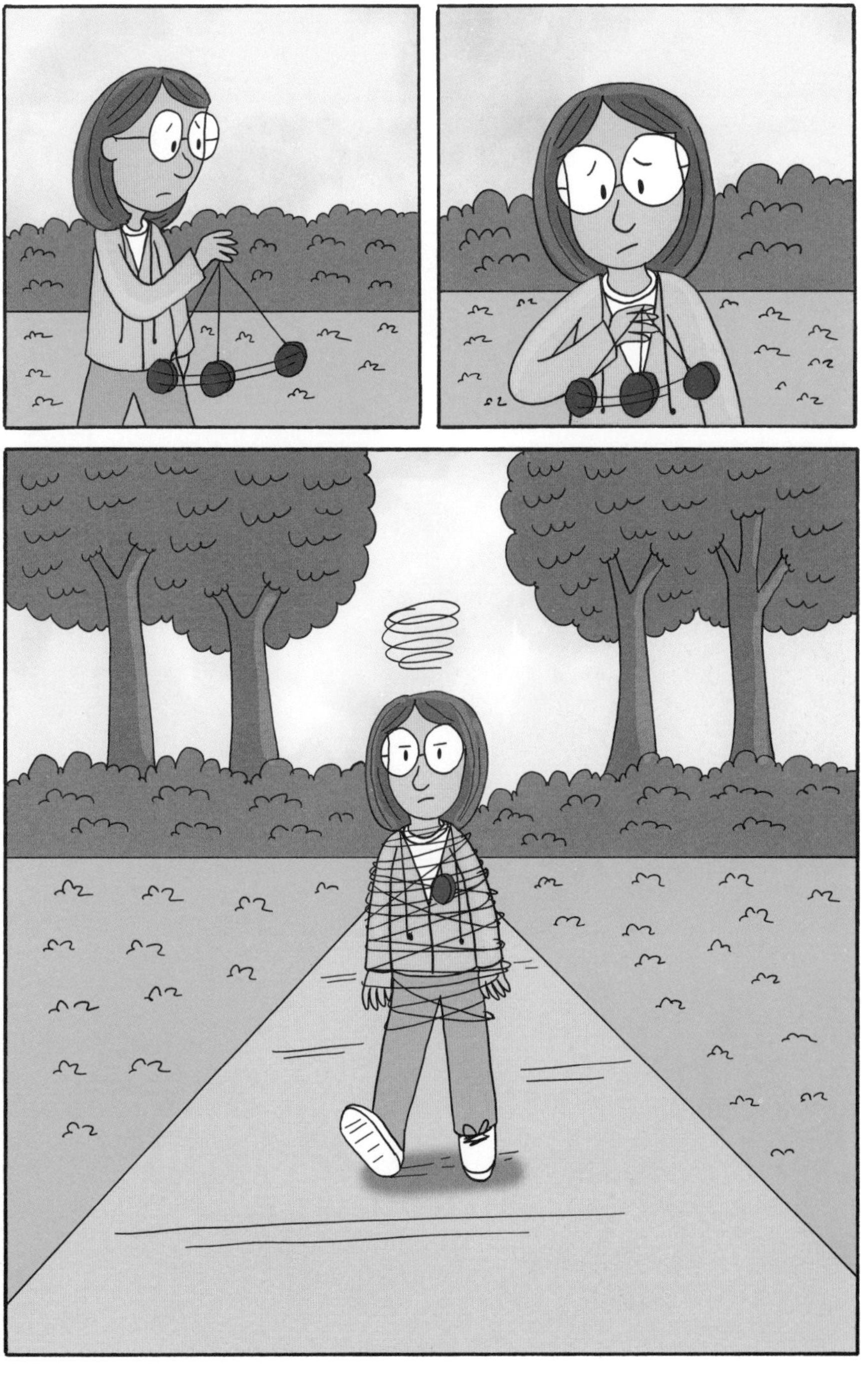

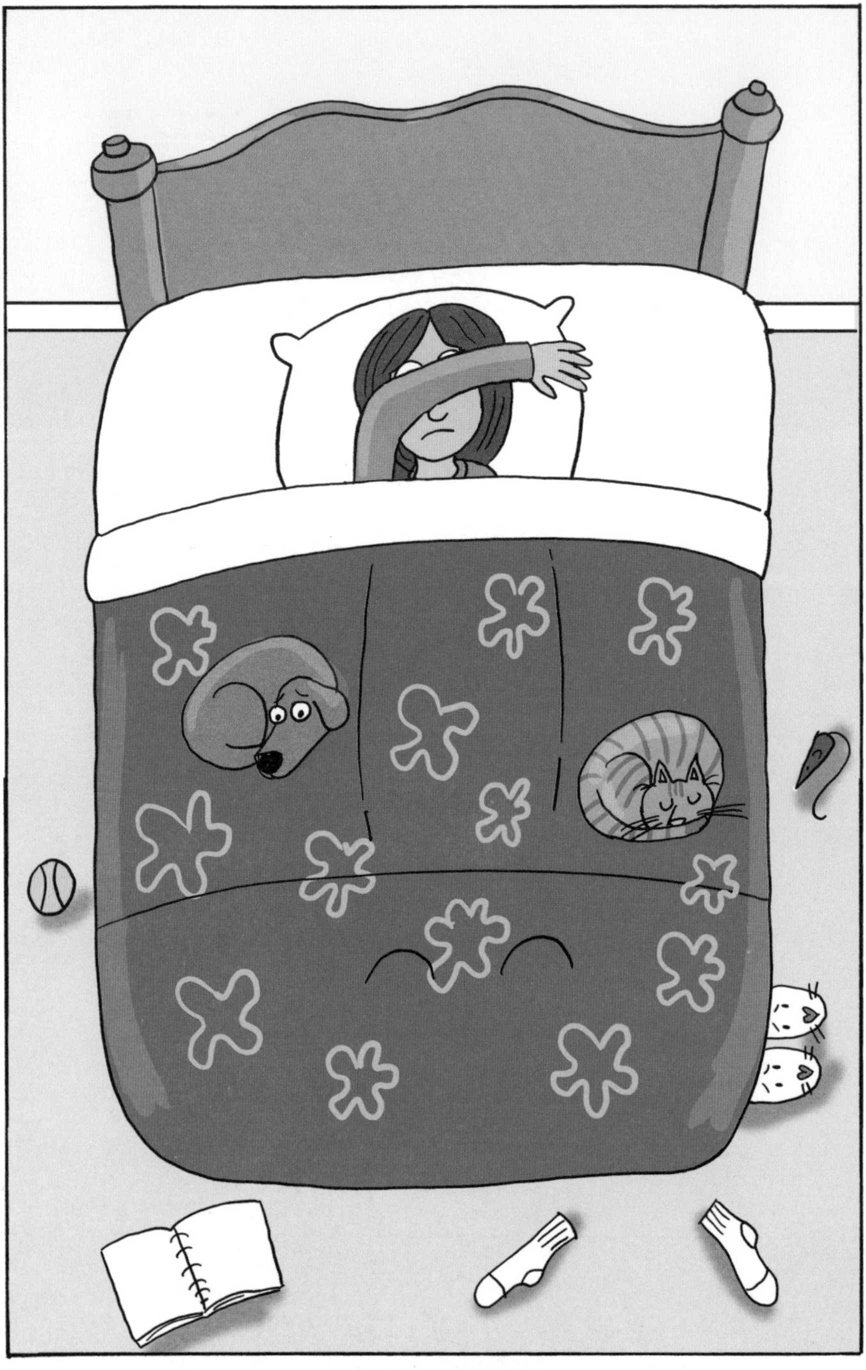

CHAPTER 16
SPECIAL DELIVERY

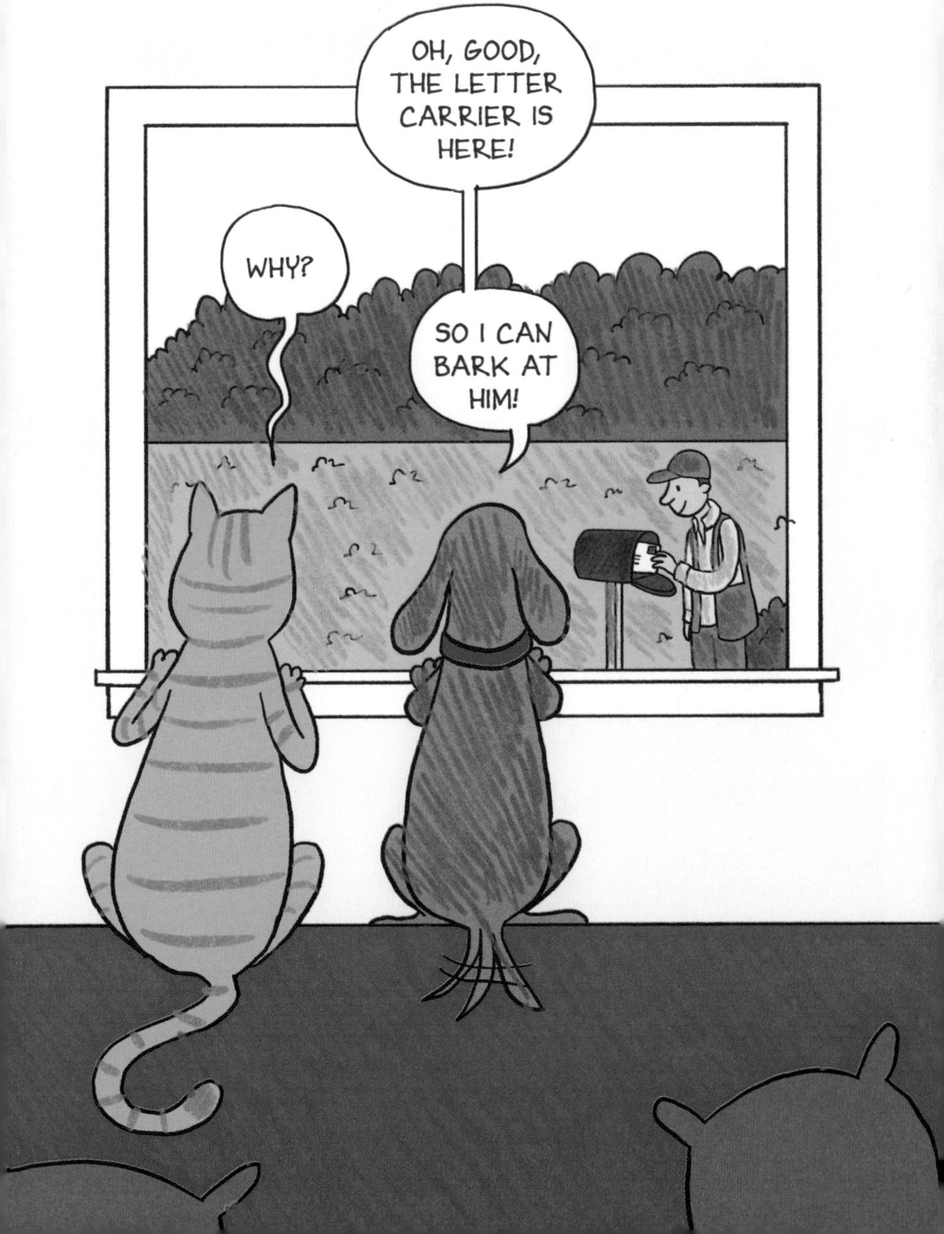
OH, GOOD, THE LETTER CARRIER IS HERE!
WHY?
SO I CAN BARK AT HIM!

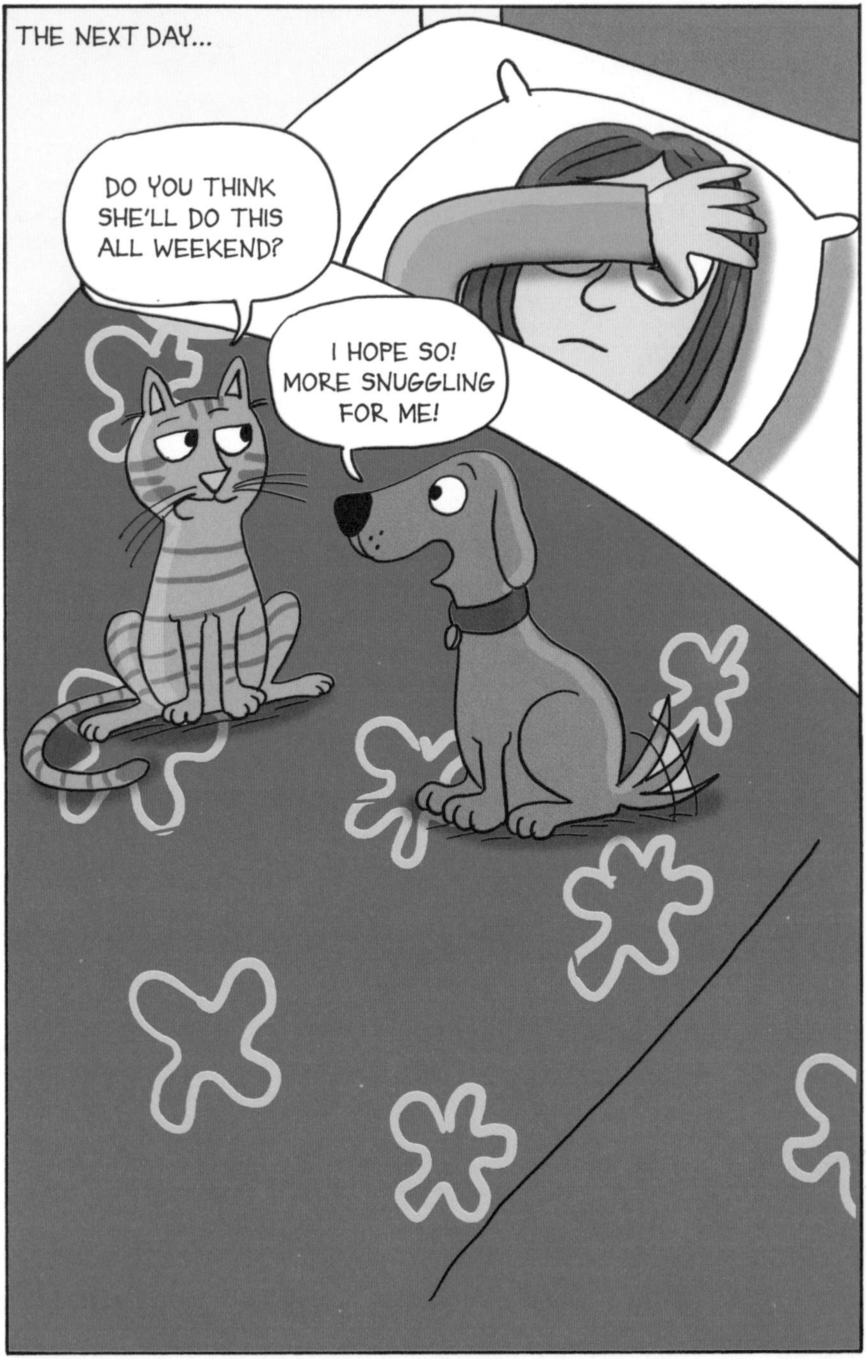
THE NEXT DAY...
DO YOU THINK SHE'LL DO THIS ALL WEEKEND?
I HOPE SO! MORE SNUGGLING FOR ME!

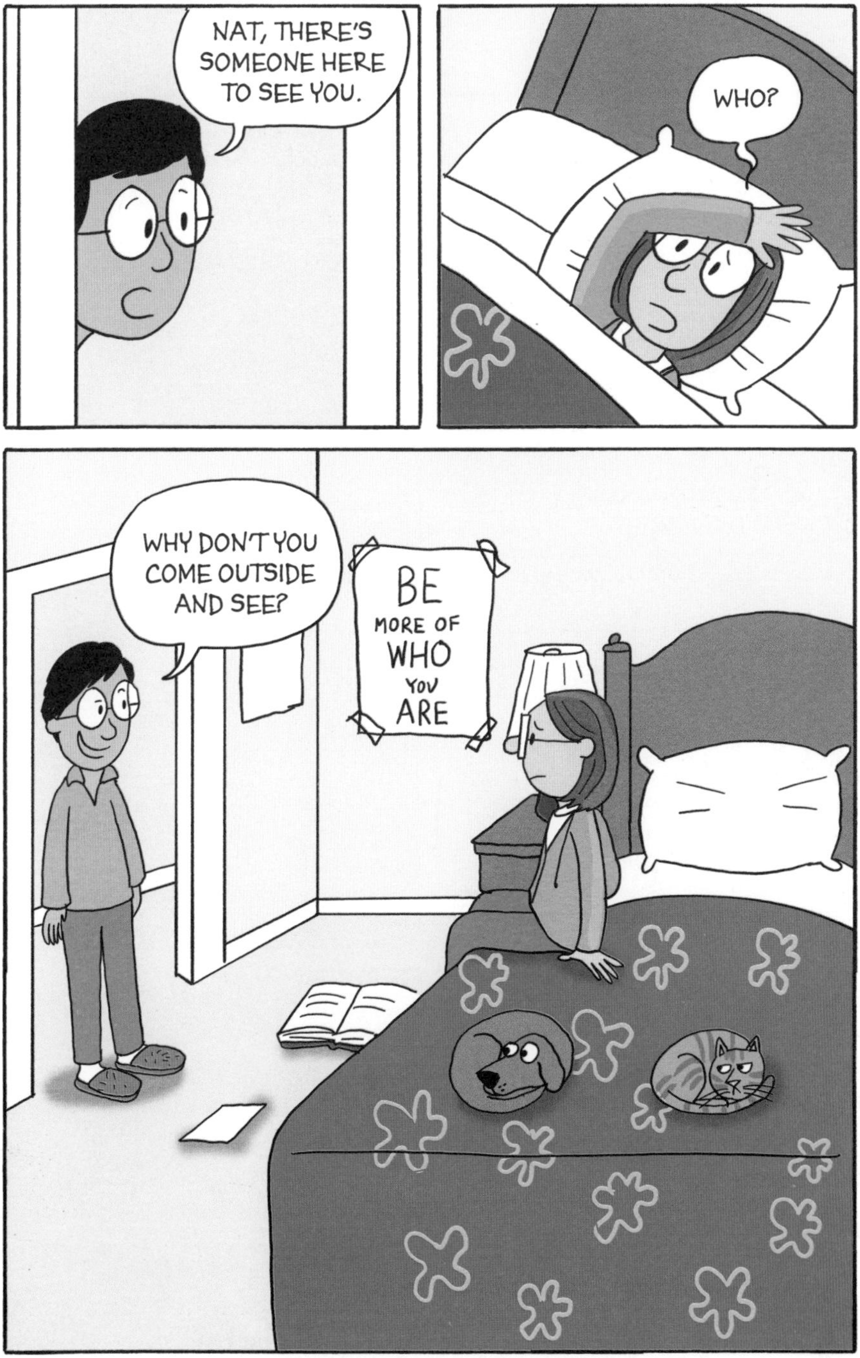
NAT, THERE'S SOMEONE HERE TO SEE YOU.
WHO?
WHY DON'T YOU COME OUTSIDE AND SEE?
BE MORE OF WHO YOU ARE

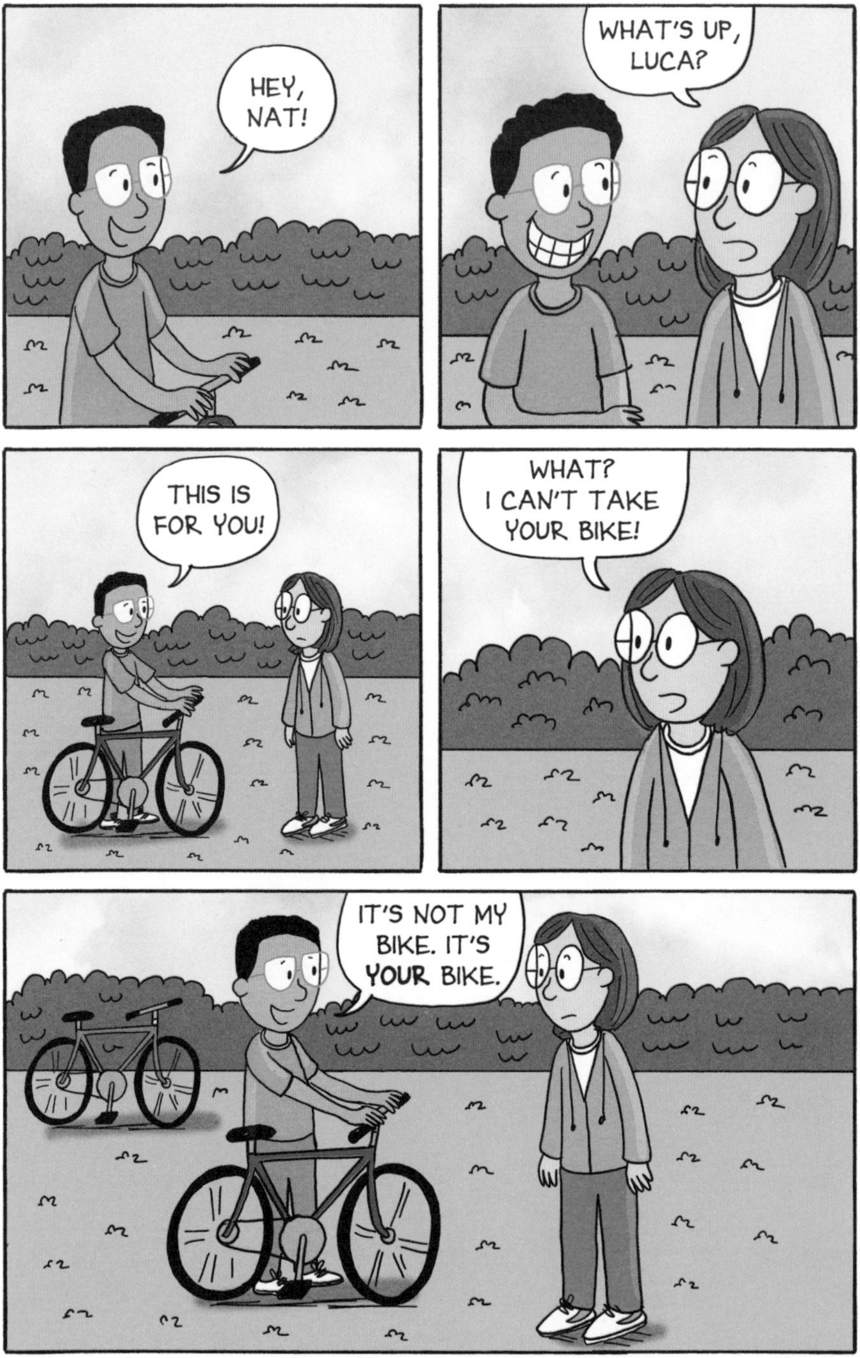
HEY, NAT!
WHAT'S UP, LUCA?
THIS IS FOR YOU!
WHAT? I CAN'T TAKE YOUR BIKE!
IT'S NOT MY BIKE. IT'S **YOUR** BIKE.

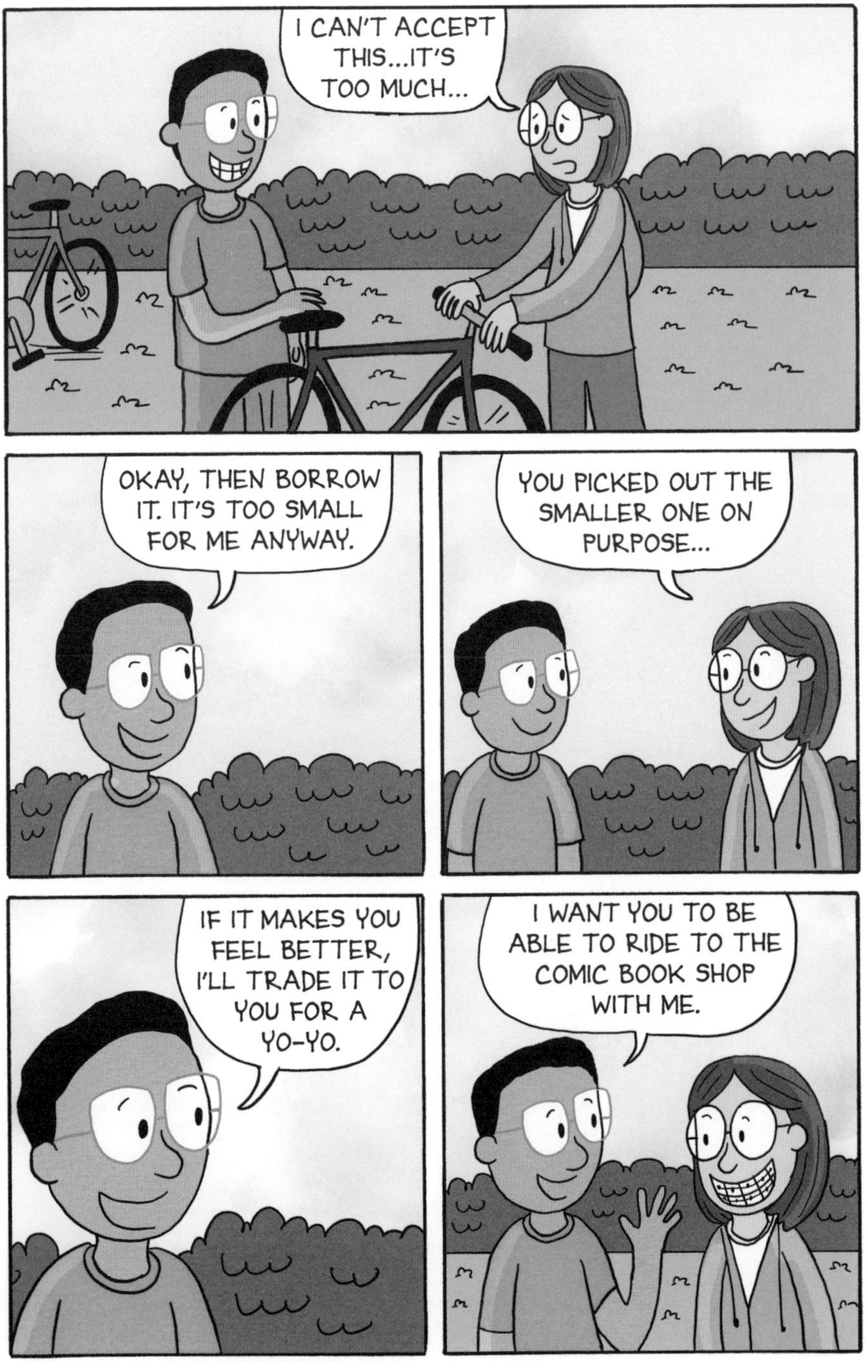
I CAN'T ACCEPT THIS...IT'S TOO MUCH...
OKAY, THEN BORROW IT. IT'S TOO SMALL FOR ME ANYWAY.
YOU PICKED OUT THE SMALLER ONE ON PURPOSE...
IF IT MAKES YOU FEEL BETTER, I'LL TRADE IT TO YOU FOR A YO-YO.
I WANT YOU TO BE ABLE TO RIDE TO THE COMIC BOOK SHOP WITH ME.

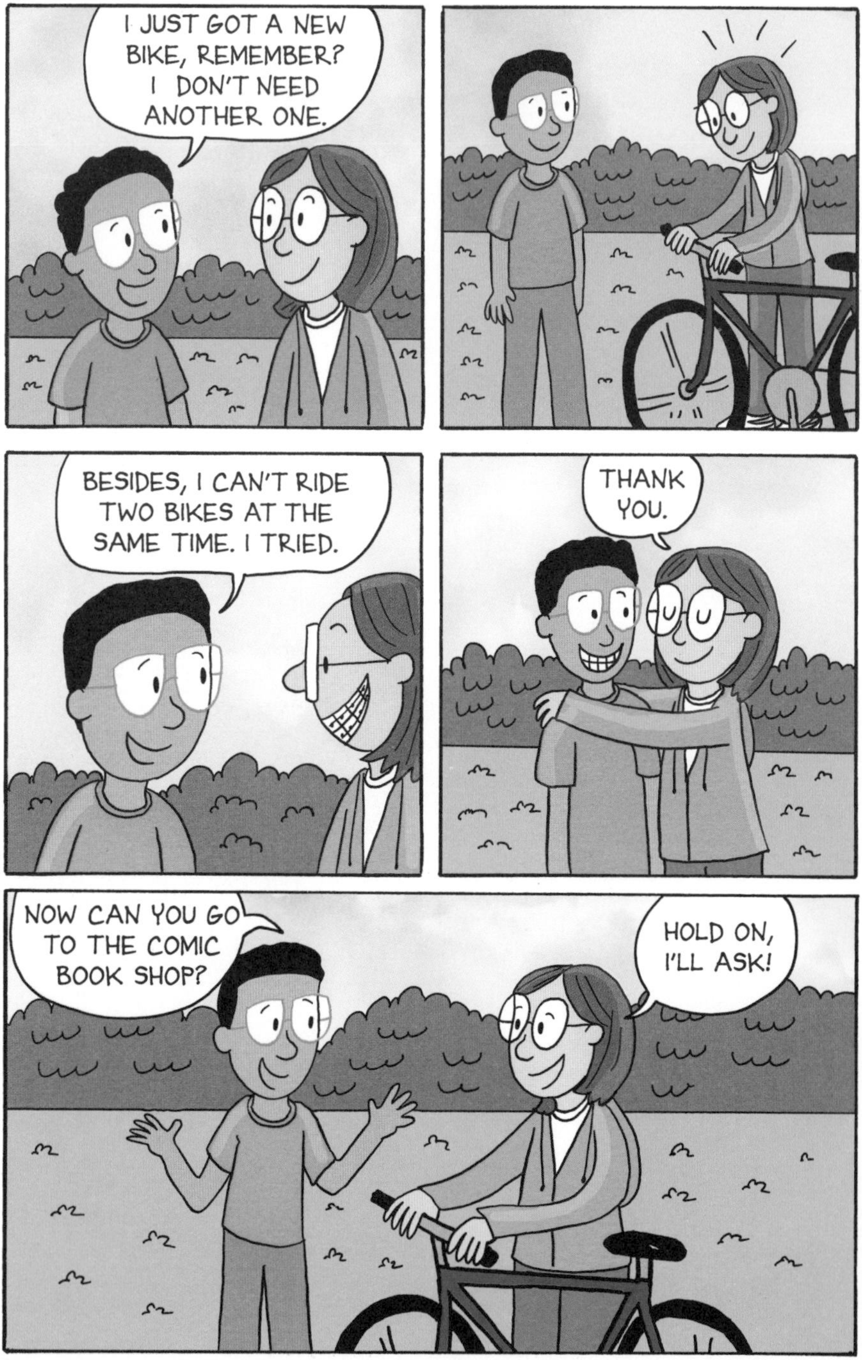
I JUST GOT A NEW BIKE, REMEMBER? I DON'T NEED ANOTHER ONE.
BESIDES, I CAN'T RIDE TWO BIKES AT THE SAME TIME. I TRIED.
THANK YOU.
NOW CAN YOU GO TO THE COMIC BOOK SHOP?
HOLD ON, I'LL ASK!

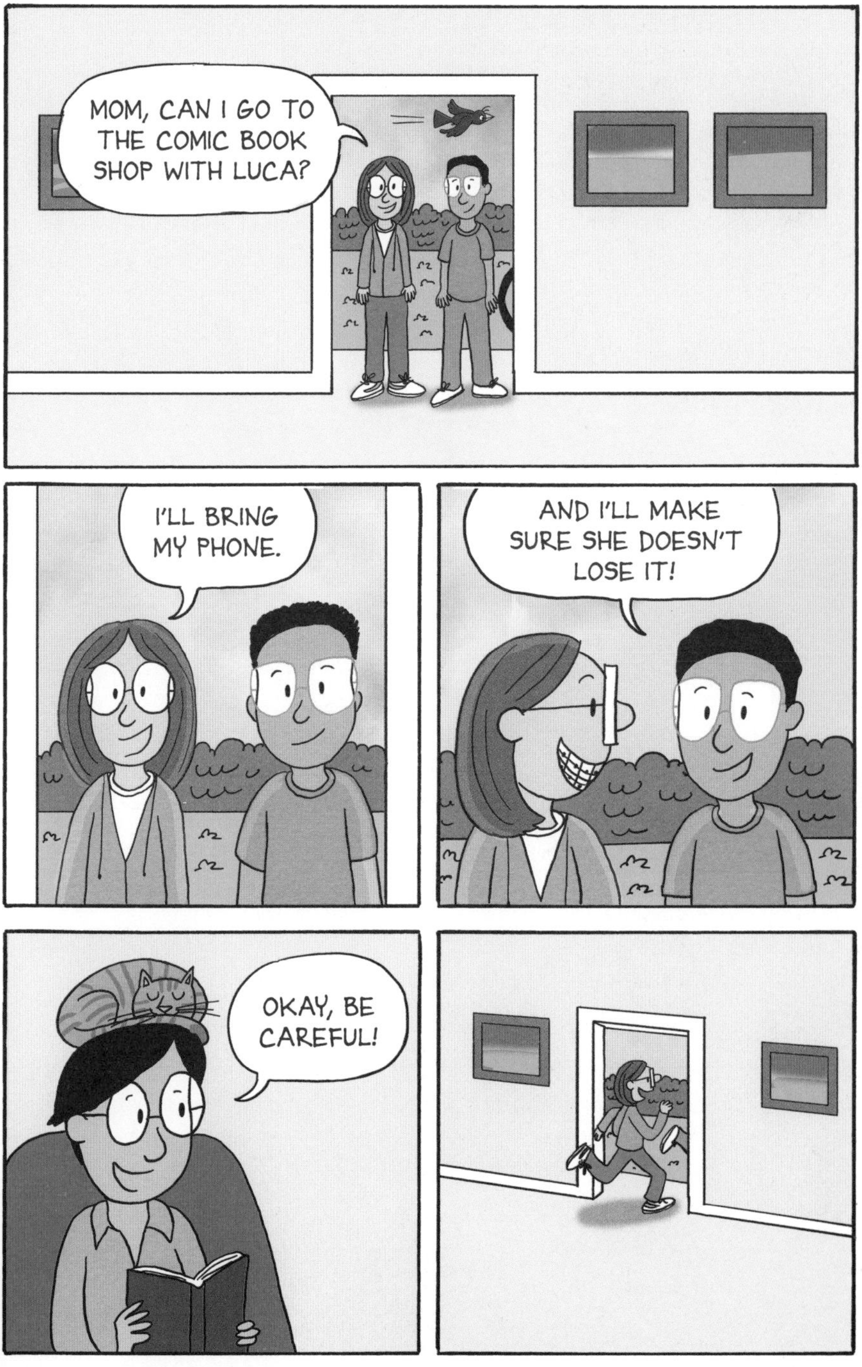
MOM, CAN I GO TO THE COMIC BOOK SHOP WITH LUCA?
I'LL BRING MY PHONE.
AND I'LL MAKE SURE SHE DOESN'T LOSE IT!
OKAY, BE CAREFUL!

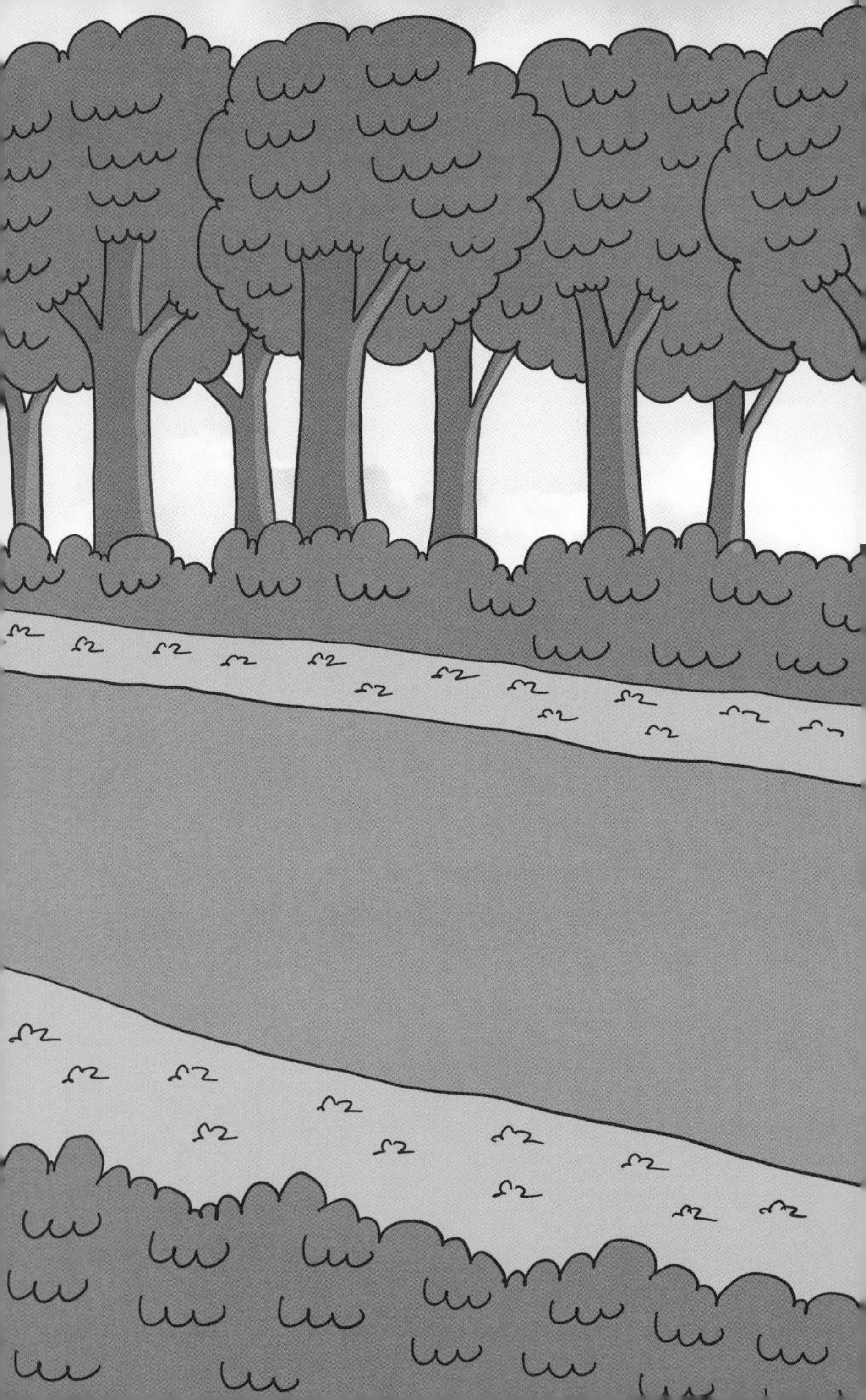

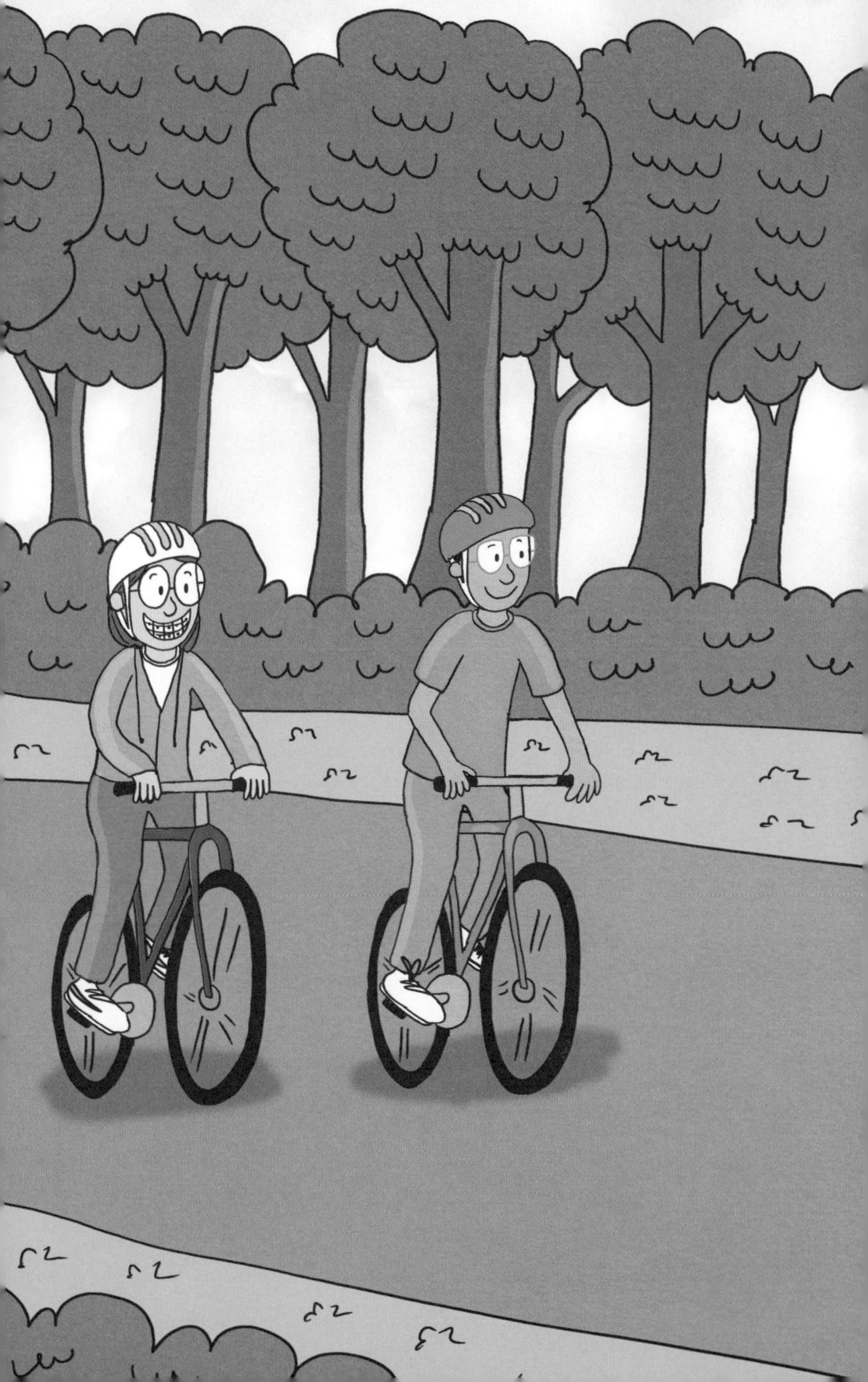

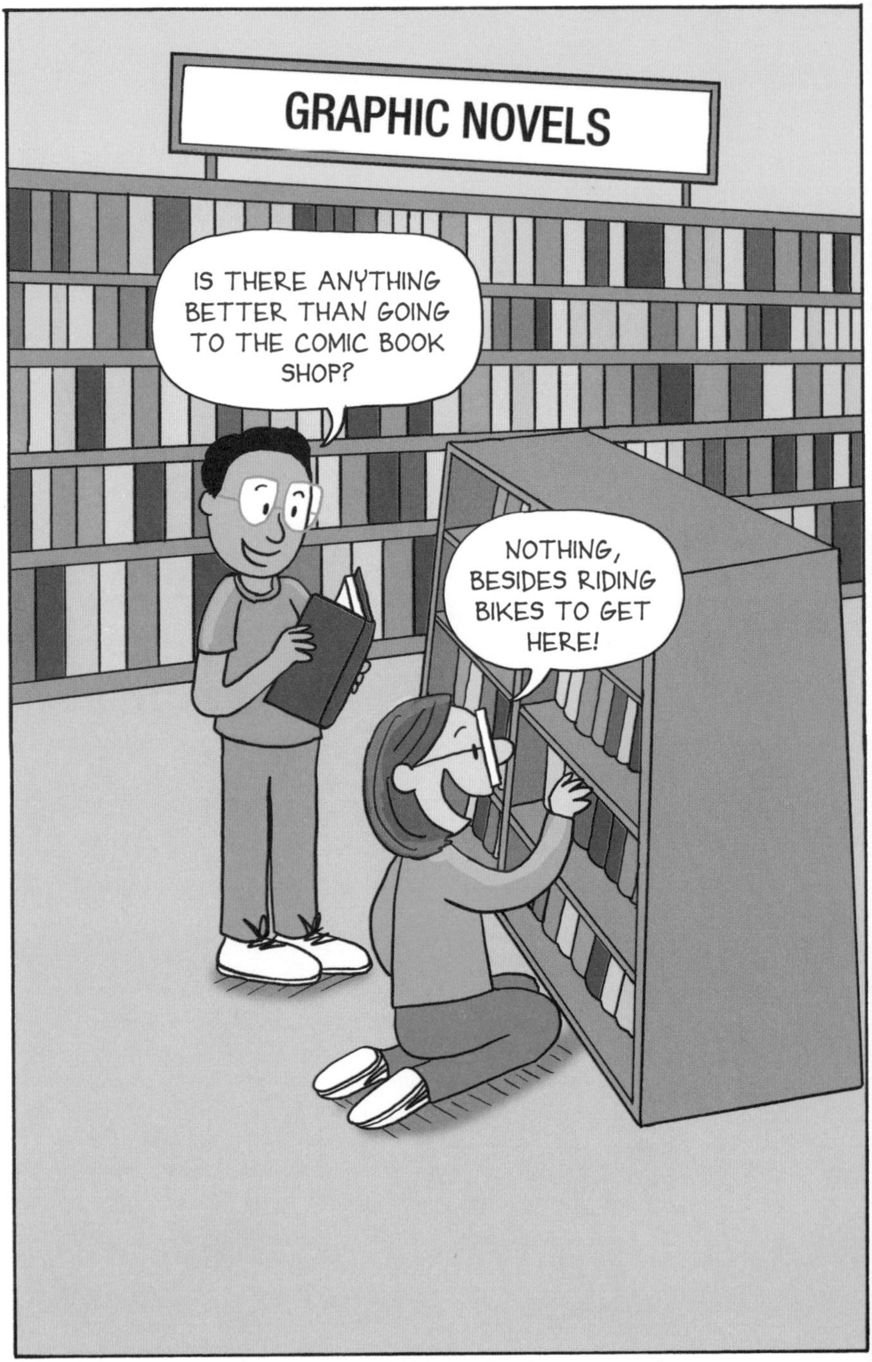
GRAPHIC NOVELS
IS THERE ANYTHING BETTER THAN GOING TO THE COMIC BOOK SHOP?
NOTHING, BESIDES RIDING BIKES TO GET HERE!

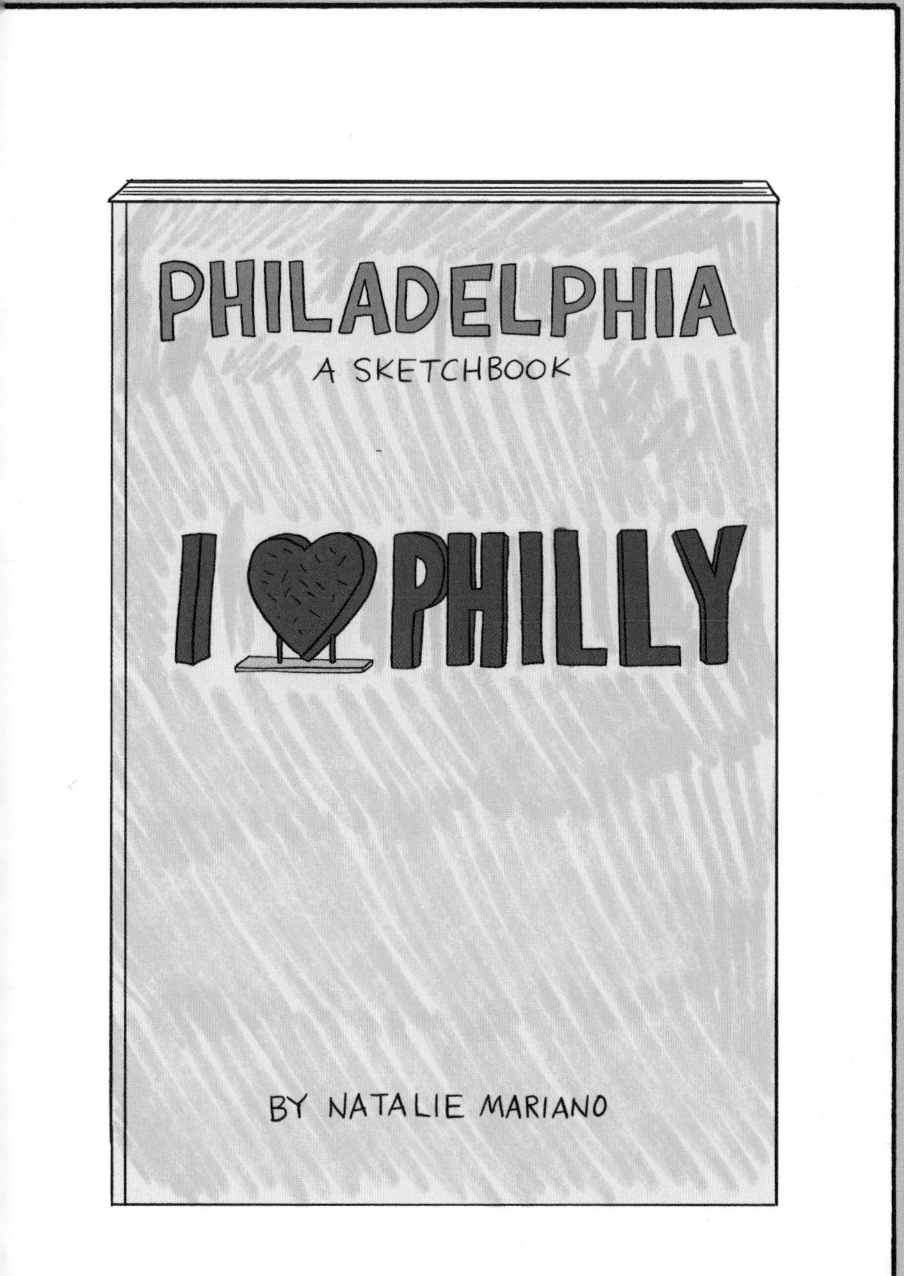
PHILADELPHIA
A SKETCHBOOK
I ♥ PHILLY
BY NATALIE MARIANO

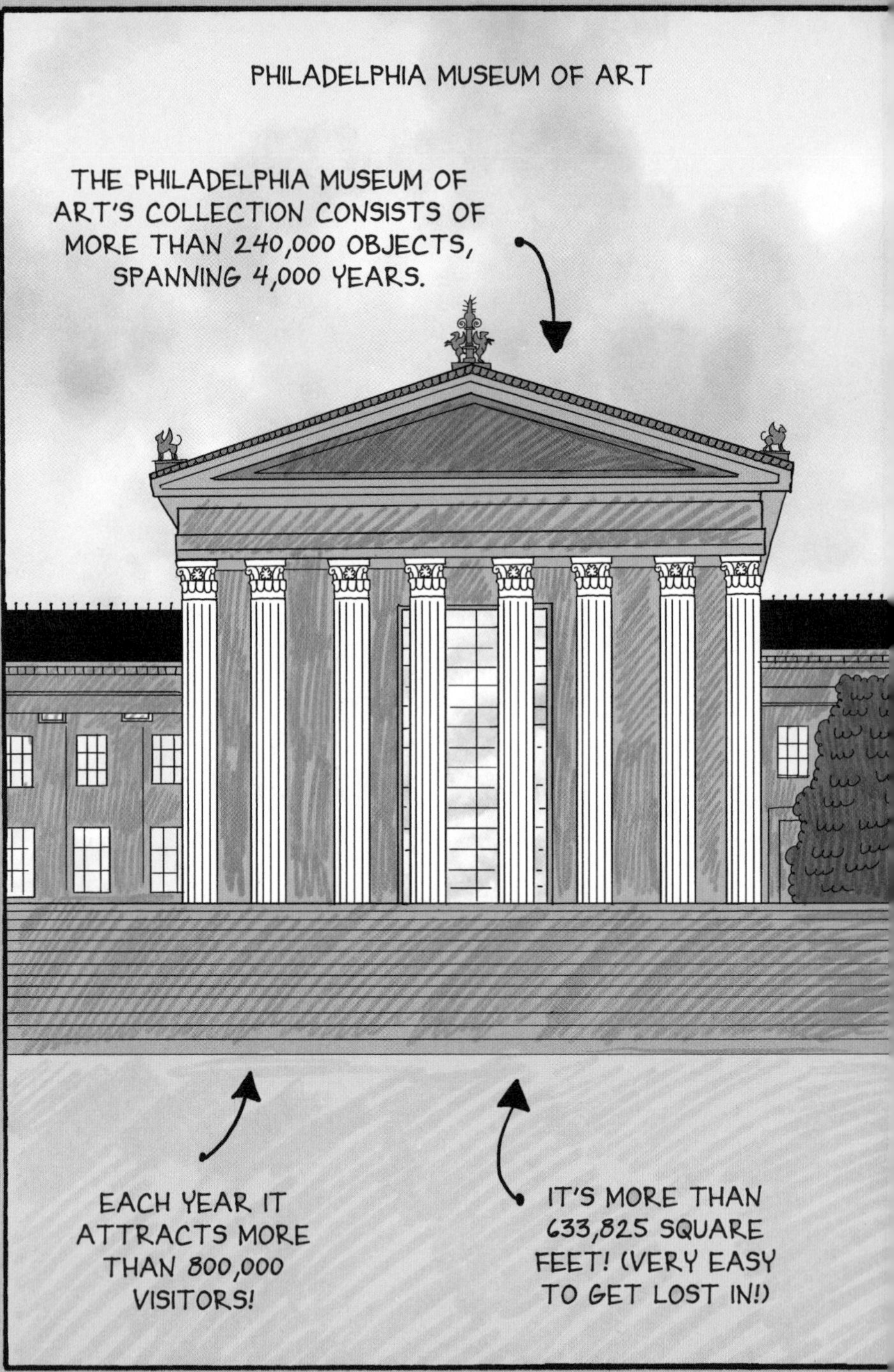
PHILADELPHIA MUSEUM OF ART
THE PHILADELPHIA MUSEUM OF ART'S COLLECTION CONSISTS OF MORE THAN 240,000 OBJECTS, SPANNING 4,000 YEARS.
EACH YEAR IT ATTRACTS MORE THAN 800,000 VISITORS!
IT'S MORE THAN 633,825 SQUARE FEET! (VERY EASY TO GET LOST IN!)

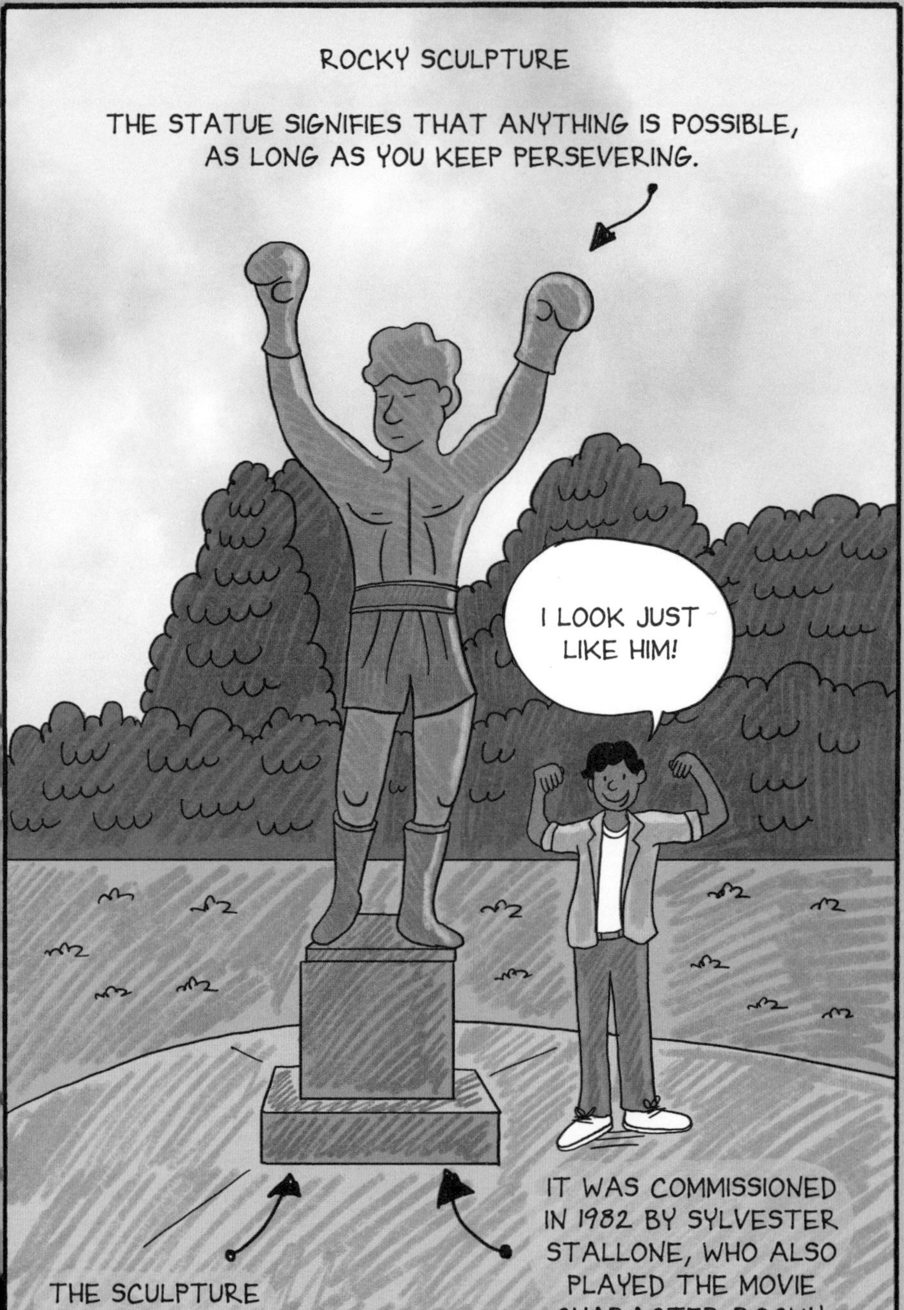
ROCKY SCULPTURE
THE STATUE SIGNIFIES THAT ANYTHING IS POSSIBLE, AS LONG AS YOU KEEP PERSEVERING.
I LOOK JUST LIKE HIM!
THE SCULPTURE IS 2,000 LBS.
IT WAS COMMISSIONED IN 1982 BY SYLVESTER STALLONE, WHO ALSO PLAYED THE MOVIE CHARACTER ROCKY.

EVEN MORE THINGS YOU CAN'T UNSEE FROM THE MÜTTER MUSEUM:

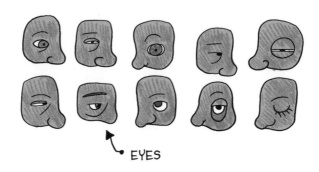

EYES

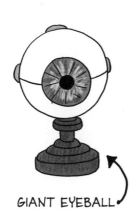

GIANT EYEBALL

BRAIN

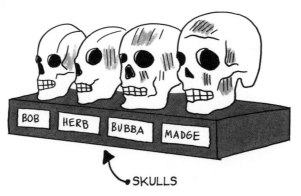

SKULLS

HATS OF PHILADELPHIA

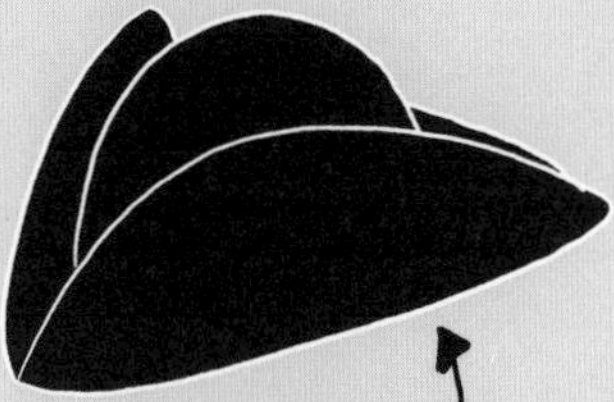

TRICORNE
SOLDIERS PINNED UP THE SIDES IN ORDER TO CHANNEL RAINWATER AWAY.

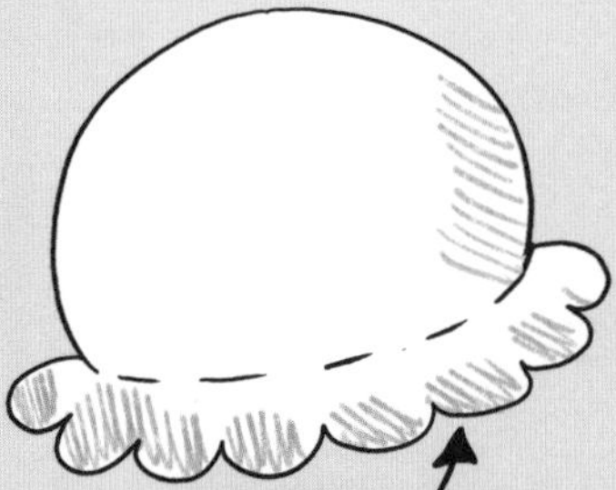

MOBCAP
GIRLS AND WOMEN TUCKED THEIR HAIR UNDER THESE CAPS TO AVOID STYLING IT.

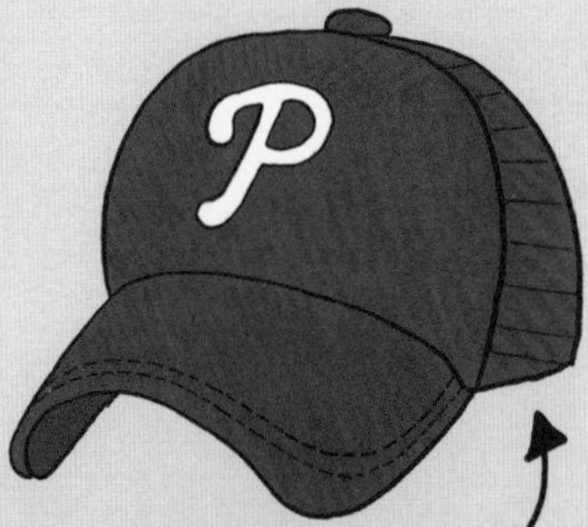
P

BASEBALL CAP
FAN FAVORITE FOR SHOWING LOVE FOR THE HOME TEAM, THE PHILADELPHIA PHILLIES.

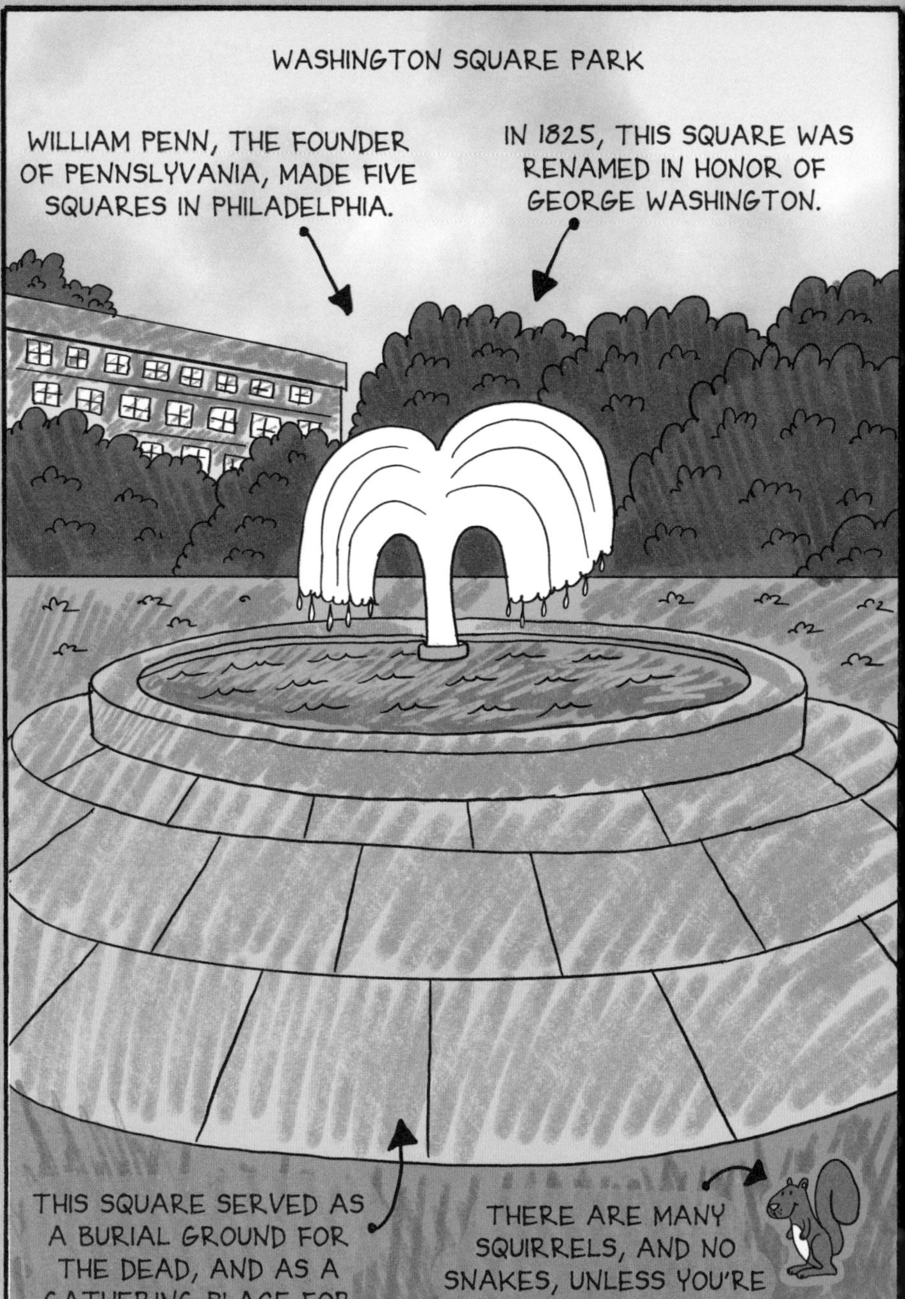
WASHINGTON SQUARE PARK
WILLIAM PENN, THE FOUNDER OF PENNSLYVANIA, MADE FIVE SQUARES IN PHILADELPHIA.
IN 1825, THIS SQUARE WAS RENAMED IN HONOR OF GEORGE WASHINGTON.
THIS SQUARE SERVED AS A BURIAL GROUND FOR THE DEAD, AND AS A GATHERING PLACE FOR THE LIVING.
THERE ARE MANY SQUIRRELS, AND NO SNAKES, UNLESS YOU'RE WITH SHAWN.

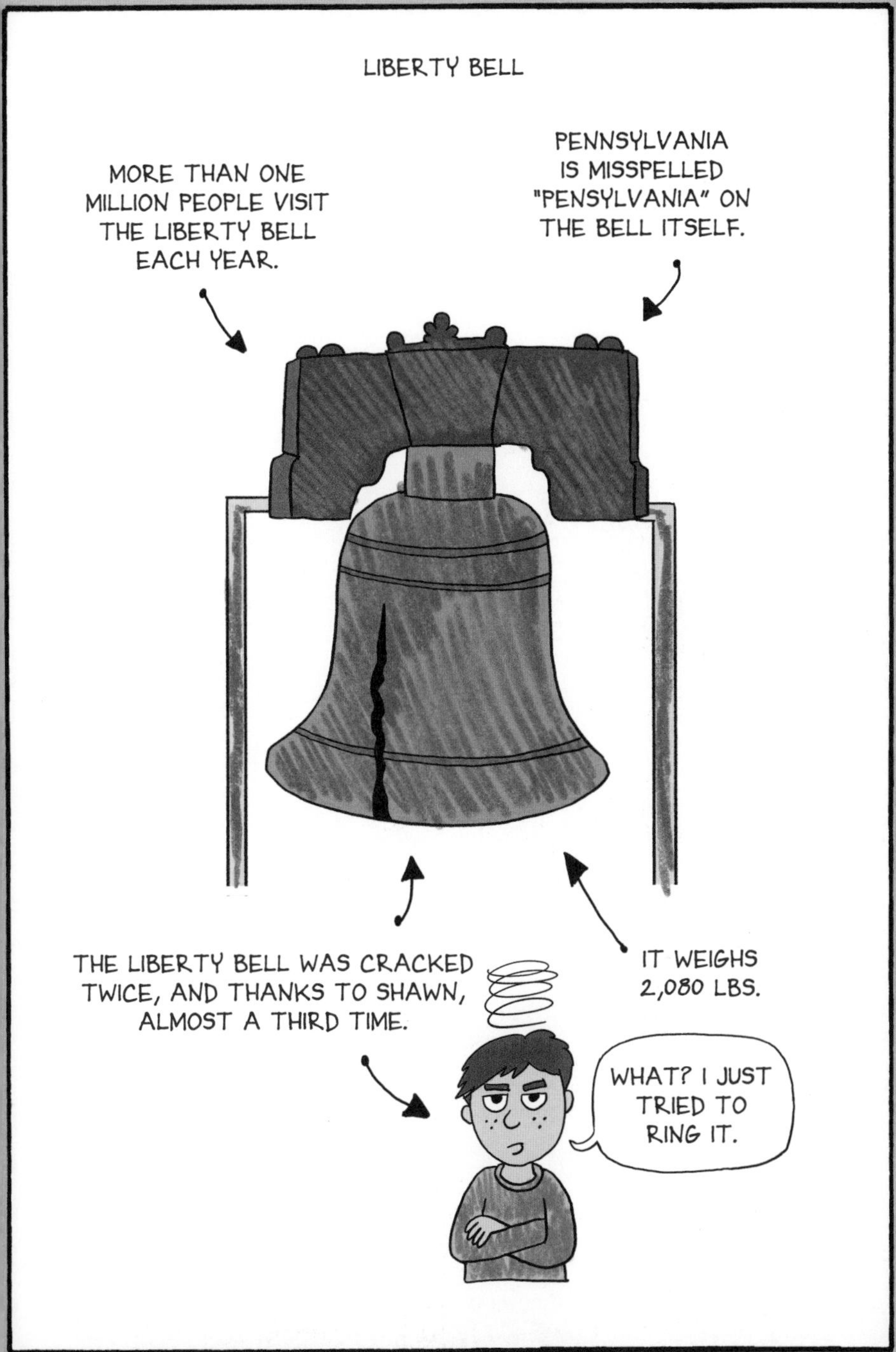
LIBERTY BELL
MORE THAN ONE MILLION PEOPLE VISIT THE LIBERTY BELL EACH YEAR.
PENNSYLVANIA IS MISSPELLED "PENSYLVANIA" ON THE BELL ITSELF.
THE LIBERTY BELL WAS CRACKED TWICE, AND THANKS TO SHAWN, ALMOST A THIRD TIME.
IT WEIGHS 2,080 LBS.
WHAT? I JUST TRIED TO RING IT.

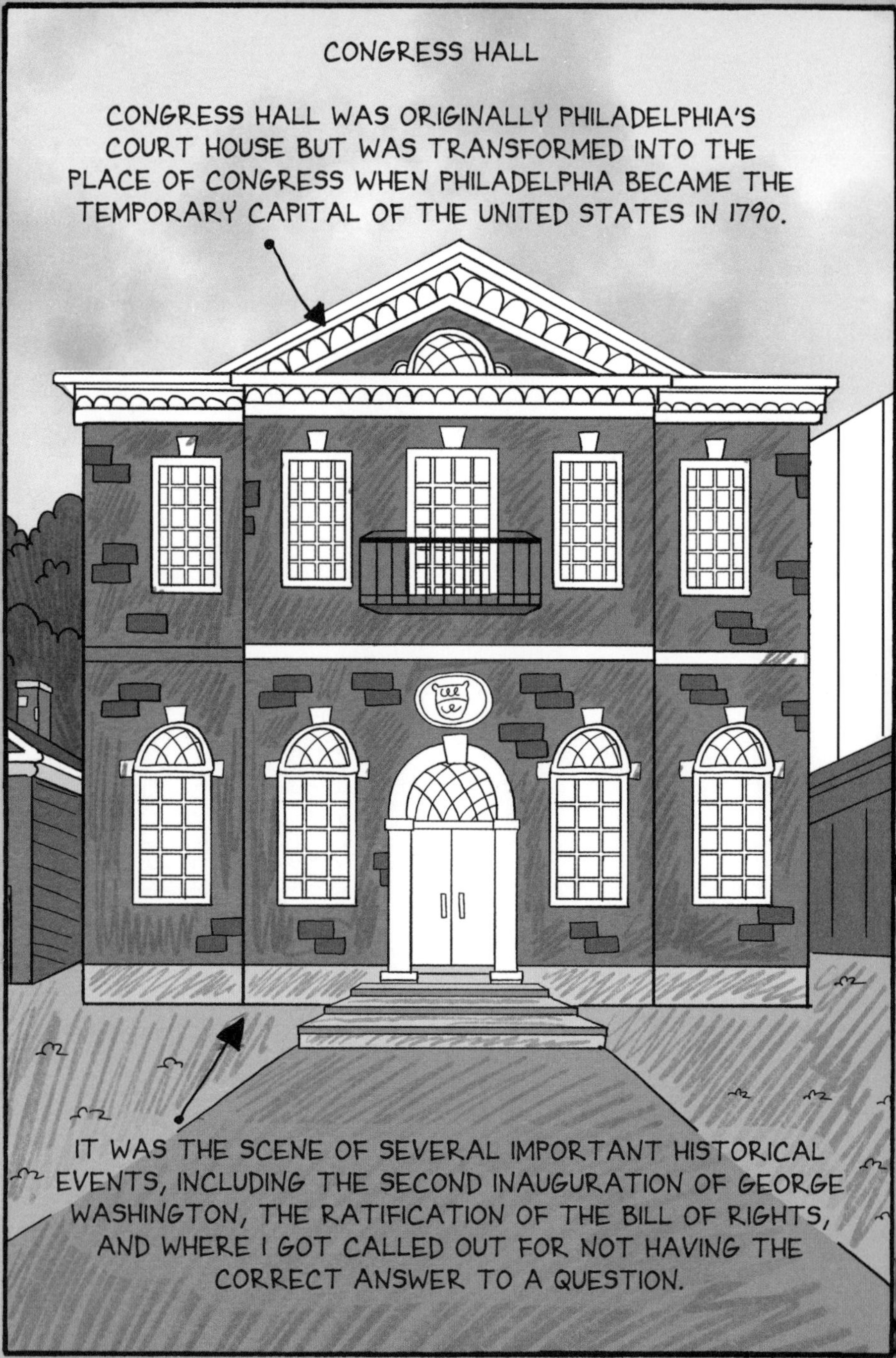
CONGRESS HALL
CONGRESS HALL WAS ORIGINALLY PHILADELPHIA'S COURT HOUSE BUT WAS TRANSFORMED INTO THE PLACE OF CONGRESS WHEN PHILADELPHIA BECAME THE TEMPORARY CAPITAL OF THE UNITED STATES IN 1790.
IT WAS THE SCENE OF SEVERAL IMPORTANT HISTORICAL EVENTS, INCLUDING THE SECOND INAUGURATION OF GEORGE WASHINGTON, THE RATIFICATION OF THE BILL OF RIGHTS, AND WHERE I GOT CALLED OUT FOR NOT HAVING THE CORRECT ANSWER TO A QUESTION.

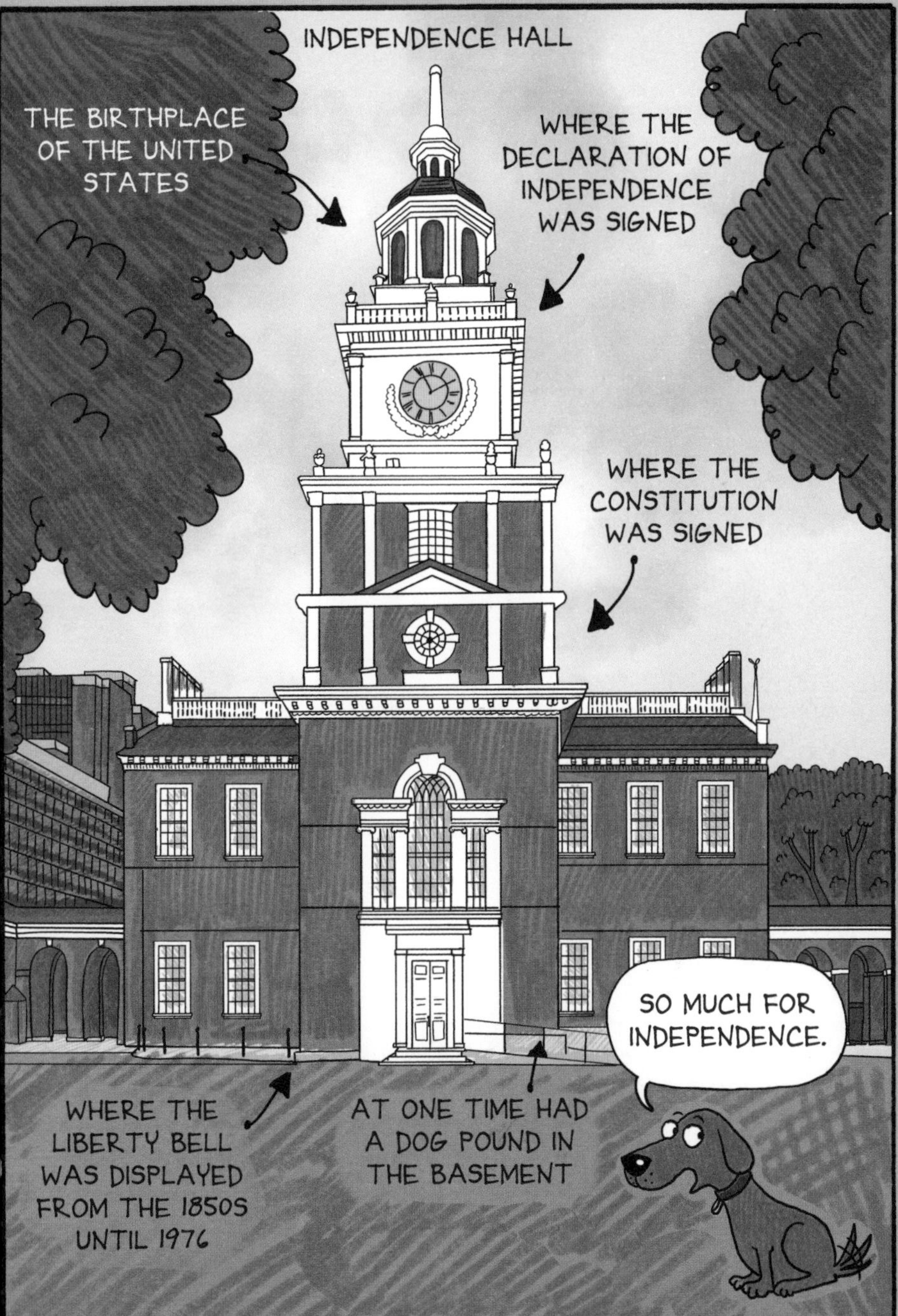
INDEPENDENCE HALL
THE BIRTHPLACE OF THE UNITED STATES
WHERE THE DECLARATION OF INDEPENDENCE WAS SIGNED
WHERE THE CONSTITUTION WAS SIGNED
WHERE THE LIBERTY BELL WAS DISPLAYED FROM THE 1850S UNTIL 1976
AT ONE TIME HAD A DOG POUND IN THE BASEMENT
SO MUCH FOR INDEPENDENCE.

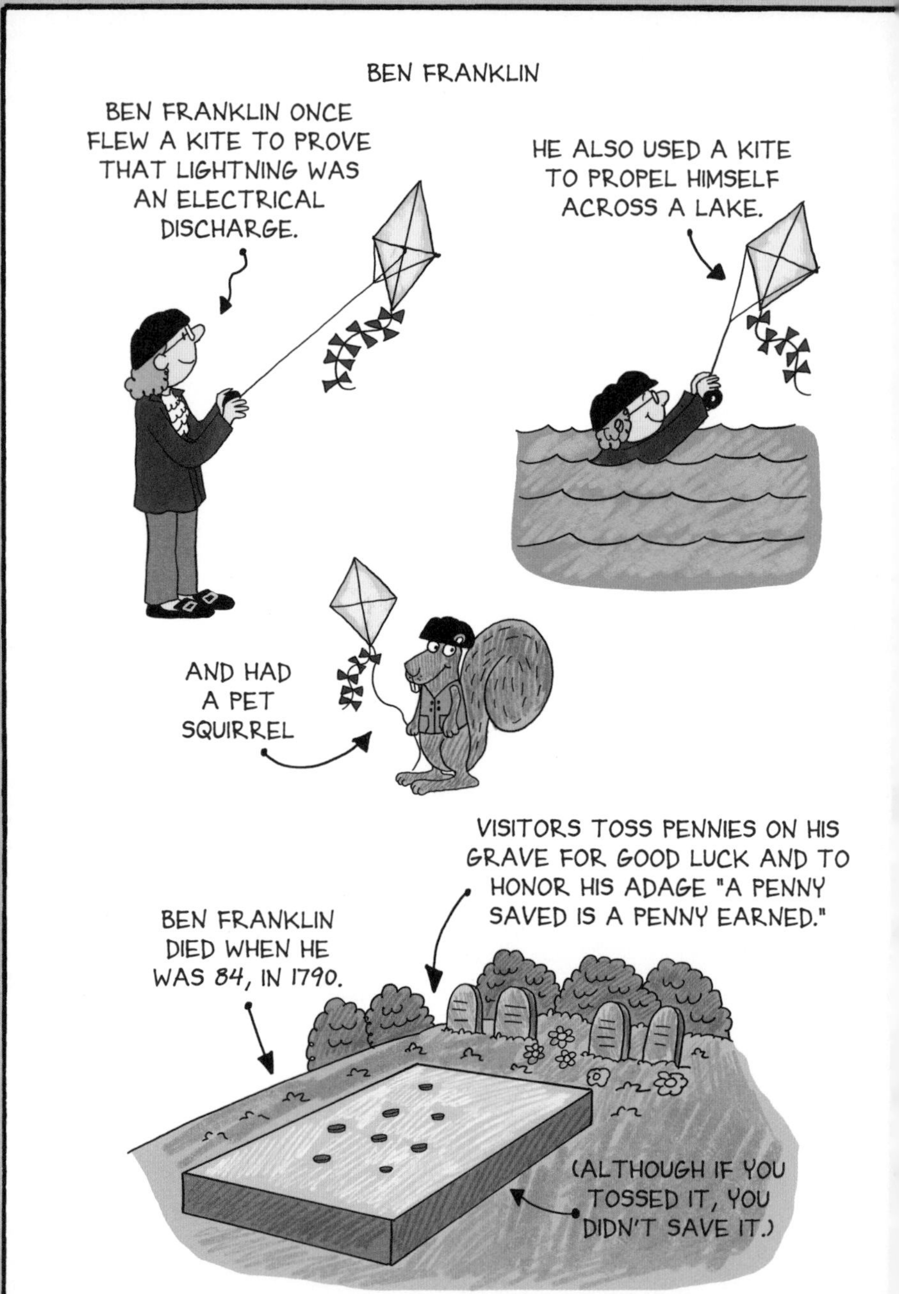
BEN FRANKLIN
BEN FRANKLIN ONCE FLEW A KITE TO PROVE THAT LIGHTNING WAS AN ELECTRICAL DISCHARGE.
HE ALSO USED A KITE TO PROPEL HIMSELF ACROSS A LAKE.
AND HAD A PET SQUIRREL
VISITORS TOSS PENNIES ON HIS GRAVE FOR GOOD LUCK AND TO HONOR HIS ADAGE "A PENNY SAVED IS A PENNY EARNED."
BEN FRANKLIN DIED WHEN HE WAS 84, IN 1790.
(ALTHOUGH IF YOU TOSSED IT, YOU DIDN'T SAVE IT.)

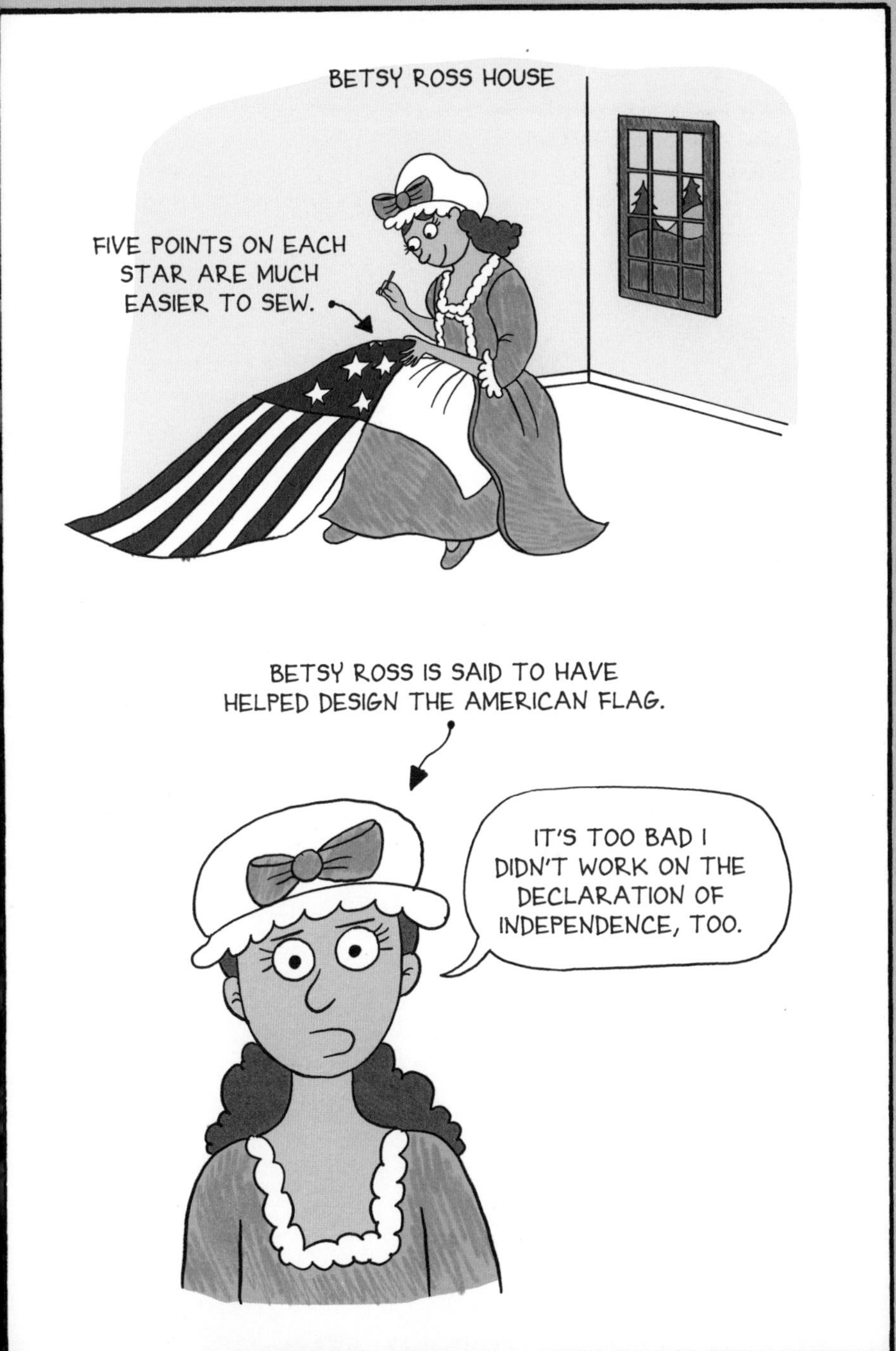
BETSY ROSS HOUSE
FIVE POINTS ON EACH STAR ARE MUCH EASIER TO SEW.
BETSY ROSS IS SAID TO HAVE HELPED DESIGN THE AMERICAN FLAG.
IT'S TOO BAD I DIDN'T WORK ON THE DECLARATION OF INDEPENDENCE, TOO.

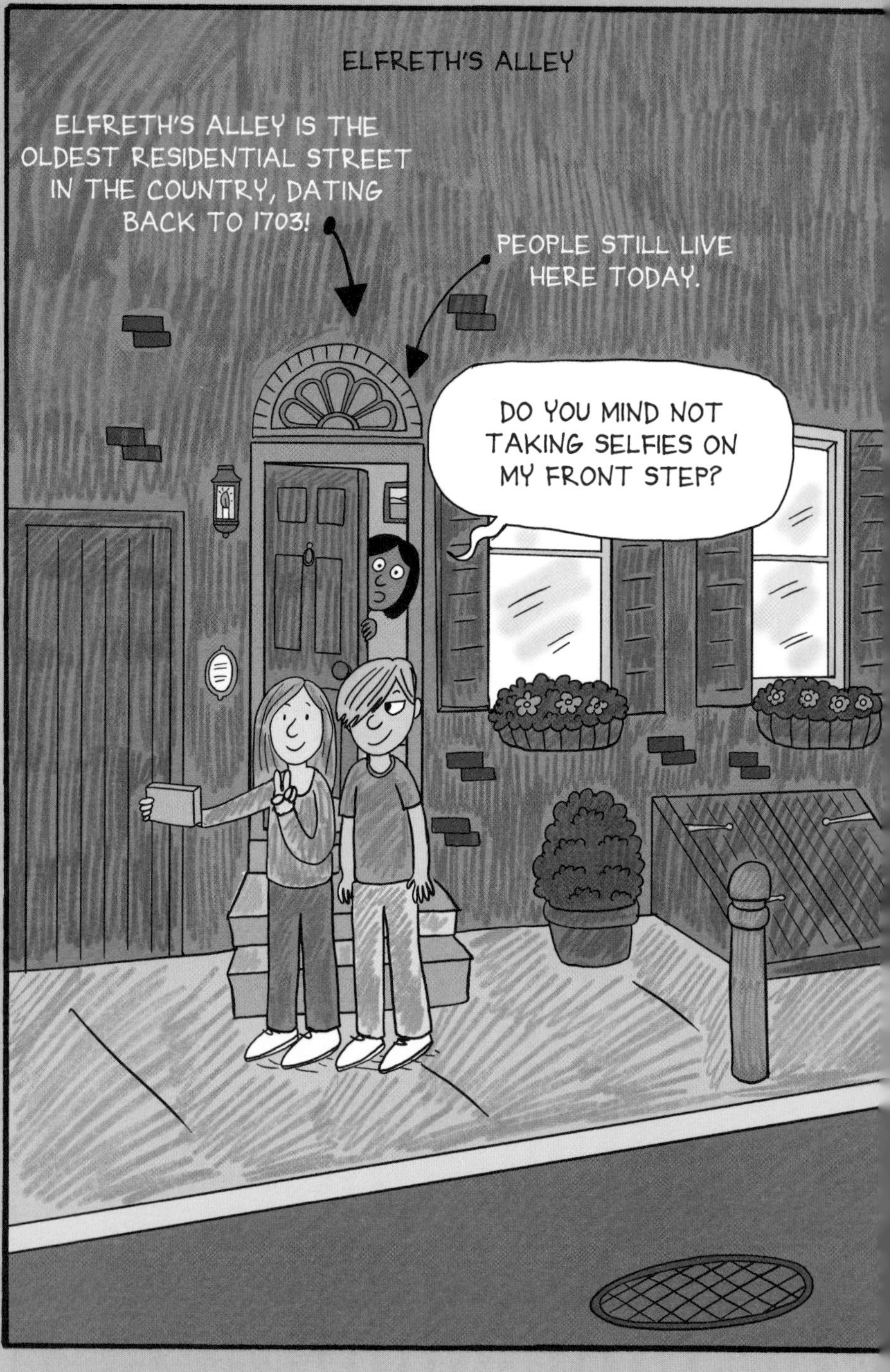
ELFRETH'S ALLEY
ELFRETH'S ALLEY IS THE OLDEST RESIDENTIAL STREET IN THE COUNTRY, DATING BACK TO 1703!
PEOPLE STILL LIVE HERE TODAY.
DO YOU MIND NOT TAKING SELFIES ON MY FRONT STEP?

CHEESESTEAK

A CHEESESTEAK IS A SANDWICH MADE FROM THINLY SLICED PIECES OF BEEFSTEAK AND MELTED CHEESE ON A ROLL.

THE SANDWICH WAS INVENTED IN THE EARLY 1930S.

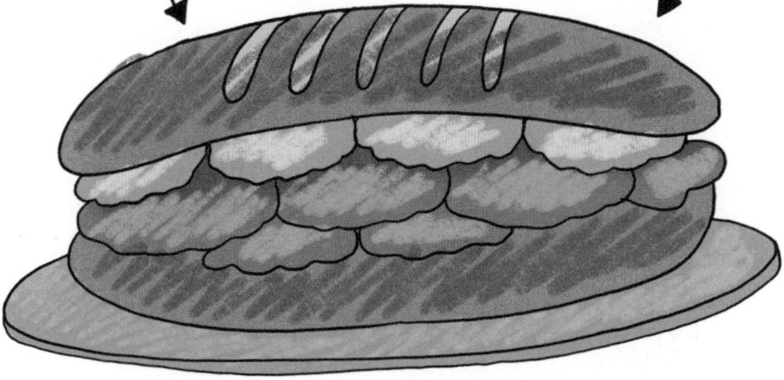

PHILADELPHIA CREAM CHEESE ISN'T FROM PHILLY. IT'S FROM NEW YORK.

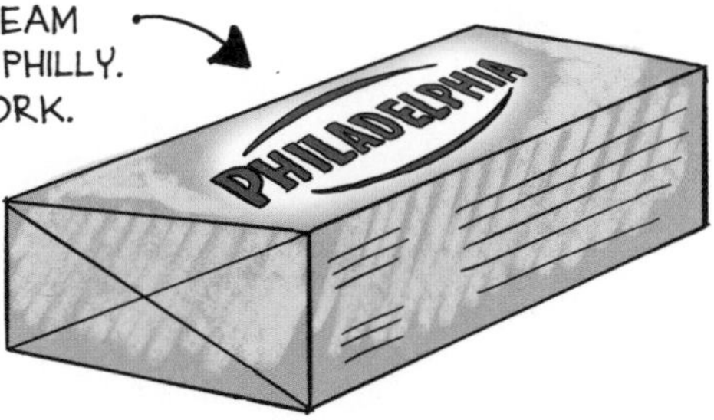
PHILADELPHIA

AUTHOR'S NOTE

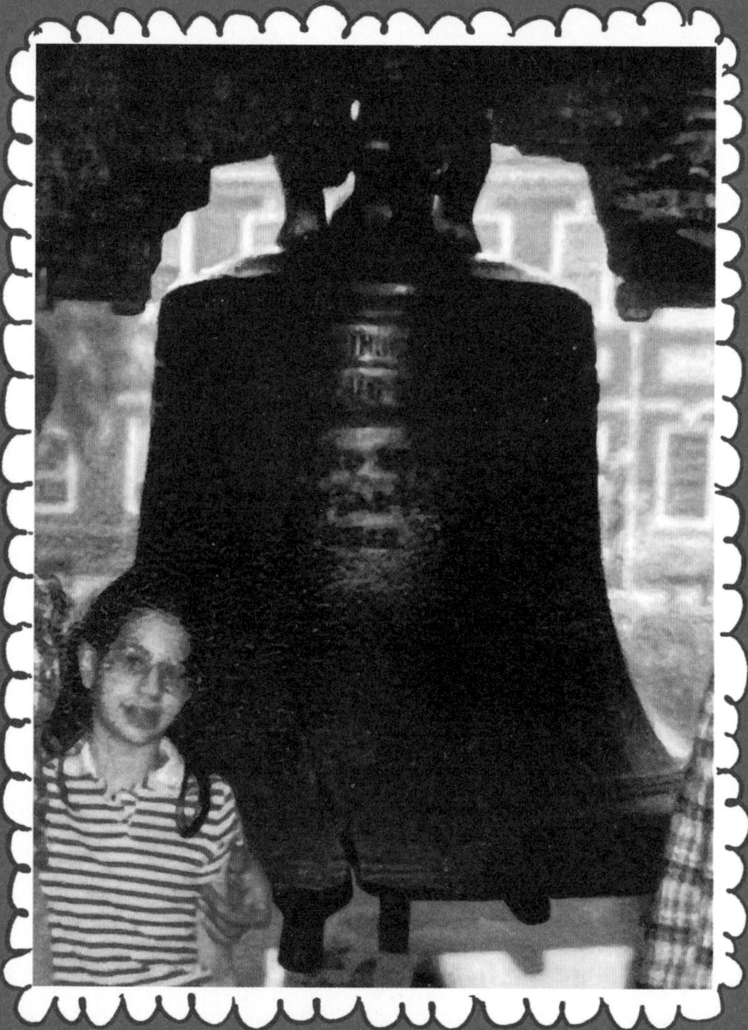

When I realized *All is Nat Lost* would be about a class trip to Philadelphia, I went to Philly to do some research. While I was in town, there were about a hundred class trips happening at that same time, so I put myself on one. I met a lovely teacher who told me all about their class trip, and that they were doing a scavenger hunt. So much of my discussion with her fueled ideas for the book!

I wandered all over the Philadelphia Museum of Art and watched many people flex in front of the Rocky sculpture. I walked past the Rodin Museum, where I saw *The Thinker*, and walked over to the Mütter Museum, where I saw many fascinating (and some really gross) things. Their exceptional staff gave me endless information and more details about Grover Cleveland's tumor than I needed to know. I went to the Liberty Bell (I did not try to ring it), Independence Hall, Congress Hall, and Betsy Ross House. I walked all over Elfreth's Alley, the whole time wondering what it would feel like to be lost.

To be authentic, I almost left my phone in the car so I could feel what it would be like to lose it, but I wasn't that brave.

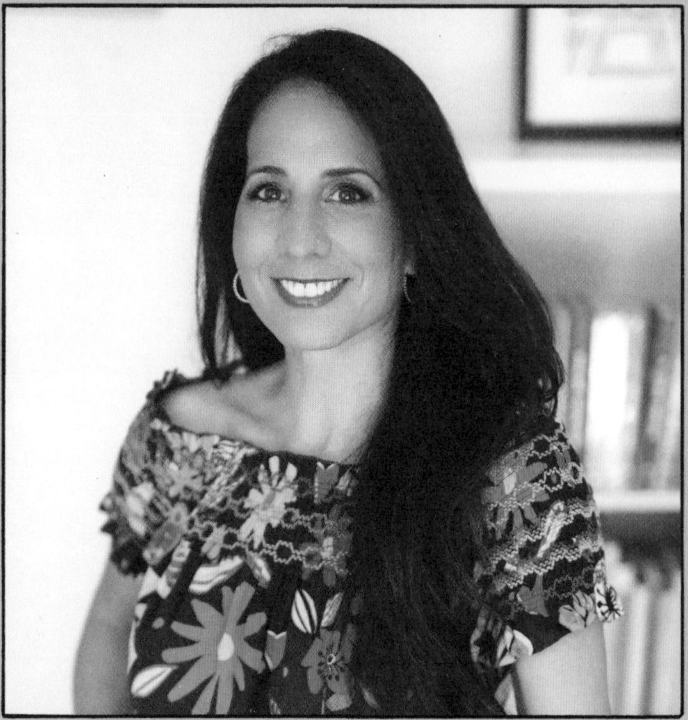

Photo credit: Kyle Norton

MARIA SCRIVAN is a *New York Times* bestselling author, award-winning syndicated cartoonist, and speaker based in Greenwich, Connecticut. Her laugh-out-loud comic, *Half Full*, appeared daily in newspapers nationwide and is available on gocomics.com. Maria licenses her work for greeting cards, and her cartoons have appeared in *MAD Magazine*, *Parade*, and many other publications. *Nat Enough*, her debut graphic novel, was an instant *New York Times* bestseller, and the follow-ups, *Forget Me Nat*, *Absolutely Nat*, and *Nat for Nothing*, also released to great acclaim. Learn more about Maria at mariascrivan.com.